Praise for Tami Hoag

'[Tami Hoag] confirms that she can turn out a police procedural as gritty, grimy and engrossing as the best of them ... Hoag is in a crowded procedural market but the quality of the writing makes *Dust to Dust* a standout novel'
Observer

'Grisly tension is not the only commodity on offer here – the internal politics of the police investigations are handled with genuine panache ... Hoag has demonstrated ... an effortless command of the thriller technique, adroitly juggling the twin demands of character and plot. The set-piece confrontations will ensure that it will take quite a lot to distract the reader from Hoag's narrative' *Crime Time*

'A top-class follow-up to Hoag's bestseller *Ashes to Ashes*'
Publishing News

'Her books are cleverly plotted, feature strong female protagonists and are extremely – often emetically – violent ... Hoag has the bestselling writer's way with a punchy sentence and keeps the surprises coming right up to the very last page' *The Times*

'First rate procedural detail with a credible crew of homicide cops, spectacularly foul-mouthed and fending off the horrors with dirty jokes. Some ornate plotting ... worth your while, though, if not for the faint-hearted'
Literary Review

'Lock the doors and windows, and turn on all the lights – Hoag has crafted a knuckle-whitening, spine-chilling thriller' *New Woman*

'Accomplished and scary' *Cosmopolitan*

With thirteen consecutive *New York Times* bestsellers to her credit, including *The Alibi Man*, *Kill the Messenger* and *Dust to Dust*, Tami Hoag has over twenty-two million books in print in more than twenty languages worldwide. Tami divides her time between Los Angeles and Palm Beach County, Florida. Visit her website at www.tamihoag.com.

By Tami Hoag

TAMI HOAG
A Thin Dark Line

An Orion paperback

First published in Great Britain in 1997
by Orion
This paperback edition published in 1998
by Orion Books Ltd,
Orion House, 5 Upper St Martin's Lane,
London WC2H 9EA

An Hachette UK company

9 10

Reissued 2011

A CIP catalogue record for this book
is available from the British Library.

ISBN 978-1-4091-2148-0

Printed and bound in Great Britain by Clays Ltd, St Ives plc

The Orion Publishing Group's policy is to use papers
that are natural, renewable and recyclable products and
made from wood grown in sustainable forests. The logging
and manufacturing processes are expected to conform to
the environmental regulations of the country of origin.

www.orionbooks.co.uk

This book is dedicated to the many victims who wait for justice, and to the law enforcement professionals who pursue that justice with dogged determination.

Author's Note

A Thin Dark Line takes place in a setting my longtime readers know is a favorite of mine – Louisiana's French Triangle. It is a place like no other in this country – ecologically, culturally, linguistically. I have done my best to bring some of the rich flavor of the region to you, in part with the occasional use of Cajun French, a patois as unique to Louisiana as gumbo. You will find a glossary for these words and phrases in the back of the book. My sources include *A Dictionary of the Cajun Language* by Rev. Msgr. Jules O. Daigle and *Conversational Cajun French* by Randall P. Whatley and Harry Jannise.

My sincere thanks and appreciation to Sheriff Charles A. Fuselier of St Martin Parish, Louisiana, for your generosity with both your time and your knowledge; for giving me the real tour of bayou country and a lesson in Lou'siana politics. The stories were great, the food was even better. *Merci!* Thanks also to Deputy Barry Reburn, my in-family consultant on police procedure. Any mistakes made or liberties taken in the name of fiction are my own.

Thanks to Kathryn Moe, Coldwell Banker Real Estate, Rochester, Minnesota, for unwittingly planting the seed of a gruesome idea when you offered to wait for the furnace inspection guy. Hope it doesn't give you nightmares. And thanks once again to Diva Dreyer for the trauma lingo.

Thank you, Rat Boy, wherever you are.

And finally, my most special thanks to Dan for never minding that I'm always on deadline.

Hide your heart under the bed and lock your secret drawer
Wash the angels from your head, won't need them anymore.
Love is a demon and you're the one he's coming for.
Oh my Lord.

—"Could I Be Your Girl"
Jann Arden Richards

Prologue

'Red is the color of violent death. Red is the color of strong feelings – love, passion, greed, anger, hatred.

Emotions – better not to have them.

Luckier not to have them.

Love,

   Passion,

      Greed,

         Anger,

            Hatred.

The feelings pull one another in a circle. Faster, harder, blurring into violence. I had no power over it.

Love,

   Passion,

      Greed,

         Anger,

            Hatred.

The words pulsed in my head every time I plunged the knife into her body.

Hatred,

   Anger,

      Greed,

         Passion,

            Love,

The line between them is thin and red.'

1

Her body lay on the floor. Her slender arms outflung, palms up. Death. Cold and brutal, strangely intimate.

The people rose in unison as the judge emerged from his chambers. The Honorable Franklin Monahan. The figurehead of justice. The decision would be his.

Black pools of blood in the silver moonlight. Her life drained from her to puddle on the hard cypress floor.

Richard Kudrow, the defense attorney. Thin, gray, and stoop-shouldered, as if the fervor for justice had burned away all excess within him and had begun to consume muscle mass. Sharp eyes and the strength of his voice belied the image of frailty.

Her naked body inscribed with the point of a knife. A work of violent art.

Smith Pritchett, the district attorney. Sturdy and aristocratic. The gold of his cuff links catching the light as he raised his hands in supplication.

Cries for mercy smothered by the cold shadow of death.

Chaos and outrage rolled through the crowd in a wave of sound as Monahan pronounced his ruling. The small amethyst ring had not been listed on the search warrant of the defendant's home and was, therefore, beyond the scope of the warrant and not legally subject to seizure.

Pamela Bichon, thirty-seven, separated, mother of a nine-year-

old girl. Brutally murdered. Eviscerated. Her naked body found in a vacant house on Pony Bayou, spikes driven through the palms of her hands into the wood floor; her sightless eyes staring up at nothing through the slits of a feather Mardi Gras mask.

Case dismissed.

The crowd spilled from the Partout Parish Courthouse, past the thick Doric columns and down the broad steps, a buzzing swarm of humanity centering on the key figures of the drama that had played out in Judge Monahan's courtroom.

Smith Pritchett focused his narrow gaze on the navy blue Lincoln that awaited him at the curb and snapped off a staccato line of 'no comments' to the frenzied press. Richard Kudrow, however, stopped his descent dead center on the steps.

Trouble was the word that came immediately to Annie Broussard as the press began to circle the defense attorney and his client. Like every other deputy in the sheriff's office, she had hoped against hope that Kudrow would fail in his attempt to get the ring thrown out as evidence. They had all hoped Smith Pritchett would be the one crowing on the courthouse steps.

Sergeant Hooker's voice crackled over the portable radio. 'Savoy, Mullen, Prejean, Broussard, move in front of those goddamn reporters. Establish some distance between the crowd and Kudrow and Renard before this turns into a goddamn cluster fuck.'

Annie edged her way between bodies, her hand resting on the butt of her baton, her eyes on Marcus Renard as Kudrow began to speak. He stood beside his attorney, looking uncomfortable with the attention being focused on him. He wasn't a man to draw notice. Quiet, unassuming, an architect in the firm of Bowen & Briggs. Not ugly, not handsome. Thinning brown hair neatly combed and hazel eyes that seemed a little too big for their sockets. He stood

3

with his shoulders stooped and his chest sunken, a younger shadow of his attorney. His mother stood on the step above him, a thin woman with a startled expression and a mouth as tight and straight as a hyphen.

'Some people will call this ruling a travesty of justice,' Kudrow said loudly. 'The only travesty of justice here has been perpetrated by the Partout Parish Sheriff's Department. Their *investigation* of my client has been nothing short of harassment. Two prior searches of Mr Renard's home produced nothing that might tie him to the murder of Pamela Bichon.'

'Are you suggesting the sheriff's department manipulated evidence?' a reporter called out.

'Mr Renard has been the victim of a narrow and fanatical investigation led by Detective Nick Fourcade. Y'all are aware of Fourcade's record with the New Orleans Police Department, of the reputation he brought with him to this parish. Detective Fourcade *allegedly* found that ring in my client's home. Draw your own conclusions.'

As she elbowed past a television cameraman, Annie could see Fourcade turning around, half a dozen steps down from Kudrow. The cameras focused on him hastily. His expression was a stone mask, his eyes hidden by a pair of mirrored sunglasses. A cigarette smoldered between his lips. His temper was a thing of legend. Rumors abounded throughout the department that he was not quite sane.

He said nothing in answer to Kudrow's insinuation, and yet the air between them seemed to thicken. Anticipation held the crowd's breath. Fourcade pulled the cigarette from his mouth and flung it down, exhaling smoke through his nostrils. Annie took a half step toward Kudrow, her fingers curling around the grip of her baton. In the next heartbeat Fourcade was bounding up the steps – straight at Renard, shouting, 'NO!'

'He'll kill him!' someone shrieked.

'Fourcade!' Hooker's voice boomed as the fat sergeant

lunged after him, grabbing at and missing the back of his shirt.

'You killed her! You killed my baby girl!'

The anguished shouts tore from the throat of Hunter Davidson, Pamela Bichon's father, as he hurled himself down the steps at Renard, his eyes rolling, one arm swinging wildly, the other hand clutching a .45.

Fourcade knocked Renard aside with a beefy shoulder, grabbed Davidson's wrist, and shoved it skyward as the .45 barked out a shot and screams went up all around. Annie hit Davidson from the right side, her much smaller body colliding with his just as Fourcade threw his weight against the man from the left. Davidson's knees buckled and they all went down in a tangle of arms and legs, grunting and shouting, bouncing hard down the steps, Annie at the bottom of the heap. Her breath was pounded out of her as she hit the concrete steps with four hundred pounds of men on top of her.

'He killed her!' Hunter Davidson sobbed, his big body going limp. 'He butchered my girl!'

Annie wriggled out from under him and sat up, grimacing. All she could think was that no physical pain could compare with what this man must have been enduring.

Swiping back the strands of dark hair that had pulled loose from her ponytail, she gingerly brushed over the throbbing knot on the back of her head. Her fingertips came away sticky with blood.

'Take this,' Fourcade ordered in a low voice, thrusting Davidson's gun at Annie butt-first. Frowning, he leaned down over Davidson and put a hand on the man's shoulder even as Prejean snapped the cuffs on him. 'I'm sorry,' he murmured. 'I wish I coulda let you kill him.'

Annie pushed to her feet and tried to straighten the bulletproof vest she wore beneath her shirt. Hunter Davidson was a good man. An honest, hardworking planter who had put his daughter through college and walked her down the aisle the day she married Donnie Bichon. Her murder

5

had shattered him, and the subsequent lack of justice had driven him to this desperate edge. And tonight Hunter Davidson would be the man sitting in jail while Marcus Renard slept in his own bed.

'Broussard!' Hooker snapped irritably, suddenly looming over her, porcine and ugly. 'Gimme that gun. Don't just stand there gawking. Get down to that cruiser and open the goddamn doors.'

'Yes, sir.' Not quite steady on her feet, she started around the back side of the crowd.

With the danger past, the press was in full cry again, more frenzied than before. Renard's entourage had been hustled off the steps. The focus was on Davidson now. Cameramen jostled one another for shots of the despondent father. Microphones were thrust at Smith Pritchett.

'Will you file charges, Mr Pritchett?'

'Will charges be filed, Mr Pritchett?'

'Mr Pritchett, what kind of charges will you file?'

Pritchett glared at them. 'That remains to be seen. Please back away and let the officers do their job.'

'Davidson couldn't get justice in court, so he sought to take it himself. Do you feel responsible, Mr Pritchett?'

'We did the best we could with the evidence we had.'

'Tainted evidence?'

'I didn't gather it,' he snapped, starting back up the steps toward the courthouse, his face as pink as a new sunburn.

Limping, Annie descended the last of the steps and opened the back door of the blue and white cruiser sitting at the curb. Fourcade escorted the sobbing Davidson to the car, with Savoy and Hooker just behind them, and Mullen and Prejean flanking them. The crowd rushed along behind them and beside them like guests at a wedding seeing off the happy couple.

'You gonna book him in, Fourcade?' Hooker asked as Davidson disappeared into the backseat.

'The hell,' Fourcade growled, slamming the door. 'He

6

didn't commit the worst crime here today. Not even if he'd'a killed the son of a bitch. Book him yourself.'

The belligerence brought a rise of color to Hooker's face, but he said nothing as Fourcade crossed the street to a battered black Ford 4X4, climbed in, and drove off in the opposite direction of the parish jail.

The sheriff would chew his ass later, Annie thought as she headed for her own radio car. But then a breach in procedure was the least of Fourcade's worries, and, if anything Richard Kudrow had said was true, the least of his sins.

2

'He's guilty,' Nick declared. Ignoring the chair he had been offered, he prowled the cramped confines of the sheriff's office, adrenaline burning inside him like a blue gas flame.

'Then why don't we have squat on him, Nick?'

Sheriff August F. Noblier kept his seat behind his desk. Rawboned and rough-edged, he was working hard to affect an air of calm and rationality, even though the concepts seemed to bounce right off Fourcade. Gus Noblier had ruled Partout Parish off and on for fifteen of his fifty-three years – three consecutive terms, one election lost to the vote hauling and assorted skullduggery of Duwayne Kenner, then a fourth victory. He loved the job. He was good at the job. Only in the last six months – since hiring Fourcade – had he found a sudden yen for antacid tablets.

'We had the damn ring,' Fourcade snapped, slicking his black hair back with one hand.

'You knew it wasn't on the warrant. You had to know it'd get thrown out.'

'No. I thought for once maybe someone in the system would use some common sense. *Mais sa c'est fou!*'

'It's not crazy,' Gus insisted, translating the Cajun French automatically. 'We're talking about the rules, Nick. The rules are there for a reason. Sometimes we gotta bend 'em. Sometimes we gotta sneak around 'em. But we can't just pretend they're not there.'

'So what the hell were we supposed to do?' Fourcade asked with stinging sarcasm and an exaggerated shrug. 'Leave the ring at Renard's house, come back, and try to get another warrant? Can't use the 'plain view' argument to get the warrant. Hell, the ring wasn't in plain sight. So then what? Track down some of Pam Bichon's family and play Twenty Questions?'

He squeezed his eyes shut and pressed his fingertips against his forehead. 'I'm thinking of something of Pam's that might be missing. Can y'all guess what that something might be? *Mais non*, I can't just come right out and tell you. That would be *against the fucking rules*!'

'Goddammit, Nick!'

Frustration pushed Gus to his feet and flooded his face with unhealthy color. Even his scalp glowed pink through the steel gray of his crew cut. He jammed his hands against his thick waist and glared at Fourcade leaning across his desk. At six-three he had a couple inches on the detective, but Fourcade was built like a light heavyweight boxer – all power and muscle and 3 percent body fat.

'And while we were all chasing our tails, trying to follow the rules,' Fourcade went on, 'you don't think Renard would be pitching that ring in the bayou?'

'You could have left Stokes there and come back. And why hadn't Renard pitched the ring already? We'd been to his house twice –'

'Third time's a charm.'

'He's smarter than that.'

Of all the things Nick had expected Gus Noblier to say to him, to insinuate, he hadn't anticipated this. He felt blindsided, then foolish, then told himself it didn't matter. But it did.

'You think I planted that ring?' he asked in a voice gone dangerously soft.

Gus blew a sigh between his lips. His narrow eyes glanced a look off Nick's chin and ricocheted elsewhere. 'I didn't say that.'

'You didn't have to. Hell, you don't think *I'm* smarter than that? You don't think if I knew what I was gonna find before I went there, I woulda had sense enough to list the ring on the goddamn warrant?'

The sheriff scowled, accentuating the sagging lines of his big face. 'I'm not the one who thinks you're a rogue cop,

Nick. That's Kudrow's game, and he's got the press playing with him.'

'And I'm supposed to give a shit?'

'You, of all people. This case has folks spooked. They're seeing killers in every shadow and they want someone put away.'

'*Renard –*'

Gus held a hand up. 'Save your breath. We all want a conviction on this. I'm just telling you how it can look. I'm just telling you how this thing can be twisted. Kudrow plants enough doubt, we'll never get this creep. I'm telling you to mind your manners.'

Nick let out the breath he'd been holding and turned away from the cluttered desk, resuming his pacing with less energy. 'I'm a detective, not a damn community relations officer. I've got a job to do.'

'You can't just do it all over Marcus Renard. Not now.'

'So I'm supposed to do what? Have a gypsy conjure me up some more suspects? Cast suspicion on someone else, just to be fair? Buy into that bullshit theory this murder is the work of a serial killer everybody knows got his ticket punched for him four years ago?'

'You can't keep leaning on Renard, Nick. Not without some solid evidence or a witness or *something*. That's harassment, and he'll sue our asses eight ways from Sunday.'

'Oh, well, God forbid he should sue us,' Nick sneered. 'A murderer!'

'A citizen!' Gus yelled, thumping the desktop between stacks of paperwork. 'A citizen with rights and a damn good lawyer to make sure we respect them. This ain't some lowlife dirtbag you're dealing with here. He's an architect, for Christ's sake.'

'He's a killer.'

'Then you nail him and you nail him by the book. I've got enough trouble in this parish with half the people thinking the Bayou Strangler's been raised from the dead and half of them spoiling for a lynching – Renard's, yours, mine. This fire's burning hot enough, I don't need you throwing gasoline on it. You don't want to defy me on this, Nick. I'm telling you right now.'

'Telling me what?' Nick challenged. 'To back off? Or you want me off the case altogether, Gus?'

He waited impatiently for Noblier's reply. It frightened him a little, how much it mattered. The first murder he'd handled since leaving New Orleans and it had sucked him in, consumed his life, consumed *him*. The Bichon murder had taken precedence over everything else on his desk and in his head. Some would have called it an obsession. He didn't think he had crossed that line, but then again maybe he was in the middle of the deep woods seeing nothing but trees. It wouldn't have been the first time.

His hands had curled into fists at his sides. Holding on to the case. He couldn't make himself let go.

'Keep a low profile, for crying out loud,' Gus said with resignation as he lowered himself into his chair. 'Let Stokes take a bigger part of the case. Don't get in Renard's face.'

'He killed her, Gus. He wanted her and she didn't want him. So he stalked her. He terrorized her. He kidnapped her. He tortured her. He killed her.'

Gus cupped his hands together and held them up. 'This is our evidence, Nick. Everybody in the state of Lou'siana can know Marcus Renard did it, but if we don't get more than what we've got now, he's a free man.'

'*Merde*,' Nick muttered. 'Maybe I *shoulda* let Hunter Davidson shoot him.'

'Then it'd be Hunter Davidson going on trial for murder.'

'Pritchett's filing charges?'

'He doesn't have a choice.' Gus picked up an arrest report from his desk, glanced at it, and set it aside. 'Davidson tried to kill Renard in front of fifty witnesses. Let that be a lesson to you if you're fixing to kill someone.'

'Can I go?'

Gus gave him a long look. 'You're not fixing to kill someone, are you, Nick?'

'I got work to do.'

Fourcade's expression was inscrutable, his dark eyes unreadable. He slipped on his sunglasses. Gus's stomach called loudly for Mylanta. He jabbed a finger at his detective. 'You keep that coonass temper in check, Fourcade. It's already landed your butt in water hot enough to boil crawfish. Blaming the cops is in vogue these days. And your name is on the tip of everyone's tongue.'

Annie loitered in the open doorway to the briefing room, a leaking Baggie of melting ice cubes pressed to the knot on the back of her head. She had changed out of her torn, dirty uniform into the jeans and T-shirt she kept in her locker. She strained to make out the argument going on in the sheriff's office down the hall, but only the tone was conveyed. Impatient, angry.

The press had been speculating even before the evidentiary hearing that Fourcade would lose his job over the screwup on the warrant, but then the press liked to make noise and understood little of the intricacies of police work. They had written much about the public's frustration with the SO's failure to make an arrest, but they brushed off the frustration of the cops working the case. They all but called for a public hanging of the suspect based on nothing more than hearsay evidence, then spun around 180 degrees and pointed their fingers at the detective in charge of the case when he finally came up with something tangible.

No one had any evidence Fourcade had planted that ring in Renard's desk drawer. It didn't make sense that he would have planted evidence but not listed that evidence on the warrant. There was every possibility Renard had put the ring in that drawer himself, never imagining his house would be searched a third time. Perpetrators of sex-related homicides tended to keep souvenirs of their victims.

12

Everything from pieces of jewelry to pieces of bodies. That was a fact.

Annie had attended the seminar on sexual predators at the academy in Lafayette three months before the Bichon murder. She took as many extra courses as she could in preparation for one day making detective. That was her goal – to work in plain clothes, dig deep into the mysteries of the crimes she now dealt with only at the outset of a case.

The crime-scene slides the class instructor had shown them had been horrific. Crimes of unspeakable cruelty and brutality. Victims tortured and mutilated in ways no sane person could ever have imagined in their worst nightmares. But then she no longer had to imagine. She had been the one to discover Pam Bichon's body.

She had been off duty the weekend the real estate agent was reported missing. On routine patrol Monday morning, Annie had found herself drawn to a vacant house out on Pony Bayou. The place had been for sale for months, though the renters had moved out only five or six weeks previous. A rusted Bayou Realty sign had fallen over on one side of the overgrown drive. Something she had read in Police magazine made Annie turn in the driveway – an article about how many female real estate agents each year are lured to remote properties, then raped or murdered.

Hidden in the brambles behind the dilapidated house sat a white Mustang convertible, top up. She recognized the car from the briefing, but ran it to be certain. The plates came back to Pamela K. Bichon, no wants, no warrants, reported missing two days previous. And in the dining room of the old house it was Pam Bichon she found … or what was left of her.

She still saw the scene too often when she closed her eyes. The nails in her hands. The mutilation. The blood. The mask. The flashbacks still awakened her in the night, the images entwining with a nightmare four years old, forcing her to rush to the surface of consciousness like a

13

swimmer coming up from the depths, running out of air. The smell still burned in her nostrils from time to time, when she least expected it. The putrid miasma of violent death. Cloying, choking, thick with the scent of fear.

A chill ran through her now, twisting and coiling in the bottom of her stomach.

The Baggie dribbled ice water down the back of her neck, and she flinched and swore under her breath.

'Hey, Broussard.' Deputy Ossie Compton sucked in his stomach and sidled past her through the doorway to the break room. 'I heard you were a cold one. How come that ice is melting?'

Annie shot him a wry look. 'Must be all your hot air, Compton.'

He gave her a wink, his grin flashing white in his dark face. 'My hot charm, you mean.'

'Is that what you call it?' she teased. 'Here I thought it was gas.'

Laughter rolled behind her, Compton's included.

'You got him again, Annie,' Prejean said.

'I quit keeping score,' she said, glancing back down the hall toward the sheriff's office. 'It got to where it was just cruel.'

The shift would change in twenty minutes. Guys coming on for the evening wandered in to BS with the day shift before briefing. The Hunter Davidson incident was the hot topic of the day.

'Man, you shoulda seen Fourcade!' Savoy said with a big grin. 'He moves like a damn panther, him! Talk about!'

'Yeah. He was on Davidson like that.' Prejean snapped his fingers. 'And there's women screaming and the gun going off and nine kinds of hell all at once. It was a regular goddamn circus.'

'And where were you during all this, Broussard?' Chaz Stokes asked, turning his pale eyes on Annie.

Tension instantly rose inside her as she returned the detective's stare.

'At the bottom of the pile,' Sticks Mullen snickered, flashing a small mouth overcrowded with yellow teeth. 'Where a woman belongs.'

'Yeah, like you'd know.' She tossed her dripping ice bag into the trash. 'You read that in a book, Mullen?'

'You think he can read?' Prejean said with mock astonishment.

'*Penthouse*,' someone suggested.

'Naw,' Compton drawled, elbowing Savoy. 'He just looks at the pictures and milks his lizard.'

'Fuck you, Compton.' Mullen rose and headed for the candy machine, hitching up his pants on skinny hips and digging in his pocket for change.

'Jesus, don't fish it out here, Sticks!'

'Christ,' Stokes muttered in disgust.

He had the kind of looks that drew a woman's eye. Tall, trim, athletic. An interesting combination of features hinted at his mixed family background – short dark hair curled tight to his head, skin that was just a shade more brown than white. He had a slim nose and a Dudley Do-Right mouth framed by a neat mustache and goatee.

His face would have looked good on a recruiting poster with its square jaw and chin, the light turquoise eyes piercing out from beneath heavy black brows. But Stokes wasn't the type in any other respect. He cultivated a laid-back, free-spirit image advertised by his unconventional clothing, which today consisted of baggy gray janitor's pants and a square-bottomed shirt printed with bucking broncos, Indian tipis, and cacti. He pulled his black straw snap-brim down at an angle over one eye.

'You steal that off Chi Chi Rodriguez?' Annie asked.

'Come on, Broussard,' he murmured with a sly smile. 'You want me. You're always looking at me. Am I right or am I right?'

'You're full of shit and you're kind of hard to miss in that getup. So where were you during all the fun? You been working the Bichon case as much as Fourcade.'

He leaned a shoulder against the doorjamb, glancing out into the hall. 'Nick's the primary. I had to go to St. Martinville. They picked up my meth dealer on a DUI.'

'And that required your personal attention?'

'Hey, I've been working to nail that rat bastard for months.'

'If they had him in their jail, what's the big hurry?'

Stokes flashed his teeth. 'Hey, no time like the present. You know what I'm saying. The warrants came out of this parish. I want Billy Thibidoux on my résumé ASAP.'

'You left Fourcade swinging in the breeze so you could have Billy Thibidoux in your jacket. Yeah, I'd want to be your partner, Chaz,' Annie said with derision.

'Nicky's a big boy. He didn't need me. And you . . .' His eyes hardened a bit, even though the smile stayed firmly in place. 'I thought we'd already covered that ground, Broussard. You had your chance. But hey, I'm a generous guy. I'd be willing to give you another shot . . . out of uniform, so to speak.'

I'd rather mud wrestle alligators in the nude. But she kept the remark to herself, when she would have readily tossed it at any of her other co-workers. She knew from experience Chaz didn't take rejection well.

He reached out unexpectedly and pressed his thumb against the darkening bruise along the crown of her left cheekbone. 'You're gonna have a shiner, Broussard.' He dropped his hand as she pulled back. 'Looks good on you.'

'You're such a jerk,' she muttered, turning away, knowing she was the only one in the department who thought so. Chaz Stokes was everybody's pal . . . except hers.

The door to the sheriff's office swung open and Fourcade stormed out, his expression ominous, his tie jerked loose at the throat of his tan shirt. He dug a cigarette out of his breast pocket.

'We're fucked!' he snapped at Stokes, not slowing his stride.

'I heard.'

Annie watched them go down the hall. Stokes had worked the Bichon case when Pam was alive and claiming Renard was stalking her. He had missed the homicide call, but had worked the murder as Fourcade's partner. They weren't being held up to public scrutiny and ridicule as a team, however. It was Fourcade's name in the papers. Fourcade, who had come to Partout Parish with a checkered past. Fourcade, who had come up with the ring. Stokes wouldn't be raked over the coals after today's court ruling. He had assured that by making himself scarce.

'Billy Thibidoux, my ass,' she grumbled under her breath.

Annie stayed late to finish her report on the Davidson incident. When she came out of the building at 5:06, the parking lot behind the law enforcement center was deserted except for a pair of trustees washing the sheriff's new Suburban. The day-shift deputies had split for home or second jobs or stools in their favorite bars. The press had taken Smith Pritchett's brief official statement on Hunter Davidson's situation and gone off to meet their deadlines.

A sense of false peace held the moment. Any stranger walking through Bayou Breaux would have remarked on the lovely afternoon. Spring had arrived unusually early, filling the air with the perfume of sweet olive and wisteria. Window boxes on the second-floor galleries of the historic business district were bursting with color and overflowing greenery, ivy trailing down the wrought iron and wood railings. Store windows had been decorated for the upcoming Mardi Gras carnival. Down on the corner, old Tante Lucesse sat on a folding chair weaving a pine-needle basket and singing hymns for passersby.

But underlying the veneer of peace was something sinister. A raw nerve of disquiet. As the sun went down on Bayou Breaux, a killer sat somewhere in the gathering gloom. That knowledge tainted the shabby beauty here like a stain seeping across a tablecloth. Murder. Whether you believed Renard was the killer or not, a murderer was loose among them, free to do as he pleased.

It wasn't the first time, which made it impossible to discount as an aberration. Death had stalked this patch of South Louisiana before. The memories had barely gone stale. The death of Pam Bichon had dredged them to the surface, had awakened fear and stirred up doubt.

Six women in five different parishes had died over an eighteen-month period between 1992 and 1993, raped, strangled, and sexually mutilated. Two of the victims had come from Bayou Breaux-Savannah Chandler and Annick Delahoussaye-Gerrard, whom Annie had known her entire life. The crimes had shocked the people of Louisiana's French Triangle into a state of near panic, and the conclusion of the case had shocked them even more.

The murders had stopped with the death of Stephen Danjermond, son of a wealthy New Orleans Garden District shipping family. The investigation had revealed a long history of sexual sadism and murder, hobbies Danjermond had practiced since his college days. Trophies from his victims had been discovered during a search of his home. At the time of his death Danjermond had been serving his first term as Partout Parish district attorney.

The story had put Bayou Breaux in the spotlight for a short time, but the glare had faded and the horror was put aside. The case was closed. The evil had been burned out. Life had returned to normal. Until Pam Bichon.

Her death was too close for comfort, too similar. All the old fears had bubbled to the surface, divided, and multiplied. People wondered if Danjermond had been the killer at all, their new panic clouding the memory of the evidence against him. Killed in a fire, he had never publicly confessed to his crimes. Other folks were eager to embrace Renard as the suspect in the Bichon killing – better a tangible evil than a nebulous one. But even with a target to point their fingers at, the underlying fear remained: a superstition, a half-conscious belief that the evil was indeed a phantom, that this place had been cursed.

Annie felt it herself – an edginess, a low-frequency hum that skimmed along her nerves at night, an instinct that heightened the awareness of every sound, a sense of vulnerability. Every woman in the parish felt it, perhaps more so this time than the last. The Bayou Strangler's victims had been women of questionable reputation. Pam Bichon had led a normal life, had a good job, came from a nice family . . . and a killer had chosen her. If it could happen to Pam Bichon . . .

Annie felt the uneasiness within her now, felt it press in around her as if the air had suddenly become more dense. The sense of being watched itched across the back of her neck. But when she turned around, it was no evil gargoyle staring at her. A small face with big sad eyes peered at her over the steering wheel of her Jeep. Josie Bichon.

'Hey, Josie,' she said, letting herself in on the passenger's side. 'Where y'at?'

The little girl laid her cheek against the steering wheel and shrugged. She was a beautiful child with straight brown hair that hung like a thick curtain to her waist and brown eyes too soulful for her years. In a denim jumper and floppy denim hat, the brim pinned up in front with a big silk sunflower, she could have been modeling for a GAP Kids fashion shoot.

'You here on your own?'

'No. I came with Grandma to see Grandpa. They wouldn't let me go in.'

'Sorry, Jose. They've got rules about letting kids into the jail.'

'Yeah. Everybody's got rules for everything when it comes to kids. I wish I could make a rule for once.' She reached out and tapped her finger against the plastic alligator that hung from the rearview mirror. The gator wore sunglasses, a red beret, and a leering grin designed to amuse, but Josie was in a place beyond amusement. 'Rule number one: No treating me like a baby, 'cause I'm not. Rule number two: No lying to me for my own good.'

'You heard about what happened in front of the courthouse?' Annie asked gently.

'It was on the radio when we were having art class. Grandpa tried to shoot the man that killed my mom, and he was arrested. At first, Grandma tried to tell me he just tripped and fell down the courthouse steps. She lied to me.'

'I'm sure she didn't mean it to be a lie, Josie. Imagine how scared she must have been. She didn't want to scare you too.'

Josie gave her an expression that spoke eloquently of her feelings on the subject. From the moment her family had been notified of her mother's death, Josie had been fed half-truths, gently pushed aside while the adults whispered concerns and secrets. Her father and her grandparents and aunts and uncles had done their best to wrap her in an insulation of misinformation, never imagining that what they were doing only hurt her more. But Annie knew.

Mama, Mama! We're home! Look what Uncle Sos got me at Disney World! It's Minnie Mouse!'

The kitchen door banged shut and she stopped in her tracks. The person sitting at the kitchen table wasn't her mother. Father Goetz rose from the chrome-legged chair, his face grave, and Enola Meyette, a fat woman who always smelled of sausage, came away from the sink drying her hands on a red checked towel.

'Allons, chérie,' Mrs Meyette said, holding out one dimpled hand. 'We go down the store. Get you a candy, oui?'

Annie had known right then something was terribly wrong. The memory still brought back the same sick twisting in her stomach she had felt that day as Enola Meyette led her from the kitchen. She could see herself clearly at nine, eyes wide with fear, a choke hold on her new stuffed Minnie Mouse, as she was pulled away from the truth Father Goetz had come to deliver: that while Annie was on her first-ever vacation trip with Tante Fanchon and Uncle Sos, Marie Broussard had taken her own life.

She remembered the gentle lies of well-meaning people, and the sense of isolation that grew with each of those lies. An isolation she had carried inside her for a long, long time.

Annie had taken it upon herself to answer Josie's questions when the sheriff's office had sent its representatives to break the news to Hunter Davidson and his wife. And Josie, perhaps sensing a kindred spirit, had made an instant and yet-to-be-severed connection.

'You could have come to the sheriff's office and asked for me,' Annie said.

Josie tapped the alligator again and watched it swing. 'I didn't want to be with people. Not if I couldn't see Grandpa Hunt and ask him what really happened.'

'I was there.'

'Did he really try to kill that guy?'

Annie chose her words with care. 'He might have if Detective Fourcade hadn't seen the gun in time.'

'I wish he had shot him dead,' Josie declared.

'People can't take the law into their own hands, Jose.'

'Why? Because it's against the rules? That guy killed my mom. What about the rules he broke? He should have to pay for what he did.'

'That's what the courts are for.'

'But the judge let him go!' Josie cried, frustration and pain tangling in a knot in her throat. The same frustration and pain Annie had heard in Hunter Davidson's broken sobs.

'Just for now,' Annie said, hoping the promise wasn't really as empty as it felt to her. 'Just until we can get some better evidence against him.'

Tears welled up in Josie's eyes and spilled over. 'Then why can't you find it? You're a cop and you're my friend. You're supposed to understand! You said you'd help! You're supposed to make sure he gets punished! Instead, you put my grandpa in jail! I hate this!' She hit her hand against the steering wheel, blasting the horn. 'I hate everything!'

Josie scrambled from the driver's seat and dashed toward the law enforcement center. Annie hopped out of the Jeep and started after her. But she pulled herself up short as she caught sight of Belle Davidson and Thomas Watson, the Davidsons' attorney, coming out the side door.

Belle Davidson was a formidable woman in a demure sweater-and-pearls disguise. A steel magnolia of the first order. The woman's lips thinned as her gaze lit on Annie. She disconnected herself from Josie's embrace and started across the lot.

'You have an awful nerve, Deputy Broussard,' she declared. 'Throwing my husband in jail instead of my daughter's murderer, then playing up to my granddaughter as if you have a right to her devotion.'

'I'm sorry you feel that way, Mrs Davidson,' Annie said. 'But we couldn't let your husband shoot Marcus Renard.'

'He wouldn't have been driven to such desperation if not for the incompetence of you people in the sheriff's department. You let a guilty man run free all over town due to carelessness and oversight. By God, I've got half a mind to shoot him myself.'

'Belle!' the lawyer whined as he caught up with his client. 'I told you, you hadn't ought to say that in front of people!'

'Oh, for God's sake, Thomas. My daughter has been murdered. People would think it strange if I *didn't* say these things.'

'We're doing the best we can, Mrs Davidson,' Annie said.

'And what have you come up with? Nothing. You're a disgrace to your uniform – when you're wearing one.'

She gave Annie's faded T-shirt a sharply dubious look that had likely sent many a Junior Leaguer home in tears.

'I'm not working your daughter's case, ma'am. It's up to Detectives Fourcade and Stokes.'

Belle Davidson's expression only hardened. 'Don't make excuses, Deputy. We all have obligations in this life that go beyond boundaries. You found my daughter's body. You saw what –' She cut herself off, glancing down at Josie. When she turned back to Annie, her dark eyes glittered with tears. 'You *know*. How can you turn your back on that? How can you turn your back on that and still show your face to my granddaughter?'

'It's not Annie's fault, Grandma,' Josie said, though the gaze she lifted to Annie's face was tainted with disappointment.

'Don't say that, Josie,' Belle admonished softly as she slipped an arm around her granddaughter's shoulders and pulled her close. 'That's what's wrong with the world today. No one will take responsibility for anything.'

'I want justice, too, Mrs Davidson,' Annie said. 'But it has to happen within the system.'

'Deputy, the only thing we've gotten within the system so far is injustice.'

As they walked away, Josie looked back over her shoulder, her brown eyes huge and sad. For an instant Annie felt as if she were watching herself walking away into the painful haze of her past, the memory pulling out from the core of her like a string.

'What happened, Tante Fanchon? Where's Mama?'

'Your maman, she's in heaven, ma 'tite fille.'

'But why?'

'It was an accident, chèrie. God, He looked away.'

'I don't understand.'

'Non, chère 'tite bête. Someday. When you get older …'

But she had hurt right then, and promises of later had done nothing to soothe the pain.

3

We'll get him one way or another, Slick.'

Fourcade cast Chaz Stokes a glance out the corner of his eye as he raised his glass. 'There's plenty of people who think we already tried "another." '

'Fuck 'em,' Stokes declared, and tossed back a shot. He stacked the glass on the bar with the half dozen others they had accumulated. 'We know Renard's our man. We know what he did. The little motherfucker is wrong. You know it and I know it, my friend. Am I right or am I right?'

He clamped a hand on Fourcade's shoulder, a buddy gesture that was met with a stony look. Camaraderie was the rule in police work, but Fourcade didn't have the time or the energy to waste on it. His focus was, by necessity, on his caseload and himself – getting himself back on the straight and narrow path he had fallen from in New Orleans.

'The state ought to plug his dick into a socket and light him up like a goddamn Christmas tree,' Stokes muttered. 'Instead, the judge lets him walk on a fucking technicality, and Pritchett throws Davidson in the can. The world's a fucking loony bin, but I guess you already knew that.'

Par for the damn course, Nick thought, but he kept it to himself, choosing to treat Stokes's invitation to share as a rhetorical remark. He didn't talk about his days in the NOPD or the incident that had ultimately forced him out of New Orleans. As far as he had ever seen, the truth was of little interest to most people, anyway. They chose to form their opinions based on whatever sensational tidbit of a story took their fancy. The fact that he had been the one to find Pamela Bichon's small amethyst ring, for instance.

He wondered if anyone would have suspected Chaz Stokes of planting the ring, had Stokes been the one to discover it. Stokes had come to Bayou Breaux from somewhere in Crackerland, Mississippi, four years ago, a regular Joe with no past to speak of. If Stokes had found the ring, would the focus now be solely on the injustice of Renard walking free, or would the waters of public opinion have been muddied anyway? Lawyers had a way of stirring up the muck like catfish caught in the shallows, and Richard Kudrow was kingfish of that particular school of bottom feeders.

Nick had to think Kudrow would have cast aspersions on the evidence regardless of who had recovered it. He didn't want to think that his finding it had tainted it, didn't want to think that his presence on the case would block Pam Bichon from getting justice.

Didn't want to think. Period.

Stokes poured another shot from the bottle of Wild Turkey. Nick tossed it back and lit another cigarette. The television hanging in one corner of the dimly lit lounge was showing a sitcom to a small, disinterested audience of businessmen who had come in from the hotel next door to bullshit over chunky glasses of Johnnie Walker and Cajun Chex mix served in plastic ashtrays.

There were no other customers, which was why Stokes had suggested this place over the usual cop hangouts. Nick would have sooner done his brooding in private. He didn't want questions. He didn't want commiseration. He didn't want to rehash the day's events. But Stokes was his partner on the Bichon case, and so Nick made this concession – to pound down a few together, as if they had something more in common than the job.

He shouldn't have been drinking at all. It was one of the vices he had tried to leave in New Orleans, but it and some others had trailed after him to Bayou Breaux like stray dogs. He should have been home working through the intricate and consuming moves of the Tai Chi, attempting to cleanse his mind, to focus the negative energy and burn it out. Instead, he sat here at Laveau's, stewing in it.

The whiskey simmered in his belly and in his veins, and he decided he was just about past caring where he was. Well on his way toward oblivion, he thought. And he'd be damn glad when he got there. It was the one place he might not see Pam Bichon lying dead on the floor.

'I still think about what he did to her,' Stokes murmured, fingers absently peeling away strips of the label from his beer bottle. 'Don't you?'

Day and night. During consciousness and what passed for sleep. The images stayed with him. The paleness of her skin. The wounds: gruesome, hideous, so at odds with what she had been like in life. The expression in her eyes as she stared up through the mask – stark, hopeless, filled with a kind of terror that couldn't be imagined by anyone who hadn't faced a brutal death.

And when the images came to him, so did the sense of violence that must have been thick in the air at the time of her death. It hit him like a wall of sound, intense, powerful, poisonous rage that left him feeling sick and shaken.

Rage was no stranger. It boiled inside him now.

'I think about what she went through,' Stokes said. 'What she must have felt when she realized ... what he did to her with that knife. Christ.' He shook his head as if to shake loose the images taking root there. 'He's gotta pay for that, man, and without that ring we got shit for a bill. He's gonna walk, Nicky. He's gonna get away with murder.'

People did. Every day. Every day the line was crossed and souls disappeared into the depths of an alternate dimension. It was a matter of choice, a battle of wills. Most people never came close enough to the edge to have any knowledge of it. Too close to the edge and the force could pull you across like an undertow.

'He's probably sitting in his office thinking that right now,' Stokes went on. 'He's been working nights, you know. The rest of his firm can't stand to have him around. They know he's guilty, same as we do. Can't stand looking at him, knowing what he did. I'll bet he's sitting there right now, thinking about it.'

Right across the alley. The architectural firm of Bowen & Briggs was housed in a narrow painted brick building that faced the bayou; flanked by a shabby clapboard barbershop and an antiques store. The same building that housed Bayou Realty on the first floor. Bowen & Briggs was likely the only place on the block inhabited tonight.

'You know, man, somebody ought to do Renard,' Stokes whispered, cutting a wary glance at the bartender. He stood at the end of the bar, chuckling over the sitcom.

'Justice, you know,' Stokes said. 'An eye for an eye.'

'I shoulda let Davidson shoot him,' Nick muttered, and wondered again why he had not. Because there was still a part of him that believed the system was supposed to work. Or maybe he hadn't wanted to see Hunter Davidson sucked over to the dark side.

'He could have an accident,' Stokes suggested. 'It happens all the time. The swamp is a dangerous place. Just swallows people up sometimes, you know.'

Nick looked at him through the haze of smoke, trying to judge, trying to gauge. He didn't know Stokes well enough. Didn't know him at all beyond what they had shared on the job. All he had were impressions, a handful of adjectives, speculation hastily made because he didn't care to waste his time on such things. He preferred to concentrate on focal points; Stokes was part of the periphery of his life. Just another detective in a four-man department. They worked independently of one another most of the time.

Stokes's mouth twisted up on one corner. 'Wishful thinking, pard, wishful thinking. Idn' that what they do down in New Orleans? Pop the bad guys and dump 'em in the swamp?'

'Lake Pontchartrain, mostly.'

Stokes stared at him a moment, uncertain, then decided it was a joke. He laughed, drained his beer, and slid off the stool, reaching into his hip pocket for his wallet. 'I gotta split. Gotta meet with the DA on Thibidoux in the morning.' The grin flashed again. 'And I got a hot date tonight. Hot and sweet between the sheets. If I'm lyin', I'm dyin'.'

He dropped a ten on the bar and clamped a hand on Nick's shoulder one last time. 'Protect and serve, pard. Catch you later.'

Protect and serve, Nick thought. Pamela Bichon was dead. Her father was sitting in jail, and the man who had killed her was free. Just who had they protected and what purpose had been served today?

'Pritchett's fit to kill somebody.'

'I'd suggest Renard,' Annie muttered, scowling at her menu.

'More apt to be your idol, Fourcade.'

She caught the sarcasm, the jealousy, and rolled her eyes at her dinner partner. She had known A.J. Doucet her whole life. He was one of Tante Fanchon and Uncle Sos's brood of actual nephews and nieces, related by blood rather than by serendipity, as she was. As children, they had chased each other around the big yard out at the Corners – the café/boat landing/convenience store Sos and Fanchon ran south of town. During their high school years, A.J. had taken on the often unappreciated role of protector. Since then he had gone from friend to lover and back as he proceeded through college and law school and into the Partout Parish District Attorney's Office.

They had yet to agree on a description for their current relationship. The attraction that had come and gone between them over the years seemed never to come or go for both of them at the same time.

'He's not my idol,' she said irritably. 'He happens to be the best detective we've got, that's all. I want to be a detective. Of course I watch him. And why should you care? You and I are not, I repeat, *not* an item, A.J.'

'You know how I feel about that too.'

Annie blew out a sigh. 'Can we skip this argument tonight? I've had a rotten day. You're supposed to be my best friend. Act like it.'

He leaned toward her across the small white-draped table, his brown eyes intense, the hurt in them cutting at her conscience. 'You know there's more there than that, Annie, and don't give me that "we're practically related" bullshit you've been wading in recently. You are no more related to me than you are related to the President of the United States.'

'Which I could be, for all I know,' she muttered, sitting back, retreating in the only way she could without making a scene.

As it was, they had become the object of speculation for another set of diners across the intimate width of Isabeau's. She suspected it was her blackening eye that had caught the other woman's attention. Out of uniform, she supposed she looked like an abused partner rather than an abused cop.

'It's not the cops Pritchett should be pissed at,' she said. 'Judge Monahan made the ruling. He could have let that ring in.'

'And left the door open for appeal? What would be the point of that?'

The waitress interrupted the discussion, bringing their drinks, her gaze cutting from Annie's battered face to A.J.

'She's gonna spit in your étouffée, you know,' Annie remarked.

'Why should she assume I gave you that shiner? I could be your high-priced, ass-kicking divorce lawyer.'

Annie sipped her wine, dismissing the subject. 'He's guilty, A.J.'

'Then bring us the evidence – obtained by legal means.'

'By the rules, like it's a game. Josie wasn't far wrong.'

'What about Josie?'

'She came to see me today. Or, rather, she came with her grandmother to see Hunter Davidson in jail.'

'The formidable Miss Belle.'

'They both tore into me.'

'What for? It's not your case.'

'Yeah, well ...' she hedged, sensing that A.J. wouldn't understand the strong pull she was feeling. Everything in its place – that was A.J. Every aspect of life was supposed to fit into one of the neat little compartments he had set up, while everything in Annie's life seemed to be tossed into one big messy pile she was continually sorting through, trying to make sense of. 'I'm tied to it. I wish I could do more to help. I look at Josie and ...'

A.J.'s expression softened with concern. He was too handsome for his own good. Curse of the Doucet men with their square jaws and high cheekbones and pretty mouths. Not for the first time, Annie wished things between them could have been as simple as he wanted.

'The case has been hell on everyone, honey,' he said. 'You've done more than your part already.'

Therein lay the problem, Annie thought as she picked at her dinner. What exactly was her part? Was she supposed to draw the boundary at duty and absolve herself of any further responsibility?

We all have obligations in this life that go beyond boundaries.

She had already gone above and beyond the call involving herself with Josie. But, even without Josie, she would have felt this case pulling at her, would have felt Pam Bichon pulling at her from that limbo inhabited by the restless souls of victims.

With all the controversy swirling around the case, Pam was being pushed out of view little by little. No one had helped her when she was alive and believed that Marcus Renard was stalking her, and now that she was dead, attention was being diverted elsewhere.

'Maybe there wouldn't be a case if Judge Edmonds had taken Pam seriously in the first place,' she said, setting her fork down and abandoning her meal. 'What's the point of having a stalking law if judges are just gonna blow off every complaint that comes their way as "boys will be boys" –'

'We've had this conversation,' A.J. reminded her. 'For Edmonds to have granted that restraining order, the law would have to be worded so that looking crossways at a woman would be considered criminal. What Pam Bichon brought before the court did not constitute stalking. Renard asked her out, he gave her presents –'

'He slashed her tires and cut her phone line and –'

'She had no proof the person doing those things was Marcus Renard. He asked her out, she turned him down, he was unhappy. There's a big leap from unhappy to psychotic.'

'So said Judge Edmonds, who probably still thinks it's okay for men to hit women over the head with mastodon bones and drag them into caves by their hair,' Annie said with disgust. 'But then that makes him about average around here, doesn't it?'

'Hey, objection!'

She broke her scowl with a look of contrition. 'It goes without saying, you're above average. I'm sorry I'm such poor company tonight. I'm gonna pass on the movie, go home, soak in the tub, go to bed.'

A.J. reached across the table and hooked a fingertip inside the simple gold bracelet she wore, caressing the tender skin of her inner wrist. 'Those aren't necessarily solitary pursuits,' he whispered, his eyes rich with a warm promise he had fulfilled from time to time in the past when the currents of their attraction had managed to cross paths.

Annie drew her hand back on the excuse of reaching for her pocketbook. 'Not tonight, Romeo. I have a concussion.'

They said their goodbyes in the tiny parking lot alongside the restaurant, Annie offering her cheek for A.J.'s goodnight kiss when he aimed for her lips. Their parting only added to the restlessness she had been feeling all day, as if everything in the world were just a half beat out of sync.

She sat behind the wheel of the Jeep, listening with one ear to the radio as A.J. drove out onto La Rue Dumas and turned south.

'You're on KJUN, all talk all the time. Home of the giant jackpot giveaway. This is your *Devil's Advocate*, Owen Onofrio. Our topic tonight: today's controversial decision in the Renard case. I've got Ron from Henderson on line one. Go ahead, Ron.'

'I think it's a disgrace that criminals have all the rights in the courts anymore. He had that woman's ring in his house. By God, that oughta be all she wrote right there. Strap him down and light him up!'

'But what if the detective planted the evidence? What happens when we can't trust the people sworn to protect us? Jennifer in Bayou Breaux on line two.'

'Well, I'm just scared sick by all of it. What's anyone supposed to think? I mean, the police are all over this Renard fella, but what if he *didn't* do it? I heard they have secret evidence that links this murder to those Bayou Strangler murders. I'm a woman lives alone. I work the late shift down at the lamp factory –'

Annie switched the radio off, not in the mood. She often listened to the talk station to get a feel for public opinion. But opinions on this case spanned the spectrum. Only the emotions were consistent: anger, fear, and uncertainty. People were nervous, easily spooked. Reports of prowlers and Peeping Toms had tripled. The waiting lists for home alarm systems were long. Gun shops in the parish were doing a brisk, grim business.

The feelings were no strangers to Annie. The lack of closure, of justice, was driving her crazy. That and her own minimal role in the drama. The fact that, even though she had been in it at the beginning, she had been relegated to bystander. She knew what role she wanted to play. She also knew no one would ever invite her into the game. She was just a deputy, and a *woman* deputy at that. There was no affirmative-action fast track in Partout Parish. A considerable span of rungs ran up the ladder from where she was to where she wanted to be.

She was supposed to wait her turn, earn her stripes, and meanwhile ... Meanwhile the need that had pushed her to become a cop simmered and churned inside her ... and Pam Bichon got lost in the shuffle ... and a killer lay watching, waiting, free to slip away or kill again.

Night had crept in over the town and brought with it a damp chill. Sheer wisps of fog were floating up off the bayou and drifting through the streets like ghosts. Across the street from where Annie sat the black padded door to Laveau's swung open and Chaz Stokes stepped out, blue neon light washing down on him. He stood on the deserted sidewalk for a moment, smoking a cigarette, looking up one side of the street and down the other. He tossed the cigarette in the gutter, climbed into his Camaro, and drove away, turning down the side street that led to the bayou, leaving an empty space at the curb in front of a weathered black pickup. Fourcade's pickup.

It struck Annie as odd. Another piece out of place. No one hung out at Laveau's. The Voodoo Lounge was the usual spot for cops in Bayou Breaux. Laveau's was the mostly empty companion to the mostly empty Maison Dupré hotel next door.

Out of place. It was that thought that pushed her out of the Jeep. Even as she told herself that lie, she could clearly see A.J.'s accusatory face in her mind. He thought she had the hots for Fourcade, for all the good that would have done her. Fourcade treated her like a fixture. She could have been a lamp or a hat rack, with all the sexual allure of either. He didn't resent her, didn't harass her, didn't joke around with her. He had no interest in her whatsoever. And her only interest was in the case. She jaywalked across Dumas to the bar.

Laveau's was a cave of midnight blue walls and mahogany wood black with age. If it hadn't been for the television in the far corner, Annie would have thought she had gone blind walking into the place. The bartender flicked a glance at her and went back to pouring a round of Johnnie Walker for the only table of patrons – a quartet of men in rumpled business suits.

Fourcade sat at the end of the bar, shoulders hunched inside his battered leather jacket, his gaze on the stack of shot glasses before him. He blew a jet stream of smoke at them and watched it dissipate into the gloom. He didn't turn to look at her, but as she approached Annie had the distinct feeling that he was completely conscious of her presence.

She slipped between a pair of stools and leaned sideways against the bar. 'Tough break today,' she said, blinking at the sting of the smoke.

The big dark eyes were on her instantly, staring out from beneath a heavy sweep of brows. Clear, sharp, showing no foggy effects from the whiskey he had consumed, burning with a ferocious intensity that seemed to emanate from the very core of him. He still didn't turn to face her, presenting her with a profile that was hawkish. He wore his black hair slicked back, but a shock of it had tumbled down across his broad forehead.

'Broussard,' Annie said, feeling awkward. 'Deputy Broussard. Annie.' She brushed her bangs out of her eyes in a nervous gesture. 'I – ah – was on the courthouse steps. We took down Hunter Davidson. I was the one at the bottom of the pile.'

The gaze slid down from her face past the open front of her denim jacket and the thin white T-shirt beneath it to the flower-sprigged skirt that hit her mid-calf to the Keds she wore on her feet ... and eased back up like a long caress.

'You out of uniform, Deputy.'

'I'm off duty.'

'Are you?'

Annie blinked at his response and at the smoke, not quite

sure what to make of the first. 'I was the first officer on the scene at the Bichon homicide. I –'

'I know who you are. What you think, *chère*, that this little bit o' whiskey pickled my brain or something?' He arched a brow and chuckled, tapping his cigarette into a plastic ashtray bristling with butts. 'You grew up here, enrolled in the academy August 1993, got hired into the Lafayette PD, came to the SO here in '95. You were the second woman deputy on patrol in this parish – the first having lasted all of ten months. You got a good record, but you tend to be nosy. Me, I think that's maybe not such a bad thing if you gonna do the job, if you looking to move up, which you are.'

Astonished, Annie gaped at him. In the months Fourcade had been in the department she had never heard him volunteer a sentence of more than ten words. She had certainly never dreamed that he knew enough about her to do so. That he seemed to know quite a lot about her was unnerving – a reaction he read without effort.

'You were the first deputy on the scene. I needed to know if you were any good, or if you mighta screwed up, or if maybe you knew Pam Bichon. Maybe you had the same boyfriend. Maybe she sold you a house with snakes under the floors. Maybe she beat you out for head cheerleader back in high school.'

'You considered me a suspect?'

'Me, I consider ever'body a suspect 'til I can find out different.'

He took a long pull on his smoke and watched her as he exhaled. 'Does this bother you?' he asked, making a small gesture with the cigarette.

She tried without success not to blink. 'No.'

'Yes, it does,' he declared as he stubbed it out in the overflowing ashtray. 'Say so. Ain't nobody in this world gonna speak up for you, *chère*.'

'I'm not afraid to speak up.'

'No? You afraid of me?'

'If I were afraid of you, I wouldn't be standing here.'

His lips twisted in a faint smirk and he gave a very French shrug that said, *Maybe, maybe no.* Annie felt her temper spike a notch.

'Why should I be afraid of you?'

His expression darkened as he turned a shot glass on the bar. 'You don't listen to gossip?'

'I take it for what it's worth. Half-truths, if that.'

'And how you decide which half is true?' he asked. 'There is no justice in this world,' he said softly, staring into his whiskey. 'How's that for a truth, Deputy Broussard?'

'It's all in your perception, I suppose.'

' "One man's justice is another man's injustice … one man's wisdom another's folly." ' He sipped at the whiskey. 'Emerson. No reporter will sum up today's events as well … or with such truth.'

'What they say doesn't change the facts,' Annie said. 'You found Pam's ring in Renard's house.'

'You don't think I put it there?'

'If you had put it there, it would have been listed on the warrant.'

'*C'est vrai*. True enough, Annie.' He gave her a pensive look. 'Annie – that's short for something?'

'Antoinette.'

He sipped his whiskey. 'That's a beautiful name, why you don't use it?'

She shrugged. 'I – well – everyone calls me Annie.'

'Me, I'm not ever'body, 'Toinette,' he said quietly.

He seemed to have gotten closer or loomed larger. Annie thought she could feel the heat of him, smell the old leather of his jacket. She knew she could feel his gaze holding hers, and she told herself to back away. But she didn't.

'I came here to ask you about the case,' she said. 'Or did Noblier pull you off?'

'No.'

'I'd like to help if I can.' She blurted the words, forced the idea out before she could swallow it back. She held up one hand to stave off his reply and gestured nervously with the other. 'I mean, I know I'm just a deputy, and technically it isn't my case, and you're the detective, and Stokes won't want me involved, but –'

'You're a helluva salesman, 'Toinette,' Fourcade remarked. 'You telling me every reason to say no.'

'I found her,' Annie said simply. The image of Pam Bichon's body throbbed in her memory, a dead thing that was too alive, that would give her no rest. 'I saw what he did to her. I still see it. I feel … an obligation.'

'You feel it,' Fourcade whispered. 'Shadow of the dead.'

He raised his left hand, fingers spread, and reached out, not quite touching her. Slowly he passed his hand before her eyes, skimmed around the side of her head, just brushing his fingertips against her hair. A shiver rippled down her body.

'It's cold there, no?' he whispered.

'Where?' Annie murmured.

'In Shadowland.'

She started to draw a breath, to tell him he was full of shit, to defuse the prickly sensation that had come to life inside her and between them, but her lungs didn't seem to function. She was aware of a phone ringing somewhere, of the canned laughter coming from the television. But mostly she was aware of Fourcade and the pain that shone in his eyes and came from somewhere deep in his soul.

'You Fourcade?' the bartender called, holding up the telephone receiver. 'You got a call.'

He slid off his stool and moved down the bar. Air rushed into Annie's lungs as he walked away, as if his aura had been pressing down on her chest like an anvil. With an unsteady hand, she raised his glass to her lips and took a drink. She stared at Fourcade as he hunched over the bar and listened to the telephone receiver. He had to be drunk. Everyone knew he wasn't quite right at his most sober.

He hung up the phone and turned toward her.

'I gotta go.' He pulled a twenty out of his wallet and tossed it on the bar.

'Stay away from those shadows, 'Toinette,' he warned her softly, the voice of too much experience. With one hand he reached up and cradled her face, the pad of his thumb brushing the corner of her mouth. 'They'll suck the life outta you.'

4

Nick walked along the boulevard between the road and the bayou. Gloved hands in the pockets of his leather jacket. Shoulders hunched against the damp chill of the night. Fog skimmed off the water and floated past like clouds of perfume, redolent with the scents of rotting vegetation, dead fish, and spider lilies. Something broke the surface with a pop and a splash. A bass snatching a late dinner. Or someone with a heavy case of boredom, tossing rocks.

Pausing by the trunk of a live oak, he stared out past the branches hung with tattered scraps of Spanish moss and looked up and down the bank. There was no one, no foot traffic, no cars crossing the little drawbridge that spanned the bayou to the north. House lights glowed amber in windows beyond the east bank. The night air had gone heavy with a thick mist that was threatening to become rain. A rainy night did nothing to entice folks outdoors without a purpose.

And my purpose?

That remained unclear.

He was close to drunk. He had given himself the excuse of dulling the pain, but instead had only fueled it. The frustration, the injustice – they were like fire under his skin. They would consume him if he didn't do something to burn them out.

He closed his eyes, took a breath, and released it, attempting to find his center – that core of deep calm within that he had spent so much time and effort building. He had worked so hard to control the rage, and it was slipping through his grasp. He had worked so hard on the case, and it was crumbling around him. He felt the chill pass over him, through him. The shadow of the dead. He felt the need pull at him. And a part of him wanted very badly to go where it would lead him.

He wondered if Annie Broussard felt that same pull or if she would even recognize it. Probably not. She was too young. Younger than he had been at twenty-eight. Fresh, optimistic, untainted. He had seen the doubt in her eyes when he had spoken of the shadows. He had also seen the naked truth when she spoke of the obligation she felt to Pam Bichon.

The key to staying sane in homicide was keeping a distance. Don't let it get personal. Don't get involved. Don't take it home with you. Don't cross the line.

He had never been good at taking any of that advice. He lived the job. The line was always behind him.

Had the shadows drawn Pam Bichon? Had she seen Death's phantom coming, felt its cold breath on her shoulders? He knew the answer.

She had complained to friends about Renard's persistent, if subtle advances. Despite her rebuffs, he had begun sending her gifts. Then came the harassment. Small acts of vandalism against her car, her property. Items stolen from her office – photographs, a hairbrush, work papers, her keys.

Yes, Pam had seen the phantom coming, and no one had listened when she tried to tell them. No one had heard her fear any more than they had heard her tortured screams that night out on Pony Bayou.

'I still think about what he did to her,' Stokes said. *'Don't you?'*

All the time. The details had saturated his brain like blood.

With his back against the tree trunk, Nick lowered himself to sit on his heels and stared across the empty street at the building that housed Bowen & Briggs. A light burned on the second floor. A desk lamp. Renard worked at the third drafting table back and on the south side of the big room there. Bowen & Briggs designed both small commercial and residential buildings, with their commercial work coming out of New Iberia and St Martinville as well as Bayou Breaux.

Renard was a partner in the firm, though his name was not on the logo. He preferred designing residential buildings, especially single-family homes, and had a liking for historical styles. His social life was quiet. He had no long-term romantic involvement. He lived with his mother, who collected Mardi Gras masks and created costumes for Carnival revelers, and his autistic brother, Victor, the elder by four years. Their home was a modest, restored plantation house – less than five miles by car from the scene of Pam Bichon's murder. Nearer by boat.

According to the descriptions of the people who worked with and knew Marcus Renard, he was quiet, polite, ordinary, or a touch odd – depending on whom you asked. But other words came to Nick's mind. Meticulous, compulsive, obsessive, repressed, controlling, passive-aggressive.

Behind the mask of ordinariness, Marcus Renard was a very different man from the one his co-workers saw every day sitting at his drafting table. They couldn't see the core component Nick had sensed in him from their first meeting – rage. Deep, deep inside, beneath layers and layers of manners and mores and the guise of mild apathy. Rage, simmering, contained, hidden, buried.

It was rage that had driven those spikes through Pam Bichon's hands.

Rage was no stranger.

The light went out in the second-story window. Out of old habit, Nick checked his watch – 9:47 P.M. – and scanned the street in both directions – all clear. Renard's five-year-old maroon Volvo sat in the narrow parking area between the Bowen & Briggs building and the antiques shop next door, an area poorly lit by a seventy-five-watt yellow bug light over the side door.

Renard would emerge from that door, climb in his car,

and go home to his mother and his brother and his hobby of designing and building elaborate dollhouses. He would sleep in his bed a free man tonight and dream the sinister, euphoric dreams of someone who had gotten away with murder.

He wasn't the first.

'*Protect and serve, pard. ...*'

The rage built. ...

'*Case dismissed.*'

... and burned hotter ...

'*I still think about what he did to her. ...*'

'*I saw what he did to her. ... I still see it. ...*'

'*Don't you?*'

Blood and moonlight, the flash of the knife, the smell of fear, the cries of agony, the ominous silence of death. The cold darkness as the phantom passed over.

The chill collided violently with the fire. The explosion pushed him to his feet.

'*He's gonna walk, Nicky. He's gonna get away with murder. ...*'

Nick crossed the street, hugged the wall of the Bowen & Briggs building, out of sight from the elevated first-floor windows. Pulling a handkerchief from his pocket, he hopped silently onto the side stoop, doused the bug light with a twist of his wrist, and dropped down on the far side of the steps.

He heard the door open, heard Renard mutter something under his breath, heard the *click, click, click* of the light switch being tried. Footsteps on the concrete stoop. A heavy sigh. The door closed.

He waited, still, invisible, until Renard's loafers hit the blacktop and he had stepped past Nick on his way to the Volvo.

'It's not over, Renard,' he said.

The architect shied sideways. His face was waxy white, his eyes bulged like a pair of boiled eggs.

'You can't harass me this way, Fourcade,' he said, the

tremor in his voice mocking his attempt at bravado. 'I have rights.'

'Is that a fact?' Nick stepped forward, his gloved hands hanging loose at his sides. 'What about Pam? She didn't have rights? You take her rights away, *tcheue poule*, and still you think you got rights?'

'I didn't do anything,' Renard said, glancing nervously toward the street, looking for salvation that was nowhere in sight. 'You don't have anything on me.'

Nick advanced another step. 'I got all I need on you, *pou*. I got the stink of you up my nose, you piece of shit.'

Renard lifted a fist in front of him, shaking so badly his car keys rattled. 'Leave me alone, Fourcade.'

'Or what?'

'You're drunk.'

'Yeah.' A grin cut across his face like a scimitar. 'I'm mean too. What you gonna do, call a cop?'

'Touch me and your career is over, Fourcade,' Renard threatened, backing toward the Volvo. 'Everybody knows about you. You got no business carrying a badge. You ought to be in jail.'

'And you oughta be in hell.'

'Based on what? Evidence you planted? That's nothing you haven't done before. You'll be the one in prison over this, not me.'

'That's what you think?' Nick murmured, advancing. 'You think you can stalk a woman, torture her, kill her, and just walk away?'

The nightmare images of murder. The false memories of screams.

'You got nothing on me, Fourcade, and you never will have.'

'*Case dismissed.*'

'You're nothing but a drunk and a bully, and if you touch me, Fourcade, I swear, I'll ruin you.'

'He's gonna walk, Nicky. He's gonna get away with murder. ...'

A face from his past loomed up, an apparition floating beside Marcus Renard. A mocking face, a superior sneer.

'You'll never pin this on me, Detective. That's not the way the world works. She was just another whore. ...'

'You killed her, you son of a bitch,' he muttered, not sure which demon he was talking to, the real or the imagined.

'You'll never prove it.'

'You can't touch me.'

'He's gonna get away with murder. ...'

'The hell you say.'

The rage burned through the fine thread of control. Emotion and action became one, and restraint was nowhere to be found as his fist smashed into Marcus Renard's face.

Annie walked out of Quik Pik with a pint of chocolate chip ice cream in a bag and a little mouse chewing at her conscience. She could have picked up the treat at the Corners, but she'd had her fill of people for one day, and a prolonged grilling by Uncle Sos was too much to face. The politics of the Renard case had him in a lather. She knew for a fact he had bet fifty dollars on the outcome of the evidentiary hearing – and lost. That, coupled with his opinion of her current platonic relationship with A.J., would have him in rare form tonight.

'Why you don' marry dat boy, 'tite chatte? Andre, he's a good boy, him. What's a matter wit' you, turnin' you purty nose up? You all the time chasin' you don' know what, éspèsces de tête dure.'

Just the imagined haranguing was enough to amplify the thumping in her head. The whole idea of buying ice cream was to be nice to herself. She didn't want to think about A.J. or Renard or Pam Bichon or Fourcade.

She had heard the stories about Fourcade. The allegations of brutality, the rumors surrounding the unsolved case of a murdered teenage prostitute in the French Quarter, the unsubstantiated accusations of evidence tampering.

'Stay away from those shadows, 'Toinette. ... They'll suck the life outta you.'

Good advice, but she couldn't take it if she wanted in on the case. They were a package deal, Fourcade and the murder. They seemed to go together a little too well. He was a scary son of a bitch.

She started the Jeep and turned toward the bayou, flicking the wipers on to cut the thick mist from the windshield. On the radio, Owen Onofrio was still prodding his listeners for reactions to the scene at the courthouse.

'Kent in Carencro, you're on line two.'

'I think that judge oughta be unpoached –'

'You mean impeached?'

As she slowed for a stop sign, her eyes automatically scanned for traffic ... and hit on a black Ford pickup with a dent in the driver's-side rear panel. Fourcade's truck, parked in front of a shoe repair place that had gone out of business two years ago.

Annie doused her lights and sat there, double-parked, engine grumbling. This was not a residential street. There were no businesses open. A third of the places on this stretch of road were vacant ... but the offices of Bowen & Briggs were located two blocks south.

She put the Jeep in gear and crept forward. She could see the building that housed Bayou Realty and Bowen & Briggs. There were no lights. There were no cars parked on the street. The sheriff had pulled the surveillance on Renard after the hearing, hoping the press would back off. Renard had been working evenings for the same reason. Fourcade was parked two blocks away.

' *"One man's justice is another man's injustice ... one man's wisdom another's folly."* '

Annie pulled to the curb in front of Robichaux Electric, cut the engine, and grabbed her big black flashlight from the debris on the floor behind the passenger's seat. Maybe Fourcade was taking it upon himself to continue the surveillance. But if that were the case, he wouldn't park two blocks away or leave his vehicle.

She pulled her Sig P-225 out of her duffel bag and stuck the gun in the waistband of her skirt, then climbed out of the Jeep. Keeping the flashlight off, she made her way down the sidewalk, her sneakers silent on the damp pavement.

'There is no justice in this world. How's that for a truth, Deputy Broussard?'

'Shit, shit, shit,' she chanted under her breath, her step quickening at the first sound from the direction of Bowen & Briggs. A scrape. A shoe on asphalt. A thump. A muffled cry.

'Shit!' Pulling the gun and flicking the switch on the flashlight, she broke into a run.

She could hear the sound of flesh striking flesh even before she entered the narrow parking lot. Instinct rushed her forward, overruling procedure. She should have called it in. She didn't have any backup. Her badge was in her pocketbook in the Jeep. Not one of those facts slowed her step.

'Sheriff's office, freeze!' she yelled, sweeping the bright halogen beam across the parking area.

Fourcade had Renard up against the side of a car, swinging at him with the rhythm of a boxer at a punching bag. A hard left turned Renard's face toward Annie, and she gasped at the blood that obscured his features. He lunged toward her, arms outstretched, blood and spittle spraying from his mouth in a froth as a wild animal sound tore from his throat and his eyes rolled white. Fourcade caught him in the stomach and knocked him back into the Volvo.

'Fourcade! Stop it!' Annie shouted, hurling herself against him, trying to knock him away from Renard. 'Stop it! You're killing him! *Arrête! C'est assez!*'

He shrugged her off like a mosquito and cracked Renard's jaw with a right.

'Stop it!'

Using the big flashlight like a baton, she swung it as hard as she could into his kidneys, once, twice. As she drew back for a third blow, Fourcade spun toward her, poised to strike.

Annie scuttled backward. She turned the full beam of the flashlight in Fourcade's face. 'Hold it!' she ordered. 'I've got a gun!'

'Get away!' he roared. His expression was feral, his eyes glazed, wild. One corner of his mouth curled in a snarl.

'It's Broussard,' she said. '*Deputy* Broussard. Step back, Fourcade! I mean it!'

He didn't move, but the look on his face slipped toward uncertainty. He glanced around with the kind of hesitancy that suggested he had just come to and didn't know where he was or how he had gotten there. Behind him, Renard dropped to his hands and knees on the blacktop, vomited, then collapsed.

'Jesus,' Annie muttered. 'Stay where you are.'

Squatting beside Renard, she stuck her gun back in her waistband and felt for the carotid artery in his neck, her fingers coming away sticky with blood. His pulse was strong. He was alive but unconscious, and probably glad for it. His face looked like raw hamburger, his nose was an indistinct mass. She wiped the blood from her hand on his shoulder, pulled the Sig again, and stood, her knees shaking.

'What the hell were you thinking?' she asked, turning toward Fourcade.

Nick stared down at Renard lying in his own puke as if seeing him for the first time. Thinking? He couldn't remember thinking. What he did remember didn't make sense. Echoes of voices from another place ... taunts ... The red haze was slowly dissipating, leaving him with a sick feeling.

'What were you gonna do?' Annie Broussard demanded. 'Kill him and dump him in the swamp? Did you think nobody would notice? Did you think nobody would suspect? My God, you're a *cop*! You're supposed to uphold the law, not take it into your own hands!'

She hissed a breath through her teeth. 'Looks like I believed the wrong half of those rumors about you, after all, Fourcade.'

'I – I came here to talk to him,' he muttered.

'Yeah? Well, you're a helluva conversationalist.'

Renard groaned, shifted positions, and settled back into oblivion. Nick closed his eyes, turned away, and rubbed his gloved hands over his face. The smell of Renard's blood in the leather gagged him.

'*C'est ein affaire à pus finir*,' he whispered. *It is a thing that has no end.*

'What are you talking about?' Broussard demanded.

Shadows and darkness, and the kind of rage that could swallow a man whole. But she knew of none of these things, and he didn't try to tell her.

'Go call an ambulance,' he said with resignation.

She looked to Renard and back, weighing the options.

'It's all right, 'Toinette. I promise not to kill him while you're gone.'

'Under the circumstances, you'll forgive me if I don't believe a word you say.' Annie glanced at Renard again. 'He's not going anywhere. You can come with me. And by the way,' she added, gesturing him toward the street with her gun, 'you're under arrest. You have the right to remain silent ...'

5

You can't arrest Fourcade. He's a detective, for Christ's sake!' Gus ranted, pacing behind his desk.

The desk sergeant had called him in from a Rotary Club dinner where he had been ingesting calories in the liquid form, trying to dull the barbed comments of Rotarians unhappy with the day's court ruling. The civic leaders of Bayou Breaux had wanted Renard's indictment as something extra to celebrate for Mardi Gras. Even with half a pint of Amaretto in him, Gus felt as if his blood pressure just might cause his head to explode.

'What the hell were you thinking, Broussard?' he demanded.

Annie's jaw dropped. 'I was thinking he committed assault! I saw him with my own eyes!'

'Well, there's got to be more to this story than what *you* know.'

'I saw what I saw. Ask him yourself, Sheriff. He won't deny it. Renard looks like he put his face in a Waring blender.'

'Fuck a duck,' Gus muttered. 'I told him, I *told* him! Where's he at now?'

'Interview B.'

It had been a fight getting him in there. Not that Fourcade had resisted in any way. It was Rodrigue, the desk sergeant, and Degas and Pitre – deputies just hanging around. *'Arresting Fourcade? Naw. Must be some mistake. Quit screwing around, Broussard. What'd he do – pinch your ass? We don't arrest our own. Nick, he's part of the Brotherhood. Whatsa matter with you, Broussard – you on the rag or somethin'? He beat up Renard? Christ, we oughta get him a medal! Is Renard dead? Can we throw a party?'*

In the end, Fourcade had pushed past them through the doorway and let himself into Interview B.

The sheriff stalked past Annie and out the door. She hustled after him, a choke hold on her temper. If she'd hauled in a civilian, no one would have questioned her judgment or her perception of facts.

The door to the interview room was wide open. Rodrigue stood with one hand on the frame and one eye on his abandoned desk, grinning as he traded comments with someone inside the room, his mustache wriggling like a woolly caterpillar on his upper lip.

'Hey, Sheriff, we're thinking maybe Nick oughta get a ticker-tape parade.'

'Shut up,' Gus barked as he bulled his way past the desk sergeant and into the room where Degas and Pitre had sprawled into chairs. Coffee cups sat steaming on the small table. Fourcade sat on the far side, smoking a cigarette and looking detached.

Gus cut a scathing look at his deputies. 'Y'all don't have nothing better to do, then why are you on my payroll? Get outta here! You too!' he snapped at Annie. 'Go home.'

'Go home? But – but, Sheriff,' she stammered, 'I was there. I'm the –'

'So was he.' He pointed at Fourcade. 'I talked to you, now I'm gonna talk to him. You got a problem with that, Deputy?'

'No, sir,' Annie said tightly. She looked at Fourcade, wanting him to meet her eyes, wanting to see … what? Innocence? She knew he wasn't innocent. Apology? He didn't owe her anything. He took a drag on his cigarette and focused on the stream of smoke.

Gus planted his hands on the back of a vacant chair and leaned on it, waiting to hear the door close behind him. And when the door closed, he waited some more, wishing he would come to in his own cozy bed with his plump, snoring wife and realize this day had all been a bad dream and nothing more.

'What do you have to say for yourself, Detective?' he asked at last.

Nick stubbed out the butt in the ashtray Pitre had obligingly fetched him. What was he supposed to say? He had no explanation, only excuses.

'Nothing,' he said.

'Nothing. Nothing?' Noblier repeated, as if the word were foreign to his tongue. 'Look at me, Nick.'

He did so and wondered which was the better choice: to allow himself an emotional response to the disappointment he saw or to block it. Emotion was what unfailingly landed him in trouble. He had spent the last year of his life learning to hold it in an iron fist deep within him. Tonight it had broken free, and here he sat.

'I took a big chance bringing you on board here,' Gus said quietly. 'I did it because I knew your papa, and I owed him something from way back. And because I believed you about that business in New Orleans, and I thought you could do a good job here.

'This is how you pay me back?' he asked, voice rising. 'You screw up an investigation and beat the hell out of a suspect? You better have something more than nothing to say for yourself, or, by God, I'll throw your ass to the wolves!

'Why'd you go near Renard when I told you not to? Why'd you have to get in his face? Jesus Christ, do you have any idea what him and that anorexic lawyer of his are gonna do to this office? Tell me you had some kind of cause to go near him. What were you even doing in that part of town?'

'Drinking.'

'Oh, great! Good answer! You left my office in a flaming temper and went and threw alcohol on it!'

He shoved the chair into the table. 'Damage control,' he muttered. 'How the fuck do we spin this? I can say you were on surveillance.'

'You told the press you pulled the surveillance.'

'Fuck the press. I tell 'em what I want 'em to think. Renard is still a suspect. We got reason to watch him. That gives you cause to be there, and it shows I believe in your innocence on that evidence-tampering bullshit Kudrow's trying to stir up. So then what? Did he provoke you?'

'Does it matter?' Nick asked. 'Never mind that he's a murderer, and the goddamn court shoulda punched his ticket for him –'

'Yeah, the court should have, but it didn't. Then Hunter Davidson tried to and you stopped him. It looks like you just wanted the job all for yourself.'

'I know what it looks like.'

'It looks like assault, at the very least. Broussard thinks I should throw your ass in jail.'

Broussard. Nick pushed to his feet, the anger stirring anew. Broussard, who hadn't said ten words to him in the six months he'd been in Bayou Breaux. Who suddenly sought him out at Laveau's. Who appeared out of nowhere with a gun and the power to arrest him.

'Will you?' he asked.

'Not if I don't have to.'

'Renard'll press charges.'

'You bet your balls he will.' Gus rubbed a hand over his face and secretly wished he'd stayed in geology all those years ago. 'He's no shit-for-brains lowlife you can stick his head in a toilet and flush a confession outta him and won't nobody listen to him when he screams about it. Kudrow's been threatening a lawsuit all along. Harassment, he says. Unlawful arrest, he says. Well, I sure as hell know what he'll say about this.'

He dropped down onto a chair. 'All in all, I think I'm gonna wish you'd finished the job and fed Renard to the gators.'

What you hanging around for, Broussard?' Rodrigue asked. Blocky and nearly bald, he stood behind his desk shuffling papers with an air of false importance, as if he hadn't been kicked out of the interview room himself.

Annie gave the sergeant a defiant glare. 'I'm the arresting officer. I've got a suspect to book, a report to file, and evidence to log in.'

Rodrigue snorted. 'There ain't gonna be no arrest, darlin'. Fourcade, he didn't do nothing ever'body in this parish hasn't wanted to do.'

'Last time I looked, assault was against the law.'

'Dat wasn't no assault. Dat was justice. Oh, yeah.'

'Yeah,' Degas chimed in. 'And you interrupted it, Broussard. There's the crime. Why didn't you let him finish the job?'

Because that would have been murder, Annie thought. That Renard deserved killing didn't enter into it. The law was the law, and she was sworn to uphold it, as were Fourcade and Rodrigue and Degas, and Gus Noblier.

'That's right,' Pitre said, swaggering toward her, pulling the handcuffs off his belt. 'Maybe we oughta be arresting you, Broussard. Obstruction of justice.'

'Interfering with an officer in the performance of his duty,' Degas added.

'I think a strip search is in order here,' Pitre suggested, reaching for her arm.

'Fuck you, Pitre,' she snapped, jerking away from him.

A salacious sneer lit his face. 'I'm up for it, sugar, if you think it'll help your case.'

'Go piss up a rope.'

'The sheriff told you to go home, Broussard,' Rodrigue said. 'You're disobeying an order. You wanna go on report?'

Annie shook her head in disbelief. He would condone brutality, and write her up for loitering. She looked at the door to the interview room, uncertain. Procedure dictated one course of action, her sheriff had ordered another. She would have given anything to know what was being said on the other side of that door, but no one was going to let her in either literally or figuratively. Gus had taken over, and Gus Noblier was absolute ruler of the Partout Parish Sheriff's Office, if not of Partout Parish itself.

'Fine,' she said grudgingly. 'I'll do the paperwork in the morning.'

She felt their eyes burning into her back all the way to the door, their hostility a tangible thing. The sensation made her feel ill. These were men she had known for two years, men she had joked with.

The mist had evolved into a steady, cold rain. Annie pulled her denim jacket up over her head and ran to the Jeep, where her ice cream had melted and was seeping through the carton into a milky puddle on the driver's side floor. A fitting end to her evening.

She sat behind the wheel, trying to imagine what would happen tomorrow, but nothing came. She had no frame of reference. She had never arrested a fellow officer.

'We don't arrest our own. Nick, he's part of the Brotherhood.'

The Brotherhood. The Code.

I broke the Code.

'Well, what the hell was I supposed to do?' she asked aloud.

The plastic alligator that hung from the mirror stared back at her with a mocking leer. Annie snapped at him with a forefinger and sat back as he danced on the end of his tether. She glanced at the paper bag she had tucked between the bucket seats. The bag her ice cream had come in. The bag she had used to collect Fourcade's bloody gloves. Each glove should have been bagged individually, but she'd made do with what she had on hand, slipping one glove in, then folding the bag and inserting the other in the top pocket created by the fold. Procedure dictated she log in the evidence, see to it that it was secured in the evidence room. Instinct kept her from running back into the station with the bag. She could still feel the burning gazes of Rodrigue and Degas and Pitre boring into her. She had broken the Code.

And yet, she had bent rules, had made concessions for

Fourcade she wouldn't have made with a civilian. She should have called a unit to the scene, but she hadn't. The jurisdiction was City of Bayou Breaux, not Partout Parish, but it seemed like betrayal to turn Fourcade over to another department. She had called an ambulance for Renard, explained nothing to the paramedics, and hauled Fourcade to the station in her own vehicle. She hadn't even called in to dispatch to warn them, because she didn't want it on the radio.

She had made concessions to Fourcade because he was a cop, and still she was being made the heavy. Men she would have joked with last night suddenly looked at her as if she were a hostile and unwelcome stranger.

She started the Jeep and rolled out of the parking lot as two cars turned in. Deputies coming on for the midnight shift. The news of Fourcade's run-in would spread like hot oil in a skillet. Her world had suddenly turned 180 degrees. Everything simple had become complex. Everything familiar had become unfamiliar. Everything light had gone dark. She looked at the rain and remembered Fourcade's whispered word: *Shadowland*.

The streets were deserted, making the traffic lights seem an extravagance. The majority of Bayou Breaux's seven thousand residents were working-class people who went to bed at a decent hour weeknights and saved their hell-raising for the weekends. Commercial fishermen, oil workers, cane farmers. What industry there was in town supported those same professions.

The core of Bayou Breaux was old. A couple of the buildings on La Rue Dumas had been standing there since before the first Acadians got off the boats from *le grand dérangement* in the eighteenth century, when the British confiscated their property in Nova Scotia and kicked them out. Many more buildings dated to the nineteenth century – some clapboard, some brick with false fronts, some in good shape, some not. Annie drove past them, temporarily oblivious to their history.

A neon light for Dixie beer glowed red in the window of T-Neg's, the nightspot in what was still called the colored part of town. The modern rage for political correctness had yet to sift into the deeper recesses of South Louisiana. She hung a right at Canray's Garage, a tumbledown filling station that looked like something from a bleak postapocalyptic sci-fi movie, with junked cars and disemboweled engines abandoned all around. The houses down this street didn't look much better. Tatty one-story cottages rose off the ground on leaning brick pilings, the houses crammed shoulder to shoulder with yards the size of postage stamps.

The properties gradually became larger, the homes more respectable and more modern the farther west she drove. The old neighborhoods gave way to subdivisions on the southwest side of town, where contractors had lined cul-de-sacs with brick pseudo-Acadian and pseudo-Caribbean plantation cottages. A.J. lived out here.

But how could she go to him? He worked for the DA. The cops and the prosecutors may have technically been on the same big team for justice, but the reality was often more adversarial than congenial. If she went over the sheriff's head and crossed the line into the DA's camp, there would be hell to pay with Noblier, and the rest of the department would see it only as further proof that she had turned on them.

And if she went to A.J. as a friend, then what? Could she expect him to separate who they were from what they did when a possible felony charge hung in the balance?

Annie pulled a U-turn and headed for the hospital. Marcus Renard's beating was her case until someone told her differently. She had a victim's statement to take.

A pristine white statue of the Virgin Mary welcomed the afflicted to Our Lady of Mercy with open arms. Spotlights nestled in the hibiscus shrubs at the base of her pedestal illuminated her all night long, a beacon to the battered. The hospital itself had been built in the seventies, during the oil

56

boom, when ready money and philanthropy were in abundant supply. A two-story brick L, it sprawled over a manicured lawn that was set back just far enough from the bayou to be both scenic and prudent in flood season.

Annie parked in the red zone in front of the ER entrance, flipping down her visor with the insignia of the sheriff's department clipped to it. Notebook in hand, she headed into the hospital, wondering if Renard would be in any condition to speak to her. If he died, would that make life easier or harder?

'We just got him moved into a room.' Nurse Jolie led her down a corridor that glowed like pearl under the soft night lighting. 'I voted for the boiler room – the boiler itself, to be precise. Do you know who beat him up? I wanna kiss that man all over.'

'He's in jail,' Annie lied.

Nurse Jolie arched a finely curved brow. 'What for?'

Annie bit back a sigh as they stopped before the door to room 118. 'Is he awake? Sedated? Can he talk?'

'He can talk through what's left of his teeth. Dr Van Allen used a local on his nose and jaw. He hasn't been given any painkillers.' A slyly sadistic smile turned the nurse's mouth. 'We don't want to mask the symptoms of a serious head trauma with narcotics.'

'Never piss off medical people,' Annie said, pretending to jot herself a note.

'Damn straight, girl.'

Jolie pushed open the door to Renard's room and held it. The room was set up as a double, but only one bed was occupied. Renard lay with the head of the bed tipped up slightly, the fluorescent light glaring down into his eyes, which were nearly swollen shut. His face looked like a mutant pomegranate. Just two hours after his beating and already the swelling and bruising made him unrecognizable. One eyebrow was stitched together. Another line of stitches ran up his chin and over his lower lip like a millipede. Cotton had been crammed up his nostrils, and what was left of his nose was swathed in bandaging and adhesive tape.

'Not a plug to be pulled,' the nurse said regretfully. She cut a glance at Annie. 'You couldn't have just hung back until Whoever put this asshole in a coma?'

'Timing has never been my strong suit,' Annie muttered with bitter irony.

'Too bad.'

Annie watched her glide away, heading back for the nurses' station.

'Mr Renard, I'm Deputy Broussard,' she said, uncapping her pen as she moved toward the bed. 'If it's at all possible, I'd like to get a statement from you as to what happened this evening.'

Marcus studied her through the slits left open in the swelling around his eyes. His angel of mercy. Beside the elevated hospital bed, she looked small. The denim jacket she wore swallowed her up. She was pretty in a tomboy-next-door kind of way, with a blackening bruise high on one cheek and her brown hair hanging in disarray. Her eyes were the color of café noir, slightly exotic in shape, their expression dead serious as she waited for him to speak.

'You were there,' he whispered, setting off a stabbing pain in his face. What little lidocaine the doctor had bothered to use was wearing off. The packing in his nose forced him to breathe through his mouth, and only added to the feeling that his head was twice its normal size. His sinuses were draining down the back of his throat, half choking him.

'I need to know what happened before I got there,' she said. 'What precipitated the fight?'

'Attack.'

'You're saying Detective Fourcade simply attacked you? No words were exchanged?'

'I came out ... of the building,' he said haltingly. Tape bound his cracked ribs so tightly he wasn't able to take in more than a teaspoon of air at a time. 'He was there. Angry

... about the ruling. Said it wasn't over. Hit me. Again ... and again.'

'You didn't say anything to him?'

'He wants me dead.'

She glanced up at him from her notebook. 'He's hardly the only one, Mr Renard.'

'Not you,' Marcus said. 'You ... saved me.'

'I was doing my job.'

'And Fourcade?'

'I don't speak for Detective Fourcade.'

'He tried ... to kill me.'

'Did he state that he meant to kill you?'

'Look at me.'

'It's not my place to draw conclusions, Mr Renard.'

'But you did,' he insisted. 'I heard you say, 'You're killing him.' You saved me. Thank you.'

'I don't want your thanks,' Annie said bluntly.

'I didn't ... kill Pam. I loved her ... like a friend.'

'Friends don't stalk other friends.'

Marcus lifted a finger to admonish her. 'Conclusion ...'

'That's not my case. I'm free to review the facts and come to any conclusion I like. Did you provoke Detective Fourcade in any way?'

'No. He was irrational ... and drunk.'

He tried to moisten his lips, his tongue butting into the jagged edges of several chipped teeth and a blank space where a tooth had been. He shifted his gaze to a plastic water pitcher on his right.

'Could you please ... pour me a drink ... Annie?'

'Deputy Broussard,' Annie said, too sharply. His use of her name unnerved her. She wanted to deny his request, but he already had enough to file suit against the department. There was no sense exacerbating the situation over so simple a task.

She set her notebook on the bedside stand, poured half a glass of water, and handed it to him. The knuckles of his right hand were skinned raw and painted orange with iodine. This was the hand he would have held the knife in as he butchered a woman he claimed to love as a friend.

He tried to sip at the water, avoiding the mended split in his lip by pressing the glass against the left corner of his mouth. A stream dribbled down his chin onto his hospital gown. He should have had a straw, but the nurses hadn't left him one. Annie supposed he'd be lucky if they hadn't poisoned the water.

'Thank you, again ... Deputy,' he said, attempting a smile that made him look more ghoulish. 'You're very kind.'

'Do you want to press charges?' Annie asked abruptly.

He made a choking sound that might have been a laugh. 'He tried to kill me. Yes ... I want to press charges. He should be ... in prison. You'll help me put him there ... Deputy. You're my witness.'

The pen stilled in Annie's hand as the prospect went through her like a skewer. 'You know something, Renard? I wish I'd never turned down that street tonight.'

He tried to shake his head. 'You don't ... want me dead ... Annie. You saved me today. Twice.'

'I already wish I hadn't.'

'You don't ... look for revenge. You look ... for justice ... for truth. I'm not ... a bad man ... Annie.'

'I'll feel better if a court decides that,' she said, closing her notebook. 'Someone from the department will get back to you.'

Marcus watched her walk away, then closed his eyes and conjured up her face in his mind's eye. Pretty, rectangular, a hint of a cleft in the chin, skin the color of fresh cream and new Georgia peaches. She believed in the good in people. She liked to help. He imagined her voice – soft, a little husky. He thought of what she might have said to him if she hadn't come in her capacity as deputy. Words of sympathy and comfort, meant to soothe his pain.

Annie Broussard. His angel of mercy.

6

The rain fell steadily, reducing the reach of the headlights, making the night close in like a tunnel. The sky seemed too low, the trees that grew thick seemed to hunch over the road. Jennifer Nolan's imagination ran wild with movie images of maniacs leaping out in front of her and cars suddenly looming up in the rearview mirror.

She hated working the late shift. But then, she hated being home at night, too. She had been raised to fear basically everything about the night: the dark, the sounds in the dark, the things that might lurk in the dark. She wished she had a roommate, but the last one had stolen her best jewelry and her television and run off with some no-account biker, and so she was living alone.

Headlights came up behind her, and Jennifer's breath caught. All anybody ever talked about anymore was murder and how women weren't safe to walk the streets. She'd heard that Bichon woman had been dismembered. That wasn't what had been reported on the news, but she'd heard it and knew it was probably true. Rumors leaked out – like the detail of the Mardi Gras mask. The police didn't want anyone to know that either, but everyone did.

Just imagining the terror that woman must have felt was enough to give Jennifer nightmares. She didn't even want to think about Mardi Gras, which was less than two weeks away, on account of that mask business. And now she had this car on her tail. For all she knew, this could have been what happened to Pam Bichon. She could have been forced off the road and herded up that driveway to her death.

The car swept up alongside her and her panic doubled. Then the car sailed on past, taillights glowing in the gloom. Relief ran through her like water. She hit the blinker and turned in at the trailer park.

She had her key in her hand as she went up the steps to the front door, the way she'd read in *Glamour*. Have the key ready to unlock the door quickly or to be used as a weapon if an attacker jumped up from the honeysuckle bush that struggled to live beside her stoop.

A lamp burned in the living room to give the impression someone was home all evening. After locking the door behind her, Jennifer hung her jacket on the coatrack and grabbed a towel off the kitchen counter to dab at her rain-wet red hair as she moved through the trailer, turning on more lights. She was careful not to step into a room until the light was on and she could see. She checked the spare bedroom, the bathroom. Her bedroom was at the end of the narrow hall. Nothing had been disturbed, no one was in the closet. A can of Aqua Net hair spray sat on the nightstand. She would use it like Mace if someone broke in during the night.

With the knowledge of safety, the tension began to subside, letting fatigue settle in. Too many nights with too little sleep, the hassle with her supervisor over the length of her coffee breaks, the past-due balance on her phone bill – each worry weighed down on her. Depressed, she brushed her teeth, took off her jeans, and climbed into bed in the T-shirt she'd worn all day. I'M WITH STUPID, it read, and an arrow pointed to the empty space in the bed beside her. She was with no one. Until 1:57 A.M.

Jennifer Nolan woke with a start. A gloved hand struck her hard across the face as she struggled to sit up and opened her mouth to scream. The back of her skull smacked against the headboard. She tried again to lurch forward, stopped this time by the feel of a blade at her throat. Her bladder released and tears welled in her eyes.

But even through the blur she could see her attacker. His image was illuminated by the green glow of the alarm clock and by the light that seeped in around the edges of the cheap miniblinds. He seemed huge as he loomed over her, the vision of doom. Terrified, she fixed on his face – a face half hidden by a feathered Mardi Gras mask.

7

Richard Kudrow was dying. The Crohn's disease that had besieged his intestinal tract for the last five years of his life had been joined in the last few months by a voracious cancer. Despite the efforts of medical science, his body was virtually devouring itself.

He had been told to quit his practice and devote his time to the hopeless task of treatment, but he didn't see the point. He knew his demise was inevitable. Work was all that kept him going. Anger and adrenaline fueled his weakened system. The focus on justice – an attainable goal – gave him a greater sense of purpose than the pursuit of a cure – an unattainable goal. In defying his doctors and his disease, he had already managed to live past all expectations.

His enemies said he was too damned mean to die. He figured the beating of Marcus Renard was going to give him another six or eight months' worth of fury to live on.

'My client was beat to within an inch of his life by your detective, Noblier. What kind of bullshit will you attempt to spread over that plain truth?'

Gus pressed his lips together. His eyes narrowed to the size of beads as he glared at Kudrow sitting across from him, gray and withering like a rotting pecan husk in his wrinkled brown suit.

'You're the bullshit expert, Kudrow. I'm supposed to swallow the rantings of your sociopathic homicidal pervert client?'

'He didn't break his own nose. He didn't break his own jaw. He did not break his own teeth out of his head. Ask your Deputy Broussard. Better yet, *I'll* ask your Deputy Broussard,' Kudrow said, pressing up out of the chair. 'I sure as hell don't trust you any farther than I could throw a grown hog.'

Gus rose with energy and thrust a finger at the lawyer. 'You stay the hell away from my people, Kudrow.'

Kudrow waved him off. 'Broussard is a material witness and Fourcade is a thug. He was a thug on the NOPD and you knew it when you hired him. That makes you culpable in the civil suit, Noblier, and, by virtue of the fact that you did not suspend Fourcade from the Bichon case after his obvious attempt to plant and manipulate evidence, you may well be guilty of collusion on the assault.'

Gus snorted. 'Collusion! You give yourself a hernia trying to drag that dead horse into court, you old goat. And you file as many goddamn civil suits as you want. You'll die poor before you get a dime out of my office. As for the rest, I don't remember anybody electing you district attorney.'

'Smith Pritchett will bring charges before you can digest the grease you ate for breakfast. He'll be all too happy to see Fourcade's ass in jail.'

'We'll see about that,' Gus grumbled. 'You don't know shit about what happened last night, and I am not obliged to talk with you about it.'

'It'll all be a matter of record.' Kudrow picked up his old briefcase, and the weight of it tilted him slightly sideways. 'It had damn well better be. Your deputy made an arrest last night. She took a statement from my client, asked if he wanted to press charges. If there isn't paperwork to go with those facts, there will be hell to pay, Noblier.'

Gus's features twisted as if he had just caught wind of day-old roadkill. 'Your client is delusional and a liar, and those are some of his better qualities,' he said, cutting past the lawyer to the front door of his office. 'Get out of here, Kudrow. I've got better things to do with my time than listen to you pass gas through your mouth all morning.'

Kudrow bared the teeth the toxins in his body had turned amber. Energy burned in his veins like rocket fuel and he envisioned it searing the cancer out of him. 'It's been a pleasure, as always, Sheriff. But not so much a pleasure as ruining you and your rogue, Fourcade, will be.'

'Why don't you just do the world a favor and drop dead,' Gus suggested.

'I'd never be that nice to you, Noblier. I plan to outlive your days in this office, if for no other reason than spite.'

'God should live that long, but you sure as hell won't, I'm glad to say.'

'We'll see who gets the last word.'

Gus slammed the door on Kudrow's back. 'Me, you rotting old turd,' he grumbled. He swung toward the side door to his secretary's office and bellowed, 'Get in here, Broussard!'

Annie's heart sank as she rose from the chair she'd been waiting in. She had listened with rapt attention to the angry voices that could be quite plainly heard through the door. The heat of the argument seemed to have physically enveloped her. She could feel sweat trickling down between her shoulder blades and moistening the armpits of her uniform.

Valerie Comb, Noblier's secretary, cut her a sideways look. A bottle blonde, she had been four years ahead of Annie in school, head basketball cheerleader and voted most likely to get pregnant on purpose, which she had done. Now divorced with three kids to feed, she placed her loyalties solidly in Noblier's corner.

Pulling in a deep breath, Annie let herself into the inner sanctum, and closed the door behind her. The sheriff stomped toward her with a bulldog glare and hands jammed at his belt line. Annie braced her feet slightly apart and locked her hands together behind her back.

'You took a statement from Marcus Renard last night?' he said in a tight voice.

'Yes, sir.'

'I told you to go home, didn't I, Broussard? Am I getting Alzheimer's or something? Did I just imagine I told you to go home?'

'No, sir.'

'Then what the hell were you doing down at Our Lady, taking a statement from Marcus Renard?'

'It had to be done, Sheriff,' she said. 'I was the officer on the scene. I knew Renard would be only too happy to charge the department with negligence, and –'

'Don't you preach procedure to me, Deputy,' he snapped. 'You don't think I know procedure? You think I don't know what I'm doing?'

'No, sir – I mean, yes, sir – I –'

'When I tell you to do something, I have a reason for it, Deputy Broussard.' He leaned toward her, his whole head as red as a radish out to the tips of his ears. 'Sometimes a situation needs to be sorted through before we proceed in the usual way. Do you understand what I'm saying here, Deputy?'

Annie held every muscle in her body stiff, too afraid that she knew exactly what he was saying. 'I saw Nick Fourcade beating the shit out of Marcus Renard, Sheriff.'

'I'm not saying you didn't. I'm saying you don't know the circumstances. I'm saying you didn't hear the call about a prowler in that part of town. I'm saying you weren't there when the offender resisted arrest.'

Annie stared at him for a long moment. 'You're saying I wasn't in the room last night when everyone was getting their story straight,' she said at last, knowing she was inviting Noblier's wrath. 'What Fourcade did last night was illegal. It was wrong.'

'And what Renard did to that Bichon girl wasn't?'

'Of course it was, but –'

'Let me tell you something here, Annie,' he said, suddenly quieter, gentler. He stepped back and sat on the edge of his desk. His expression was serious, frank, absent of the bluster he regularly blew at the world.

'The world isn't black and white, Annie. It's shades of gray. The world don't follow no procedure handbook. The law and justice are not always the same thing. I'm not

67

saying I condone what Fourcade did. I'm saying I *understand* what Fourcade did. I'm saying we take care of our own in this department. That means you don't go off half-cocked and try to arrest a detective. That means you don't run and take a statement when I tell you to go home.'

'I can't change the fact that I was there, Sheriff, or that Renard knows I was there. How would it look if I *hadn't* taken his statement?'

'It might look like he was confused about the chain of events. It might look like we were giving him the night to recover before we troubled him further. It might look like we were sorting out the jurisdictional questions here.'

Or it might have looked like they were ignoring the victim of a brutal beating, turning their heads the other way because the perpetrator was a cop. It might have looked like they were stalling for time until they could come up with a story.

Annie turned toward the wall that held a pictorial essay on the illustrious career of August F. Noblier. The sheriff in his younger, trimmer days grinning and shaking hands with Governor Edwards. An array of photographs through the years with lesser politicians and celebrities who had passed through Partout Parish during the years of Gus's reign. She had always respected him.

'You did what you did, and we'll deal with it, Deputy,' he said, as if *she* was the one who had broken the law. Annie wondered if he had given Fourcade a reprimand or a pat on the back. 'The point is, we could have dealt with the situation more cleanly if you'd stayed on the page with me. You know what I'm saying?'

Annie said nothing. It wouldn't have done any good to point out that she hadn't been given the opportunity to stay on the page, that the book had been slammed shut on her last night, that she had been cut loose and excluded from the proceedings like an outsider. She wasn't sure which was worse – being shut out or being included in a conspiracy.

'I don't want you talking to the press,' Noblier said, going around behind his desk to settle himself into his big leather executive's chair. 'And I don't want you talking to Richard Kudrow under any circumstances. You understand me?'

'Yes, sir.'

' "No comment." Can you manage that?'

'Yes, sir.'

'And, most of all, I don't want you talking to Marcus Renard. You got that?'

'Yes, sir.'

'You were off duty, which is why you didn't hear that 10–70 call that went out. You stumbled into a situation and contained it. Is that what happened?'

'Yes, sir,' she whispered, the sick feeling in the pit of her stomach swelling like bread dough.

Noblier stared at her in silence for a moment. 'How did Kudrow know you tried to arrest Fourcade? Has he already talked to you?'

'He left a message on my answering machine this morning while I was out running.'

'But you didn't talk to him?'

'No.'

'Did you tell Renard you arrested Fourcade?'

'No.'

'Did you Mirandize Fourcade in front of him?'

'Renard was unconscious.'

'Then Kudrow was bluffing, that ugly son of a bitch,' Gus muttered to himself. 'I hate that man. I don't care that he's dying. I wish he'd hurry up and get it over with. Have you filed an arrest report?'

'Not yet.'

'Nor will you. If you've started that paperwork, I want it shredded. Not thrown away. Shredded.'

'But Renard is going to press charges –'

'That doesn't mean we have to make it easy for him. Go ahead and write up his complaint, write up your preliminary report, but you did not arrest Fourcade. Get your sergeant's initials on the paperwork, then bring the file straight to me.

'I'm personally taking charge of the case,' he said, as if he were trying out the phrase for a future official statement. 'It's an unusual situation – allegations being made against one of my men. Requires my undivided attention to see to it justice is served.

'And don't look at me like that, Deputy,' he said, pointing an accusatory finger. 'We're not doing anything Richard Kudrow hasn't done time and again for the scum he represents.'

'Then we're no better than they are,' Annie murmured.

'The hell we're not,' Noblier growled, reaching for the telephone. 'We're the good guys, Annie. We work for Lady Justice. It's just that she can't always see what's what with that damned blindfold on. You're dismissed, Deputy.'

The women's locker room in the Partout Parish Sheriff's Department had originally been a janitor's closet. There had been no women on the job when the building was designed in the late sixties, and the blissful chauvinists on the planning committee hadn't foreseen the possibility. Their shortsightedness meant male officers had a locker room with showers and their own rest room, while female personnel got a broom closet that had been converted during the 1993 remodeling.

The only light was a bare bulb in the ceiling. Four battered metal lockers had been salvaged out of the old junior high school and transplanted along one wall. A cheap frameless mirror hung on the opposite wall above a tiny porcelain sink. When Annie had first come on the job, someone had drilled a peephole half a foot to the left of the mirror from the men's room on the other side. She now checked the wall periodically for new breaches of privacy, filling the holes with spackling compound she kept in her locker alongside her stash of candy bars.

She was the only female deputy who used the room with

any regularity, and currently the only female patrol officer. There were two women who worked in the jail, and one female plainclothes juvenile officer, all of whom had come on before the broom closet had been converted and had adjusted to life without it. Annie thought of the room as her own and had tried to spruce it up a little by bringing in a plastic potted palm and a carpet remnant for the concrete floor. A poster from the International Association of Women Police brightened one wall.

Annie sat on her folding chair and faced the door. She couldn't bring herself to face the women in the poster. She was late for patrol, had missed the morning briefing. There was no doubt in her mind that every uniform in the place knew Noblier had called her into his office, and why. Sergeant Hooker had announced the first the minute she stepped into the building. The looks she had drawn from the rest of the men had hinted strongly at the second.

She looked at the file folder on her lap. She had gone so far as to type out the arrest report on Fourcade last night. It had given her a small sense of control to sit at her typewriter at home and put down in black and white what she had seen, what she had done. She had felt a sense of validation for just a little while there in the dead of night. Sheriff Noblier had smashed it flat beneath the weight of his authority this morning.

He wanted her to file a false report. She was supposed to lie, justify brutality, violate God knew how many laws.

'And no one sees anything wrong with that picture but me,' she muttered.

Anxiety simmered like acid in her stomach as she left the locker room and headed down the hall.

Hooker rolled an eye at her as she passed the sergeant's desk. 'See if you can't contain yourself to arresting *criminals* today, Broussard.'

Annie reserved comment as she signed herself out. 'I have to be in court at three o'clock.'

'Oh really? You testifying for us or against us?'

'Hypolite Grangnon – burglary,' she said flatly.

Hooker narrowed his little pig eyes at her. 'Sheriff wants those reports on his desk by noon.'

'Yes, sir.'

She should have gone straight to the report room and gotten it over with, but she needed air and space, some time on the road to clear her head, and a cup of coffee that didn't taste like boiled sweat socks. She let herself out of the building and sucked in air that smelled of damp earth and green grass.

The rain had subsided around five A.M. Annie had lain awake all night listening to it assault the roof over her head. Finally giving up on the idea of rest, she had forced herself to get out of bed and work out with the free weights and pull-up bar that gave her second bedroom such a decorative flair.

As she worked her aching muscles, she watched for dawn to break over the Atchafalaya basin. There were mornings when the sunrise boiled up over the swamp like a ball of flame and the sky turned shades of orange and pink so intense they seemed liquid. This morning had come in with rolling, angry slate-colored clouds that carried the threat of a storm with a bully's arrogance.

A storm would have suited her, she thought, except that a spring rainstorm would blow over and be forgotten, while the metaphorical storm in which she had landed herself would do neither.

'Deputy Broussard, might I have a moment of your time?'

Annie jerked around toward the source of the low, smooth voice. Richard Kudrow stood propped against the side of the building, holding the front of his old trench coat together like a flasher.

'I'm sorry. No. I don't have time,' she said quickly, stepping off the sidewalk and heading across the parking lot toward her cruiser. She cast a nervous glance over her shoulder at the building.

'You'll have to talk to me sooner or later,' the lawyer said, falling in step beside her.

'Then it'll have to be later, Mr Kudrow. I'm on duty.'

'Taxpayer time. Need I point out to you, Miss Broussard, that I myself pay mightily into August Noblier's fat coffers and am, therefore, technically, one of your employers?'

'I'm not interested in your technicalities.' She unlocked the car door with one hand while balancing her clipboard, files, and ticket books in the other arm. 'It's my sergeant who's gonna kick my butt if I don't get to work.'

'Your sergeant? Or Gus Noblier – for talking to me?'

'I don't know what you mean,' she lied. She added the car keys to the pile on her arm and started to pull the cruiser's door open.

'Can I hold something for you?' Kudrow offered gallantly, reaching toward her.

'No,' Annie snapped, twisting away.

The sudden movement sent the pile sliding off the clipboard. The keys, the ticket books, the files tumbled to the ground, the Renard file spilling its contents. Panicking, Annie dropped the clipboard and fell to the blacktop on her hands and knees, chanting expletives, scrambling to scrape the papers back into the folder before the wind could take them. Kudrow crouched down, reaching for the notebook that had blown open, its pages of details and observations and interview notes fluttering, as tantalizing to a lawyer as a glimpse of lacy underwear. Annie snatched it out of his hand, then saw his liver-spotted hand reach next for the arrest form she hadn't filed and hadn't shredded.

She lunged for it, cracking her elbow hard on the blacktop, crumpling the form in her fist as she grabbed it.

'I've got it. I've got it,' she stammered. Turning her face away from Kudrow, she closed her eyes and mouthed a silent thank-you to God. She clutched the mess of papers and folders and clipboard to her chest, rose awkwardly, and backed around the open door of the squad car.

73

Kudrow watched her with interest. 'Something I shouldn't see, Miss Broussard?'

Annie's fingers tightened on the crumpled arrest form. 'I have to go.'

'You were the officer on the scene last night. My client claims you saved his life. It took courage for you to stop Fourcade,' he said, bracing the car door open as Annie slid behind the wheel. 'It takes courage to do the right thing.'

'How would you know?' Annie grumbled. 'You're a lawyer.'

The gibe bounced off his jaundiced hide. She could feel the heat of his gaze on her face, though she refused to look at him. A faint, fetid scent of decay touched her nose, and she wondered if it was the bayou or Kudrow.

'The abuse of power, the abuse of office, the abuse of public trust – those are terrible things, Miss Broussard.'

'So are stalking and murder. It's *Deputy* Broussard.' She turned the key in the ignition and slammed the door shut.

Kudrow stepped back as the car rolled forward. He pulled his coat closed around him as the spring breeze swept across the parking lot. Disease had skewed his internal thermometer to where he was always either freezing or on fire. Today he was cold to the marrow, but his soul was burning up with purpose. If he could have been half a step quicker, he would have been holding an arrest report in his hand. An arrest report on Nick Fourcade, the thug who was *not* sitting in a jail cell this morning, thanks to August F. Noblier.

'I'll ruin you both,' he murmured as he watched the squad car turn onto the street. 'And there's the lady who's going to help me do it.'

8

As Annie had suspected, word of Renard's run-in with Fourcade had already hit the streets. Late-shift cops and nurses from Our Lady had carried what pieces of the tale they had to Madame Collette's diner, where the breakfast waitresses doled it out with announcements of the morning blue plate special. The smell of gossip and dissatisfaction was as thick in the air as the scent of bacon grease and coffee.

Annie endured a hail of barbed comments as she went to the counter for her coffee, only to be told by a hostile waitress the restaurant was 'out of coffee.' The patrons of Madame Collette's had passed judgment. The rest of Bayou Breaux would not be far behind.

They wanted someone to be guilty – in their minds if not in the courts, Annie thought. People felt betrayed, cheated by a system that seemed suddenly to favor the wrong side. They wanted to put this latest atrocity behind them and go on as if it hadn't happened. They were afraid they never would be able to do so. Afraid that maybe evil ran under the parish like an aquifer someone had tapped into by mistake, and no one knew how to plug the leak and send the force back underground.

At Po' Richard's, the woman at the drive-up window handed Annie her coffee and wished her a nice day, obviously out of the news loop. The brew was Po' Richard's usual: too black, too strong, and bitter with the taste of chicory. Annie dumped it into her spill-proof mug, added three fake creams, and headed out of town.

The radio crackled to life, reminding her that she was hardly the only person in the parish with trouble.

'All units in the vicinity: Y'all got a possible 261 out to the Country Estates trailer park. Over.'

Annie grabbed her mike as she punched the accelerator. 'One Able Charlie responding. I'm two minutes away. Out.'

When no response came back, she tried the mike again. The radio crackled back at her.

'10–1, One Able Charlie. You're breaking up. Must be something wrong with your radio. You're where? Out.'

'I'm responding to that 261 in Country Estates. Out.'

Nothing came back. Annie hung up the mike, annoyed with the glitch, but more concerned with the call: a sexual assault. She'd caught a handful of rape cases in her career. There was always an extra emotional element to deal with at a rape call. She wasn't just another cop. It wasn't just another call. She went in not only as an officer, but as a woman, able to provide the victim with the kind of support and sympathy no male officer could offer.

The Country Estates mobile-home park sat in exactly the middle of nowhere between Bayou Breaux and Luck, which qualified it as country. The place bore no resemblance to an estate. The name suggested a certain tidy gentility. Reality was a dozen rusting relic trailer houses that had been plunked down on a two-acre weed patch back in the early seventies.

Jennifer Nolan's trailer was at the back of the lot, a pink and once-white model with an OPERATION ID crime-watch sticker on the front door. Annie knocked on the storm door and announced herself as a deputy. The inside door cracked open two inches, then five.

If the face that stared out at her had ever been pretty, Annie doubted it ever would be again. Both lips were ballooning, both split open. The brown eyes were nearly swollen shut.

'Thank God, you're a woman,' Jennifer Nolan mumbled. Her red hair hung in frizzy strings. She had wrapped herself in a pink chenille robe that she clutched together over her heart as she shuffled painfully away from the door.

'Ms Nolan, have you called an ambulance?' Annie asked, following her into the small living room.

76

The trailer reeked of tobacco smoke and the kind of mildew that grows under old carpets. Jennifer Nolan lowered herself with great care to a boxy plaid sofa.

'No, no,' she mumbled. 'I don't want … Everyone will look.'

'Jennifer, you need medical attention.'

Annie squatted down in front of her, taking in the obvious signs of psychological shock. There was a good chance Jennifer Nolan wasn't fully aware of the extent of her injuries. She probably felt numb, stunned. The mental self-protection mechanisms of denial may have kicked in: How could this terrible thing have happened to her, it couldn't be real, it was just a terrible nightmare. Already her logic was skewed: She worried about the appearance of an ambulance, but not the cop car.

'Jennifer, I'm going to call an ambulance for you. Your neighbors won't know what it's coming here for. Our main concern is your well-being. Do you understand? We want to make sure you're taken care of.'

'Judas,' Sticks Mullen muttered, letting himself in without knocking. 'Looks like somebody already took care of her.'

Annie shot him a glare. 'Go call for an ambulance. My radio's out.'

She turned back to the victim, even though Mullen made no move to obey her. 'Jennifer? How long ago did this happen?'

The woman's gaze drifted around the room until it hit on the wall clock. 'In the night. I – I woke up and he – he was just there. On top of me. He – he – *hurt* me.'

'Did he rape you?'

Her face contorted, squeezing tears from her swollen eyes. 'I t-try to be s-so careful. Why – why did this happen?'

Annie skipped the question, not wanting to tell her that carefulness didn't always make a difference. 'When did he leave, Jennifer?'

She shook her head a little. Whether she couldn't or didn't want to recall was unclear.

'Was it dawn yet? Or was it still dark?'

'Dark.'

Meaning their rapist was long gone.

'Great,' Mullen muttered.

Annie took in Jennifer Nolan's appearance once again – the stringy hair, the bathrobe. 'Jennifer, did you bathe or take a shower after he left?'

The tears came harder. 'He – made me. An – and I *had* – to,' she said in an urgent whisper. 'I couldn't stand – the way I felt. I – felt him *all over me*!'

Mullen shook his head in disgust at the lost evidence. Annie gently rested a hand on Jennifer Nolan's forearm, careful to avoid touching the ligature marks that encircled the woman's wrist, just in case some fiber remained embedded in the skin.

'Jennifer, did you know the man who did this to you? Can you tell us what he looks like?'

'No. No,' she whispered, staring at Mullen's shoes. 'He – he was w-wearing a mask.'

'Like a ski mask?'

'No. No.'

She reached a trembling hand for a pack of Eve 100s and a white Bic lighter on the end table. Annie intercepted the cigarettes without a word and set them aside. It was probably too much to hope that Jennifer Nolan hadn't brushed her teeth or smoked a cigarette after the rapist had left the scene, but oral swabs would have to be taken nonetheless. Any trace left behind by the rapist could provide a key to identifying him.

'Horrible. Like f-from a nightmare,' the woman said, as spasms rocked her body. 'Feathers. Black feathers.'

'You mean an actual mask,' Annie said. 'From Mardi Gras.'

Chaz Stokes arrived on the scene eating a breakfast burrito.

He was in one of his usual getups: baggy brown suit pants with a brown and yellow shirt that belonged in a fifties bowling alley. A crumpled black porkpie hat rode low over the rims of wraparound shades that were a testimony to the kind of night he'd had. The sun was nowhere in sight.

'She took a *bath*,' Mullen said, striding down off the rusty metal steps of the trailer. 'At least she didn't do the fucking laundry. We got a crime scene.'

Annie hustled after him. 'The rapist *made her* take a bath. Big difference, jerk. You of all people should be able to relate to a woman wanting to bathe after sex.'

'I don't need your mouth, Broussard,' Mullen snapped. 'I don't know what you're even doing in a uniform after last night.'

'Oh, pardon me for arresting someone who was breaking the law.'

'Nicky's a brother,' Stokes said, throwing the butt end of his breakfast into a patch of dead marigolds along the side of Jennifer Nolan's trailer. 'You turned on one of our own. What's the deal with that, Broussard? He come on to you or something? Everybody knows you think you're too good to do a cop.'

'Yeah, well, look what I've got to pick from,' Annie sneered. 'In case you're interested, there's a rape victim sitting just inside that open door, asshole. She says the guy was wearing a black feather Mardi Gras mask.'

Stokes winced. 'Jesus H., now we got us some kind of copycat.'

'Maybe.'

'What's that supposed to mean? Renard didn't do her and he did Pam Bichon. Or you got some other opinion on Bichon?'

Annie chewed back the temptation to point out no one had proven Renard guilty of anything. Stokes punched her buttons. He said black, she said white. Hell, she *believed* Renard was their killer.

'What are you?' Mullen said, curling his lip. 'Hot for

79

Renard's shriveled little dick or something? You're all of a sudden his little cheerleader. Nick and Chaz say he did Bichon, he did Bichon.'

'Go start knocking on doors, Broussard,' Stokes ordered as the ambulance rolled into the trailer park. 'Leave the detecting to a real cop.'

'I can help process the scene,' Annie said as he popped the trunk of his Camaro.

The department wasn't large enough or busy enough to warrant a separate crime-scene unit. The detective who caught the call always brought the kits and supervised as officers on the scene pitched in to dust for prints and bag evidence.

Stokes's trunk was crammed with junk: a rusted toolbox, a length of nylon towrope, a dirty yellow rain slicker, two bags from McDonald's. Three bright-colored plastic bead necklaces from a past Mardi Gras celebration had become tangled around a jack handle. Stokes pulled out a latent fingerprints kit and a general evidence collection kit from the neater end of the junk pile.

Stokes cut Annie a sideways look. 'We don't need your kind of help.'

She walked away because she didn't have a choice. Stokes outranked her. The idea of him and Mullen processing the scene made her cringe. Stokes was a slacker, Mullen a moron. If they missed something, if they screwed up, the case could be blown. Of course, if Jennifer Nolan's description of events was accurate – not a guarantee with a badly shaken victim – there would be precious little evidence to collect.

Annie walked around the back side of the trailer, putting off the KOD duty. The attacker had come into Jennifer Nolan's trailer in the middle of the night, gaining entrance through the back door, which was not visible from any other trailer in the park. The chances of a neighbor having seen anything would be slim to none. The phone line had been cut clean. Nolan had made her call to 911 from the home of her nearest neighbor, an elderly woman named Vista Wallace, whom Nolan said was very hard-of-hearing.

Annie took a Polaroid of the torn screen door and the inside door that had been easily jimmied and left ajar. There would be no fingerprints. Nolan said her attacker had worn gloves. He had attacked her in her bed, tying her to the bed frame using strips of white cloth he had brought with him. There was no evidence of seminal fluid on the sheets, indicating that the rapist had either used a condom or hadn't ejaculated during the attack.

From her studies, Annie knew that contrary to popular belief, sexual dysfunction was fairly common among sex offenders. Rape was about power and anger, hurting and controlling a woman. Motivation that came out of rage against a particular woman in the rapist's past or against the entire gender, stemming from some past wrong. The attack on Jennifer Nolan had been premeditated, organized, indicating that it was primarily about power and control. The rapist had come prepared, wearing the mask, bringing with him something to jimmy the door and the white cloth ligatures to tie up his victim.

The Bayou Strangler's signature had been a white silk scarf around the throat of his victim. The bindings in this case would be close enough to generate a lot of gossip if word leaked out. Lack of semen could also be pointed out as a similarity. But in the Bayou Strangler cases the women had been violently brutalized and their bodies left exposed to the elements so that such evidence would most likely have broken down.

The primary difference between the Bayou Strangler cases and Jennifer Nolan's was that Jennifer Nolan was still alive. She had been attacked in her home, rather than taken to another location; raped, but not murdered or mutilated. Those were also the differences between Jennifer Nolan's case and Pam Bichon's, and yet the press was bound to draw correlations. The mask was going to be big as a shock factor.

Annie wondered if either the similarities or the differences in the cases had been intentional. If she wondered it, so would everyone else. The level of fear in Partout Parish was going to be pushed to heights that hadn't been seen in four years. It had been bad enough when Pam Bichon had been killed. But at least a great many people had focused on Renard as the killer. Marcus Renard had been in Our Lady of Mercy when Jennifer Nolan was attacked.

God, what a mess, Annie thought, her gaze on the ground. The sheriff's office had come under enough criticism for the Bichon case. Now they had a masked rapist running around loose, and while Jennifer Nolan was being attacked, the cops had been busy arresting each other. That was how the press would paint it. And right smack in the middle of that painting would be Annie's own face.

The ground around the back side of the trailer was nothing but weedy gravel for several feet, then the 'estate' gave way to woods with a floor of soft rotted leaves. Annie worked her way from one end of the trailer to the other, looking for anything – a partial footprint, a cigarette butt, a discarded condom. What she found at the north end of the trailer was a fan-shaped black feather about one inch in length, caught in a tuft of grass and dandelions. She took a snapshot of the feather where it lay, then tore a blank sheet of paper from her pocket notebook, folded it around the feather, and slipped it in between the pages of the notebook for safekeeping.

Where had the rapist parked his vehicle? Why had he chosen this place? Why had he chosen Jennifer Nolan? She claimed to have no men in her life. She lived alone and worked the night shift at the True Light lamp factory in Bayou Breaux. The factory would seem the logical starting point to nose around for suspects.

Of course, Annie wasn't going to get the chance to interview anyone but the neighbors. The case belonged to Stokes now. If he wanted help, he sure as hell wouldn't come to her for it. Then again, maybe the rapist *was* a neighbor. A neighbor wouldn't have to worry about hiding his vehicle. A neighbor would be aware of Jennifer Nolan's schedule and the fact that she lived alone. Maybe that KOD duty wouldn't be so boring after all.

The ambulance was driving out of the trailer park as she came around the end of the Nolan home. A woman with a toddler on one hip and cigarette in hand stood in the doorway of a trailer two down the row. At another trailer, a heavyset old guy in his underwear had pulled back a curtain to stare out.

Annie bagged the feather and took it inside. She found Stokes in the bathroom picking pubic hairs out of the tub with a tweezers.

'I found this behind the trailer,' she said, setting the bag on the vanity. 'It looks like the kind of feather they use in masks and costumes. Maybe our bad guy was molting.'

Stokes arched a brow. '*Our?* You got nothing to do with this, Broussard. And what the hell am I supposed to do with a feather?'

'Send it to the lab. Compare it to the mask left on Pam Bichon –'

'Renard did Bichon. That's got nothing to do with this. This is a copycat.'

'Fine, then send it to the lab, get Jennifer Nolan to draw a sketch of the mask the rapist was wearing, and see if you can't track down a manufacturer. Maybe –'

'Maybe you don't know what the hell you're talking about, Broussard,' he said, straightening from the tub. He folded the pubic hairs in a piece of paper and set it on the back of the toilet. 'I told you before, I don't want you around. Get outta here. Go write some tickets. Practice for your new job as a meter maid. That's all you're gonna be, sweetheart. If I'm lyin', I'm dyin'. You don't rat out a brother and stay on the job.'

'Is that a threat?'

He reached out with a forefinger and pressed it hard

against the bruise on her cheek. His eyes looked as flat and cold as glass. 'I don't make threats, sugar.'

Annie gritted her teeth against the pain.

'Better get your story straight about what happened with Renard last night,' he said.

'I know exactly what happened.'

Stokes shook his head. 'You chicks just don't know shit about honor, do you?'

She pushed his hand away. 'I know it doesn't involve committing a felony. I'll go talk to those neighbors now.'

9

Nick stood in the pirogue, his gaze focused on a watery horizon, his mind concentrating completely on his slow, precise movements. *Balance ... grace ... calm ... breathe ... harmonize mind, body, spirit ... sense the water beneath the boat – fluid, yielding ... become as the water ...*

Despite the cool of the day, sweat beaded on his forehead and soaked through his sleeveless gray sweatshirt. Biceps and triceps flexed and trembled as he moved. The strain came not from the Tai Chi form, but from within, from the battle to remain focused.

Move slowly ... without force ... without violence ...

A scene from the night broke his concentration for a heartbeat. *Renard ... blood ... force ... violence ...* The sense of harmony he had been seeking pulled away from him and was gone. The pirogue jerked beneath his feet. He dropped to the seat of the boat and cradled his head in his hands.

He had built the boat himself from cypress and marine plywood, and painted it green and red like the old swampers had done years ago to identify themselves as serious fishermen and trappers. He had been glad to come back to the swamp. New Orleans was a discordant place. Looking back, he had always felt spiritually fractured there. This was where he had come from: the Atchafalaya – over a million acres of wilderness strung along the edges with a garland of small towns like Bayou Breaux and St. Martinville, and smaller towns like Jeanerette and Breaux Bridge, and places that seemed too small and inconsequential to have names, though they did.

He had passed his boyhood some miles removed from one of those places, on a house barge tethered to the bank of a nameless lake. He remembered his father as a swamper, fishing and trapping, before the oil boom hit and he took a job as a welder and moved the family to Lafayette. They had lived richer there, but not better. Armand Fourcade had confessed more than once he had left a part of his soul in the swamp. Only since coming back had Nick begun to realize what his father had meant. Here he could feel whole and centered. Sometimes.

This was not one of those times.

Reluctantly, he picked up his paddle and started the boat toward home. The sky was hanging low, dulling the color of the swamp, tinting everything a dingy gray: the fragile new lime green leaves of the tupelos that stood like sentinels in the water, the lacy greenery of the willows and hackberry trees that covered the islands, the few yellow-tops that had been tricked into opening by the warmth that had come too early in the season. This day was cool, but if the weather heated up again, the bright flowers would soon crowd the banks, and white-topped daisy fleabane and showy black-eyed Susans would grow down to the water's edge to blend in with the tangles of poison ivy and alligator weed and ratten vine.

The swamp was usually bursting with life in the spring. Today it seemed to be holding its breath. Waiting. Watching.

Just as Nick was waiting. He had set something in motion last night. Every action produces reaction; every challenge, a response. The thing hadn't ended with Gus sending him home. It had hardly begun.

He guided the pirogue through a channel studded with deadhead cypress stumps, and around the narrow point of an island that would double in size when the spring waters receded. His home sat on the bank two hundred yards west, an Acadian relic that had been poorly updated as modern conveniences became available to the people of rural South Louisiana.

He was remodeling the place himself, a room at a time, restoring its charm and replacing cheap fixes with quality.

Mindless manual labor afforded an acceptable outlet for the restlessness he once would have tried to douse with liquor.

He spotted the city cruiser immediately. The car sat near his 4X4. A white uniformed officer stood beside the car with a stocky black man in a sharp suit and tie and an air of self-importance discernible even from a distance. Johnny Earl, the chief of the Bayou Breaux PD.

Nick guided the pirogue in alongside the dock and tied it off.

'Detective Fourcade,' Earl said, moving toward the dock, holding his gold shield out ahead of him. 'I'm Johnny Earl, chief of police in Bayou Breaux.'

'Chief,' Nick acknowledged. 'What can I do for you?'

'I think you know why we're here, Detective,' the chief said. 'According to a complaint made this morning by Marcus Renard, you committed a crime last night within the incorporated municipality of Bayou Breaux. Contrary to what Sheriff Noblier seems to think, that's a police matter. I assured DA Pritchett I would see to this myself, even though it pains me to have cause. You're under arrest for the assault of Marcus Renard – and this time it's for real. Cuff him, Tarleton.'

Annie took the stairs to the second floor of the courthouse, trying to imagine how she might escape having a private conversation with A.J. If she could slip into the courtroom just as the case against Hypolite Grangnon was called, then skip as soon as she had testified ...

She'd had enough confrontations for one day. She hadn't been able to so much as fill her cruiser with gas without getting into it with somebody. But the capper had been getting called to the Bayou Breaux Police Department.

The interview with Johnny Earl had seemed like the longest hour of her life. He had personally taken charge of the case and personally grilled her like a rack of ribs, trying to get her to admit to having arrested Fourcade at the scene of the incident. She stuck to the story the sheriff had force-fed her, telling herself the whole time that it wasn't that far from the truth. She hadn't heard any radio call about a prowler – because there hadn't been one. She hadn't really arrested Fourcade – because no one else in the department would let her.

Earl hadn't swallowed a word of it. He'd been a cop too long. But busting Noblier's chops over the cover-up was only secondary on his agenda. He had Fourcade in custody and would make as much political hay off that as possible. He didn't need her true confession to make the sheriff look bad, and he knew it. In fact, he might have been just as well off without it. This way he could allege the corruption in the sheriff's office was widespread, reaching into all echelons. He could count her as a co-conspirator.

Conspiracy, giving a false statement. What's next? To what new low can I aspire? Annie asked herself as she turned down the corridor that led past the old courtrooms. *Perjury.* Sooner or later she would be coming to this courthouse to testify against Fourcade.

The hall was clogged with loitering lawyers and social workers and people with vested interests in the cases being heard. The door to Judge Edmonds's courtroom swung open, nearly bowling over a public defender. A.J. stepped into the hall. His gaze immediately homed in on Annie.

'Deputy Broussard, may I see you in my office?' he said.

'B-but the Grangnon trial –'

'Is off. He copped a plea.'

'Swell,' she said without enthusiasm. 'Then I can get back on patrol.'

He leaned close. 'Don't make me drag you, Annie, and don't think I'm not mad enough to do it.'

The secretaries in the outer office of the DA's domain sat up like show dogs as A.J. stormed through, oblivious to their batting eyelashes. He tossed his briefcase into a chair as he entered his own office and slammed the door shut behind Annie.

'Why the hell didn't you call me?' he demanded.

'How the hell *could* I call you, A.J.?'

'You get in the middle of Fourcade trying to kill Renard, and you don't bother to mention that to me? Jesus, Annie, you could have been hurt!'

'I'm a cop. I could be hurt any day of the week.'

'You weren't even on duty!' he ranted, tossing his hands up. 'You told me you were going home! How did this happen?'

'A cruel twist of fate,' she said bitterly. 'I was in the wrong place at the wrong time.'

'That's not quite how Richard Kudrow put it when he dropped this little bomb on Pritchett this morning. He hailed you as a heroine, the only champion for justice in an otherwise morbidly corrupt department.'

'The department is not corrupt,' she said, hating the lie. What was a cover-up of police brutality if not corruption?

'Then why wasn't Fourcade in jail this morning? You arrested him, didn't you? Kudrow claims he saw the report, but there's no report on file at the sheriff's department. What's up with that? Did you arrest him or not?'

'And you wonder why I didn't call you,' Annie muttered, staring to the left of him. Better to look at his diploma from LSU than to lie to his face. 'I can do without this third-degree bullshit, thank you very much.'

'I want to know what happened,' he said, stepping into her field of vision, wise to all her argument strategies. 'I'm concerned about you, Annie. We're friends, right? You're the one who kept saying it last night – we're best friends.'

'Oh yeah, *best friend*,' she said sarcastically. 'Last night we were best friends. And now you're a DA and I'm a deputy, and you're pissed off because you looked bad in front of your boss this morning. That's it, isn't it?'

'Dammit, Annie, I'm serious!'

'So am I! You tell me that isn't true,' she demanded. 'You look me in the eye and tell me you're not trying to use our friendship to get information you couldn't get any other way. You look at me and tell me you would have accosted any other deputy in the hall in front of two dozen people and dragged him in here like a child.'

A.J. snapped his teeth together as he turned his face away. The disappointment that pressed down on Annie was almost as heavy as the inescapable sense of guilt. Hands clamped on top of her head, she walked past him to the window.

'You don't have any idea what I've fallen into,' she murmured, staring out at the parking lot.

'It's simple,' he said. The voice of reason, calm and charming as he came up behind her. 'If you caught Fourcade breaking the law, then he belongs in jail.'

'And I have to testify against him. Rat out another cop – a detective, no less.'

'The law is the law.'

'Right is right. Wrong is wrong,' she said, nodding her head with each beat as she turned to face him once more. 'I'm glad life is so easy for you, A.J.'

'Don't give me that. You believe in the law as much as I do. That's why you stopped Fourcade last night. It's for the courts to mete out punishment, not Nick Fourcade. And you had damn well better testify against him!'

'Don't threaten me,' Annie said quietly. He took a step toward her, already contrite, but she held her hands up and backed away. 'Thanks for your compassion, A.J. You're a real friend, all right. I'm so glad I turned to you in my time of need. I'll look forward to getting your subpoena.'

'Annie, don't –' he started, but she waved him off as she pushed past him. 'Annie, I –'

She slammed the door on whatever he had been about to say. At the same time, the door to Smith Pritchett's corner office flew open and a quartet of angry men bulled their way into the hall, with Pritchett himself in the lead. The chief of police came close on his heels, followed by Kudrow and Noblier. Annie pressed her back against the door to let them pass, her heart tripping as Kudrow nodded to her.

'Deputy Broussard,' he said smoothly. 'Perhaps you should join us in –'

Noblier muscled the lawyer to the side. 'Butt out, Kudrow. I need a word with my deputy.'

'I'm sure you do,' Kudrow said with a chuckle. 'Need I remind you, witness tampering is a serious offense, Noblier?'

'You make me want to puke, lawyer,' Gus snarled. 'You get a murderer off and go after the cops. Somebody oughta turn you ass-end up and knock some decency into you.'

Kudrow shook his head, smile in place. 'You even preach brutality. How the press will prick up their ears when they hear about this.'

'His guts aren't the only thing that's cancerous in him,' Gus grumbled as Kudrow followed the others down the hall. 'That man's soul is black with rot.

'He pulled Pritchett's tail,' he said, seeming to talk to himself. 'That's my fault. I should have called Pritchett myself last night. Now he's got it into his head this is some kind of pissing contest. That man has an ego bigger than my granddaddy's dick.

'And Johnny Earl ... I don't know who put the bug up his ass. The man is contrary. Doesn't understand the rhythms of life around here. That's what happens when the city council hires outsiders. They bring in Johnny Fucking Earl from Cleveland or some goddamn place where don't nobody know jack about life in this place. The man has an attitude. He thinks I'm some lazy, crooked, racist cracker out of a goddamn movie. Like I don't have blacks working in my department. Like I'm not friends with blacks. Like I didn't win thirty-three percent of the black vote in the last election.'

He turned his attention squarely on Annie with a ferocious scowl as he backed her toward Pritchett's empty office. 'I told you not to talk to Kudrow.'

'I didn't talk to him.'

'Then what's this bullshit he's spewing about an arrest

report?' he whispered. 'And how come your sergeant told me he saw the two of you in the goddamn parking lot not twenty feet from the building?'

'I didn't tell him anything.'

'And that's exactly what you're gonna say at this press conference, Deputy. Nothing.'

Annie swallowed hard. 'Press conference?'

'Come on,' he ordered as he strode down the hall.

Pritchett opened the show with a statement about Marcus Renard's alleged attack. He announced Detective Nick Fourcade had been taken into custody by the Bayou Breaux PD. He promised to get to the bottom of the allegations and expressed outrage at the idea of anyone attempting to circumvent the justice system.

Kudrow, looking wan and tragic, quietly reminded everyone of Fourcade's checkered past, and asked that justice be served. 'I will state again my client's innocence. He has been proven guilty of nothing. In fact, while he lay in the hospital last night, put there by Detective Fourcade, the real criminal was at large and may well have committed a brutal rape.'

And then began the feeding frenzy.

The questions and comments of the reporters were pointed and barbed. They had been chasing the story of Renard in one form or another for better than three months with no solid conclusion as to his innocence or guilt. While they couldn't find sympathy for the officers who had endured the same frustration, they didn't hesitate to vent their own. They went after everybody, sided with no one, and homed in on the chance for fresh blood.

'Sheriff, is that true – that another woman was attacked last night?'

'No comment.'

'Deputy Broussard, is it true you formally arrested Detective Fourcade last night?'

Annie squinted into the blinding light of a portable sun gun as Gus nudged her forward. 'Ah – I can't comment.'

'But you *are* the officer who called in the ambulance. You *did* return to the sheriff's department with Detective Fourcade.'

'No comment.'

'Sheriff, if Renard was in the hospital while this other woman was being attacked, doesn't that prove his innocence?'

'No.'

'Then you're confirming the attack occurred?'

'Deputy Broussard, can you confirm taking a statement from Mr Renard at the hospital last night? And if so, why was Detective Fourcade not in custody this morning?'

'Ah – I –'

Gus leaned in front of her at the microphone. 'Detective Fourcade was responding to a report of a prowler in the area. Deputy Broussard was off duty and did not hear the call. She came across a situation she found questionable, contained it, and accompanied Detective Fourcade back to the sheriff's department. It's as simple as that.

'I immediately suspended Detective Fourcade with pay, pending further investigation. And that's where this case stands as far as I'm concerned. My department has nothing to hide, nothing to be ashamed of. If the district attorney wants to have the police investigate the matter, I welcome the scrutiny. I stand behind my people one hundred percent, and that's all I have to say on the matter.'

Pritchett stepped back up to the microphone, determined to have the last word, while Gus herded Annie away from the podium toward the door. Annie kept at Noblier's heels like a faithful dog and wondered if that made her some kind of hypocrite. She expected the sheriff to protect her but not Fourcade. *I didn't try to kill anyone. All I did was lie and file a false report.*

Disgusted with herself, with her boss, with the vultures trying to pick at her on the fly as she made her escape from the courthouse and went to her cruiser, she kept her mouth shut and her eyes forward. The mob split into factions then, some of them running back up the courthouse steps as Kudrow emerged, some trailing after Noblier as he drove away in his Suburban. Half a dozen tailed Annie to the law enforcement center and chased her across the parking lot to the officers' entrance to the building.

Hooker stood in the foyer, staring out at the show, arms crossed over his round belly. 'Where's the follow-up report on that cemetery vandalism?'

'I turned it in two days ago.'

'The hell you did.'

'I did!'

'Well, I don't have it, Broussard,' he stated. 'Do it again. Today.'

'Yes, sir,' Annie said, biting down on the urge to call him a liar. Hooker was an asshole, but fair in that he usually treated everyone with equal disrespect.

'Like it's not bad enough to have to do paperwork once,' she grumbled as she came up on the briefing room. 'I get to do mine twice.'

'Who you want to do twice, Broussard?' Mullen sneered. He and Prejean stood in the hall, drinking coffee. 'Your little pervert friend, Renard? I hear when he nails a woman, she stays nailed to the floor.' He snickered, flashing his bad teeth.

'Very funny, Mullen,' Annie said. 'And in such good taste. Maybe you could get a job doing stand-up comedy down at the funeral home.'

'I'm not the one gonna be looking for a job, Broussard,' he returned. 'We heard about you going over to the townies to suck Johnny Earl's dick.'

'I hate to spoil your sordid daydreams, but I didn't go over there because I wanted to, and the chief wasn't exactly happy when I left.'

Mullen smirked. 'Can't even get a blow job right?'

'You'll sure as hell never find out.'

Annie looked to Prejean, who was usually quick with a smile and a smart remark when she bested Mullen. He looked at her now as if he didn't know her. The snub hurt.

'That's okay, Prejean,' she said. 'It's not like I ever covered for you when your wife was working nights and you wanted a little extra time at lunch to, shall we say, satisfy your appetite.'

Prejean looked at his shoes. Annie shook her head and walked away. She needed ten minutes alone, just to sit down and regroup. Ten minutes to marshal her disappointment and corral the fear that was beginning to skitter around inside her. She had fallen into a deep hole and no one was reaching in to help her out. Instead, the men she had thought were her comrades stood around the rim, ready to kick dirt on her.

She headed for her locker room. But she knew before she even set foot inside that her sanctuary had been breached.

The smell hit her as she turned the doorknob – sickening, rotten. She flipped the light switch and barely managed to clamp her hand over her mouth before the scream could escape.

Hanging from a length of brown twine tied to the single bulb in the ceiling, the cord knotted together with its long, skinny tail, was a dead muskrat.

The muskrat had been skinned from the base of its tail to the base of its skull, the pelt left dangling down past its head. Annie stared at it, nausea rising up her esophagus. Air currents and the weight of its body twisted the rodent to and fro like a grotesque mobile. One hind leg was missing, suggesting the muskrat had met its untimely end in the steel jaws of a trap, as thousands did every year in South Louisiana.

Aware that her tormentor could have been watching through a fresh hole in the wall, Annie moved toward the muskrat, then stepped around it. She took in every detail – the knotted tail, the naked muscle, the piece of paper that had been stabbed to the corpse with a nail.

The note read: *Turncoat bitch.*

10

Broussard ratted you out,' Stokes said, curling his fingers through the wire mesh of the holding cell. 'Man, I can't believe she did this to you. I mean, it's one thing that she won't sleep with me. Some women are just masochists that way. But ratting out another cop ... man, that's low.'

Stokes shouldn't have been allowed into the city jail holding cells. At least not as a visitor. Prisoners in holding had the right to see their attorneys, and that was all. But, as always, Stokes had known somebody and talked his way in.

'Goddamn, you think maybe she's a lesbian?' he asked, as the idea struck him.

An image of Annie Broussard came to Nick as he prowled his cell – her eyes widening, a hint of a blush spreading across her cheeks as he reached out and passed his hand too close to her.

'I don't care,' he said.

'Maybe you don't, but she's just taken on a whole new role in my fantasy life,' Stokes admitted. 'Damn, but I've always had a thing for lesbians. Pretty ones,' he qualified. 'Not the butch dykes. Don't you ever picture beautiful women naked together? Man, that gets my dick twitching.'

'She arrested me,' Nick stated flatly, impatient with Stokes. The man had no focus.

'Well, yeah, she'll be a bad lesbian in my fantasies. A black leather bitch with a whip. Man hater.'

'How'd she happen to be there?' Nick asked.

'Damn bad luck, that's for sure.'

Nick had mixed feelings about that. If Annie Broussard hadn't come along, he would have killed Renard. She had, in fact, saved him from himself, and for that he was thankful. But her motives troubled him.

'She thinks I should be held accountable.'

97

Maybe it was as simple as that. Maybe she was that idealistic. Having never been an idealist himself, he had a hard time accepting the prospect. In his experience, people were usually motivated by one thing: self-gain. They could couch their intentions in a million different guises, give no end of excuses, but most everything came down to one thought: *What's in it for me?* What was in it for Annie Broussard? Why had she suddenly popped up in his life?

'She's a pain in the ass,' Stokes said. 'Little Miss By-the-Book. I caught a rape case this morning out in that white-trash trailer park going toward Luck. She's out there butting into every damn thing. "You gonna send that nose hair to the lab?" ' he mocked in a high falsetto. ' "Maybe it's rapist nose hair. Maybe this guy did Bichon. Maybe he's the Bayou Strangler." '

'What made her think it was tied to Bichon?'

Chaz rolled his eyes. 'The guy wore a mask. Like that's an original idea. Christ,' he muttered. 'Whoever thought they should let broads on the job?'

He glanced over his shoulder, checking the door. The city jail was about a thousand years old and had no surveillance cameras in its holding cell areas. City cops had to listen in on conversations the old-fashioned way.

'Well, she's damn near the only one who thinks you should pay for this, man,' he muttered. 'Not even God himself would call you on it. An eye for an eye, you know what I mean?'

'I know what you mean. I'm supposed to be an avenging angel.'

'Hell, you should have been the Invisible Man. No one would have been the wiser if Broussard hadn't stuck her nose in it. Renard would be roasting in hell, case closed.'

'That's what you thought?' Nick said softly, stepping toward the chain-link that caged him in. 'When you called me at Laveau's – you thought I'd go over to Bowen and Briggs and kill him?'

'Jesus!' Stokes hissed. 'Keep your voice down!'

Nick leaned close to the wire mesh, slipping his fingers through just above Stokes's. 'Whatsa matter, *pard*?' he whispered. 'You worried about a conspiracy beef?'

Stokes jerked back, looking shocked, offended, hurt even. 'Conspiracy? Shit, man, we were drunk and talking trash. Even when I called you and told you he was over there, I never thought you'd really do it! I'm just saying I wouldn't blame you if you had. I mean, good riddance – am I right or am I right?'

'You're the one wanted to go to that particular bar.'

''Cause no one else hangs there, man! You can't think I was setting you up! Jesus, Nicky! We're brothers of the badge, man. I'm the closest thing to a friend 'you got. I don't know how you can even think it. It wounds me, Nicky. Truly.'

'*I'll* wound you, Chaz. I find out you fucked me over, you'll wish your mama and daddy never got past first base.'

Stokes stepped away from the cell. 'I don't believe what I'm hearing. Man oh man! Stop being so fuckin' paranoid. I'm not your enemy here.' He tapped his breastbone with one long forefinger. 'Hell, I called you a lawyer. The guys are gonna cover it. They all agreed –'

'I pay my own way.'

'You didn't do anything the rest of us hadn't had wet dreams about for the last three months.'

'What lawyer?'

'Wily Tallant from St Martinville.'

'That bastard –'

'– is slick as snot,' Stokes finished. 'Don't think of him as being on the other side of the fence. Think of him as the man who's gonna open the gate so you can get back on your own side. That ol' boy can make Lucifer look like the poor misunderstood neglected child of a dysfunctional family. By the time he's through, you'll probably end up with a commendation and the keys to the fucking city, which is what you deserve.'

He leaned toward the mesh again, slipping a hand inside

his jacket and pulling out a cigarette like a magician. 'That's all I want, pard,' he said, passing the cigarette through the wire. 'I want everybody to get what they deserve.'

Annie stayed in the locker room for twenty minutes fighting to compose herself. Twenty minutes of staring at that skinned muskrat.

There was no way of knowing where it had come from or who had hung it, not without questioning people, looking for witnesses, making a fuss. Mullen was a sound bet, but she knew a half dozen deputies who did some trapping for extra income. Still, skinning would have been Mullen's touch. Annie had always pegged him for the sort of kid who had pulled the wings off flies.

Turncoat bitch.

Holding her breath against the sweet-putrid scent of decaying rodent, she cut the thing down with her pocket-knife and grimaced as it hit the floor with a soft thud. She tore up the note, then pilfered a cardboard box from the garbage in the office supply room and used it for a coffin. She had no intention of taking the thing to Noblier and making a bad situation worse. And there was no leaving it. After she rewrote her final report on the cemetery vandal-ism and filed it, she grabbed the box and her duffel bag and left. She could toss the corpse in the woods after she got home, and Mother Nature would give it a proper disposal.

The drive home usually calmed her after a bad day. Today it only made her feel more alienated. Daylight was nearly gone, casting the world in the strange gray twilight of bad dreams. The woods looked forbidding, uninviting; the cane fields were vast, unpopulated seas of green. Lamps burned in the windows of the houses she passed; inside families were together, eating supper, watching television.

Always in times like this, she became acutely aware of her lack of a traditional family. This was when the memories crept up from childhood: her mother sitting in a rocking chair looking out at the swamp, a wraithlike woman, surreal, pale, detached, never quite in the present. There had always been a distance between Marie Broussard and the world around her. Annie had been keenly aware of it and frightened by it, fearing that one day her mother would just slip away into another dimension and she would be left alone. Which was exactly what had happened.

She had had Uncle Sos and Tante Fanchon to look after her, and she couldn't have loved them more, but there was always, would always be, a place inside her where she felt like an orphan, disconnected, separate from the people around her ... as her mother had been. The door to that place was wide open tonight.

'You're on the air with Owen Onofrio, KJUN, all talk all the time. Home of the giant jackpot giveaway. We're up over nine hundred dollars now. What lucky listener will pocket that check? It could happen any time, any day.

'On our agenda tonight: Murder suspect Marcus Renard was allegedly attacked and beaten last night by a Partout Parish sheriff's detective. What do you have to say about that, Kay on line one?'

'I say there ain't no justice, that's what I say. The world's gone crazy. They put that dead woman's daddy in jail, too, and everyone I know says he's a hero for trying to do what the courts wouldn't. Killers and rapists have more rights than decent people. It's crazy!'

Annie switched the radio off as she turned in at the Corners. There were three cars in the crushed shell lot. Uncle Sos's pickup, the night clerk's rusty Fiesta, and off to one side, a shiny maroon Grand Am that made her groan aloud. A.J.

She sat for a moment just staring at the place she had called home her whole life: a simple two-story wood-frame building with a corrugated tin roof. The wide front window acted as a billboard, with half a dozen various ads and messages for products and services. A red neon sign for Bud,

101

a placard that read ICI ON PARLE FRANÇAIS, another sign handwritten in Magic Marker HOT BOUDIN & CRACKLINS.

The first floor of the building housed the business Sos Doucet had run for forty years. Originally a general store that served area swampers and their families who had come in by boat once or twice a month, it had evolved with the times and economic necessity into a landing for swamp tours, a café, and a convenience store that did its biggest business on the weekends when fishermen and hunters – 'sports,' Uncle Sos called them – stocked up to head out into the Atchafalaya basin. The tourists loved the rustic charm of the scarred old cypress floor and ancient, creaking ceiling fans. The locals were happier with the commercial refrigerators that kept their beer cold and handy, and the two-for-one movie rentals on Monday night.

The second-floor apartment had been home to Sos and Fanchon during the first years of their marriage. Prosperity had allowed them to build a little ranch-style brick house a hundred yards away, and in 1968 they had rented the apartment to Marie Broussard, who had shown up on the porch one day, pregnant and forlorn, as mysterious as any of the stray cats that had come to make their home at the Corners.

"Bout time you got home, *chère*!" Uncle Sos called, leaning out the screen door.

Annie climbed out of the Jeep with her duffel bag strapped over one shoulder and the muskrat box in her other hand.

'What you got in the box? Supper?'

'Not exactly.'

Sos came out onto the porch, barefoot, in jeans and a white shirt with the sleeves rolled halfway up his sinewy forearms. He wasn't a tall man, but even at sixtysomething his shoulders suggested power. His belly was as flat as an anvil, his skin perpetually tan, his face creased in places like fine old leather. People told him he resembled the actor Tommy Lee Jones, which always brought a sparkle to his eyes and the retort that, hell no, Tommy Lee Jones resembled *him*, the lucky son of a bitch.

'You got comp'ny, *chère*,' Sos said with a sly grin that nearly made his eyes disappear. 'Andre, he's here to see you.' He lowered his voice in conspiracy as she stepped up onto the porch. His face was aglow. 'Y'all had a little lovers' spat, no?'

'We're not lovers, Uncle Sos.'

'Bah!'

'Not that it's any of your business, by the way, for the hundredth time.'

He jerked his chin back and looked offended. 'How is that not my business?'

'I'm a grown-up,' she reminded him.

'Then you smart enough to marry dat boy, *mais* no?'

'Will you *ever* give up?'

'Mebbe,' he said, pulling open the screen door for her. 'Mebbe when you make me a grandpapa.'

A bouquet of red roses and baby's breath sat on the corner of the checkout counter, as out of place as a Ming vase. The night clerk, a crater-faced kid as skinny as a licorice whip, was running *Speed* on the VCR.

'Hey, Stevie,' Annie called.

'Hey, Annie,' he called back, never taking his eyes off the set. 'What's in the box?'

'Severed hand.'

'Cool.'

'Aren't you gonna say hello to Andre?' Sos said irritably. 'After he come all the way out here. After he sent you flowers and all.'

A.J. had the grace to look sheepish. He leaned back against a display counter of varnished alligator heads and other equally gruesome artifacts that titillated the tourists. He hadn't changed out of his suit, but had shed his tie and opened the collar of his shirt.

'I don't know,' Annie said. 'Should I have my lawyer present?'

'I was out of line,' he conceded.

'Try left field. On the warning track.'

'See, *chère*?' Sos smiled warmly, motioning her to close the distance. 'Andre, he knows when he's licked. He come to kiss and make up.'

Annie refused to be charmed. 'Yeah? Well, he can kiss my butt.'

Sos arched a brow at him. 'Hey, that's a start.'

'I'm tired,' Annie declared, turning back for the door. 'Good night.'

'Annie!' A.J. called. She could hear him coming behind her as she rounded the corner of the porch and started up the staircase to her apartment. 'You can't just keep running away from me.'

'I'm not running away. I'm trying to ignore you, which, I promise you, is preferable to the alternative. I'm not very happy with you at the moment –'

'I said I was sorry.'

'No, you said you were out of line. An admission of wrongdoing is not an apology.'

Two cats darted around her feet and onto the landing, meowing. A calico hopped up on the railing and leaned longingly toward the muskrat box. Annie held it out of reach as she opened the door. She hadn't intended to bring the thing into her apartment, but she couldn't very well dispose of it with A.J. breathing down her neck.

She set the box and her duffel on the small bench in the entry and proceeded past the telephone stand in the living room, where the light on her answering machine was blinking like an angry red eye. She could only imagine what was waiting for her on the tape. Reporters, relatives, and disgruntled strangers calling to express their opinions and/or try to wheedle information out of her. She walked past the machine and went into the kitchen, flipping on the lights.

A.J. followed, setting the vase of roses on the chrome-legged kitchen table.

'I'm sorry. I *am*,' he said. 'I shouldn't have jumped all over you about Fourcade, but I was worried for you, honey.'

'And it had nothing to do with you being caught flat-footed with Pritchett.'

He sighed through his nose. 'All right. I admit, the news caught me off guard, and, yes, I thought you should have told me because of our relationship. I would like to think that you would turn to me in that kind of situation.'

'So that you could turn to Smith Pritchett and spill it all, like a good lieutenant.'

Annie stood on the opposite side of the table, her lower back pressing against the edge of the counter at the sink. 'This is just another example of why this relationship thing isn't going to work out,' she said, her voice going a little rusty under pressure. 'Here I am and there you are and there's this – this – *stuff* between us.' She used her hands to illustrate her point. 'My job and your job, and when is it about the job and when is it about us. I don't want to deal with it, A.J. I'm sorry. I don't. Not now.'

Not now, when she suddenly found herself caught up in the storm Fourcade had created. She needed all her wits about her just to keep her head above water.

'I don't think this is the best time for us to have this conversation,' A.J. said softly, coming toward her, gentleness and affection on his face. 'It's been a rough day. You're tired, I'm tired. I just don't want us mad at each other. We're too good friends for that. Kiss and make up?' he whispered.

She let her eyes close as he settled his mouth against hers. She didn't try to stop her own lips from moving or her arms from sneaking around his waist. He pulled her closer, and it seemed as natural as breathing. His body was strong, warm. His size made her feel small and safe.

It would have been easy to go to bed with him, to find comfort and oblivion in passion. A.J. enjoyed the role of lover-protector. She knew exactly how good it felt to let him take that part. And she knew she couldn't go there tonight. Sex would solve nothing, complicate everything. Her life had gotten complicated enough.

A.J. felt her enthusiasm cool. He raised his head an inch or two. 'You know, you can hurt a guy making him stop like this.'

'That's a lie,' Annie said, appreciating his attempt at humor.

'Says who?'

'Says you. You told me that when I was a sophomore and Jason Benoit was trying to convince me I would cripple him for life if I didn't let him go all the way.'

'Yeah, well, *I* would've crippled him if he had.' He touched the tip of her nose with his forefinger. 'Friends again?'

'Always.'

'Who ever thought life could be so complicated?'

'Not you.'

'That's a fact.' He glanced at his watch. 'Well, I suppose I should go home and take a cold shower or page through the Victoria's Secret catalog or something.'

'No work?' Annie asked, following him to the door.

'Tons. You don't want to hear about it.'

'Why not?'

He turned and faced her, serious. 'Fourcade's bond hearing tomorrow.'

'Oh.'

'Told you so.' He started to open the door, then hesitated. 'You know, Annie, you're gonna have to decide whose side you're on in this thing.'

'I'm either for you or against you?'

'You know what I mean.'

'Yeah,' she admitted, 'but I don't want to talk about it tonight.'

A.J. accepted that with a nod. 'If you decide you do want to talk, and you want to talk to a friend ... we'll work around the rest.'

Annie kept her doubts to herself. A.J. pulled the door

106

open, and three cats darted into the entry and pounced on the muskrat box, growling.

'What *is* in that box?'

'Dead muskrat.'

'Jeez, Broussard, anybody ever tell you you've got a morbid sense of humor?'

'A million times, but I'm also in denial.'

He smiled and winked at her as he stepped out onto the landing. 'I'll see you around, kiddo. I'm glad we're friends again.'

'Me, too,' Annie murmured. 'And thanks for the flowers.'

'Ah – sorry.' He pulled a face. 'I didn't send them. Uncle Sos assumed ...'

Annie held a hand up. ''Nough said. That's okay. I wouldn't expect you to.'

'But feel free to let me know who did, so I can go punch the guy in the nose.'

'Please. One assault a week is my limit.'

He leaned down and brushed a kiss to her cheek. 'Lock your door. There's bad guys running around out there.'

She shooed the cats out of the entry and went back into the apartment. The bouquet sat dead center on her kitchen table, looking almost as out of place there as it had in the store. Her apartment was a place for wildflowers in jelly jars, not the elegance of roses. She plucked the white envelope from its plastic stem and extracted the card.

Dear Ms Broussard,

I hope you don't think roses inappropriate, but you saved my life and I want to thank you properly.

Yours truly,
Marcus Renard

11

He wondered what she'd thought of the flowers. She should have seen them by now. She worked the day shift. He knew because the news reports about his beating identified her as 'an off-duty sheriff's deputy.' She had been on duty at the courthouse yesterday, and had helped save him from Davidson's attack. She had been on duty the morning Pam's body had been found. She had been the one to find it.

There was a thread of continuity running through all this, Marcus reflected as he gazed out the window of his workroom. He had been in love with Pam; Annie had discovered Pam's body. Pam's father had tried to kill him; Annie had stopped him. The detective in charge of Pam's case had tried to kill him; Annie had again come to his rescue. *Continuity*. In his drug-numbed mind he pictured the letters of the word unraveling and tying themselves into a perfect circle, a thin black line with no beginning and no ending. *Continuity*.

He moved his pencil over the paper with careful, feather-light strokes. Fourcade hadn't damaged his hands. There were bruises – defensive wounds – and his knuckles had been skinned when he fell to the ground, but nothing worse. His eyes were still nearly swollen shut. Cotton packing filled both nostrils, forcing him to breathe through his mouth, the air hissing in and out between his chipped teeth because his broken jaw had been wired shut. Stitches crisscrossed his face like seams in a crazy quilt. He looked like a gargoyle, like a monster.

The doctor had given him a prescription for painkillers and sent him home late in the day. None of his injuries were life-threatening or needed further monitoring, for which he was glad. He had no doubt the nurses at Our

Lady of Mercy would have killed him if given ample opportunity.

The Percodan dulled the throbbing in his head and face, and took the bite out of the knifing pains in his side where Fourcade had cracked three of his ribs. It also seemed to blur the edges of all sensory perception. He felt insulated, as if he were existing inside a bubble. The volume of his mother's voice had been cut in half. Victor's incessant muttering had been reduced to a low hum.

They had both been right there when Richard Kudrow brought him home. Agitated and irritated by the interruption of their routines.

'Marcus, you had me worried sick,' his mother said as he made his way painfully up one step and then another onto the veranda.

Doll stood leaning against a pillar, as if she hadn't the strength to keep herself upright. As tall as both her sons, she still gave the impression of being a birdlike woman, fine boned, almost frail. She had a habit of fluttering one hand against her breastbone like a broken wing. Despite the fact that she was an excellent seamstress, she wore dowdy five-and-dime housedresses that swallowed her up and made her look older than her fiftysome years.

'I didn't know what to think when the hospital called. I was just terrified you might die. I barely slept for worrying on it. What would I do without you? How would I cope with Victor? I was nearly ill with worry.'

'I'm not dead, Mother,' Marcus pointed out.

He didn't ask why she hadn't come to the hospital to see him, because he didn't want to hear how she hated to drive, especially at night – on account of her undiagnosed night blindness. Never mind that she had hounded him to buy her a car years ago so that she wouldn't have to feel dependent upon him. She rarely took the thing out of the carriage shed they used as a garage. And he didn't want to hear how she was afraid to leave Victor, and how she disliked hospitals and believed them to be the breeding

109

grounds for all fatal disease. The last would set Victor off into his germ litany.

His brother stood to one side of the door, his face turned away, but his eyes glancing back at Marcus, wary. Victor had a way of holding himself that was stiff and slightly cockeyed, as if gravity affected him differently from normal people.

'It's me, Victor,' Marcus said, knowing it was hopeless to attempt to put Victor at ease.

Victor had been in his teens before he figured out that putting on a hat didn't turn one person into another being. Voices coming from a telephone had baffled him into his twenties, and sometimes still did. For years he would never do anything more than breathe into the receiver because he couldn't see the person speaking to him, and, therefore, that person did not exist. Only crazy people responded to the voices of people who did not exist, and Victor was not crazy; therefore, he would not speak to faceless voices.

'Mask, no mask,' he mumbled. 'The mockingbird. *Mimus polyglottos*. Nine to eleven inches tall. No mask. Sound and sound alike. More common than similar shrikes. The common raven. *Corvus corax*. Very clever. Very shrewd. Like the crow, but not a crow. A mask, but no mask.'

'Victor, stop it!' Doll said, her voice scratching up toward shrillness. She sent Marcus a long-suffering look. 'He's been on his rantings all day long. I'd like to have lost my mind worrying about you, and here was Victor droning on and on and on. It was enough to make me see red.'

'Red, red, very red,' Victor said, shaking his head as if a bug had crawled into his ear.

'That lawyer of yours had better make the sheriff's department pay for the suffering they've caused this family,' Doll harped, following Marcus into the house. 'Those people are rotten to the core, every last one of them.'

'Annie Broussard saved my life,' Marcus pointed out. 'Twice.'

Doll made a sour face. 'Annie Broussard. I'm sure she's no better than any of the rest. I saw her on the television. She didn't have a thing to say about you. You blow everything out of proportion, Marcus. You always have.'

'I was there, Mother. I know what she did.'

'You just think she's pretty, that's all. I know how your mind works, Marcus. You are your father's son.'

It was meant to be an insult. Marcus didn't remember his father. Claude Renard had left them when Marcus was hardly more than a toddler. He had never come back, had severed all ties. There were times when Marcus envied him.

He closed his eyes now and let a wave of Percodan wash the memory from his battered brain. The miracles of modern chemistry.

He had gone straight to his bedroom and shut out his mother's incessant whining with a pill and two hours of unconsciousness. When he came to, the house was quiet. Everyone had settled back into their routines. His mother retreated to her room every night at nine to watch television preachers and work her word puzzles. She would be in bed by ten and would complain all the next morning that she had barely slept. According to Doll, she hadn't slept through a night in her life.

Victor went to bed at eight and rose at midnight to study his nature books or work on elaborate mathematical calculations. He would go to bed again at four a.m. and rise for the day precisely at eight. Routine was sacred to him. He equated routine with normalcy. The least deviation could set him off into a spell of upset, causing him to rock himself and mumble, or worse. Routine made him happy.

If only my own life were so simple. Marcus didn't like being the center of anyone's attention. He preferred to be left alone to do his work and to work at his hobbies.

His workroom was located just off his bedroom and had probably been a study or a nursery at one time in the house's history. He had claimed the small suite as his own the first time he had walked through the house with Pam.

111

She had been his real estate agent when he had come to Bayou Breaux to interview with Bowen & Briggs – another strand in the thread of continuity.

The suite was on the first floor at the back of the house and you had to walk through one room to get to the other. A worktable held his latest project, a Queen Anne dollhouse with elaborate gingerbread and heart-shaped shingles on the roof. Houses he had designed and built over the years were displayed on deep custom-built shelves along one long wall. He entered them in competitions at fairs and sold all but the most special to him.

But it wasn't the dollhouse that claimed his attention tonight. Tonight he had risen from bed to sit at his drawing table. He worked to bring a mental image from his mind to the page.

Pam had been a lovely woman – small, feminine, her dark hair cut in a sleek, shoulder-length bob, her smile bright, her brown eyes sparkling with life. She had her nails done every Friday. She shopped at the most exclusive stores in Lafayette, and always looked as if she had just stepped from the pages of *Southern Living* or *Town and Country*.

Annie was pretty in her own way. She was taller than Pam, but by no more than an inch; sturdier than Pam, but still small. He pictured her, not in the slate blue sheriff's department uniform, but in the long, flowered skirt she had worn last night. He rid her of the sloppy denim jacket and put her instead in a white cotton camisole. Delicate, almost sheer, teasing him with the shadows of her small breasts.

In his mind's eye, he combed her hair back neatly and secured it at the nape of her slender neck with a white bow. She had a retroussé nose; a hint of a cleft gave her chin a certain stubborn quality. Her eyes were a deep, rich brown, like Pam's, but with a tantalizing tilt at the corners. He was fascinated with the shape of them – slightly exotic, slightly almond-shaped, like a cat's. Her mouth was nearly as intriguing. A very French mouth – the lower lip full, the upper lip a delicate cupid's bow. He had never seen her smile. Until he had, he would superimpose Pam's smile onto her face.

He set his pencil aside and assessed his work.

He had missed Pam these past three months, but he could feel the ache of that loneliness beginning to subside. In his drug-induced haze, he visualized having been parched all that time. Now a fresh source of wine was ebbing closer, tantalizing him. He tried to imagine the taste on his tongue. Desire stirred lazily in his blood, and he smiled.

Annie. His angel.

12

Bail hearings in Partout Parish were held Monday, Wednesday, and Friday mornings, a schedule carefully structured to produce revenue. Anyone bailed out on Friday had the weekend to break another law or two, for which they would have to be bailed out again come Monday. Wednesday was thrown in for good measure and civil liberties.

The presiding judge, as luck would have it, was old Monahan. Nick groaned inwardly as Monahan emerged from his chambers and took his seat on the bench. Cases were called. A mixed bag of petty offenses on this Friday morning: drunk and disorderly, shoplifting, possession with intent to distribute, burglary. The defendants, their eyes downcast like dogs that had been caught soiling the carpet, stood beside their lawyers. Some of the accused looked ashamed, some embarrassed, some were just used to playing the game.

The gallery of the courtroom filled steadily as the cases were dealt with in short order, one scumbag loser at a time. If these people going before him were losers, Nick thought, then what did that make him? Every person who came before the court claimed to have a good reason for what he or she had done. None was as good as his, but he doubted getting up and telling the court he had only done the job the court had shirked would win him any points with Monahan.

The esteemed members of the press filling the pews behind him were no doubt drooling for precisely that kind of dramatic statement. They waited restlessly through the preliminary goings-on, eager for the main event. Monahan seemed irritated by their presence, his mood more churlish than usual. He barked at the attorneys, snapped at the defendants, and set bail amounts at the high end of the spectrum.

Nick had exactly three thousand two hundred dollars in the bank.

'Don't piss off His Honor, Nick, my boy,' Wily Tallant murmured, leaning toward Nick. 'I do believe he's got an Irish headache today. Don't meet his eyes. If you can't look contrite, look contemplative.'

Nick looked away. Tallant was a sly, scheming bastard – good qualities in a defense attorney, but that didn't mean he had to like the man. He only had to listen to him.

The lawyer was nearly a head shorter than Nick, with a lean, European elegance about him. His thin, dark hair was slicked back neatly, accentuating the distinguished lines of his face. He wore black suits year-round and a Rolex that cost more than Nick made in four months. Wily's clients may have been scumbags, but they tended to be scumbags with money.

Nick scanned the crowd again. A number of cops had found their way into the balcony that had been the gallery for black spectators in the days of open segregation. He spotted a couple of sheriff's deputies, a couple of Bayou Breaux uniforms. Broussard was not among them. He thought she might have come. This was what she wanted: him facing the music.

In the balcony front row, Stokes touched the brim of the ball cap he wore low over a pair of Ray-Bans. Quinlan, another of the SO detectives, sat beside him, along with Z-Top McGee, a detective from the city squad they had worked with a time or two.

It struck Nick as odd that anyone other than Stokes had come. He had spent no time cultivating friendships here. More likely their attachment to him was through the job. The Brotherhood. He was one of them, and here but for the grace of God ... Ultimately, their concern was for themselves, he decided. A comforting cynical thought.

115

He dropped his gaze to the main gallery seating, skimming the faces of the reporters who had hounded him from the outset of the Bichon case, and one who had hounded him longer than that – a face familiar from New Orleans. New Orleanians generally cared little what went on beyond the boundaries of the Big Easy. The Cajun parishes were a separate world. But this one had smelled Nick's blood in the water and had come hungry. Unexpected, but not surprising.

The surprises sat ahead of the New Orleans hack. Belle Davidson and, two rows in front of her, her erstwhile son-in-law, Donnie Bichon. What were they doing here? Hunter Davidson was not among the unfortunate waiting their turn before the judge. Pritchett would want to downplay that bail hearing. Pressing charges against a grieving father would be unpopular with his constituents. Pressing charges against 'a rogue cop' for the same crime was an altogether different matter.

'State of Lou'siana versus Nick Fourcade!'

Nick followed Tallant through the gate to the defense table. Pritchett had remained silent through the previous proceedings, letting ADA Doucet deal with the petty stuff, saving himself for the feature attraction. He rose from his chair and buttoned his suit coat, twitching his shoulders back and smoothing a hand over his silk tie. He looked like a little gamecock preening his feathers and scratching the dirt before a fight.

'Your Honor,' he intoned loudly. 'The charges here are extremely egregious: aggravated assault and attempted murder perpetrated by a member of the law enforcement community. We're dealing not only with a felony, but with a gross abuse of power and a betrayal of the public trust. It's an absolute disgrace. I –'

'Save your preaching for another pulpit, Mr Pritchett,' Judge Monahan barked as he snapped the cap off a bottle of Excedrin and dumped a pair of pills into his hand.

The judge glared at Nick, black eyebrows creeping down over piercing blue eyes.

'Detective Fourcade, I cannot begin to express my disgust at having you before my bench on this matter. You have managed to turn an ugly situation hideous, and I am not inclined to be forgiving. Could you possibly have anything to say for yourself?'

Wily leaned forward, his fingertips just resting on the defense table. 'Revon Tallant for the defense. Your Honor, my client wishes to enter a plea of not guilty at this time.' He enunciated each word as precisely as a poet. 'As usual, Mr Pritchett has jumped to all manner of extreme conclusions without having heard the facts of the situation. Detective Fourcade was simply going about the business of his job –'

'Beating the snot out of people?' Pritchett said.

'Apprehending a suspected burglar, who chose to resist arrest and fight.'

'Resist and fight? The man had to be hospitalized!' Pritchett shouted. 'He looks like he ran headlong into a steel beam!'

'I never said he was good at it.'

Laughter rippled through the gallery. Monahan banged his gavel. 'This is not a humorous matter!'

'I quite agree, Your Honor,' Pritchett said. 'We had ought to take a dim view of law enforcement officers crossing the line into vigilantism. A sheriff's deputy caught Detective Fourcade red-handed – in the literal sense. She will testify –'

'This isn't the trial, Mr Pritchett,' Monahan cut in. 'I am in no mood to listen to lawyers go on and on for the benefit of the press and the sheer love of the sound of their own voices. Get on with it!'

'Yes, Your Honor.' Pritchett swallowed his pride, his cheeks tinting pink. 'In view of the seriousness of the charges and the brutality of the crime, the state requests bail in the amount of one hundred thousand dollars.'

The words hit Nick like a ball bat.

Wily tossed his head back and rolled his big sloe eyes. 'Your Honor, Mr Pritchett's predilection for drama aside –'

'Your client is a law enforcement officer who stands accused of beating a man senseless, Mr Tallant,' Monahan said sharply. 'That's all the drama I need.' He consulted his clerk for his schedule, shaking the Excedrin tablets in his hand like a pair of dice. 'Preliminary hearing set for two weeks from yesterday. Bail in the amount of one hundred thousand dollars, cash or bond. Pay the clerk if you can. Next case!'

Nick and Tallant moved away from the defense table as the next defendant and his attorney came in. Nick stared at Pritchett across the room. The DA's small mouth was screwed into a self-satisfied smirk.

'I'll have Monahan recused from the case before the hearing,' Wily murmured, moving with Nick toward the side door, where a city cop waited to escort him back to jail. 'He's obviously too biased to hear the case. However, there's nothing I can do about Pritchett. That man wants your head on a pike, my boy. You made him look bad with that unfortunate evidentiary matter the other day. That's a felony in Smith Pritchett's book. Can you make bail?'

'Hell, Wily, I can barely pay you. I might get ten thousand if I hock everything I own,' Nick said absently, his attention suddenly on the gallery.

Donnie Bichon had risen from his seat and came forward, lifting a hand tentatively, like an uncertain schoolboy trying to attract the teacher's attention. He was a handsome kid – thirty-six going on twenty – with a short nose and ears that stuck out just enough to make him perpetually boyish. He had played third-string forward at Tulane and had a tendency to walk with his shoulders slightly hunched, as if he were ready to drive to the basket at any second. Everyone on the business side of the bar stopped what they were doing to look at him.

'Your Honor? May I approach the bench?'

Monahan glared at him. 'Who are you, sir?'

'Donnie Bichon, Your Honor. I'd like to pay Detective Fourcade's bail.'

Construction business must be doing better than I thought,' Nick said, moving around Donnie Bichon's office, rolling a toothpick between his teeth.

He had allowed the drama in the courtroom to unfold, not because he wanted Bichon's money, but because he wanted to know the motive behind the magnanimous gesture.

The press had gone wild. Headline frenzy. Monahan had ordered the courtroom cleared. Smith Pritchett had stormed from the room in a fit of temper at having his thunder stolen. After Donnie paid the clerk, they had all run the media gauntlet out of the courthouse and down the steps. Déjà vu all over again.

Nick had jumped into Wily's money green Infiniti and they had driven clear to New Iberia to shake the tail of reporters behind them. By the time they doubled back to Bayou Breaux on country roads, the press had gone off to write their stories. Nick had Wily drop him off at the house, where he grabbed the keys to his truck and left, skipping the shower and change of clothes he needed badly. He needed other things more. Answers.

The office gave the impression that Bichon Bayou Development was a solid company – sturdy oak furnishings, masculine colors, a small fortune in wildlife prints on the walls. Nick's investigation had told a different tale. Donnie had built the company on the back of Bayou Realty, Pam's business, and pissed away his opportunities to put it on solid financial ground. According to one source, the divorce would have cleanly severed the attachment between BBD and Pam's company, and Donnie would have been left to get business sense or die.

Nick traced a fingertip over the graceful line of a hand-carved wooden mallard coming in for a landing on the credenza. 'When I checked your company out, looked to me like you were in hock up to your ass, Donnie. You nearly went belly-up eighteen months ago. You hid land in Pam's company to keep from losing it. How is it you can write a check for a hundred thousand dollars?'

Donnie laughed as he dropped into the oxblood leather chair behind his desk. He had opened his collar and rolled up the sleeves of his pin-striped shirt. The young businessman at work.

'You're an ungrateful bastard, Fourcade,' he said, caught somewhere between amusement and irritation. 'I just bailed your ass out of jail and you don't like the smell of my money? Fuck you.'

'I believe I thanked you already. You paid for my release, Donnie, you didn't buy me.'

Donnie broke eye contact and straightened a stack of papers on his desk. 'The company's worth a lot on paper. Assets, you know. Land, equipment, houses built on spec. Bankers love assets more than cash. I have a nice line of credit.'

'Why'd you do it?'

'You're kidding, right? After what Renard did to Pam? And ol' Hunter and you are sitting in jail and he's out walking around? That's crazy. The courts are a goddamn circus nowadays. It's time somebody did the right thing.'

'Like kill Renard?'

'In my dreams. Perverted little prick. *He's* the criminal, not you. That was my statement. That deputy that hauled you in should have just minded her own damn business, let nature take its own course and finish this thing. Besides, I'm told I'm not out anything, unless you decide to skip town.'

'Why cash?' Nick asked. 'You pay a bail bondsman only ten percent for the bond.'

And get a fraction of the publicity, he thought. Donnie crossing the bar to write out a huge check had been a climactic moment. It hadn't been Donnie's first taste of the spotlight.

He had been right there soaking it up from the day Pam's body had been discovered. He had immediately offered a fifty-thousand-dollar reward for information leading to an arrest. He had cried like a baby at the funeral. Every newspaper in Louisiana had printed the close-up of Donnie with his face in his hands.

In the outer office, the telephone was ringing off the hook. Reporters looking for comments and interviews most likely. Every story that ran was free advertising for Bichon Bayou Development.

Donnie glanced away again. 'I wouldn't know anything about that. I never bailed anybody out of jail before. Christ, will you sit down? You're making me nervous.'

Nick ignored the request. He needed to move, and having Donnie nervous wasn't an altogether bad thing.

'Will you be able to go back to work on the case?'

'When hell freezes over. I'm on suspension. My involvement would taint the case because of my obvious bias against the chief suspect. At least, that's what a judge would say. I'm out, officially.'

'Then I'd better hope you have something else to keep you in Partout Parish, hadn't I? I sure as hell can't afford to lose a hundred grand.'

'Some folks would say you can afford to lose it now more than you could have when your wife was alive,' Nick said.

Donnie's face went tight. 'We've been down that road before, Detective, and I mightily resent you going down it again.'

'You know it's been a two-pronged investigation all along, Donnie. That's standard op. You bailing me outta jail won't change that.'

'You know where you can stick your two prongs, Fourcade.'

Shrugging, Nick went on. 'Me, I've had a lotta time on my hands in the last twenty-four hours. Time to let my mind wander, let it all turn over and over. It just seems … fortuitous … that Pam was killed before the divorce went

121

through. Once the insurance company coughs up and you sell off Pam's half of the real estate company, you won't need that line of credit.'

Donnie surged to his feet. 'That's it, Fourcade! Get outta my office! I did you a good turn, and you come in here and abuse me! I should have left you to rot in jail! I didn't kill Pam. I couldn't possibly. I loved her.'

Nick made no move to leave. He pulled the toothpick from his mouth and held it like a cigarette. 'You had a funny way of showing it, Tulane: chasing anything in a skirt.'

'I've made mistakes,' Donnie admitted angrily. 'Maturity was never my strong suit. But I *did* love Pam, and I *do* love my daughter. I could never do anything to hurt Josie.'

The very thought seemed to distress him. He turned away from the school portrait of his daughter that sat on a corner of his desk.

'Is she living with you yet?' Nick asked quietly.

There had been rumors of a custody battle brewing within the divorce war. Something that seemed more like petty meanness on Donnie's part than genuine concern for his daughter's well-being. As in countless divorce cases, the child became a tool, a possession to be bickered over. Donnie liked his freedom too well for full-time fatherhood. Visitation would suit his lifestyle better than custody.

Nick had long ago discounted Josie as a motive for murder. It was the money angle that bothered him, and the land Donnie had hidden in Bayou Realty's assets. Even when he swore up and down Renard was their boy, the money issue kept tugging at him. It was a loose thread and he couldn't simply let a loose thread dangle. He would worry at it until it could be tied off one way or another. If it meant looking his gift horse in the mouth, then so be it. Donnie had decided on his own to bail him out. Nick felt no obligation.

'She's with Belle and Hunter,' Donnie said. 'Belle thought they could provide a more stable environment for the time being. Then Hunter goes off with a gun and tries to commit murder in broad daylight. Some stability. Of course, the press is making him out to be a celebrity. If he doesn't go to prison, they'll probably make a movie about him.'

The fight had run out of him. His shoulders slumped and he suddenly seemed older.

'Why are you dredging all this up again? You still believe Renard did it. I mean, I know some people are saying things after that rape the other night – all that Bayou Strangler bullshit and whatnot. But that's got nothing to do with this. You're the one found Pam's ring in Renard's house. You're the one put him in the hospital. Why are you dogging my ass? I'm the best friend you had today.'

'Habit,' Nick replied. 'Me, I tend to be suspicious by nature.'

'No shit. Well, I'm not guilty.'

'Ever'body's guilty of something.'

Donnie shook his head. 'You need help, Fourcade. You're clinically paranoid.'

A sardonic smile curved Nick's mouth as he tossed his toothpick in the trash and turned for the door. '*C'est vrai*. That's true enough. Lucky for me, I'm one of the few people who can make a living off it.'

Nick left Bichon Bayou Development through the back door, made his way down two alleys, and cut across the backyard of a house where a teenage girl in a yellow bikini was stretched out on a shiny metallic blanket trying to absorb ultraviolet rays. With headphones and sun goggles, she was oblivious to his passing.

He had parked in the weedy side lot of a closed welding shop, the truck blending in with an array of abandoned junk. He climbed into the cab, rolled the windows down, and sat there, smoking a cigarette and thinking as the radio mumbled to itself.

'You're on KJUN with Dean Monroe. Our topic this afternoon: the release on bail of Partout Parish detective,

123

Nick Fourcade, who stands accused of brutalizing murder suspect Marcus Renard. Montel in Maurice, speak your mind.'

'He done this kind of thing before and he got off. I thinks we all gots to be scared when cops can plant evidence and beat people up and just get off –'

Nick silenced the radio, thinking back to New Orleans. He had paid in ways worse than prison. He had lost his job, lost his credibility. He had crashed and burned and was still struggling to put the pieces back together. But he had more urgent things than the past to occupy his mind today.

Maybe Donnie Bichon was filled with regret for the demise of his marriage and the death of the woman he had once loved. Or maybe his remorse was about something else altogether. Except for the hideous brutality of the murder, Donnie had been an automatic suspect. Husbands always were. But Donnie seemed more the sort who would have choked his ex in a moment of blind fury, not the sort who could have planned a death like Pam's and carried it out. It took cold hate to pull off a murder like that.

'Renard did it,' Nick murmured. The trail, the logic led back to Renard. Renard had fixated on her, stalked her, killed her when she rejected him. Nick believed he'd done it in Baton Rouge shortly before moving here, but that woman's death had been ruled accidental and never investigated as a homicide.

Renard was their guy, he could feel it in the marrow of his bones. Still, there was something off about the whole damn deal.

Maybe it was the fact that no one had ever been able to prove Renard was the one stalking Pam. Hell, the word *stalking* never even appeared in the reports. That was how doubtful the cops and the courts had been. Renard had openly sent her flowers and small gifts. There was nothing menacing in that. Pam had thrown the gifts back at him in the Bowen & Briggs office one day, not long before her death.

No one had ever seen Renard going into Pam's office or her house out on Quail Drive when she wasn't there, and yet someone had stolen things from her desk and from her dresser. Someone had left a dead snake in her pencil drawer. Renard had access to the office building, but so did Donnie. No one had identified Renard as the prowler Pam had reported several times to 911 from her home, but someone had slipped into her garage and cut the tires on her Mustang. She had received so many hang-up and breather calls at home, she had taken an unlisted number. But there was not a single call listed in the phone company records from Renard's home or business number to Pam Bichon's.

Renard was meticulous, compulsively neat. Careful. Intelligent. He could have pulled it off. The flowers and candy could have been part of the game. Perhaps he had sensed all along she would never have him. Perhaps it was resentment that drove his fixation. Affection was the perfect cover for a deep-seated hatred.

Then again, perhaps Donnie had harassed Pam in a foolish and misguided attempt to get her back. Donnie had never been in favor of the divorce. He had argued it was not in Josie's best interest, but it was not in Donnie's best interest – financially. Pam had asked him to move out in February – a year ago, now. A trial separation. They went to a few counseling sessions. By the end of July it had been plain in Pam's mind that the marriage was over, and she filed the papers. Donnie had not taken the news well.

The harassment began the end of August.

Donnie could have pulled those tricks to scare her. He had the capacity for juvenile behavior. But again, there was no evidence. No witnesses. No phone records. A search of his home following the murder had turned up nothing. Donnie wasn't that smart.

'You need a break, Fourcade,' he muttered.

Like the snap of a hypnotist's fingers, the trance was shattered. He didn't need a break. He was off the case. He didn't want to let it go, and yet, he had thrown it away with both hands by going after Renard.

He had replayed that night in his head a hundred times. In his head, he made the right choices. He didn't accept Stokes's invitation to Laveau's. He didn't pour whiskey on his wounded pride. He didn't listen to Stokes's eye-for-an-eye nonsense. He didn't take that phone call, didn't go down that street.

And Annie Broussard didn't walk out of the blue and into his life.

Where the hell had she come from? And why?

He didn't believe in coincidence, had never trusted Fate.

The possibilities rubbed back and forth in his mind and chafed his temper raw. He put the truck in gear, and rolled out of the parking lot.

The hell he was off this case.

13

Friday. Payday. Everyone was in a hurry to get to the bank, get to the bars, get home to start the weekend. Friday was a big speeding-ticket day. Friday nights were good for brawls and DUIs.

Annie preferred the tickets. With more people packing guns every day, brawls had become a little too unpredictable to be fun. Then there was the whole AIDS scare and the threats of lawsuits. The only cops she knew who still liked brawls were the boneheaded type who sweated testosterone, and short guys with big chips on their shoulders. Little guys always wanted to fight to prove their manhood. The Napoleon complex.

Just one more reason to be glad she didn't have a penis. The few skirmishes she had jumped into had been enough to win her a chipped tooth, two cracked ribs, and the respect of her fellow deputies. Men were that way. Being able to take a punch somehow made you a better person.

She wondered if any of them remembered those past brawls. It seemed not. When she had reported to the briefing room this morning, she had taken a seat at one of the long tables, and every deputy at the table got up and moved. Not a word was spoken, but the message was clear: They no longer considered her one of them. Because of Fourcade, a man who had befriended none of them and yet was lionized by them all for the mere fact that he had external genitalia. Men.

She had wanted to hear about the follow-up on the Jennifer Nolan rape, but the closest she was going to come to the case was rewriting her initial report, which Hooker had 'misplaced'. She had interviewed half a dozen of Nolan's neighbors yesterday, getting only one potentially useful piece of information: Nolan's former roommate had run off with a biker. Two of the doors she had knocked on had gone unanswered. She had passed all the information on to Stokes and doubted she would ever hear another word about it unless she read it in the paper.

She thought about the rape in fragments: the mask, the violence, the absence of seminal fluid, the ligatures, the fact that he made her bathe afterward. The fact that he hadn't spoken a single word during the ordeal. Verbal intimidation and degradation were standard fare in most rapes. She wondered which would be more terrifying: an attacker who threatened death or the ominous uncertainty of silence.

Careful. The word kept coming back to her. The rapist had been careful to leave no trace. He seemed to be perfectly aware of what the cops would need to nail him. That pointed to someone with experience and maybe a record. Someone should have been checking personnel records at the True Light lamp factory to see if any of Nolan's co-workers was an ex-con. But it wasn't her job, and it never would be if Chaz Stokes had anything to say about it.

Annie checked her watch again. Another half hour and she could head back to Bayou Breaux. She had pulled the cruiser off the road into the turnaround lot of a ramshackle vegetable stand that had blown down in the last big storm. The position was shaded by a sprawling live oak and gave her a view of two blacktop roads that converged a quarter mile south of the small town of Luck – a hot spot on Friday nights. Every rough character in the parish headed down to Skeeter Mouton's roadhouse on Friday night. Bikers, roughnecks, rednecks, and criminal types, all gathered for the popular low-society pursuits of beer, betting, and breaking heads.

A red Chevy pickup was coming fast out of town. Annie clocked it with the radar as it cruised past, the driver hanging a beer can out the window. Sixty-five in a forty zone and a DUI to boot. Jackpot. She hit the lights and siren and pulled him over half a mile down the road. The truck had a rebel-flag sunscreen in the back window and a bumper sticker that read USA Kicks Ass.

Nothing like a drunken redneck to make a day truly suck the big one.

'One Able Charlie,' she radioed in. 'I got a speeder on twelve, two miles south of Luck. Looks like he's drinking. Lou'siana tags Tango Whiskey Echo seven-three-three. Tango Whiskey Echo seven-three-three. Over.'

She waited a beat for the acknowledgment that didn't come, then tried again. Still no response. The silence was more than annoying; it was disturbing. The radio was her link to help. If a routine stop turned into trouble, Dispatch had her location and the tag number on the vehicle she had pulled over. If she didn't call them back in a timely fashion, they would send other units.

'10–1, One Able Charlie. We didn't catch that. You're breaking up again. Say again. Over.'

It was a simple thing to interrupt a radio transmission. All it took was one other deputy keying his mike when he heard her calling in and she was cut off. Cut off from communication, cut off from help.

Disgusted at the possibility, Annie grabbed her clipboard and ticket book and got out of the car.

'Step out of the vehicle, please,' she called as she approached the truck from the rear.

'I wadn' speedin',' the driver yelled, sticking his head out the open window. He had small mean eyes and a mouth that drew into a tight knot. The dirty red ball cap he wore was stitched with a yellow TriStar Chemical logo. 'You cops ain't got nothin' better to do than stop me?'

'Not at the moment. I'll need to see your license and registration.'

'This is bullshit, man.'

He swung open the door of the truck, and an empty Miller Genuine Draft can tumbled out onto the verge and rolled under the cab. He pretended not to notice as he stepped down with the extreme caution of a man who knows he has lost his equilibrium to booze. He wasn't any taller than Annie, a little pit bull of a man in jeans and a Bass Master T-shirt stretching tight over a hard beer belly. A *short*, drunken redneck.

'I don't pay taxes in this parish so y'all can harass me,' he grumbled. 'Goddamn gov'ment's tryin' to run my life. This here's supposed to be a free fuckin' country.'

'So it is as long as you're not drunk and driving sixty-five in a forty. I need your license.'

'I ain't drunk.' He pulled a big trucker's wallet on a chain out of his hip pocket and fumbled around to extract his license, which he held out in Annie's general direction. His fingers were stained dark with grease. A tattoo of a naked blue woman with bright red nipples reclined on his forearm. Classy.

Vernell Poncelet. Annie stuck the license under the clip on her board.

'I wadn' speedin',' he insisted. 'Them radar guns is always wrong. You can clock a goddamn tree doing sixty.'

Suddenly his squinty eyes widened in surprise. 'Hey! You're a woman!'

'Yep. I've been aware of that for some time now.'

Poncelet put his head on one side, studying her, until he started to tip over. He swung an arm to point at her and righted himself in the process.

'You're the one was on the news! I seen you! You turned in that cop what beat up that killer rapist!'

'Stay right here,' Annie said coolly, backing toward the squad. 'I need to run your name and tags.' And call for a backup. She had the feeling Vernell wasn't going down without a fight. Short guys.

'What kinda cop are you?' Poncelet shouted, staggering after her. 'You want killer rapists runnin' 'round loose? An' you're giving me a ticket? That's bullshit!'

Annie gave him the evil eye. 'Stand where you are!'

He kept coming, thrusting a finger at her as if he meant

130

to run her through with it. 'I ain't takin' no fuckin' ticket from you!'

'The hell you're not.'

'You let a rapist run around loose. Maybe you wanna get lucky, huh? You fuckin' bitch –'

'That's it!' Annie tossed the clipboard on the hood of the cruiser and reached for the cuffs on her belt. 'Up against the truck! Now!'

'Fuck you!' Poncelet made a wobbly 180-degree turn and started back for his truck. 'Let a real cop stop me. I ain't takin' no shit from a broad.'

'Up against the truck, stubby, or this is gonna get so real it'll hurt.' Annie stepped in behind him, slapped a cuff around his right wrist, and pulled his arm up behind his back. 'Up against the goddamn truck!'

She stepped into him, trying to turn him with pressure on his arm. Poncelet staggered, throwing her off balance, then swung around to take a punch at her. Their feet tangled in a clumsy dance and they went down in a heap on the side of the road, wrestling, grunting.

Poncelet swore in her face, his breath hot and acetous with beer gases bubbling up from his belly. He groped for a handhold to right himself, grabbing Annie's left breast. Annie kicked him in the shin and caught him in the mouth with her elbow. Poncelet got one knee under him and tried to surge to his feet, one hand swinging hard into Annie's nose.

'Son of a bitch!' she yelled as blood coursed down over her lips. She came to her feet and ran Poncelet headlong into the side of the truck.

'You picked the wrong day to fuck with me, shorty!' she snarled, closing the other cuff tight around his free wrist. 'You're under arrest for every stinkin' crime I can think of!'

'I want a real cop!' he bellowed. 'This is America. I got rights! I got the right to remain silent –'

'Then why don't you?' Annie barked, shoving him toward the cruiser.

'I ain't no crim'nal! I got rights!'

'You've got shit for brains, that's what you've got. Man, you have dug yourself a hole so deep, you're gonna need a ladder to see rock bottom.'

She pushed him into the backseat and slammed the door. Traffic passed by on the blacktop road to Mouton's. A kid with a goatee leaned out the window of a jacked-up GTO and gave her the finger. Annie flipped it back at him and climbed in behind the wheel of her car.

'You're a feminazi, that's what you are!' Poncelet shouted, kicking the back of the seat. 'You're a goddamn feminazi!'

Annie wiped the blood off her mouth with her shirt-sleeve. 'Watch your mouth, Poncelet. You start quoting Rush Limbaugh to me, I'll take you out in the swamp and shoot you.'

She glanced at herself in the rearview mirror and swore as she pulled the radio mike. With the black eye from Wednesday and the bloody nose, she looked as if she'd gone five rounds with Mike Tyson.

'One Able Charlie. I'm bringing in a drunk. Thanks for nothing.'

Poncelet was still screaming when Annie escorted him to Booking. She had stopped listening, her own anger muting his words to an annoying roar in the background. What if Poncelet had hurt her? What if he had gotten hold of her gun? Would anyone have known the difference?

The Deputies' Association had voted to pay Fourcade's legal bills. She wondered if they'd also taken a vote on getting her killed. She hadn't been invited to the meeting.

The shift was changing – guys going in and out of the locker room, hanging around the briefing room. Time for bullshit and bad jokes over strong coffee. The relaxed smiles froze and vanished when Annie came down the hall.

'What?' she challenged no one in particular. 'Disappointed to see me in one piece?'

'Disappointed to see you at all,' Mullen muttered.

'Yeah? Well, now you know how the whole female population feels when they see you coming, Mullen. What did you think?' she demanded. 'That keying me out on the radio would make me disappear?'

'I don't know what you're talking about, Broussard. You're hysterical.'

'No, I'm pissed off. You got a problem with me, then be a man and bring it to me instead of pulling this adolescent bullshit –'

'You're the problem,' he charged. 'If you can't handle the job, then leave.'

'I can handle the job. I was *doing* my job –'

'What the hell's going on out here?' Hooker bellowed, stepping into the hall.

Too angry for circumspection, Annie turned toward the sergeant. 'Someone's covering my transmissions.'

'That's bullshit,' Mullen said.

'Musta been something wrong with your radio,' Hooker said. Annie wanted to kick him.

'Funny how I suddenly can't get a radio that works.'

'You got bad vibes, Broussard,' Mullen said. 'Maybe the wire in your bra is screwing up your reception.'

Hooker glared at him. 'Shut the fuck up, Mullen.'

'It's not the radio,' Annie said. 'It's the attitude. Y'all are acting like a bunch of spoiled little boys, like I ruined everybody's fun. Someone was breaking the law and I stopped him. That's my job. If y'all have a problem with that, then you don't belong in a uniform.'

'We know who doesn't belong here,' Mullen muttered.

The silence was absolute. Annie looked from one deputy to another, a lineup of stony faces and averted eyes. They may not all have felt as strongly as Mullen, but no one was standing up for her, either.

Finally, Hooker spoke. 'You got proof somebody did you wrong, Broussard, then file a grievance. Otherwise, quit

133

your goddamn whining and go do your paperwork on that drunk.'

No one moved until Hooker had disappeared back into his office. Then Prejean and Savoy walked away, breaking the standoff. Mullen started down the hall, leaning toward Annie as he passed.

'Yeah, Broussard,' he murmured. 'Quit your whining or somebody'll give you something to whine about.'

'Don't threaten me, Mullen.'

He raised his brows in mock fear. 'What you gonna do? Arrest me?' The expression turned stony. 'You can't arrest us all.'

14

Late July: Pam makes it known around the office that she means to divorce Donnie. They have been separated since February. Renard begins to show an interest in her. Drops into the realty office to chat, to show his concern for her, etc.

August: Renard clearly has a crush. He sends Pam flowers and small gifts, asks her to lunch, asks her out for drinks. She goes with him only in a group, tells her partner she wants to be sure Renard doesn't get the wrong idea about their friendship, though she admits she thinks it's rather sweet the way he's trying to court her. She tries to stress to Renard they are just friends.

Late August: Pam begins to receive breather and hang-up calls at home.

September: Small items go missing from Pam's office and from her home. A paperweight, a small bottle of perfume, a small framed photo of herself and daughter Josie, a hairbrush. She can't pinpoint when the items were taken. Renard is hanging around, shows more concern than seems appropriate. Pam begins to feel uncomfortable around him. Breather and hang-up calls continue.

9/25: On leaving for work, Pam discovers her tires slashed (car parked in unlocked garage). Calls the sheriff's department. Responding deputy: Mullen. Pam expresses her concerns about Renard, but there is no evidence he committed the crime. Detective assigned to investigate alleged harassment: Stokes.

10/02 1:00 A.M.: Pam reports a prowler outside her home. No suspect apprehended. Renard interviewed regarding incident. Denies involvement. Expresses concern for Pam.

10/03: Renard comes to Pam's office, expresses concern for her in person.

10/09 1:45 A.M.: Pam again reports a prowler. No suspect apprehended.

10/10: On leaving house for school bus, Josie Bichon discovers the mutilated remains of a raccoon on the front step.

10/11: Renard comes to Pam's office again to express concern for her safety and for Josie's safety. Unnerved, Pam tells him to leave. Clients waiting to meet with her confirm her level of upset.

10/14: On arriving at her office, Pam finds a dead snake in her desk drawer. Later that day Renard approaches her yet again to express his concern for her. Says something to the effect that a single woman, like Pam, has much to fear, that any number of bad things might happen to her. Pam perceives this as a threat.

10/22: On returning home from work, Pam finds house has been vandalized: clothing cut up, bedding smeared with dog waste, photos of herself defaced. No suspect fingerprints recovered from scene. No witnesses. Pam calls Acadiana Security to have home system installed. Later realizes a spare set of house and office keys has gone missing. Can't pinpoint when she last saw them.

10/24: Renard gives Pam an expensive necklace for her birthday. Pam, extremely angry, confronts Renard in his office with her suspicions, returns all small gifts he had given her during the months of August and September. In front of witnesses, Renard denies all charges of stalking.

10/24: Pam consults attorney Thomas Watson about a restraining order against Renard.

10/27: Watson petitions the court on Pam's behalf for a restraining order against Marcus Renard. Request denied for lack of sufficient cause. Judge Edwards refuses to 'blacken a man's reputation' with no more reason than 'a woman's unsubstantiated paranoia.'

10/31: Pam sees a prowler outside her house. Tries to call sheriff's department. House phones are dead. Calls on cellular. No suspect apprehended. Phone line had been cut. Back door of house smeared with human waste.

11/7: Pam Bichon reported missing.

Annie read through her notes. Laid out in this linear fashion, it seemed so simple, so obvious. A classic pattern of escalation. Attraction, attachment, pursuit, fixation, increasing hostility at rejection. Why hadn't anyone else seen it for what it was and stopped it?

Because a pattern was all they had. There was absolutely nothing to tie Renard to the stalking. His public reaction to Pam's accusations had been confusion, hurt. How could she think he would ever harm her? Not once in those months preceding Pam Bichon's murder had Renard expressed to any of his co-workers anger or hostility toward her. Quite the contrary. Pam had complained to friends about Renard. They offered support to her face and questioned her sanity behind her back. He seemed so harmless.

With the divorce looming and the settlement potentially affecting his business, Donnie Bichon had seemed a more likely candidate for villain. But Pam had insisted Renard was her stalker.

What a nightmare, Annie thought. To be so certain this man was a danger, but unable to convince anyone else.

Annie rose from her kitchen table to prowl the apartment. Half past nine. She'd been staring at those notes for an hour, cross-referencing newspaper articles, referring to photocopies of magazine articles and textbook passages on stalkers. She had kept track of the case all along – out of a sense of obligation, and to continue her self-education toward one day making detective. She had purchased a three-ring binder, storing all news clippings in one section, notes in another, personal observations in another. If not for the news clippings, it would have been a thin notebook. She had conducted no interviews. It wasn't her case. She was only a deputy.

Fourcade probably had two notebooks – murder books, the detectives called them. But Fourcade was off the case. Which left Chaz Stokes in charge. Stokes had been the detective assigned to check out the initial harassment charges. If he had been able to come up with anything at the time, maybe Pam would still be alive today.

Annie wandered restlessly into the living room. Out of old habit, she fell into a slow, measured pace along the length of her coffee table and back. The table consisted of a slab of glass balanced on the back of a five-foot-long taxidermied alligator, a relic Sos had once kept hung suspended from the ceiling of the store until one of the wires broke, and the gator swung down and knocked a tourist flat. Annie had taken the creature in like a stray dog and named it Alphonse.

She walked back and forth from one end of Alphonse to the other, pondering the current situation, ignoring the occasional ringing of the phone. She let the machine pick up – reporters and cranks. No one she wanted to deal with. No one who could solve her need to find justice for Pam Bichon.

She might have been able to talk Fourcade into letting her help with the investigation if it hadn't been for the incident with Renard. Now Stokes had the case and she would never ask Stokes. She would have struck out with him even if she hadn't arrested Fourcade. Stokes had never been able to get over the fact that she didn't find him irresistible. Nor would he let it go. He had taken her simple, polite 'No, thank you' first as a challenge, then as a personal insult. In the end, he had accused her of being a racist.

'It's because I'm black, isn't it?' he charged.

They were in the parking lot at the Voodoo Lounge. A hot summer night full of bugs and bats swooping to eat the bugs. Heat lightning sizzled across the southern sky out over the Gulf. The humidity made the air feel like velvet against the skin. They'd gone to the bar with others as a group, as they often did on Friday night. A bunch of cops looking to unwind a little. Stokes had too much to drink, mouthed off enough about her being frigid that Annie had walked out in disgust.

She gaped at his accusation.

'Go ahead. You might as well admit it. You don't want to be seen with the mulatto guy. You don't want to go to bed with a nigger. Say it!'

'You're an idiot!' she declared. 'Why can you not accept the fact that I'm simply not attracted to you? And *why* am I not attracted to you? Let me count the reasons: It could be that you have the maturity of a high school junior. It could be that you have an ego the size of Arkansas. Maybe it's because you have no interest in a conversation that doesn't center on you. It's got nothing to do with what kind of people are climbing around in your family tree.'

'Climbing? Like they're monkeys? You're calling my people monkeys?'

'No!'

He came toward her, his face hard with anger. Then a car drove in the lot and some people came out of the bar, and the tension of the moment snapped like a twig.

The scene was so vivid in Annie's memory that she could almost feel the heat of the night on her skin. She opened the French doors at the end of her living room and stepped out onto the little balcony, breathing in the cool damp air and the fecund smell of the swamp. There was just enough moonlight to silver the water and outline the eerie silhouettes of the cypress trees.

Funny, she'd never really thought about it, but she could relate in a small way to Pam Bichon's experience. She did know what it was like to deal with men who wouldn't take no for an answer. Stokes. A.J. Uncle Sos, for that matter. The difference between them and Renard was the difference between sanity and obsession.

'Men,' she said aloud to the white cat that jumped up on the balcony railing to beg for attention. 'Can't live with 'em, can't open pickle jars without 'em.'

The cat offered no opinion.

In all fairness, it wasn't just men, Annie knew. Stalkers came in both sexes. New studies were showing that these people were unable to shut off that focus. The impulse, the fixation, was always there. *Simple obsessionals*, the shrinks called them. Often these men and women seemed perfectly rational and normal. They were doctors, lawyers, car mechanics. Their level of schooling or intelligence didn't matter. But regarding the object of their fixation, their brains weren't wired right. Some moved on to what was known as *erotomania*, a condition in which the person imagined and actually believed there was an ongoing romantic relationship with the object of the fixation.

A simple obsessional or an erotomaniac – ahe wondered which description applied to Marcus Renard. She wondered how he could hide either so well from everyone around him.

Somewhere out in the swamp a bull alligator gave a hoarse roar. Then the shriek of a nutria split the air like a woman's scream. The sound razored along Annie's nerves. She closed her eyes and saw Pam Bichon lying on that floor, moonlight pouring in the window, spilling across her naked corpse. And deep inside her mind, Annie thought she could hear Pam's screams ... and the screams of Jennifer Nolan ... and the women who had died four years ago at the hands of the Bayou Strangler. Screams of the dead.

'It's cold there, no?'

'Where?'

'In Shadowland.'

Goosebumps racing over her flesh, Annie stepped back inside the apartment, closed the doors, and locked them.

'Nice place you got here, 'Toinette.'

Heart in her throat, she wheeled around. Fourcade stood just inside the front entry, leaning back against the wall, ankles crossed, hands in the pockets of his old leather jacket.

'What the hell are you doing here?'

'Not much of a lock you got on this door.' He shook his head in reproach as he straightened from the wall. 'You'd think a cop would know better. Especially a lady cop, no?'

He moved toward her with deceptive laziness. Even halfway across the room Annie could sense the tension in him. She sidestepped slowly, putting the coffee table between them. Her gun was in her duffel bag, which she had abandoned in the entry. Careless.

Her best hope was to get out. And then what? The store had closed at nine. Sos and Fanchon's house was a hundred yards away and they were out dancing just like every other Friday night of the year. Maybe she could get to the Jeep.

'What do you want?' she asked, edging toward the door. Her keys hung on a peg above the light switch. 'You want to beat *me* up, too? You haven't committed your daily quota of sins? You want to get rid of the witness? You should know enough to hire out that kind of job. You'll be the obvious suspect.'

He had the nerve to appear amused. 'You think I'm the devil now, don'tcha, 'Toinette?'

Annie broke for the door, grabbed for the keys with one hand, and knocked them to the floor. With the other hand, she grabbed the knob, twisted, pulled. The door didn't budge. Then Fourcade was on her, trapping her, hands planted against the door on either side of her head.

'Running out on me, 'Toinette?'

She could feel his breath on the back of her neck, laced with the scent of whiskey.

'That's not very hospitable, *chère*,' he murmured.

She was trembling. And he was enjoying it, the son of a

bitch. She willed herself to control the shaking, forced herself to turn and face him.

He stood as close as a lover. 'We have so much to talk about. For instance, who sent you to Laveau's that night?'

Nick watched her face like a hawk. Her reaction was spontaneous – surprise or shock, a touch of confusion.

'What'd you think, 'Toinette? That I was too drunk to figure it out?'

'Figure what out? I don't know what you're talking about.'

His mouth twisted in derision. 'I'm in this department six months, you never say boo to me. All of a sudden you show up at Laveau's in a pretty skirt, batting your eyelashes. You want in on the Bichon case –'

'I *did* want in.'

'Then there you are on that street. Just happen to be passing by –'

'I *was* –'

'The hell you were!' he roared, enjoying the way she flinched. He wanted her frightened of him. She had reason to be frightened of him. 'You followed me!'

'I did not!'

'Who sent you?'

'No one!'

'You been talking to Kudrow. Did he set it up? I can't believe Renard would go for it. What if I came at him with a gun or a knife? He'd be stupid to take the chance just to ruin me. And he's not stupid.'

'No one –'

'On the other hand, maybe that was Kudrow's justice, heh? He has to know Renard is guilty. So Kudrow gets him off to save his own rep. Works it so I kill Renard. Renard is dead and I'm caged up with the red hats in Angola, twenty-five to life.'

He's insane, she thought. She'd seen what he was capable of. She cut a glance at the duffel bag sitting on the bench.

Two feet away. The zipper was open. If she was fast … If she was lucky …

'I don't have a clue what you're talking about,' she said, keeping her mouth in motion to buy time. 'Kudrow's trying to jam me up with the department so I don't have anyone to turn to but his side. I wouldn't work for him if he paid in gold bullion.'

Fourcade didn't seem to hear her.

'Would he chance all that?' he mused to himself. 'That's the question. 'Course, he'd only have to pay off the blackmail 'til he's dead, and that won't be long …'

With all the power she could muster, Annie brought her right knee up into his groin, then dropped to the floor as Fourcade staggered back, doubled over, swearing.

'*Fils de putain! Merde!* Fuck! Fuck!'

Oh please oh please oh please. She plunged her hand into the duffel bag and groped for the Sig. Her fingertips grazed the holster.

'Lookin' for this?'

The Sig appeared before her eyes in the palm of Fourcade's hand, one finger hooked through the trigger guard. He had dropped to his knees behind her and now pulled her head back by a handful of hair and shoved his body into hers, pinning her against the bench.

'You fight dirty, 'Toinette,' he murmured. 'I like that in a woman.'

'Fuck you, Fourcade!'

'Mmm …' he purred, pressing against her, pressing his rough cheek against hers. 'Don't give me ideas, *'tite belle.*'

Slowly, he rose, his hand still tangled in her hair, drawing her up with him.

'You, you're not much of a hostess, 'Toinette,' he said, directing her toward the kitchen where the light was bright and cheery. 'You haven't even offered me a chair.'

'Sorry, I flunked home ec.'

'I'm sure you have other talents. A flair for decorating, I see.'

He took in the small kitchen with amazement. Someone had painted a dancing alligator on the door of the ancient refrigerator. Canisters in the likeness of stair-step dough-boys lined one counter. The wall clock was a plastic black cat whose eyes and tail twitched back and forth with the passing seconds.

One chair was pulled out at the chrome-legged table. He sat her down. Snatching up the pen she had left on the tabletop, he backed up to the counter.

Annie stared at him. Some of the wildness had gone out of his eyes, though his gaze was no less intense. He stood with his arms crossed in front of him, her gun dangling from his big hand as if it were a toy.

'Now, where were we before you tried to kick my balls up to my back teeth?'

'Oh … somewhere between delusional and psychotic.'

'Was it Kudrow? He buy you and Stokes?'

'Stokes?'

'What? You thought you were getting all the pie? Stokes got me into that bar. Why go there? Nobody ever goes there. To be away from the grunts, he tells me. And Bowen & Briggs, that just happens to be right across the alley. How fucking handy. Then along comes little 'Toinette to keep an eye on me while ol' Chaz goes his merry way.'

'Why would I let Kudrow buy me?' she asked. A futile attempt at reason, she supposed. 'Yours isn't the only career taking a beating here, you know. I'll be mopping out jail cells before this is over. Kudrow doesn't have enough money to make up for that.'

Nick tipped his head to one side and considered. He hadn't eaten all day, but had fed on anger and frustration and suspicion, and washed it all down with a few belts of whiskey. And now something black and rotten surfaced in the brew and slipped out of his mouth in a whisper.

'Duval Marcotte.'

Son of a bitch. The pieces fit with oily ease. The similarity of the cases would appeal to Marcotte's sense of irony. And he sure as hell knew how to buy cops. The face of the New Orleans reporter at the courthouse came back to him. Shit. He should have seen it coming.

He pounced at Annie, making her bolt back in the chair. 'What'd he give you? What'd he promise you?'

'Duval Marcotte?' she said, incredulous. 'Are you out of your mind? Oh, Christ, look who I'm asking!'

He leaned down into her face, wagging the nose of the Sig like a finger. 'He'll take your soul, *chère*, or worse. You think *I'm* the devil? *He's* the devil!'

'Duval Marcotte is the devil,' Annie repeated. 'Duval Marcotte, the real estate magnate from New Orleans? The philanthropist?'

'That son of a bitch,' he muttered, pacing along the counter. 'I shoulda killed him when I had the chance.'

'I don't know Duval Marcotte, other than to see him on the news. Nobody bought me. I was in the wrong place at the wrong time. Believe me, I regret it.'

'I don't believe in coincidence.'

'Well, I'm sorry, but I don't have any other explanation!' she shouted. 'So shoot me or leave me the hell alone!'

Turning possibilities over in his mind, Nick reached back and scratched behind his ear with the nose of the gun.

'Jeez! Will you be careful with that thing!' she yelled. 'If you don't shoot me, I'd rather not be left to scrape your brains off my cupboards.'

'What? This gun?' He twirled it on his finger. 'It's not loaded. I figured it might be too tempting.'

Relief surged through Annie, and she rubbed her hands over her face. 'Why me?'

'That was my question.'

'I've told you all I know, which is exactly nothing. I would no more be in league with Chaz Stokes than I would be with someone like Marcotte. Stokes hates me. Besides, who sets up a frame that completely relies on the framee actually committing the crime? That's stupid. If someone wanted to set you up, why not just kill Renard and make it

145

look like you're the guy? That's a piece of cake. So why don't you just take your elaborate conspiracy theories to Oliver Stone. Maybe he'll make a movie about you.'

Setting the empty gun aside, Nick leaned back against the counter. 'You got a mouth on you, *chère*.'

'Being terrorized brings out the bitch in me.'

He almost laughed. The urge to do so surprised him almost as much as Annie Broussard surprised him. He pressed his lips together and stared at her. She returned his stare, indignant, angry. If she was as innocent as she professed, then she had to think he was insane. That was all right. Perceived psychosis carried certain advantages.

'Tell me something,' she said. 'Did you go to Bowen and Briggs that night of your own accord?'

He thought of the phone call, but answered the real truth. 'Yes.'

'And you made your own decision to beat up Renard?'

He hesitated again, knowing the answer wasn't so simple, remembering the flashbacks that had burst in his head that night like fireworks. But in the end he could answer only one way. *'Oui.'*

'Then how is this anyone's fault but your own?'

Annie waited for his answer. He had never struck her as the kind of man who would shirk his responsibilities. Then again, she hadn't believed he was crazy either.

'Stokes didn't put you in that alley,' she said. 'Nobody held a gun to your head. You did what you did, and I was unlucky enough to catch you. Quit trying to blame everyone else. You made your own choices and now you have to live with the consequences.'

'C'est vrai,' he murmured. Just like that, the frenetic energy was shut off and he seemed to go still from deep within. 'Me, I did what I did. I lost control. I can't think of many people who deserved a beating more than Renard, and I feel no remorse for providing it – other than the impact it will have on my own life.'

'What you did was wrong.'

146

'In that force ultimately defeats itself. I disappointed myself that night,' he admitted. 'But the tendency is for every aspect of this existence to continue to be what it is, *mais oui?* Interfere with its natural state and the thing will resist. Fundamentally, I find it difficult to embrace a philosophy of nonaction. Therein lies the crux of my problem.'

He had taken a hard left turn on her once again. From raving maniac to philosopher in a span of moments.

'You pled not guilty,' she said. 'But you admit that you are.'

'Nothing is simple, *chérie.* I go down for a felony, I'm off the job forever. That's not an option.'

'The resistance of a being against interference to its natural state.'

He smiled unexpectedly, fleetingly, and for a heartbeat was extraordinarily handsome. 'You're a good student, *chère.*'

'Why do you do that?'

'What?'

'Call me *chère*, like you're a hundred years old.'

The smile this time was sad, wry. He came to her slowly and lifted her chin with his hand. 'Because I am, *jeune fille*, in ways that you will never be.'

He was too close, bending down so that she could see every year, every burden in those eyes. His thumb brushed across her lower lip. Unnerved, she turned her face away.

'So what's your beef with Duval Marcotte?' she asked, sliding out of the chair, walking toward the other end of the table.

'It's personal,' he said, taking her seat.

'You were quick enough to throw it out a while ago.'

'When I thought you might be involved.'

'So I've been absolved of guilt?'

'For the moment.' His attention caught on the papers spread out across the table. 'What's all this?'

'My notes on the Bichon homicide.' Slowly, she moved

147

back toward him. 'Why do you think Marcotte might be involved? Is there some kind of connection to Bayou Real Estate?'

'There hasn't been to this point. It all seemed very straightforward,' Nick said as he took a quick inventory of what she had compiled. 'Why are you doing this?'

'Because I care about what happens. I want to see her killer punished, legally. I believed he would be – until Wednesday. As much as it pains me to admit this at the moment, I had faith in your abilities. Now, with Stokes in charge of the investigation, and attention being diverted elsewhere, I'm not so sure Pam will get justice.'

'You don't trust Stokes?'

'He likes things to be easy. I don't know if he has the talent to clear this case. I don't know if he would apply it if he did have it. Now you're telling me you think he set you up. Why would he do that?'

'Money. The great motivator.'

'And who involved with the case would want to see you go down besides Renard and Kudrow?'

He didn't answer, but the name had taken root in his mind like a noxious weed. Duval Marcotte. The man who had ruined him.

Annie moved toward the counter. 'I need some coffee,' she said, as calmly as if this man hadn't burst into her home and held a gun to her head. But her hands were trembling as she turned on the faucet. Breath held deep in her lungs, she reached for the tin coffee canister on the counter and carefully peeled the lid off. She flinched when Fourcade spoke again.

'So what you gonna do, 'Toinette?'

'What do you mean?'

'You want to see justice done, but you don't trust Stokes to do it. I go within spitting distance of Renard, I get tossed back in the can. So what you gonna do? You gonna see 'bout getting some justice?'

'What can I do?' she asked. A bead of sweat trickled down

148

her temple. 'I'm just a deputy. They don't even let me talk on the radio these days.'

'You already been working the case on your own.'

'*Following* the case.'

'You wanted in on it. Bad enough to ask me. You wanna be a detective, *chère*. Show some initiative. You already got a knack for sticking your pretty nose in where it don't belong. Be bold.'

'Is this bold enough for you?' She turned with a five-inch-long, nine-millimeter Kurz Back-Up in hand, chambered a round with quick precision, and pointed it dead at Fourcade's chest.

'I keep this little sweetheart in the coffee tin. A trick I learned from *The Rockford Files*. Call my bluff if you want, Fourcade. No one will be too surprised to hear I shot you dead when you broke into my house.'

She expected anger, annoyance at the very least. She didn't expect him to laugh out loud.

'Way to go, 'Toinette! Good girl! This is just the kinda thing I'm talking 'bout. Initiative. Creativity. Nerve.' He rose from his chair and moved toward her. 'You got a lotta sass.'

'Yeah, and I'm about to hit you in the chest with a load of it. Stand right there.'

For once, he listened, assuming a casual stance two feet in front of the gun barrel, one leg cocked, hands settled at the waist of his faded jeans. 'You're pissed at me.'

'That would be an understatement. Everybody in the department is treating me like a leper because of you. You broke the law and I'm getting punished for it. Then you come into my house and – and terrorize me. *Pissed* doesn't begin to cover it.'

'You're gonna have to get over it if you're gonna work with me,' he said bluntly.

'Work with you? I don't even want to be in the same room with you!'

'Ah, that ...'

149

He moved quickly, knocking her gun hand to the side and up. The Kurz spat a round into the ceiling, and plaster dust rained down. In seconds Fourcade had the gun out of her hand and had her drawn up hard against him with one arm pulled up behind her back.

'... that would be untrue,' he finished.

He let her go abruptly and went back to the table, scanning her papers on the case. 'I can help you, 'Toinette. We want the same end, you and I.'

'Ten minutes ago you thought I was part of a conspiracy against you.'

He still didn't know that she wasn't, he reminded himself. But she wouldn't have gone to all the trouble of building a casebook on Pam Bichon's murder if she wasn't truly interested in seeing it solved.

'I want the case cleared,' he said. 'Marcus Renard belongs in hell. If you want to make that happen, if you want justice for Pam Bichon and her daughter, you'll come to me. I've got ten times what you've got lying here on this table – statements, complaints, photographs, lab reports, duplicates of everything that's on file at the sheriff's department.'

This was what she had wanted, Annie thought: To work with Fourcade, to have access to the case, to try – for Josie's sake and to silence the phantom screams in her own mind. But Fourcade was too volatile, too wired, too unpredictable. He was a criminal, and she was the one who had run him in.

'Why me?' she asked. 'You should hate me more than the rest of them do.'

'Only if you sold me out.'

'I didn't, but –'

'Then I can't hate you,' he said simply. 'If you didn't sell me out, then you acted on your principles and damned the consequences. I can't hate you for that. For that, I would respect you.'

'You're a very strange man, Fourcade.'

He touched a hand to his chest. 'Me, I'm one of a kind, 'Toinette. Ain'tcha glad?'

Annie didn't know whether to laugh or cry. Fourcade laid her weapon on the table and came toward her, serious again.

'I don't wanna let go of this case,' he said. 'I want Renard to go down for what he did. If I can't trust Stokes, then I can't work through him. That leaves you. You said you felt an obligation to Pam Bichon. You want to meet that obligation, you'll come to me. Until then ...'

He started to lower his head. Annie's breath caught. Anticipation tightened her muscles. Her lips parted slightly, as if she meant to tell him no. Then he touched two fingers to his forehead in salute, turned, and walked out of her apartment and into the night.

'Holy shit,' she whispered.

She stood there as the minutes ticked past. Finally she went out onto the landing, but Fourcade was gone. No taillights, no fading purr of a truck engine. The only sounds were the night sounds of the swamp: the occasional call of nocturnal prey and predator, the slap of something that broke the surface of the water and dived beneath once more.

For a long time she stared out at the night. Thinking. Wondering. Tempted. Frightened. She thought of what Fourcade had said to her that night in the bar. *Stay away from those shadows, 'Toinette. ... They'll suck the life outta you.*

He was a man full of shadows, strange shades of darkness and unexpected light. Deep stillness and wild energy. Brutal yet principled. She didn't know what to make of him. She had the distinct feeling that if she accepted his challenge, her life would be altered in a permanent way. Was that what she wanted?

She thought of Pam Bichon, alone with her killer, her screams for mercy tearing the fabric of the night, unheeded,

151

unanswered. She wanted closure. She wanted justice. But at what price?

She felt as if she were standing on the edge of an alternate dimension, as if eyes from that other side were watching her, waiting in expectation for her next move.

Finally she went inside, never imagining that the eyes were real.

'I feel a sense of limbo, as if I'm holding my breath. It isn't over. I don't know that it will ever be over.

The actions of one person trigger the actions of another and another, like waves.

I know the wave will come to me again and sweep me away. I can see it in my mind: a tide of blood.

I see it in my dreams.

I taste it in my mouth.

I see the one it will take next.

The tide has already touched her.'

15

The call came at 12:31. Annie had double-checked the locks on her doors and gone to bed, but she wasn't sleeping. She picked up on the third ring because a call in the dead of night could have been something worse than a reporter. Sos and Fanchon could have been in an accident. One of their many relatives might have fallen ill. She answered with a simple hello. No one answered back.

'Ahhh ... a breather, huh?' she said, leaning back against her pillows, instantly picturing Mullen on the other end of the line. 'You know, I'm surprised you guys didn't start in with calls two nights ago. We're talking simple, no-brain harassment. Right up your alley. I have to say, I was actually expecting the "you fucking bitch" variety. Big bad faceless man on the other end of the line. Oooh, how scary.'

She waited for an epithet, a curse. Nothing. She pictured the dumbfounded look on Mullen's face, and smiled.

'I'm docking you points for lack of imagination. But I suppose I'm not the first woman to tell you that.'

Nothing.

'Well, this is boring and I have to work tomorrow – but then, you already knew that, didn't you?'

Annie rolled her eyes as she hung up. A breather. Like that was supposed to scare her after what she'd been through tonight. She switched off the lamp, wishing she could turn off her brain as easily.

The pros and cons of Fourcade's offer were still bouncing in her head at five A.M. Exhaustion had pulled her under into sleep intermittently during the night, but there had been no rest in it, only dreams full of anxiety. She finally gave up and dragged herself out of bed, feeling worse than she had when she'd crawled between the sheets at midnight. She splashed cold water on her face, rinsed her mouth out, and pulled on her workout clothes.

Her brain refused to shut down as she went through her routine of stretching and warm-up. Maybe Fourcade's offer was all part of a revenge plot. If his compadres in the department hated her enough to get back at her, why wouldn't he?

'If you didn't sell me out, then you acted on your principles and damned the consequences. I can't hate you for that. For that, I would respect you.'

Damned if she didn't believe he meant it. Did that make her an astute judge of character or a fool?

She hooked her feet into the straps on the incline board and started her sit-ups. Fifty every morning. She hated every one.

Fourcade's ravings about Duval Marcotte, the New Orleans business magnate, should have been enough to put her off for good. She had never heard any scandal attached to Marcotte – which should have made her suspicious. Nearly everyone in power in New Orleans had his good name smeared on a regular basis. Nasty politics was a major league sport in the Big Easy. How was it Marcotte stayed so clean? Because he was as pure as Pat Boone ... or as dark as the devil?

What difference did it make? What did she care about Duval Marcotte? He couldn't possibly have anything to do with the Bichon case ... except there was that real estate connection.

Annie moved from the incline board to the chin-up bar. Twenty-five every morning. She hated them nearly as much as the sit-ups.

What if she went to Fourcade? He was on suspension, charged with multiple counts of assault. What kind of trouble could she get in with the sheriff or with Pritchett? She was a witness for the prosecution, for God's sake. Fourcade shouldn't have come within a mile of her and vice versa.

Maybe that was why he had made the offer. Maybe he

thought he could win some points, get her to soften toward him. If he was helping her with the Bichon case, letting her investigate, maybe she wouldn't remember so clearly the events of that night outside Bowen & Briggs.

But Fourcade didn't seem the kind of man for subterfuge. He was blunt, tactless, straightforward. He was more complicated than French grammar, full of rules with irregularities and exceptions.

Annie let herself out of the apartment, jogged down the stairs and across the parking lot. A dirt path led up onto the levee and the restricted-use gravel levee road. She ran two miles every morning and despised every step. Her body wasn't built for speed, but if she listened to what her body wanted, she'd have a butt like a quarter horse. The workout was the price she paid for her candy bar habit. More than that, she knew that being in shape might one day save her life.

So what was the story with Stokes? Could someone have bought him or was Fourcade simply paranoid? If he was paranoid, that didn't mean someone *wasn't* out to get him. But a setup still didn't make sense to Annie. Stokes had taken Fourcade to Laveau's, true, but Stokes had left. How could he be certain Fourcade would find his way to Bowen & Briggs to confront Renard?

The phone call.

Fourcade had taken a call, then split. But if Stokes had meant to set up Fourcade, wouldn't he have had a witness lined up? Did she know he hadn't? Stokes himself could have been watching the whole thing play out with some civilian flunky by his side waiting to step into the role of witness for the prosecution. What sweet irony for him that Annie had stumbled into the scene. She and Fourcade could cancel each other out.

She dragged herself back up to her apartment, showered, and dressed in a fresh uniform, then dashed down to the store with a Milky Way in hand.

'Dat's no breakfast, you!' Tante Fanchon scolded. She

straightened her slender frame from the task of wiping off the red checkered oilcloths that covered the tables in the café portion of the big room. 'You come sit down. I make you some sausage and eggs, *oui?*'

'No time. Sorry, Tante.' Annie filled her giant travel mug with coffee from the pot on the café counter. 'I'm on duty today.'

Fanchon waved her rag at her foster daughter. 'Bah! You all the time workin' so much. What kinda job for a purty young thing is dat?'

'I meet lots of eligible men,' Annie said with a grin. 'Of course, I have to throw most of them in jail.'

Fanchon shook her head and fought a smile. '*T'es trop grand pour tes culottes!*'

'I'm not too big for my pants,' Annie retorted, backing toward the door. 'That's why I run every morning.'

'Running.' Fanchon snorted, as if the word gave her a bad taste.

Annie turned the Jeep out of the lot onto the bayou road. She had the juggling act down – coffee mug clamped between her thighs, candy bar and steering wheel in her left hand while she shifted and turned on the radio with her right.

'You're on KJUN. All talk all the time. Home of the giant jackpot giveaway. Every caller's name is registered – including yours, Mary Margaret in Cade. What's on your mind?'

'I think gambling is a sin and your jackpot is gambling.'

'How's that, ma'am? There's no fee.'

'Yes, there is. There's the price of the long-distance call if a person don't live in Bayou Breaux. How can y'all sleep nights knowing people take the food out the mouths of their children so they can make those calls to sign up for your jackpot?'

Traffic picked up with every side-road intersection. People headed into Bayou Breaux to work or do their Saturday errands, or continued on up to Lafayette for a day in the city. Sports headed to the basin for a day of fishing. A big

157

old boat of a Cadillac pulled out onto the blacktop ahead of her. Annie hit the clutch and the brake and reached for the shift, glancing down just enough for something odd to catch her eye. Her duffel bag, on the floor in front of the passenger seat, was moving, the near end rising up slightly.

She turned her head to look, and her heart vaulted into her throat. Slithering out from under the duffel, its body already edging past the gearshift toward her, was a mottled brown snake as thick as a garden hose. *Copperhead.*

'Jesus!'

She bolted sideways in her seat, jerking the wheel left. The Jeep swerved into the southbound lane, eliciting angry honks from oncoming traffic. Annie looked up and swore again as a ton truck bore down on her, horn blaring. A white-knuckle grip on the steering wheel, she hit the gas and gunned for the ditch.

The Jeep was airborne for what seemed like an eternity. Then the world was a jarred blur in every window. The impact bounced her off the seat and bounced the snake off the floor. Its thick, muscular body hit her across her thighs and fell back down.

Annie was barely aware of killing the engine. Her only thought was escape. She threw her shoulder against the door, tumbled out of the Jeep, and slammed the door shut behind her. Her heart was thumping like a trip-hammer. Her breath came in ragged, irregular jerks. She hugged the front fender to steady herself.

'Ohmygod, ohmygod, ohmygod.'

Up on the road, several cars had pulled to the shoulder. One driver had climbed out of his pickup.

'Please stay with your vehicles, folks! Move it along! I'll handle this.'

Annie raised her head and peered through the strands of hair that had fallen in her face. A deputy was coming toward her, his cruiser parked on the shoulder with the lights rolling.

'Miss?' he called. 'Are you all right, Miss? Should I call an ambulance?'

Annie straightened up so he could see her uniform. She recognized him instantly, even if he couldn't manage the same with her. York the Dork. He walked as if he had a permanent wedgie. A Hitler mustache perched above his prim little mouth. It twitched now as realization dawned.

'Deputy Broussard?'

'There's a copperhead in my Jeep. Somebody put a copperhead in my Jeep.'

While she probably wouldn't have died from a bite, the possibility was there. She certainly could have been killed in the accident, and she may not have been the only casualty. She wondered if her harasser had considered that when he'd been planting his little reptile friend, then wondered which answer would have upset her more.

'A copperhead!' the Dork chirped with a sniff. He peered into the Jeep. 'I don't see anything.'

'Why don't you climb in and crawl around on the floor? When it bites your ass we'll know it's real.'

'It was probably just a belt or something.'

'I know the difference between a snake and a belt.'

'Sure you weren't just looking in the mirror, putting your lipstick on, and lost control of the vehicle? You might as well tell the truth. It wouldn't be the first time I heard that story,' he said with a chortle. 'You gals and your makeup ...'

Annie grabbed him by the shirtsleeve and hauled him around to face her. 'Am I wearing lipstick? Do you see any lipstick on this mouth, you patronizing jerk? There's a snake in that Jeep and if you 'little lady' me again, I'll wrap it around your throat and choke you with it!'

'Hey, Broussard! You're assaulting an officer!'

The shout came from the road. Mullen. He had parked on the shoulder – a piece-of-crap Chevy truck with a bass boat dragging behind. Encased in tight jeans, his legs were skinny as an egret's. He compensated with a puffed-up green satin baseball jacket.

159

'She claims there's a copperhead in there,' York said, hooking a thumb at the Jeep.

'Yeah, like he doesn't already know that,' Annie snapped.

Mullen made a face at her. 'There you go again. Hysterical. Paranoid. Maybe you need to get your hormones adjusted, Broussard.'

'Fuck you.'

'Oooh, verbal abuse, assaulting an officer, reckless driving ...' He swaggered around to the passenger side to look in the window. 'Maybe she's drunk, York. You better put her through the paces.'

'The hell you will.' Annie rounded the hood. 'Keying me out on the radio was bad enough, and I can take the crap at the station, but somebody other than me could have gotten killed with this stunt. If I can find one scrap of evidence linking you to this –'

'Don't threaten me, Broussard.'

'It's not a threat, it's a promise.'

He sniffed the air. 'I think I smell whiskey. You better run her in, York. The stress must be getting to you, Broussard. Drinking in the morning on your way to work. That's a shame.'

York looked apprehensive. 'I didn't smell anything.'

'Well, Christ,' Mullen snapped. 'She's seeing snakes and driving off the damn road. Tag the vehicle and take her in!'

Annie planted her hands on her hips. 'I'm not going anywhere until you get that snake out of my Jeep.'

'Resisting,' Mullen added to her list of sins.

'I think we'd better go in to the station to sort this out, Annie,' York said, straining to look apologetic.

He reached for her arm and she yanked it away. There was no out. York couldn't let her get back into her vehicle if there was a question of her sobriety, and she'd be damned if she was going to go through the drunk drill for them like a trick poodle.

'Uh – I think you better sit in the back,' he said as she reached for the passenger-side door on his cruiser.

Annie bit her tongue. At least she had driven Fourcade to the station in her own vehicle, calling as little attention to the situation as possible. No one was going to offer her the same courtesy.

'I need my duffel bag,' she said. 'My weapon is in it. And I want that Jeep locked up.'

She watched as he went back into the ditch and said something to Mullen. York went around to the driver's side and pulled the keys, while Mullen opened the passenger's door, hauled her duffel out, then bent back into the vehicle. When he emerged again, he had hold of the writhing snake just behind its head. It looked nearly four feet in length, big enough, though copperheads in this part of the country regularly grew bigger. Mullen said something to York and they both laughed, then Mullen swung the snake around in a big loop and let it fly into a field of sugarcane.

'Just a king snake!' he shouted up at Annie as he came toward the car with her bag. 'Copperhead! You *must* be drunk, Broussard. You don't know one snake from the next.'

'I wouldn't say that,' Annie shot back. 'I know what kind of snake you are, Mullen.'

And she stewed on it all the way in to Bayou Breaux.

Hooker was in no mood for dealing with the aftermath of a practical joke, malicious or otherwise. He ranted and swore from the moment York escorted her into the building, directing his wrath at Annie.

'Every time I turn around, you're in the middle of a shit pile, Broussard. I've about had it up to my gonads with you.'

'Yes, sir.'

'You got some kind of brain disorder or something? Deputies are supposed to be out arresting crooks, not each other.'

'No, sir.'

161

'We never had this kind of trouble when it was just men around here. Throw a female into the mix and suddenly everybody's got some kind of hard-on.'

Annie refrained from pointing out that she'd been on the job here two years and had never had any trouble to speak of until now. They stood inside Hooker's office, which a maintenance person had painted chartreuse while Hooker was gone having angioplasty in January. The perpetrator of that joke had yet to come forward. The door stood wide open, allowing anyone within earshot to listen to the diatribe. Annie held on to the hope that this would be the last of the humiliation. She could weather the storm. Hooker would eventually run out of insults or have a stroke, and then she could go out on patrol.

'I've had it, Broussard. I'm tellin' you right now.'

From somewhere down the hall came another raised voice. 'What do you mean, *you can't find it*?' Annie recognized Smith Pritchett's nasal whine. Dispatch was down the hall. What would Pritchett want from them? What would Pritchett want badly enough to come in on a Saturday?

'Y'all are telling me you keep these 911 tapes for-frigging-ever, but you don't have the *one* tape from the night of Fourcade's arrest?'

A pulsing vein zigzagged across Pritchett's broad forehead like a lightning bolt. He stood in the hall outside the dispatch center in a lime green Izod shirt, khakis, and golf spikes, a nine iron in hand.

The woman on the other side of the counter crossed her arms. 'Yessir, that's what I'm tellin' you. Are you callin' me a liar?'

Pritchett stared at her, then wheeled on A.J. 'Where the hell is Noblier? I told you to call him.'

'He's on his way,' A.J. promised. Bad enough that Pritchett had sent him on this quest on Saturday morning – a surprise attack, he called it – now they could all have a

162

knock-down-drag-out brawl besides. He bet his money on the dispatch supervisor. Even though Pritchett was armed, she had to outweigh him by eighty pounds.

He would have saved the news that the tape was missing, but Pritchett was like an overeager five-year-old at Christmas. He had called in on his cellular phone from the third tee. While Fourcade's lawyer had yet to submit a written account of his client's version of events, Noblier had stated the detective had been responding to a call of a possible prowler in the vicinity of Bowen & Briggs. A bald-faced lie, certainly. The 911 tapes would confirm it as such, and the dispatch center in the sheriff's office handled all 911 calls in the parish. But the 911 tape from that fateful night was suddenly nowhere to be found.

The door to the sheriff's office swung open, and Gus came into the hall in jeans and cowboy boots and a denim shirt, the pungent aroma of horses hanging on him like bad cologne. 'Don't get your shorts in a knot, Smith. We'll find the damn tape. This is a busy place. Things get mislaid.'

'Mislaid, my ass.' Pritchett shook the nine iron at the sheriff. 'There's no tape because there's no damn call on the tape referring to a prowler in the vicinity of Bowen and Briggs.'

'Are you calling me a liar? After all the years I've backed you? You are a small, ungrateful man, Smith Pritchett. You don't believe me, you talk to my deputies on patrol that night. Ask them if they heard the call.'

Pritchett rolled his eyes and started down the hall toward the sheriff, his spikes thundering on the hard floor. 'I'm sure they'd tell me they heard the archangels singing Dixieland jazz if they thought it would get Fourcade off,' he shouted above the racket. 'It's a damn shame this has to come between us, Gus. You've got a bad apple in your barrel. Cut him out and be done with it.'

Gus squinted at him. 'Maybe the reason we don't have that tape is that Wily Tallant came and got it already. As exculpatory evidence.'

'What?' Pritchett squealed. 'You would just blithely hand something like that over to a *defense attorney*?'

Gus shrugged. 'I'm not saying it happened. I'm saying it might have.'

A.J. stepped in between them. 'If Tallant has it, he'll have to disclose it, Smith. And if the tape is gone, then they have nothing but biased hearsay that the call ever came in. It's no big deal.'

Other than the fact that Pritchett had just been embarrassed again.

'I don't know, Gus,' Pritchett lamented as they stepped out into the warm spring sunshine. 'Maybe you've been at this too long. Your sense of objectivity has become warped. Just look at Johnny Earl: He's young, smart, untainted by the corruptions of time and familiarity. And he's black. A lot of people think it's time for a black sheriff in this parish – it's progressive.'

Gus blew a booger onto the sidewalk. 'You think I'm afraid of Johnny Earl? Might I remind you, I carried thirty-three percent of the black vote in the last election, and I was running against *two* blacks.'

'Don't bring it up, Gus,' Pritchett said. 'It just calls to mind those ugly vote-hauling allegations made against you.'

He started toward his Lincoln, where his caddy stood, waiting to drive him back to the country club. 'Doucet!' he barked. 'You come with me. We have charges to discuss. What all do you know about the statutes on conspiracy?'

Gus watched the lawyers climb into the Lincoln, then stomped back into the station, muttering, 'Dickhead college-boy prick. Threaten me, you little –'

'Sheriff?'

The bark came from Hooker. Gus rubbed a hand against his belly. Hell of a Saturday this was turning out to be. He stopped in front of Hooker's open door and stared inside.

'My office, Deputy Broussard.'

'You think someone put that snake in your Jeep.'
    'Yes, sir. It couldn't have gotten there any other way.'
    'And you think another deputy put it there?'
    'Yes, sir, I –'
    'Nobody else could have had access to the vehicle?'
    'Well –'
    'You keep it locked at home, do you?'
    'No, sir, but –'
    'You got proof another deputy did it? You got a witness?'
    'No, sir, but –'
    'You live over a goddamn convenience store, Deputy. You telling me no one stopped at the store last night? You telling me folks weren't in and out of that parking lot to do this deed or see it done?'
    'The store closes at nine.'
    'And after that, damn near anybody could have put that snake in your Jeep. Isn't that right?'
    Annie blew out a breath. *Fourcade*. Fourcade could have done it, had motive to do it, was disturbed enough to do it. But she said nothing. The snake seemed an adolescent prank, and Fourcade was no adolescent.
    'Hell, I've seen the inside of your Jeep, girl. That snake coulda hatched there, for all I know.'
    'And you think it was a coincidence that York was patrolling that stretch of road this morning,' Annie said. 'And that Mullen just happened along.'
    Gus gave her a steady look. 'I'm saying you got no proof otherwise. York was on patrol. You ran off the road. He did his job.'
    'And Mullen?'
    'Mullen's off duty. What he does on his own time is no concern of mine.'
    'Including interfering in the duty of another officer?'
    'You're a fine one to talk on that score, Deputy,' he said.

'York ran you in 'cause he thought you mighta been drinking.'

'I wasn't drinking. They did it to humiliate me. And Mullen was the ringleader. York was just his stooge.'

'They found a half-empty pint of Wild Turkey under your driver's seat.'

Dread swirled in Annie's stomach. She could be suspended for this. 'I don't drink Wild Turkey and I don't drink in my vehicle, Sheriff. Mullen must have put it there.'

'You refused to go through the drill.'

'I'll take a Breathalyzer.' She realized she should have insisted on it at the scene. Now her career was crumbling beneath her feet because she'd been too proud and too stubborn. 'I'll take a blood test if you want.'

Noblier shook his head. 'That was an hour ago or better, and you weren't but five miles from home when you had the accident. If you had anything in your system, it's probably gone by now.'

'I *wasn't* drinking.'

Gus swiveled his big chair back and forth. He rubbed at the stubble on his chin. He never shaved on Saturday until his evening toilet before taking the missus out for dinner. He did love his Saturdays. This one was going to hell on a sled.

'You been under a lotta strain recently, Annie,' he said carefully.

'I *wasn't* drinking.'

'And you was kicking up dirt yesterday, saying someone keyed you out on the radio?'

'Yes, sir, that's true.' She decided to keep the muskrat incident to herself. She felt too much like a tattling child already.

A frown creased his mouth. 'This is all because of that business with Fourcade. Your chickens are coming home to roost, Deputy.'

'But I –' Annie cut herself off and waited, foreboding pressing down on her as the silence stretched.

166

'I don't like any of this,' Gus said. 'I'll give you the benefit of the doubt about the drinking. York should have given you the Breathalyzer and he didn't. But, as for the rest of the bullshit, I've had it. I'm pulling you off patrol, Annie.'

The pronouncement hit her with the force of a physical blow, stunning her. 'But, Sheriff –'

'It's the best decision I can make for all concerned. It's for your own good, Annie. You come off patrol until this all blows over and settles down. You're out of harm's way, out of sight of the many people you have managed to piss off.'

'But I didn't do anything wrong!'

'Yeah, well, life's a bitch, ain't it?' he said sharply. 'I got people telling me you're trouble. You're sitting here telling me everybody's out to get you. I ain't got time for this bullshit. Every puffed-up muck-a-muck in the parish is on my case on account of Renard and this rapist, and the Mardi Gras carnival isn't but a week off. I'm telling you, I'm sick of the whole goddamn mess. I'm pulling you off patrol until this situation blows over. End of story. Are you on tomorrow?'

'No.'

'Fine, then take the rest of the day for yourself. Report to me Monday morning for your new assignment.'

Annie said nothing. She stared at Gus Noblier, disappointment and betrayal humming inside her like a power line.

'It's for the best, Annie.'

'But it's not what's right,' she answered. And before he could reply, she got up and walked out of the room.

16

It cost $52.75 to get the Jeep out of the impound lot. Financial insult added to ego injury. Steaming, Annie made the lot attendant dig through all the junk on the floor and check every inch of the interior for unpleasant surprises. He found none.

She drove down the block to the park and sat in the lot under the shade of a sprawling, moss-hung live oak, staring at the bayou.

How simple it had been for Mullen and his moron cohorts to get what they wanted – her off the job – and she had been powerless to stop it. A thumb on a radio mike switch, a planted pint of Wild Turkey, and she was off the street. The hypocrisy made her mad enough to spit. Gus Noblier was well known for ordering a little after dinner libation *to go*, yet he pulled her off the job on the lame and unsubstantiated suggestion that maybe she'd had a little something to spike her morning coffee.

Her instinctive response was to fight back, but how? Put a bigger snake in Mullen's truck? As tempting as that idea was, it was a stupid one. Retribution only invited an escalation of the war. Evidence was what she needed, but there wouldn't be any. Nobody knew better than a cop how to cover tracks. The only witnesses would be accessories. No one would come forward. No one would rat out a brother cop to save a cop who had turned on one of their own.

'You're getting down and dirty with Dean Monroe on KJUN. The hot topic this morning is still the big decision that went down in the Partout Parish Courthouse on Wednesday. A murder suspect walks on a technicality, and now two men sit in jail for violating *his* rights. Lindsay on line one, what's on your mind?'

'Injustice. Pam Bichon was my friend and business

partner, and it infuriates me that the focus on her case has shifted to the rights of the man who terrorized and killed her. The court system did nothing to protect her rights when she was alive. I mean, wake up, South Lou'siana. This is the nineties. Women deserve better than to be patronized and pushed aside, and to have our rights be considered below the rights of murderers.'

'Amen to that,' Annie murmured.

A wedding party had come into the park for photographs. The bride stood in the center of the Rotary Club gazebo looking impatient while the photographer's assistant fussed with the train of her white satin gown. Half a dozen bridesmaids in pale yellow organdy dotted the lawn around the gazebo like overgrown daffodils. The groomsmen had begun a game of catch near the tomb of the unknown Confederate war hero. Down on the bank of the bayou, two little boys in black tuxes busied themselves throwing stones as far as they could into the water.

Annie stared at the ripples radiating out from each splash. Cause and effect, a chain of events, one action the catalyst for another and another. The mess she found herself in hadn't begun with her arrest of Fourcade, or Fourcade's attack on Renard. It hadn't begun with Judge Monahan's dismissal of the evidence or the search that had uncovered that evidence. It had all begun with Marcus Renard and his obsession with Pam Bichon. Therein lay the dark heart of the matter: Marcus Renard and what the court system had inadvertently allowed him to do. Injustice.

Not allowing herself to consider the consequences, Annie started the Jeep and drove away from the park. She needed to take positive action rather than allow herself to be caught up in the wake of the actions of others.

She needed to do something – for Pam, for Josie, for herself. She needed to see this case closed, and who was going to do that, who was going to find the truth? A department that had turned on her? Chaz Stokes, whom

Fourcade accused of betrayal? Fourcade, who had betrayed the law he was sworn to serve?

Turning north, she headed toward the building that housed Bayou Realty and the architectural firm of Bowen & Briggs.

The Bayou Realty offices were homey, catering to the tastes of women, offering an atmosphere that stirred the feminine instinct to nest. A pair of flowered chintz couches, plump with ruffled pillows, created a cozy L off to one side of the front room. Framed sales sheets with color photographs of homes being offered stood in groupings on the glass-topped wicker coffee table like family portraits. Potted ferns basked in the deep brick window wells. The scent of cinnamon rolls hung in the air.

The receptionist's station was unoccupied. A woman's voice could be heard coming from one of the offices down the hall. Annie waited. The bell on the front door had announced her entrance. Nerves rattled inside her.

'*Be bold*,' Fourcade had told her.

Fourcade was a lunatic.

The door to the second office on the right opened and Lindsay Faulkner stepped into the hall. Pam Bichon's partner looked like the kind of woman who was elected homecoming queen in high school and college and went on to marry money and raise beautiful, well-behaved children with perfect teeth. She came down the hall with the solid, sunny smile of a Junior League hospitality chairwoman.

'Good mornin'! How are you today?' She said this with enough familiarity and warmth that Annie nearly turned around to see if someone had come in behind her. 'I'm Lindsay Faulkner. How may I help you?'

'Annie Broussard. I'm with the sheriff's department.' A fact no longer readily apparent. She had changed out of her coffee-stained uniform into jeans and a polo shirt. She had tucked her badge into her hip pocket but couldn't bring herself to pull it out. She'd be in trouble enough as it was if Noblier caught wind of what she was up to.

Lindsay Faulkner's enthusiasm faded fast. Irritation flickered in the big green eyes. She stopped just behind the receptionist's desk and crossed her arms over the front of her emerald silk blouse.

'You know, you people just make me see red. This has been hell on us – Pam's friends, her family – and what have you done? Nothing. You know who the killer is and he walks around scot-free. The incompetence astounds me. My God, if you'd done your jobs in the first place, Pam might still be alive today.'

'I know it's been frustrating, Ms Faulkner.' It's been frustrating for us as well.'

'You don't know what frustration is.'

'With all due respect, yes, I do,' Annie said plainly. 'I was the one who found Pam. I would like nothing better than to have this case closed.'

'Then go on upstairs and arrest him, and leave the rest of us alone.'

She marched back down the hall. Annie followed.

'Renard is upstairs right now?'

'Your powers of deduction are amazing, Detective.'

Annie didn't correct her presumption of rank. 'It must be like salt in the wound – having to work in the same building with him.'

'I hate it,' she said flatly, going into her office. 'Bayou Realty owns the building. If I could terminate their lease tomorrow, the whole lot of them would be out in the street, but once again the law is on *his* side.

'The gall of that man!' Her expression was a mix of horror and hatred. 'To come here and work as if he's done nothing wrong at all, while every day I have to walk past that empty office, Pam's office –'

She sat for a moment with a hand to her mouth, staring out the window at the parking lot.

'I know you and Pam were very close,' Annie said quietly,

slipping into a chair in front of the desk. She extracted a small notebook and pen from her hip pocket and positioned the notebook on her thigh.

Lindsay Faulkner produced a small linen handkerchief seemingly from thin air and blotted delicately at the corners of her eyes. 'We were best friends from the day we met at college. I was Pam's maid of honor. I'm Josie's godmother. Pam and I were like sisters. Do you have a sister?'

'No.'

'Then you can't understand. When that animal murdered Pam, he murdered a part of me, a part that can't be buried in a tomb. I will carry that part inside me for the rest of my life. Deadweight, black with rot; something that used to be so bright, so full of joy. He has to be made to pay for that.'

'If we can convict him, he'll get the death penalty.'

A little smile twisted at Faulkner's lips. 'We opposed capital punishment, Pam and I. Cruel and unusual, barbaric, we said. How naïve we were. Renard doesn't deserve compassion. No punishment could be cruel enough. I've tortured that man to death in my imagination more times than I can count. I've lain awake nights wishing I had the courage ...'

She stared at Annie, the light of challenge in her eyes. 'Will you arrest me? The way they arrested Pam's father?'

'He did a sight more than imagine Renard dead.'

'Pam was Hunter's only daughter. He loved her so, and now he carries that dead piece inside him too.'

'Did you suspect Renard was the one harassing Pam?'

Guilt passed over the woman's face, and she looked down at her hands lying on the desktop. 'Pam said it was him.'

'And you thought ... ?'

'I've been over this with the others,' she said. 'Don't you people talk to one another?'

'I'm trying to get a fresh perspective. Male detectives have a male point of view. I may pick up on something they

172

didn't.' A good argument, Annie thought. She'd have to remember it when Noblier called her on the carpet for overstepping her bounds.

'He seemed so harmless,' Lindsay Faulkner whispered. 'You watch the movies, you think maniacs are supposed to look a certain way, act a certain way. You think a stalker is some lowlife with no job and a double-digit IQ. You never think, 'Oh, I bet that architect upstairs is a psychopath.' He's been here for years. I never – He hadn't ...'

'We can't always see trouble coming,' Annie offered gently. 'If he'd given you no reason to suspect him –'

'Pam did, though. Not all along, but last summer, after she and Donnie split up. Renard started hanging around more, and it bothered her – the gifts he sent her, his manner around her. And when the harassment started, she didn't want to say anything at first, but she thought it was him.'

'Who did you think – ?'

'Donnie,' she said without hesitation. 'The harassment started not long after she told him she wanted the divorce. I thought he was trying to scare her. It seemed like the kind of thing he would think of. Donnie's emotional development arrested at about sixteen. I even called him on it, read him the riot act.'

'How did he react?'

She rolled her eyes. 'He accused me of poisoning Pam against him. I told him I'd tried that years ago, and she went and married him anyway. Pam always looked at Donnie and saw his potential. She couldn't believe he wouldn't live up to it.'

'It must be very unpleasant for you now – trying to resolve the business issues.'

'It's a mess. The divorce would have cut Donnie cleanly away from the realty company. Pam would have worded her new will so her half of the business went to Josie in a trust. I would have had the option of buying it out with the partner insurance we were planning to buy. We'd never gotten around to that before – the partner insurance. We just never thought about it. I mean, we were both young and healthy.' She paused. 'Anyway, none of those changes happened before ...'

Annie decided she liked this woman, liked her strength and her anger on her friend's behalf. She hadn't expected this kind of caring and conviction from a former debutante. She had expected hanky-wringing passive grief. *My prejudice*, she thought.

'Now what happens?' she asked.

'Now I have to deal with Donnie, who has the business acumen of a tick. He's being extra obnoxious because months before the marriage split up, Donnie's company was in a financial bind and Pam agreed to hide some land for him in the realty so the bank wouldn't take it.'

'Hide it?'

'Bichon Bayou Development "sold" these properties to Bayou Realty on paper. In reality, we were just holding them out of harm's way.'

'And you still have them?'

Her smile was slightly feral. 'Yes. But now Donnie holds Pam's half of the business, so technically the properties are partly his. However, before he can do anything with them, he has to have *my* approval. We're currently at a standoff. He wants his property back and I want full ownership of the business. The latest wrinkle is that Donnie suddenly thinks Pam's half of this business is worth double what it is. He's trying to play hardball, threatening me with some nebulous *other buyer* from New Orleans.'

Annie's pen went still on the paper. 'New Orleans?'
New Orleans. Real estate. Duval Marcotte.

Lindsay shook her head at the ridiculousness of the idea. 'What would anyone in New Orleans want with Bayou Breaux?'

'You think he's bluffing?'

'*He* thinks he's bluffing. I think he's an idiot.'

'What would you do if he sold his half to this buyer?'

174

'I don't know. Pam and I started this business together. It's important to me for that reason, you know, as something we built and shared as friends. And it's a strong little business; we do well enough. I enjoy it. I *will* sell this building if I get the chance,' she admitted, turning to look out at the parking lot. 'There are too many bad memories now. And that bastard upstairs. I keep picturing Detective Fourcade beating him to death. I –'

She stopped. Annie sat very still. Out in the front room the door opened and the bell announcing potential clients tinkled pleasantly.

'Broussard,' Faulkner murmured with accusation. 'You're the one who stopped him. My God. I thought you said you wanted this resolved.'

'I do.'

She rose with the poise and grace of old Southern breeding. 'Then why didn't you just walk away?'

'Because that would have been murder.'

Lindsay Faulkner shook her head. 'No, that would have been justice. Now, you'll excuse me,' she said, moving to the door. 'You will leave these offices. I have nothing further to say to you.'

Annie let herself out the rear exit of the realty office and stood in the hall. To her right was the door to the parking area where Fourcade had attacked Renard. Before her rose the stairs to the second floor and the offices of Bowen & Briggs. Renard was up there.

She thought of going up the stairs. The cop in her wanted to study Marcus Renard, try to pick him apart, figure him out, see how he would fit into the range of stalkers she had studied in books. A deeper instinct held her in place. He had called her his heroine, had sent her roses. She didn't like it.

The decision was taken away from her when the door at the top of the stairs swung open and Renard stepped out. He looked grotesque, like a monster from one of the

175

Grimms' grimmer fairy tales. The troll under the bridge. Moderate swelling distorted features dotted with bruises the hues of rotten fruit. For a second, he didn't see Annie, and she thought of stepping back into the Bayou Realty office. Then the second was lost.

'Annie!' he exclaimed as best he could with his jaw wired shut. 'This is an unexpected pleasure!'

'It's not a social call,' Annie said flatly.

'Following up on my attack?'

'No. I came to see Ms Faulkner.'

He put a hand on the stair railing and leaned against it. Beneath the bruises he was pale. 'Lindsay is a hard, uncharitable woman.'

'Gee, and she says such nice things about you.'

'We used to be friends,' he claimed. 'In fact, we went out a time or two. Did she mention that?'

'No.' Lie or not, she wanted to hear more. The cop in her shoved the cautious woman aside. 'There's never been any mention of that anywhere.'

'I never brought it up,' he said. 'It seemed both irrelevant and indelicate.'

'How so?'

'It was years ago.'

'She's very vocal in accusing you of murder. I'd think you'd want to discredit her. Why haven't you said something?'

'I'm saying it now,' he said softly, his gaze beaming down on her. 'To you.'

It was an offer. He would give her things he wouldn't give anyone else. Because he thought she was his guardian angel.

'I was about to take my lunch break,' Renard said, easing his way down the steps. 'Would you join me?'

The offer struck her as so … ordinary. She believed this man to be a monster of the worst sort. The sight of Pam Bichon's body flashed in her mind. The brutality of the crime seemed bigger, stronger, more powerful than the man standing before her.

'I don't want to be seen with you,' she said bluntly. 'My life is difficult enough at the moment.'

'I'm not going out. I can't,' he admitted. 'My life is difficult, as well.'

The side door to the parking area opened, and a delivery boy stepped in with a white deli bag.

'Mr Briggs?' He looked up at Renard, his eyes widening. 'Man, that musta been some car wreck you was in.'

Renard pulled out his wallet without comment.

'I'll share my gumbo,' he offered Annie as the delivery boy left.

'I'm not hungry,' Annie said, but she didn't turn away. Marcus Renard was at the heart of everything, the rock in the pond that had set wave after wave rippling through life in Bayou Breaux.

'I'm not a monster,' Renard said. 'I'd like the chance to convince you of that, Annie.'

'You shouldn't talk to me without your lawyer.'

'Why not?'

Why not indeed? Annie thought. She was alone. She had no wire, no tape recorder. Even if he confessed, it wouldn't matter. Kudrow was the attorney of record; without his presence nothing Renard said would be admissible in court. He could confess to a dozen murders and not hang for one of them.

She weighed her options. They were in a place of business. She could still hear muffled voices coming from Bayou Realty. She was a cop. He wouldn't be stupid enough to try anything here, and he was in no condition to try. She wanted to know what drove him. What was it about Pam Bichon that had caught hold of this otherwise seemingly ordinary man and pulled him over the edge?

'All right.'

The offices of Bowen & Briggs encompassed a single, huge open space with a wood floor that had been sanded blond and varnished to a hard gloss. Gray upholstered modular walls set off various office and conference spaces on the west side. The east side was studded with half a dozen drafting tables and work centers. Renard took his bag to a table in the southeast corner, a space set aside for relaxing, drinking coffee, having lunch. A radio on the counter played classical music.

Annie followed him at a distance, taking her time to assess the place and wishing she had worn her backup weapon.

'You're in trouble.'

She jerked around toward Renard. He was busy lifting his lunch from the deli bag.

'You said your life is difficult now,' he prompted. 'You're in trouble because of Fourcade?'

'I'm in trouble because of you.'

'No.' He motioned her to the chair across from him and took his own seat. Fragrant steam billowed up as he pried the lid off the cup of gumbo, dark roux and sassafras filé. 'You would be in trouble because of me if I were Pam's murderer. I'm not. I should think you'd be convinced of that after that poor Nolan woman was attacked.'

'Unrelated cases. One thing has nothing to do with the other,' Annie said.

'Unless they're both the work of the Bayou Strangler.'

'Stephen Danjermond was the Bayou Strangler, and he's dead. The evidence against him was conclusive.'

'So was the evidence Fourcade planted in my desk. That doesn't make me a killer.'

Annie stared at him. She'd gone over the chronology of events. All the pieces fit. But he swore he was innocent. Was he just an accomplished liar or had he convinced himself of his innocence? She'd seen it happen. People embraced a persecution complex like a security blanket. Nothing was ever their fault. Someone else caused them to be selling dope. It was the fault of the rotten cops that they got busted. But she didn't think a persecution complex fit

178

either Renard or Pam's murder. That was about something else entirely. Obsession.

'I want you to understand, Annie – May I call you Annie?' he asked politely. 'Deputy Broussard is a bit difficult for me, all things considered.'

'Yes,' Annie said, though she didn't like the idea of his using her first name. She didn't like the idea of it in his mouth, rolling over his tongue. She didn't like the idea of giving him anything, of acquiescing to any wish of his, no matter how small.

'I want you to understand, Annie,' he started again. 'I loved Pam like –'

'Like a friend. I know. We've been over this.'

'Are you working on her case now? Will you try to catch her killer?'

'I want her killer brought to justice,' she said, evading the specifics of her involvement with the case. 'You understand what that means, don't you?'

'Yes.' He lifted a spoon of gumbo to his stitched lip. 'I wonder if you do.'

Annie ignored the ominous import and pressed on. 'You said you went out with Lindsay Faulkner. Forgive me for saying so, but I have a hard time picturing that.'

'I don't always look this way.'

'You don't seem ... compatible.'

'We weren't, as it happened. I believe Lindsay may have – How shall I suggest this? Other preferences.'

'You think she's a lesbian?'

He made a little shrug and looked down at his meal, seeming uncomfortable with the topic he had raised.

'Because she wouldn't sleep with you?' Annie said bluntly.

'Heavens, no. We had dinner. I never expected more. It was clear we wouldn't progress that far. It was her ... her *way* with Pam. She was very protective. Jealous. She didn't like Pam's husband. She didn't like any man showing an interest in Pam.'

179

He took another spoon of gumbo and sipped it between his teeth.

'Are you gonna try to tell me you think Pam's partner killed her? In a jealous lesbian rage?'

'No. I don't know who killed her. I wish I did.'

'Then what's your point?'

'That Lindsay dislikes me. She wants to blame someone for Pam's death. She's chosen me.'

'*Everyone* has chosen you, Mr Renard. You *are* the primary suspect.'

'*Convenient* suspect,' he corrected her. 'Because I liked Pam. Because people think of me as a stranger here – they forget I was born here, lived here as a boy. They find it strange that I'm single and live with my mother and a brother who frightens people with his autism.'

'Because Pam believed you were stalking her,' Annie countered. 'Because you hung around her even after she told you to get lost. Because you had motive, means, opportunity, and no viable alibi for the night of the murder.'

'I was in Lafayette –'

'Going to a store that had already closed by the time you got to the Acadiana Mall. Bad luck, that. If the store had been open, you might have witnesses to corroborate your story.'

He looked at her steadily, and his voice was even when he spoke. 'I went there for supplies, not an alibi.'

'You can spare me the story,' Annie said. 'I've memorized the time line. At five-forty Lindsay Faulkner left the office and noted that your car was still in the parking lot. Pam was meeting with clients to write up an offer on a house. At eight-ten you stopped at Hebert's Hobby Shop and purchased a number of items, among them blades for an X-Acto knife.'

'A common tool for dollhouse builders.'

'Pam's clients left her office at eight-twenty. They were the last people to see Pam alive – with the exception of her killer. Meanwhile, Hebert's didn't have everything you needed –'

'French doors for my current project.'

'So you drove to Acadiana Mall in Lafayette, intending to visit the hobby store there, but it was closed,' she pressed on. 'And on your way back you claim you developed car trouble – origin unknown – and sat along a back road for two hours before you got going again with the aid of an anonymous Good Samaritan no one has been able to track down in the three months since. You say you got home around midnight, but you have no one to confirm that because your mother was gone to Bogalusa to visit her sister. That's your story.'

'It's the truth.'

'Meanwhile, the medical examiner in Lafayette puts Pam's death around midnight, give or take, just a few miles from your home.'

'I *didn't* kill her.'

'You were obsessed with her.'

'I was infatuated,' he admitted, rising slowly from his chair. He went to a small refrigerator tucked into the lower cupboards and withdrew two bottles of iced tea. 'I wish she could have returned my feelings, but she didn't and I accepted that.'

He set the bottles on the table, pushing one in Annie's direction.

'Her husband had a far more compelling obsession than I.' He eased back into his chair, picked up a paper napkin, and dabbed at the spittle that had collected in the corners of his wired mouth as he struggled with speech. 'He didn't want to let her go. I think she was afraid of him. She told me she didn't dare see other men until the divorce was final.'

A convenient story to put off a man, Annie thought, though she couldn't dismiss the possibility it was true. It was common knowledge Donnie hadn't wanted the divorce. Lindsay Faulkner confessed to thinking Donnie had been the one harassing Pam. Rumors of a fight over Josie had been whispered around, though it seemed Donnie had no ground to stand on in that arena. He had been the cheat in the marriage. Pam had done nothing to threaten her standing as custodial parent.

'But then,' Renard murmured, staring down into his tea, 'maybe that was just an excuse. I think she was seeing someone for a short time.'

'Why would you think that?'

He couldn't answer her. The only way he would know was if he had watched her, followed her. He wouldn't admit to that, *couldn't* admit to it. The stalking was the basis for the whole case against him. If he admitted to stalking Pam Bichon, and if in that admission he revealed he had seen her with another man, that only added to his motive to kill her. Jealousy. She had spurned him for another.

Annie got up from the table. 'I've heard enough, thank you. Pam was tortured and murdered by her estranged husband, her secret lesbian partner, and/or a mystery lover you can't name or identify. Couldn't have been you that killed her. You're a victim of a malicious conspiracy. Never mind that you had motive, means, opportunity, and a crappy alibi. Never mind that the detectives found Pam's stolen ring in your house.'

Renard rose, too, and limped along beside her as she moved toward the door. 'There is more than one kind of obsession,' he said. 'Fourcade is obsessed with this case. He planted that ring. He's done that kind of thing before. He has a history.

'I have no history. *I've* never hurt anyone. *I'd* never been arrested before this.'

'Maybe that just means you're good at it,' Annie said.

'I *didn't* do it.'

'Why should I believe you? More to the point: Why are you so bent on convincing me? You're a free man. The DA's got nothing on you.'

182

'For now. How long before Fourcade or Stokes manufactures something else? I'm an innocent man. My reputation has been ruined. They won't be satisfied until they have my life one way or another. Someone has to find the truth, Annie, and so far, you're the only one looking.'

'I'm looking,' she said in a cool voice. 'I don't guarantee you're gonna like what I find.'

Marcus held the door for her and watched as she descended the stairs and walked out of the building. She moved in a way that seemed unself-conscious, fresh. Freer than Pam in her physicality, in her gestures. Pam's free-spirit soul sister. He found comfort in the thought. Continuity.

He had pinned his heart on Pam, but Annie would set him free. He was sure of it.

17

The Bayou Realty office was closed and locked when Annie went around to the front of the building. Too bad. She wanted to see the look on Lindsay Faulkner's face when she told her Marcus Renard had her pegged for a lesbian.

Of course, there was the chance that it was true. Annie knew little about her. No one had ever looked that closely at Faulkner, as far as Annie knew. There had been no reason. With the business set up as it was at the time of Pam's death, Faulkner had no financial motive to kill her, and no other motive would have been considered. Women didn't kill other women in the manner Pam Bichon had died.

Annie crossed the street to the Jeep and glanced up at the building as she turned the key in the ignition. Renard was standing at a second-story window, looking out at her.

He swore he was innocent, that he loved Pam. He wanted Annie to find the truth.

Find the truth or muddy the waters? she wondered. She had just stepped into the investigation and already there were factors to consider she hadn't seen before. Fourcade had been down these twisted trails already. His offer hung in her mind like a seductive promise, something she should resist.

Turning away from Renard, she put the Jeep in gear and headed across town.

Donnie surveyed the scene from the seat of a backhoe, a bottle of Abita beer in hand. The Mardi Gras parade float taking shape before him was for Josie. She had talked him into it, those big brown eyes bright with excitement. Unable to deny her anything, he had organized a crew from the staff of Bichon Bayou Development and set them to

184

work. He had envisioned Josie spending hours here with him as the flatbed became a crêpe-paper, fairy-tale kingdom, but Belle Davidson had taken her to Lake Charles for the day 'to get away from the atmosphere' in Bayou Breaux.

'To get away from me, more like,' he muttered.

He tipped his bottle up only to find it empty. He scowled and tossed it down into the bucket of the backhoe, where it shattered against the remains of several other brown bottles. The sound pierced through the country music blaring from the radio. Several heads turned in his direction from the float, but no one said anything.

People had grown wary of his moods since Pam's death. They walked around him on eggshells, hedging their bets in case the cops were wrong about Marcus Renard, in case Donnie was the resurrection of the Bayou Strangler. He was sick of it. He wanted it all behind him. It *should* have been behind him.

'Goddamn cops,' he grumbled.

'Sounds like maybe I should come back.'

Annie had let herself in a side door of the big shed where the construction company stored some of its heavy equipment.

Donnie glared down at her from his throne. 'Do I know you?'

'Annie Broussard, sheriff's office.' This time she flashed the badge. *Be bold.*

'Oh, Christ, now what? Did my check bounce? I don't care if it did. You can throw Fourcade back in the hoosegow, the ungrateful son of a bitch.'

'Why do you say that?'

He opened his mouth to complain, then swallowed it back. Fourcade was on suspension, off the case. No sense dredging up old suspicions with a new cop.

'The man is unstable, that's all,' he said as he climbed down from the backhoe. 'So, you're Fourcade's replacement. What happened to the other guy, that black guy – Stokes?'

185

'Nothing. He's still on the case.'

'Not that I care,' he said, bending to dig another bottle out of the old Coleman cooler that sat beside the backhoe's tire. 'You want my opinion: That guy is lazy. He was on the case when Renard started hassling Pam, and all he wanted to do was make time with her. Always looked to me like Fourcade was the brains of the pair. It's too damn bad he's off the case, except of course that he's nuts.'

He twisted the top off the bottle and tossed it into the backhoe bucket with the rest of the trash. 'Too damn bad he didn't get to close the case for good in that alley. You want a beer?'

'No, thanks.' Annie dipped her head a little, letting her bangs fall into her eyes, hoping recognition wouldn't dawn on Donnie as it had with Lindsay Faulkner.

'On duty?' He laughed. 'That never stopped any cop I ever knew – Gus Noblier included. What are you, new?'

'I need to ask you a couple questions.'

'I swear, that's all you people do – ask questions. You got more answers now than you know what to do with.'

'I spoke with Lindsay Faulkner this morning.'

His face twisted in distaste. 'Did she tell you I'm the Antichrist? The woman hates me. You would have thought she was Pam's big sister. They were that close. As close as women get without being lesbians.'

'She told me you're going to sell Pam's half of the business.'

'I've got my hands full with my own business. I have no desire to have Lindsay for a partner and she has no desire to have me.'

'She said you may have a buyer from New Orleans. Is that true?'

He slanted her a sly look. 'A good businessman doesn't tip his hand too far.'

'Are you telling me it's a bluff?' She smiled back, like a friend wanting in on the secret. 'Because a name came up and I could just make a couple phone calls ...'

'What name?' She could feel him drawing back from her, raising his shields.

'Duval Marcotte.'

'It's a bluff,' he declared flatly. 'Make all the calls you want.'

He scratched at the stubble on the knob of his chin and gestured toward the float. 'What do you think of the masterpiece?'

Annie looked at the work in progress: a cheap pine framework covered with chicken wire. It could have been anything. Two women in cutoffs and tight T-shirts were stuffing chicken-wire holes with squares of blue crêpe paper, talking, laughing, oblivious to the larger problems of the world.

'It's a castle,' Donnie explained. 'My daughter's idea. She picked a scene from *Much Ado About Nothing*. Can you believe that? Nine years old and she's into Shakespeare.'

'She's a very bright girl.'

'She wanted to help build it, but her grandmother had other ideas. Another Davidson woman conspiring against me.'

'Will Belle and Hunter challenge you for custody?'

He hunched his shoulders, still staring at the float. 'I don't know. Probably. I suppose it'll depend on whether Hunter goes to prison. I've got that in my favor: I haven't tried to kill anybody recently – or ever,' he amended, glancing down at Annie. 'That was a joke.'

'You want Josie to live with you full-time?'

'She's my daughter. I love her.'

As if it were as simple as that. As if he had managed to totally separate Donnie the Daddy from Donnie the Don Juan.

'Rumor had it, you would have fought Pam for her.'

'Oh, Christ, that again?' Impatience pulled at his features, making him look petulant. 'You've got your killer. Why don't you go hound him? I didn't do anything to Pam. I didn't kill her for the insurance or for the business or in a rage or anything else. I *couldn't* do anything to Pam. I was sure as hell in no condition that night to do anything to anybody. I drank too much, got a ride home from a friend, and passed out.'

'I know all that,' Annie said. 'I'm not looking at you as a suspect, Mr Bichon.' Though it had occurred to her more than once that drunkenness was easily faked and Donnie had as much motive as anyone – more than most.

According to the news reports, he had shown up at the Voodoo Lounge that night between nine and ten, and had been dropped off at home by his friend around eleven-thirty. Pam had last been seen at eight-twenty and had died around midnight. There were windows of opportunity on both ends of Donnie's story.

'I was just wondering what grounds you had to challenge Pam for custody.'

'Why? Pam is dead. What difference does it make now?'

'If Pam was involved with someone –'

'Renard killed her!' he roared suddenly. The cords in his neck stood out, as taut as guy wires. He spiked his bottle on the cement floor of the shed, shards of glass exploding outward, beer foaming like peroxide in a raw wound. 'He killed her! Now do your fucking job and put him away for it!'

He shoved past Annie and strode for the door. The float crew stared, mouths agape. Mary Chapin Carpenter shouted from the radio – 'I Take My Chances'.

Annie hustled after him. The brilliance of the afternoon nearly blinded her as she emerged from the shed. Squinting, she shaded her eyes with her hand. Donnie stood at the chain-link fence that corralled the possessions of his company, staring at the train tracks that ran behind the property.

'Look, I'm just trying to get at the whole truth,' she said, stepping up beside him. 'I wouldn't be doing my job if I didn't ask questions.'

'It's just – It's dragged on and on.' He swallowed and his

Adam's apple bobbed like cork. His eyes stayed on the tracks. 'Why can't it just be over? Pam's gone. ... I'm so tired of it. ...'

He wanted the wounds to heal and disappear with no scars, no reminders. It was a good detective's job to keep picking and picking at those wounds. The trick was knowing when to dig and when to stand back. Annie had thought she would be able to read Donnie Bichon, know him for a liar if he was one. But the emotions that had caught him up were a tangled skein; she couldn't tell grief from remorse, fear from arrogance.

'I could have been a better husband,' he murmured. 'She could have been a better wife. You can think what you want of me for saying it.'

In the distance a train whistle blew. Donnie seemed not to have heard it. He was lost in memories.

'I just wanted what was mine,' he whispered, blinking against the threat of tears. 'I didn't want to lose her. I didn't want to lose Josie. I thought maybe if I scared her ... threatened custody ...'

If he scared her how? Was custody the only threat he'd made? Annie drew a breath to ask what he meant, but held it as he turned toward her.

'You look like her, you know,' he said, his voice strangely dreamy. 'The shape of your face ... the hair ... the mouth ...'

He reached out as if to touch her cheek, but pulled back at the last instant. She wondered if it was sanity or the fear of breaking some inner spell that stopped him. Either way, it unnerved her. She didn't welcome comparison with a woman who had met such a brutal end.

'I miss her,' Donnie admitted. 'Always want what I can't have. I used to think that was ambition, but it's just ... need.'

'What about Pam? What did she need?'

The train whistle blew again, louder, nearer.

'To be free of me,' he said simply, his expression bleak. 'And now she is.'

Annie watched him walk away, not back to the building but to a pearl white Lexus parked near the side gate. Behind her the Southern Pacific train whined past, wheels chattering over the connections in the track.

She had been working the case a matter of hours, and she felt as if she had stepped into a maze that appeared deceptively simple from the outside but was in reality a complex labyrinth, dark corridor full of mirrors. A small part of her wanted to turn back. A larger part of her wanted to go deeper, learn more. The mystery pulled at her, beckoned her. *Temptation*. The word came to her like a whispered secret from a hidden co-conspirator.

Fourcade. He was the guardian at the gate, her self-appointed guide if she would accept his offer. He held the map of the maze and the knowledge of the players. The trick would be deciding if he was friend or foe, if his offer was genuine or a trap. There seemed only one way to find out.

18

Even on a bright day the house had a sinister look. The brilliant spring sun failed to remove the shawl of shadows that fell down from the newly leafed trees. Shrouded in murky light and gray with neglect, it squatted amid the sprouting growth like a toothless crone, ugly and abandoned.

Nick stared at the house from the pirogue, fascinated by the possibility that evil could linger in a place like a scent. The house hadn't been bad off at the time of the murder. Recently vacated by renters at the time, and scheduled for some renovation work, the electricity had still been turned on. Since the murder, the place had been let go. Kids had thrown rocks through the windows. The stigma of death clung to it like grime.

Nick would not go inside. Some people would have called him superstitious, but they would have been people who had never stepped close to the boundary between good and evil; they didn't know the power or the possibilities. Still, it was telling that on a day as fine as this one, when other parts of Pony Bayou were thick with weekend fishermen, there were none within a quarter mile of this place.

He had set out in the pirogue intending to distance himself from thoughts of the case. But this place had drawn him like a magnet.

Another battle lost, and so he would give himself over to the obsession until a conclusion could be reached.

Would it be over now, he wondered, *had I killed Renard that night?*

Pony Bayou here was narrow, even this time of year, when the brown water was high and spilling into the forest. The banks were crowded with hackberry saplings and tangles of dewberry and poison ivy. The limbs of the black

191

willow and water locust reached out over the column of water from both sides, like bony fingers stretching to touch one another.

The trees were alive with the sounds of birds excited by the early arrival of spring. The songs and shrieks and squawks blended into a cacophony that seemed to take on an especially discordant and unnerving quality. And on every available limb, log, and stump, water snakes had crawled out to sun themselves in an eerie ritual of spring. The forest along the banks seemed hung with reptiles, like dark, muscular ropes of live bunting.

Taking up the push-pole, Nick rose at the back of the pirogue and sent it gliding north and west. The route was twisted, his passing witnessed by no one. Nature claimed the land here for several miles and no man in recent history had challenged Her. Then the channel widened slightly and the forest came to an abrupt halt on the western bank, marking the edge of the first piece of domesticated property away from the murder scene. Marcus Renard's home.

The house stood a hundred yards or so away, elegant in its simplicity. Clean lines, plain columns. The modest home of a modest indigo planter in a past century. Tall French windows opened onto a brick veranda where Victor Renard sat at a patio table.

Victor was slightly bigger than Marcus, thicker bodied. While he had the social awareness of a small child, he had the physical strength of a thirty-seven-year-old man and had once been turned out of a group home for destroying a bed in a fit of temper. Emotions – his own or those of others – were difficult for him to comprehend or process. The autistic mind seemed unable to decode feelings. For the most part, he expressed none, though odd things would sometimes trigger agitation and occasionally anger. At the same time, Victor was mathematically gifted, able to easily work equations that could stump college students, and he could name the genus and species of thousands of animals and plants and describe each in textbook detail.

People around Bayou Breaux didn't understand Victor Renard's condition. They were frightened of him. They mistook him for being retarded or schizophrenic. He was neither.

Nick had considered it his duty to discover these things about Victor and his autism. An arsenal of information was far more useful to a detective than any other kind of weapon. The smallest, seemingly insignificant fact or detail could prove to be the one piece that made the rest of the puzzle work.

Victor Renard's mind was itself a complex mystery. If somewhere in the labyrinth he held a clue to his brother's guilt, Nick suspected they would never know. If they could ever bring Marcus to trial, Smith Pritchett would never attempt to use Victor as a witness. Aside from the familial connection, Victor's autism precluded him from appearing reliable or even coherent in court.

Nick leaned lightly against the push-pole, holding the pirogue against the slow current. He stood at the edge of his legal boundary. Kudrow had sought and been granted a temporary restraining order for his client, specifically outlining how near Nick could come to him. If he tested those limits too strongly or too often, he could be brought up on stalking charges. The irony both amused and disgusted him.

He watched as Victor became aware of him, sitting up straighter, then reaching for a pair of binoculars on the table. He came up out of his chair as if someone had set it on fire. He rushed twenty yards across the lawn, his gait strange, his arms straight down at his sides. He stopped and raised the binoculars again. Then he dropped the binoculars on the strap around his neck and began to rock himself from side to side in jerky, irregular movements, like a windup toy gone wrong.

'Not now!' Victor shouted, pointing at him. 'Red, red! Very red! Enter out!'

When Nick made no move to leave, Victor rushed

forward another ten steps, wrapped his arms tight around his chest, and rocked himself around in a circle. Strange, piercing shrieks tore from him.

At the house, one of the French doors opened and Doll Renard rushed onto the veranda. Her agitation almost equaled her son's. She started toward Victor, then turned back toward the house. Marcus emerged, and limped across the lawn to his brother.

'Very red!' Victor screamed as Marcus took hold of his arm. 'Enter out!'

He screamed again as Marcus took the binoculars from him.

Nick expected shouting, then remembered Renard's fractured jaw and felt not remorse, but discomfort at the power of his own anger. Renard came toward the bank.

'You're violating the court order,' he said, hands curled into fists at his sides.

'I think not,' Nick said. 'I'm on a public waterway.'

'You're a criminal!'

Nick clucked his tongue. 'A matter of perspective, that.'

'We're calling the police, Fourcade!'

'This is the jurisdiction of the sheriff's office. You really think they'll come to your aid? You have no friends there, Marcus.'

'You're wrong,' Renard insisted. 'And you're breaking the law. You're harassing me.'

Yards behind him, Victor had fallen to his knees to rock himself. His banshee shrieks drove the birds from the trees.

Nick looked innocent. 'Who, me? I'm just fishing.' Lazily he straightened away from the push-pole, moving the pirogue from the bank. 'Ain't no law against fishing, no.'

He let the craft drift backward, following the curve of the land until his view of Renard's house and his brother was gone and only Renard himself remained in his line of vision. *Focus*, he thought. *Focus, calm, patience. Exist within the current, and the goal will be reached.*

Annie sat in an old ladder-back chair with a seat woven from the rawhide of some unfortunate long-dead cow. The view of the bayou was pretty from Fourcade's small gallery. She wondered if Fourcade ever idled his motor long enough to appreciate it. He didn't seem a man to care about such things, but then he had proven to be full of surprises, hadn't he?

It didn't surprise her that he lived in such a remote, inaccessible place. He was a remote, inaccessible man. It surprised her that his yard was neat, that he was obviously working on the house.

Her stomach growled. She'd been waiting an hour. Fourcade's truck was here, but Fourcade was not. God only knew where he'd gone. The sun was going down and her resolve was running out in direct proportion to her increasing need for a meal. To occupy her mind she tried to imagine a hiding spot in the Jeep where she might have tucked away an emergency Snickers and forgotten about it. She'd already been through the glove compartment and looked under the seats. She concluded that Mullen had stolen the candy, and was perfectly happy to waste another few moments hating him for it.

A pirogue came into view, skating through a patch of cypress deadheads. Nerves tightened in Annie's stomach, and she rose from the chair. Fourcade guided the boat in alongside the dock, took his time tying off the pirogue and walking up the bank. He wore a black T-shirt that fit him like a coat of paint and fatigue pants tucked into a pair of trooper boots. He didn't smile. He didn't blink.

'How did you find this place?' he asked.

'I'd be a poor candidate for detective if I couldn't manage to dig up an address.' Annie stepped behind the chair, resting her hands on its back.

'That you would, *chérie*. But no. You got initiative. You came to take the bull by the horns, *oui?*'

'I want to see what you have on the case.'

He nodded. 'Good.'

195

'But you have to know up front this doesn't change what happened Wednesday night. If that's what you're really after, then say so now and I'll just go on home.'

Nick studied her for a moment. She kept one hand close to the open flap of her faded denim jacket. She doubtless had the Sig Sauer handy. She didn't trust him. He didn't blame her.

He shrugged. 'You saw what you saw.'

'I'll have to testify. That doesn't make you angry? That doesn't make you want to – oh, say, plant a live snake in my Jeep?'

He leaned toward her and gently patted her cheek. 'If I wanted to hurt you, *chère*, I wouldn't leave it up to no snake.'

'Should I be relieved or afraid for my life?'

Fourcade said nothing.

'I don't trust you,' she admitted.

'I know.'

'If you pull any more of that crazy shit like you did last night, I'm gone,' she declared. 'And if I have to shoot you, I will.'

'I'm not your enemy, 'Toinette.'

'I hope that's true. I have enough of them right now. And I have them because of you,' Annie pointed out.

'Who ever said life was fair? Sure as hell wasn't me.'

He turned and walked away. He didn't invite her in; he expected her to follow him. No social niceties for Fourcade. They passed through the parlor, a room furnished with a toolbox and a sledgehammer. The floor was covered with a dirty canvas drop cloth. The kitchen was an absolute contrast – clean, bright, newly Sheetrocked, and painted the color of buttermilk. As tidy as a ship's galley. Nothing adorned the walls. Fresh herbs grew in a narrow tray on the windowsill above the sink.

Fourcade went to the sink to wash his hands.

'What changed your mind?' he asked.

'Noblier pulled me off patrol because the other deputies

196

won't play nice. I gotta figure he won't promote me into your job anytime soon. So, if I want in on this case, you're my ticket.'

He expressed no sympathy, and asked for no details about her trouble with Mullen or the others. It was her problem, not his.

'Get yourself assigned to Records and Evidence,' he said, turning around, drying his hands on a plain white towel. 'You can read the files all day, study the reports.'

'I'll see what I can do. It's up to the sheriff.'

'Don't be passive,' he snapped. 'Ask for what you want.'

'And you think I'll just get it?' Annie laughed. 'You're really not from this planet, are you, Fourcade?'

His face grew hard. 'You won't get anything you don't ask for one way or another, sugar. You better learn that lesson fast, you want this job. People don't just give up their secrets. You gotta ask, you gotta pry, you gotta dig.'

'I know that.'

'Then do it.'

'I will. I *have*,' she insisted. 'I spoke with Donnie Bichon today.'

Fourcade looked surprised. 'And?'

'And he seems like a man with a conscience problem. But then maybe you don't wanna hear that – the two of you being so close and all.'

'I have no ties to Donnie Bichon.'

'He bailed you out of jail to the tune of a hundred thousand dollars.'

He rested his hands at the waist of his fatigue pants. 'As I said to Donnie, I will say to you: He bought my freedom, he did not buy me. No one buys me.'

'A refreshing policy for a New Orleans cop.'

'I'm no longer in New Orleans. I didn't assimilate well.'

'That's not what I've been reading,' Annie said. 'I spent the better part of the afternoon at the library. According to the *Times-Picayune*, you were the quintessential corrupt cop. You got a lotta ink down there. None of it good.'

197

'The press is easily manipulated by powerful people.'

Annie winced. 'Oooh, you know, it's remarks like that that lead people to draw unflattering conclusions about your sanity.'

'People think what they want. I know the truth. I lived the truth.'

'And your version of the truth would be what?' she pressed.

He simply stared at her, and she saw the bleakness of a soul who had lived a long, hard life and had seen too much that wasn't good.

'The truth is that I did my job too well,' he said at last. 'And I made the mistake of caring too deeply for justice in a place that has none, existentially speaking.'

'Did you beat that suspect?'

He said nothing.

'Did you plant that evidence?'

He bowed his head for a moment, then turned his back to her and pulled a cast-iron skillet from a lower cupboard.

She wanted to go to him, demand the truth, but she was afraid to get that near him. Afraid something might rub off on her – his intensity, his compulsion, the darkness that permeated his being. She was already involving herself in this case beyond the call of duty. She didn't want to go beyond reason, and she had a strong feeling Fourcade could take her there in a heartbeat.

'I need an answer, Detective.'

'It's irrelevant to the present case.'

'Prior bad acts inadmissible on the ground they may taint the opinion of the court? Bull. More often than not they establish a pattern of behavior,' Annie argued. 'Besides, we're not in court; we're in the real world. I have to know who I'm dealing with, Fourcade, and I already told you, I'm not long on trust at the moment.'

'Trust is of no use in an investigation,' he said, moving between stove, refrigerator, and butcher block. He set an assortment of vegetables on the chopping block and selected a knife of frightening proportions.

'It is with regards to partners,' Annie insisted. 'Did you plant that ring in Renard's desk?'

He looked up at her then, unblinking. 'No.'

'Why should I believe you? How do I know Donnie Bichon didn't pay you to plant it? He could have paid you to kill Renard the other night, for all I know.'

He sliced into a red bell pepper as if it were made of thin paper. 'Now who's paranoid?'

'There's a difference between healthy suspicion and delusion.'

'Why would I invite you into the investigation if I was dirty?'

'So you can use me like a puppet to achieve your own end.'

He smiled. 'You are far too smart for that, 'Toinette.'

'Don't waste your flattery.'

'I don't believe in flattery. Me, I say what's true.'

'When it suits you.'

She sighed as they came around the circle again. A conversation with Fourcade was like shadowboxing – all effort and no satisfaction.

'Why me?' she asked. 'Why not Quinlan or Perez?'

'It's a small division. We live in each other's pockets. One itches, another one scratches. You're outside the circle – that's an advantage.' He flashed the grin again, bright with a charm he never used. 'You're my secret weapon, 'Toinette.'

She tried one last time to talk herself out of this lunacy. But she didn't want to, and he knew it.

'You feel an obligation, a tie to Pam Bichon,' he said, 'and to those who've gone before her. You feel the shadows. That's why you're here. That and you know we want the same end, you and I: Renard in hell.'

'I want the case cleared,' Annie said. 'If Renard did it –'

'He did it.'

'– then fine. I'll dance in the street the day they send him from Angola to the next life. If he didn't do it –'

He jabbed the point of the knife into the butcher block. '*He did it.*'

Annie said nothing. She had to be out of her mind to come here to him.

'It's simple,' he said, calmer. He pulled the knife out of the block and began to dice an onion. 'I have what you need, 'Toinette. Facts, statements, answers to questions you have yet to ask. All of it can be checked if need be. You have an inquisitive mind, a free will, an appropriate skepticism. I have no power over you ...' The knife stilled. He looked at her from under his brow. 'Do I?'

'No,' she said quietly, glancing away.

'Then we can proceed. But first, we eat.'

19

They ate. Stir-fried vegetables and brown rice. No meat. Odd that a man who chain-smoked would be a vegetarian, but Annie knew that she would have to become desensitized to Fourcade's contradictions. To expect the unexpected seemed a wise course, though one not easily settled into.

'You had two years at college. Why'd you quit?' he demanded, stabbing his fork into his dinner. He ate the way he did everything – with vehemence and no wasted movement.

'They wanted me to declare a major.' She felt uncomfortable with the idea that he had raided her personnel file. 'It seemed ... restrictive. I was interested in lots of things.'

'Lack of focus.'

'Curiosity,' she retorted. 'I thought you liked my inquisitive nature.'

'You need discipline.'

'Look who's talking.' Annie frowned at him, pushing her rice around with her fork. 'What happened to your Taoist principles of nonresistant existence?'

'Often incompatible with police work. With regards to religions, I take what's useful to me and apply it where appropriate. Why did you become a cop?'

'I like helping people. It's different every day. I like solving mysteries. I get to drive a hot car. How about you?'

Words like *power* and *control* came to mind, but those were not the words he gave her.

'It's factual, logical, essential. I believe in justice. I believe in the struggle for the greater good. I believe the collective evil metastasizes with malignancies in the souls of individuals.'

'So it wasn't just the cool uniforms?'

Fourcade looked bemused.

'You enrolled in the academy in August '93,' he said. 'Just after the whole Bayou Strangler thing. Connection?'

'You know so much about me – you tell me.'

He ignored the suggestion of affront in her voice. He made no apologies for overstepping a boundary. 'You went to school with the fifth victim, Annick Delahoussaye-Gerrard. You were friends?'

'Yeah, we were friends,' she said.

She took her plate to the sink and stood looking out the window, seeing nothing. Night had wrapped itself around the house. Fourcade had no yard light. Of course he wouldn't. Fourcade would be one with the dark.

'We were best friends when we were little,' she said. 'The families called us the Two Annies. But, you know, we grew apart, ran with different crowds. Her folks ran a bar – it's the Voodoo Lounge now. They sold out after Annick was killed.

'I ran into her maybe a month before it happened. She was waitressing at the bar. She was getting divorced. I told her she should come up to Lafayette for a weekend, that we'd catch up and have some fun. But you know, that weekend never came. I suppose I didn't really mean for it to. We didn't have much in common anymore. Anyway, then came the news ... and then the funeral.'

Nick watched her reflection in the window. 'Why do you think it hit you so hard if you'd grown so far apart?'

'I don't know.'

'Yes, you do.'

She was silent for a moment. He waited. The answer lay within her grasp. She didn't want to reach for it.

'We were two sides of the same coin once,' she said at last. 'A flip of the coin, a twist of fate ...'

'It could have been you.'

'Sure, why not?' she said. 'You know, you read about a crime in the paper and you think how terrible for the victims, and then you turn the page and move on. It's so different when you know the people. The press called her by name for a week, then she became Victim Number Five and they were on to the next big headline. I saw what that crime did to her family, to her friends. I started thinking it would be good to try to make a difference for people like the Delahoussayes.'

Nick got up from the table and brought his plate to the sink to nest with hers. 'That's a good reason, 'Toinette. Honor, social responsibility.'

'Don't forget the hot car.'

'That's unnecessary.'

'The car?'

'The mask you wear,' he said. 'The effort you go to to hide the truth beneath layers of insignificant mannerisms and humor. It's a waste of energy.'

Annie shook her head. 'It's called having a personality. You oughta try it sometime. I'm betting it would improve your social life.'

The retort was made an instant before she realized what he had really said – that he lived with the protective pretenses stripped away from his soul; his needs, his thoughts, his feelings lay like raw and exposed nerve endings. She would never have thought of him as vulnerable, knew he would never think of himself as such. How strange to see him that way. She wasn't sure it was something she wanted to see.

'A waste of time,' he said again, turning away. 'We've got a job to do. Let's get to it.'

He had turned the *grenier*, the loft that made up the second half-story of the house, into a study. The bed tucked into the far corner seemed like an afterthought, a grudging concession to the occasional need for sleep. A masculine place, with heavy wood furnishings, and an almost monkish quality in its sense of order. The bookcases were lined with titles, hundreds of books shelved by subject in alphabetical order. Criminology, philosophy, psychology, religion. Everything from aberrant behavior to the mysteries of Zen.

A ten-foot-long table held the reams of paperwork the Bichon homicide had generated. Photocopies of every statement, every lab report. Numbered binders filled with Fourcade's notes. A bulletin board behind the table held maps: one of a three-parish area, one of Partout Parish, one of the immediate Bayou Breaux area including the murder scene and Renard's home. Red pins marked significant sites. Fine red lines drawn between sites were annotated with exact mileage.

A second bulletin board held copies of the crime scene photos – stark, hard reality cast in the harsh light of a camera flash.

'Wow,' Annie murmured. 'I guess you believe in bringing your work home with you.'

'It's a duty, not a hobby.' He stood in front of one of the bookcases. 'You want a time clock and no worries, get a job at the lamp factory. You want to pass the buck on the tough stuff, stay in uniform.' He hit her with the Hard Stare. 'Is that what you want, 'Toinette? You wanna stay on the surface where everything is simple and safe, or do you want to go deeper?'

Once again she had the feeling he was the guardian at the gate of some secret world, that if she crossed the threshold, there would be no going back. She resented the idea.

'I want to be a detective,' she said. 'I want to help clear this case. I'm not pledging my allegiance to the Dark Lord or becoming a Jedi knight. I want to *do* the job, not *be* the job.'

That was Fourcade, the Zen detective. Disapproval hung on him like mist.

'It's a job, not a religion,' Annie said. 'You were born out of your time, Fourcade. You'd have made a hell of a Zealot.'

Her gaze shifted to the table, to the bulletin board and the pictures of Pam Bichon's grisly death. She wanted

Fourcade's resources. She didn't have to embrace his doctrine of obsessive-compulsive behavior.

'I want this solved,' she said. 'End of story.'

She selected Donnie Bichon's file folder and opened it.

'Why did you go to him?' Fourcade asked. 'We looked at him and cleared him.'

'Because Lindsay Faulkner says he's fixing to sell Pam's half of the realty business.'

The news hit Nick like a rock to the chest. He had taunted Donnie with the idea just yesterday, never imagining the man would be fool enough to make such a move so soon after Pam's death. 'When did you hear this?'

'This morning. I stopped by the realty office.' She hesitated, weighing the pros and cons of telling the whole truth.

'You stopped by and what?' he demanded. 'If we're partners, we're partners, *chère*. No holding back.'

She took a deep breath as she set the file aside. 'She said Donnie claims he has a possible buyer on the hook … in New Orleans. Donnie told me it was a bluff.'

Nick had managed to all but banish the idea of Marcotte's involvement. It seemed too far-fetched. He couldn't imagine he had ever meant enough to Marcotte for him to inflict vengeance after all this time. Besides, Marcotte had gotten what he wanted back when, so what would be the point of dragging out the game?

Unless what he wanted now was Bayou Realty, and Nick's involvement was mere coincidence or karma. The question was: If Marcotte was involved, was the murder a result of that involvement or was his involvement a by-product of the crime?

'*C'est ein affaire à pus finir*,' Nick whispered.

'I figure it's a bluff,' Annie said. 'We – *you've* got Donnie's phone records from the period when Pam was being harassed. If the sale of the business was a motive for him to get rid of her, then he would have been in contact with his buyer during that time. Not from his home, if he had any sense, but no one would think twice about him calling New Orleans from the office. We can check it out.

'But I say if Donnie has this fat cat on the hook, why would he even bother to play games with Lindsay Faulkner?' she went on. 'And if he was afraid of having the sale raise a red flag with the cops, then why do anything out in the open? It's not that hard to hide deals. In fact, Donnie's done it before. He had Pam hiding property for him so he wouldn't lose it to the bank. Did you know about that?'

'Yes.'

Nick forced himself to move. *Forward* had become a mantra months ago. Move forward physically, psychologically, spiritually, metaphorically. Movement seemed to pull taut the lines upon which facts and ideas aligned themselves in his mind. Movement maintained order. So he moved forward and tried not to be spooked by the shadow that followed him.

'I'll go over the records,' he said. 'But I doubt the sale of the business has anything to do with the murder. It's more likely scavengers moving in, taking advantage of an opportunity. A woman killed the way Pam was – that's no money murder. People killed for money reasons – they fall down steps, they drown, they disappear.'

He stopped in front of the table, his gaze on the photographs. 'This ... this was personal. This was hate. Contempt. Control. Rage.'

'Or made to look so after the fact.'

'No,' he whispered. 'I can feel it.'

'Did you know her?' she asked quietly.

'She sold me this place. Nice lady. Hard to believe someone could have hated her this way.'

'Renard claims he loved her – like a friend. He insists he's being railroaded. He wants me to find the truth for him.' Her lips twisted. 'Gee, I'm a popular girl lately.'

He didn't pick up on the irony. He concentrated instead on Renard. 'You spoke with him? When? Where?'

'This morning. In his office. He invited me up. He's

laboring under the misconception that I'm sympathetic toward him.'

'He trusts you?'

'I had the great luck to save his sorry ass – twice in one day. He seems to think just because I won't let individuals murder him, I won't want the state to do it, either.'

'You can get close to him, then,' Fourcade murmured. 'That's something Stokes and I could never do. He regarded us as the enemy from the first. Stokes had been riding him already for the harassment, before the murder. You come to him from a whole other direction.'

'I don't like the way your mind is bending,' Annie said. She went to one of the bookcases and stared at the titles. 'I told him flat out I think he did it.'

'But he wants to win you over, yes?'

'I don't know that I'd put it quite like that.'

Fourcade turned her around, his hands cupping her shoulders, and looked at her as if he was seeing her for the first time. '*Mais oui*. Oh, yeah. The hair, the eyes, 'bout the same size. You fit the victim profile.'

'So do half the women in South Lou'siana.'

'But *you* came into *his* life, *chère*. Like it was meant to be.'

'You're creeping me out, Fourcade.' She tried to wriggle away from his touch. 'You talk like he's a serial killer.'

'The potential is there. The psychopathology is there,' he said, and began pacing. 'Look at him: mid-thirties, white, single, intelligent, domineering mother, absent father, unsuccessful in maintaining relationships with women. It's classic.'

'But he doesn't have any criminal history. No pattern of escalating aberrant behavior.'

'Maybe, maybe not. Before he moved here, he had a girlfriend back in Baton Rouge. She died an untimely death.'

'The papers said she died in a car accident.'

'She was burned beyond recognition in a single-car crash on some back road not long after she told her mother she

207

was going to break it off with Renard. She thought he was too possessive. "Smothering" was the word she used with her mother.'

He had obviously gone to the source for his information. The only thing the papers had gotten out of Elaine Ingram's mother was that she found Marcus Renard 'very pleasant and a gentleman' and that she wished her daughter had married him. If he'd been a monster then, no one had seen it ... except perhaps Elaine.

'The mother doesn't think he killed her,' Annie said.

Fourcade looked impatient. 'It doesn't matter what she thinks. It matters what he did. It matters that he might have killed her. It matters that he might have had that kind of rage in him before and that he might have killed out of that rage.

'Look at this murder,' he said, gesturing to the photos. 'Rage, power, domination, sexual brutality. Not unlike your Bayou Strangler.'

'Are you saying you think maybe Renard did those women four years ago?' Annie asked. 'He moved back here in '93. You think he was the Bayou Strangler?'

Fourcade shook his head. 'No. I've been over those files. I've talked to the people who ended up pinning it on Danjermond: Laurel Chandler and Jack Boudreaux. They live up on the Carolina coast now. Too many bad memories 'round here, I guess, with her losing her sister to the Strangler and all. They tell a pretty convincing tale. The investigation backed them up.'

He stopped to stare at the crime scene photos. 'Besides, there are differences in the murders. Pam Bichon wasn't strangled to death.'

He touched a finger to one of the photos, a close-up of the bruising on the throat. 'She was choked manually – these bruises are thumbprints – and her hyoid bone was cracked. He probably choked her unconscious at some point. We can only hope so for her sake. But asphyxiation wasn't the cause of death. Loss of blood from the primary stab wounds was the cause of death.' He moved his finger to a shot of the woman's savaged bare chest. 'Because of the pattern of the blood splatters, I believe she was stabbed several times in the chest while she was standing, then fell to the floor. The choking happened sometime after she went down but before she was dead. Otherwise you wouldn't have this kind of bruising.

'The Strangler, he used a white silk scarf around the throat to kill his victims – that was his signature. And he tied them down with strips of white silk. See here? No ligature marks on Bichon's wrists or ankles.'

'But the sexual mutilation –'

He shook his head. 'Similar, but not the same by any means. Danjermond tortured his victims extensively before he killed them. The mutilation of Bichon was largely postmortem, suggesting it was about anger, hatred, disrespect, rather than any kind of erotic sadism – which was the case with the Strangler. That boy got off on it in a big way. Renard was pissed.

'And then there's the victim profile,' he said. 'The Strangler hunted women who were easily accessible: women who hung out in bars, looking for men, liked to pass a good time. That wasn't Pam Bichon.

'No,' he declared. 'The cases are unrelated. The way I see it, Renard fixated on Pam when he thought she might become available to him – when she separated from Donnie. He probably built a whole fantasy around her, and when she refused to cooperate in turning the fantasy into reality, he went over the line to the dark side.'

He turned and his gaze swept down over Annie. 'And now he's lookin' at you, *chère*.'

'Lucky me,' Annie muttered.

Fourcade ignored the sarcasm. 'Oh yeah,' he said, moving closer. 'You're being presented with a rare opportunity, 'Toinette. You can get close to him, open him up, see what's in his head. He lets you close enough, he'll give himself away.'

209

'Or kill me, if your theory holds true. I'd rather come across a nice piece of evidence, thanks anyway. The murder weapon. A witness who could put him at the scene. A trophy.'

'We found his trophy – the ring. Don't expect to find another. We never even found the gifts Pam gave back to him. We never found the other things he'd taken from her. He's too smart to make the same mistake twice – and that's what we need, sugar: for him to make a mistake. You could be it.' He brushed her bangs with his fingertips, caressed her cheek. The pad of his thumb skimmed the corner of her mouth. 'He could fall in love with you.'

She didn't like the way her pulse was pounding. She didn't like the way she saw Pam Bichon's corpse from every angle – torn, ragged, bloody; the feather mask a grotesque contrast.

'I'm not bait for your bear trap, Fourcade,' she said. 'If I can get something out of Renard, I will, but I'm not getting close enough for him to lay a finger on me. I don't want to get under his skin. I don't want to get inside his head – or yours, for that matter. I want justice, that's all.'

'Then go after it, *chère*,' he said, too seductively. 'Go after it … every way you can.'

20

They should be made to pay for what they've put us through,' Doll Renard declared. She moved around the dining room like a hummingbird, flitting here, flitting there, resting nowhere.

'You've said that ten times,' Marcus grumbled.

'Eight.' Victor corrected him automatically and without smugness. 'Eight times. Repetition, multiplication. Two times four times, eight times. Even. Equal, *equals*. Equals sometime *equal*, sometime *odd*.'

He shook his head disapprovingly at the trick of the language.

Doll shot him a look of disgust. 'I'll say it 'til I'm blue. The Partout Parish Sheriff's Department has ruined our lives. I can't go anywhere without people staring and whispering. And most of the time they don't bother to whisper. 'There's that Doll Renard,' they say. 'How can she show her face after what her boy did?' It's even worse than after your father betrayed us. Of course, you wouldn't remember that. You were just a little boy. People are hateful, that's all.'

'I didn't do anything wrong,' Marcus reminded her. 'I'm innocent until proven guilty. Tell them that.'

She sniffed and flitted from the sideboard to the corner china cupboard. 'I wouldn't give them the satisfaction. Besides, they would just throw up to me how everyone knows you panted after that Bichon woman and she didn't want you.'

'Throw up,' Victor said, rocking from side to side on his chair.

It had taken an hour to calm him from the fit Fourcade had brought on, and he was still agitated. He was supposed to be helping polish the silver, but had decided tarnish was

211

bacteria and refused to touch any of it. Bacteria, he believed, would run up his arms and gain access to his brain through his ear canals. 'Vomit. Puke. Spew. *Dis*gorge. *Re*gorge. Discharge – like excrement.'

'Victor, stop it!' Doll snapped, her bony hand fluttering over her heart. 'You're making us nauseous.'

'Talk – vomit words. Sound and sound alike,' he said, his eyes glazing over as he looked at something inside his scrambled brain.

Marcus tuned them both out, staring at his hands. He rubbed a jeweler's cloth up and down the stem of a marrow spoon and contemplated the uselessness of the thing. People didn't eat bone marrow anymore. The practice suggested a voraciousness that had gone out of vogue. To devour a creature's flesh, then crack its bones to suck out the very marrow of its life seemed a rapacious act. The hunger to consume a being whole was frowned upon, repressed.

He wondered if a need repressed deeply enough, long enough, eventually went into a person's marrow, reachable only if the bones were broken open. He wondered what would drain out of his own marrow. His mother's would be black as tar, he suspected.

'He beat you,' she reiterated, as if he needed reminding of Fourcade's sins. 'You could be permanently disfigured. You could be disabled. You could lose your job. It's a pure wonder they haven't fired you after everything that's gone on.'

'I'm a partner, Mother. They can't fire me.'

'Who will come to you with work? Your reputation is ruined – *and* mine. I've lost every single costume order I've gotten for Mardi Gras. And that man has the gall to come here, to harass us, and the sheriff's department does nothing! Nothing! I swear, we could all be murdered in our beds, and they would do nothing! They should be made to pay for what they've put us through.'

'Nine,' Victor said.

He rose abruptly from his chair as the hall clock struck eight, and hurried from the room.

'There he goes,' Doll muttered bitterly, her features pinching tight. 'He'll sleep like the dead. I can't remember the last time I had a decent night's sleep. Every night now I dream about my Mardi Gras masks. All the joy of them has been robbed from me. You know what people say. They say the mask found on that dead woman was from my collection, and, even though I know it wasn't, even though I can account for every single one of them, even though I know people are motivated by jealousy because my collection has won prizes year after year during Carnival, it's just robbed the joy from me.'

If his mother had ever had a moment's joy in her life, Marcus had never heard about it until after it had been 'robbed' from her, as if she were aware of the emotion only after the fact. He set the marrow spoon down and folded the jeweler's cloth.

'I called Annie Broussard,' he said. 'Perhaps she can do something about Fourcade.'

'What could *she* possibly do?' Doll asked sourly, annoyed at having the attention shifted from her own suffering.

'She stopped him from killing me,' he pointed out. 'I need to lie down. My head is pounding.'

Doll clucked her tongue. 'It's no wonder. You could have a brain injury. A blood vessel could burst in your head months from now, and then where would we be?'

I would be free of you, Marcus thought. But there were simpler ways to escape than death.

He went into his bedroom, pausing there only to take a Percodan from the drawer in the nightstand. Pills couldn't be left in the medicine chest where Victor would find them. Victor believed all pills to be both remedial and preventative. As a teenager he had twice had his stomach pumped to empty him of aspirin, stomach aids, vitamins and Midol.

Marcus broke the painkiller into pieces, worked them into his mouth, and washed them down with Coca-Cola – a

213

practice his mother had harped against all his life. Doll believed Coca-Cola would react with drugs like alcohol and render a person comatose. He took an extra swig for spite and carried the can into his workroom.

Tension and anger kept him from going to his drawing table. He moved around the room hunched over because his ribs were especially sore. Everything hurt more tonight because of Fourcade. Because of Fourcade, he had hurried across the lawn, strained muscles, raised his blood pressure.

That bastard damn well would pay for what he'd done. Kudrow would see to that. Criminal charges, a civil suit. By the time the dust settled, what was left of Fourcade's career would be in shreds. The idea pleased Marcus enormously – using the very system his tormentors had tried to destroy him with to destroy his tormentors. He would ruin Stokes too if he could. Donnie Bichon had already destroyed Pam's trust and made her suspicious of all men. But Marcus would have eventually won her if she hadn't called the sheriff's department. Stokes had wasted no opportunity to turn Pam against him, planting doubts in her mind at every turn.

Marcus often wondered what might have been had Pam not misconstrued his interest and called the sheriff's office. They could have had something nice together. He had pictured it a thousand times: the two of them living a quiet, suburban kind of life. Friends and lovers. Husband and wife.

In the last few months Marcus had developed a strong dislike and disrespect for the sheriff's office and officers. Except Annie. Annie wasn't like the rest of them. Her heart was pure. The politics of the system had yet to corrupt her sense of fairness.

Annie would look for the truth, and when she found it he would make her his.

Victor rose at midnight, as he always did. He hadn't slept well. Fragmented dreams had driven into his brain like

214

shards of stained glass. The colors disturbed him. Very red colors. *Red* like blood and *black* too. Dark *and* light. Light the color of urine.

The colors were too intense. Intensity was painful. Intensity could be very white or very red. White intensity came from soft and coolness; from certain feelings he couldn't name or describe; from specific visual images – semicolons and colons, phrases in parentheses, and horses. White intensity also came from a collection of precious words: *luminous, mystique, marble, running water.* He especially had to steel himself against the words. *Luminous* could produce such white intensity he would be rendered speechless and immobile.

And just a fine degree to the right of white intensity was red intensity. Like a circle with *Start* and *Stop* together. Very red intensity came from *heaviness*, pressure, the smell of cheddar cheese and of animal waste – but not human waste, even though humans were animals. *Homo sapiens.* Red words were *sluice* and *bunion* and sometimes *melon*, but not always. *Very* red words he couldn't verbalize, even in his own mind. He pictured them as objects he could allow himself only glimpses of. *Jagged, erect, slab, mucus.*

Very red intensity squeezed his brain and magnified his senses a hundredfold until the smallest sound was a piercing shriek and he could see and count each individual hair on a person's head and body. The sensory overload caused panic. Panic caused shutdown. Start and stop. Sound and silence.

His senses were full now, like water goblets lined up on a quivering, narrow ledge, the water moving, lapping at the rims and over them. *Mask*, he thought. Mask equaled *change* and sometimes *deception*, depending on red or white.

Victor stood in his room near the desk for a long time and listened to the fluorescent bulb in the lamp. Sizzle, hot *and* cold. An almost white sound. He felt time pass, felt the earth move in minute increments beneath his feet. His brain counted the passing moments by fractions until the

Magic Number. At that precise instant, he broke from his stillness and let himself out of his room.

The house was silent. Victor preferred silence with darkness. He moved more freely without the burden of sound or light. He went down the hall and stood at the door to his mother's hobby room. Mother forbade him access to the room, but when Mother was asleep her thoughts and wishes ceased to exist – like television, On and Off. He counted by fractions in his mind to the Magic Number and let himself into the room, where he turned on the small yellow light of the sewing machine.

Dress forms stood here and there like headless women garbed in the elaborate costumes Mother had made for past Carnivals. The forms made Victor uneasy. He turned away from them, turned to the wall where the masks were displayed. There were twenty-three, some small, some of smooth shiny fabric, some large, some covered with sequins, some stitched like needlepoint faces with a pro-truding penis where the nose should have been.

Victor chose his favorite and put it on. He liked the sensation it gave him inside, though he couldn't name the feeling. Mask equaled change. Change, transformation, *transmutation*. Pleased, he let himself out of the room, went down the stairs and out into the night.

21

Kay Eisner had learned to hate men at an early age, courtesy of an uncle who had found her too tempting as a seven-year-old. No man she'd known in the thirty years since had caused her to change her opinion. She scoffed at the book that claimed men were from Mars. Men were from hell, and how every woman on the planet didn't see it was beyond her. War was a bloody game played by men. Politics was a power game played by men. Crime was a cancer in society, perpetrated and spread predominantly by men. The prisons were overflowing with men. Rapists and killers prowled the streets.

It pained her to have to work for a man, but men ran the world, so what were her choices? Arnold Bouvier was her foreman, but every hand doing the dirty work gutting catfish in his plant belonged to a woman. They were working extra shifts and overtime these days, on account of Lent coming up. Catholics all over America would be stocking up on frozen fish.

Kay had worked the Saturday second shift, thinking all the while that the overtime pay would bring her that much closer to her dream of going into business for herself. She wanted to sell collectible dolls by mail order, and deal with as few men face-to-face as she could.

She double-checked the locks on her doors – front and back – before going into the bathroom. Her work clothes went immediately into a diaper bucket with water, detergent, and bleach to combat the stink of fish. She turned the shower as hot as she could stand it and scrubbed her skin with Yardley lavender soap. The room was thick with steam by the time the hot water ran out.

Kay cracked open the window to cool things off. She dried her curly hair with a threadbare towel, never looking

217

at herself in the mirror above the sink. She couldn't stand looking at the body that had betrayed her time and again throughout her life by attracting the attention of men.

Men were the scourge of the earth. She thought so no less than ten times a day. Thinking it now, she pulled on a shapeless nightshirt, went out of the bathroom and down the hall to her bedroom. She remembered the open bathroom window just as she lay down to sleep, her body aching with fatigue. She couldn't leave it. A rapist was prowling around the parish.

As if Kay had conjured him up from her nightmares, he emerged from the darkness of her closet as she started to rise. A demon in black, faceless, soundless. Terror cut through her like a spear. She screamed once before he struck her hard across the face and knocked her backward onto the bed. Twisting onto her stomach, she tried to pull herself across the mattress. But even as her instincts pushed her to escape, a fatalistic sense of inevitability filled her. The tears that came as he grabbed her by the hair were as much from hatred as from pain. Hate for the man about to rape her, and hate for herself. She wouldn't get away. She never had.

22

He remembered a woman. Or he had dreamed about a woman. Reality and its opposite floated around in his brain like the stuff in a Lava lamp. He groaned and shifted positions, sprawling on his belly. The rustling of the sheets was magnified to the sound of newspaper crumpling right next to his ear. That was when he remembered the booze – lots of it. He needed to pee.

A hand settled low on his back and a warm breath, stale with the smell of cigarettes, caressed his ear.

'Rise and whine, Donnie. You got some explaining to do.'

Fourcade.

Donnie bolted up and turned, twisting the sheet around his hips. He cracked his skull on the headboard and winced as pain bounced around inside his head.

'Jesus! Fuck! What the hell are you doing here?' he demanded. 'How'd you get in my house?'

Nick moved away from the bed, taking in the state of Donnie's bachelor habitat. Coming through the kitchen and living room he had surmised that Donnie had a cleaning woman, but not a cook. The kitchen garbage was full of frozen dinner cartons. A decorator had coordinated the town house so that it felt more like a hotel suite than a home. This had been a model to entice prospective buyers into the Quail Court condo development – until the unfortunate demise of Donnie's marital state. He had commandeered the model when he separated from Pam.

'That's nasty language for a Sunday morning, Tulane,' Nick said. 'What's the matter with you? You got no respect for the Sabbath?'

Donnie gaped at him, bug-eyed. 'You're a fucking lunatic! I'm calling the cops.'

He snatched the receiver off the phone on the night-stand. Nick stepped over and pressed the plunger down with his forefinger.

'Don't try my patience, Donnie. It ain't what it used to be.' He took the receiver away, recradled it, and sat down on the edge of the bed. 'Me, I wanna know what kind of game you're playing.'

'I don't know what the hell you're talking about.'

'I'm talking about you jerking Lindsay Faulkner's chain, telling her you gonna sell the realty. Telling her you got some big catfish on the hook down in New Orleans. That where you got the money to bail me out, Donnie?'

'No.'

''Cause that would have a very poetic irony about it. You kill your wife, collect the insurance, sell her business, use the money to bail out the cop that tried to kill the suspect.'

Donnie pressed the heels of his hands to his aching eyes. 'Jesus, I have told you and told you, I did *not* kill Pam. You know I didn't.'

'You're not wasting any time making a buck off her. Why didn't you tell me Friday about this pending deal?'

'Because it's none of your business. I have to take a piss.'

He threw back the covers and climbed out on the other side of the bed. He walked like a man who had fallen out of a moving car and rolled to a hard stop in the gutter. Black silk boxers hung low on his hips. He hadn't managed to take his socks off before succumbing to unconsciousness. They drooped around his ankles. The rest of his clothes lay where he'd dropped them as he'd peeled them off on his way to the bed.

Nick rose lazily and still beat him to the door of the master bath.

'You're dragging it low to the ground this morning, Tulane. Long night?'

'I had a few. I'm sure you can relate. Let me in the bathroom.'

'When we're through.'

220

'Fuck. Why'd I ever get hooked up with you?'

'That's what I wanna know,' Nick said. 'Who's your big money man, Donnie?'

He looked away and blew out a breath. He grimaced at the smell of himself as he inhaled – smoke, sweat, and sex. He wondered vaguely where the woman was. 'No one. I lied. It was a bluff. I told that little Cajun gal.'

'Uh-huh, and she's going over those phone records we pulled on you, Donnie,' he lied. 'She's gonna know ever'body you know by the time she's through.'

'I thought you were out of this, Fourcade. You're off the case. You're suspended. What do you care who I called or why?'

'I got my reasons.'

'You're insane.'

'So I hear people say. But, you know, it doesn't matter much to me, true or not. My existence is my perception, my perception is my reality. See how that works, Tulane? So, when I ask are you trying to swing a deal with Duval Marcotte, you need to answer me, because you're right here in my reality right now.'

Donnie closed his eyes again and shifted his weight from one foot to the other.

'We're gonna stand here 'til you wet yourself, Donnie. I want an answer.'

'I need cash,' he said with resignation. 'Lindsay wants to buy out Pam's share of the business. But Lindsay's a ball buster and she'd love nothing more than to screw me out of what she can. I want back the property Pam hid for me and I want every dime I can get out of Lindsay. I made up a little leverage, that's all.'

'You think she's stupid?' Nick said. 'You think she won't call your bluff?'

'I think she's a bitch and I'm not above doing something just to aggravate her.'

'You're just gonna piss her off, Donnie, same as you're

221

pissing me off. You think *I'm* stupid? I'll find out if what you're telling me is a lie.'

'I gotta see if I can withdraw that bail,' Donnie muttered up to the ceiling.

Nick patted his cheek as he stepped away from the door. 'Sorry, *cher*. That check's been cashed and the cat is outta the bag. Hope you don't live to regret it.'

'I already have,' Donnie said, ducking into the bathroom, penis in hand.

Annie turned the Jeep in at the drive to Marcus Renard's home. It was a pretty spot ... and a secluded one. She didn't like the second part, but she had made it clear to Renard over the phone that other people knew she was visiting him – a little insurance in case he was toying with the idea of dismembering her. She didn't tell him the person who knew she was coming here was Fourcade.

While she had been with Fourcade last night, forming their uneasy alliance, Renard had been calling her at home, leaving the message that Fourcade had paid him a visit earlier in the day. In calling, Renard had saved her from the job of formulating an excuse to see him.

'I couldn't think who else to turn to, Annie,' he'd said. 'The deputies wouldn't help. They'd sooner see that brute kill me. You're the only one I feel I can turn to.'

The idea, while it might have overjoyed Fourcade, gave Annie no comfort. She had told Fourcade she wouldn't play the role of bait, yet here she was. Assessing the suspect in his home environment, she told herself. She wanted to see Renard with his guard down. She wanted to see him interact with his family. But if Renard perceived this visit as a social call, then she was essentially bait whether she intended to be or not. Semantics. Perception was reality, Fourcade would say.

That son of a bitch. Why hadn't he told her he had come here? She didn't like the idea of him having a hidden agenda in all this.

The driveway broke free of the trees, and a lawn the size of a polo field stretched off to the left. The expanse was nothing fancy, just a close-cropped boundary meant to discourage wildlife from getting too near the house. She passed an old carriage shed that had been painted to match the house. Fifty yards farther into the property stood the home itself, graceful and simple, painted the color of old parchment with white trim and black shutters. She parked behind the Volvo and started toward the front gallery.

'Annie!'

Marcus came out, careful not to let the screen door slap shut behind him. More of the swelling had gone out of his face, but there was still no definition to his features. Most people would recoil from the sight of him, despite the fact that he was neatly dressed in crisp khakis and a green polo shirt.

'I'm so glad you've come.' He enunciated his words more clearly today, though it took an effort. He held his hands out toward her as if she were a dear distant cousin and might actually take hold of them. 'Of course, I was hoping you might have called me back last night. We were all so upset.'

'I got in late,' she said, noting the slight censure in his voice. 'By the sound of it, there was nothing to be done by that point.'

'I suppose not,' he conceded. 'The damage was done.'

'What damage?'

'The upset – to me, to my mother, most especially to my brother. It took hours to calm him. But we don't have to stand out here and discuss it. Please come in. I wish you could have accepted the invitation to dinner. It's been so long since we've entertained.'

'This isn't a social call, Mr Renard,' Annie reminded him, drawing the line clearly between them. She moved into the hall, took it in at a glance – forest green walls, a murky pastoral scene in a gilt frame, a brass umbrella stand. Victor Renard peered down at her between the white balusters of the second-floor landing, where he sat with his knees drawn up like a small child, as if he thought he could make himself invisible by compacting his frame.

Ignoring his brother, Marcus led the way through the dining room to the brick veranda that faced the bayou. 'It's such a lovely afternoon, I thought we could sit out.'

He pulled out a chair for her at the wrought iron table. Annie chose her own chair and settled herself, careful to adjust her jacket so that the tape recorder in the pocket didn't show. The recorder had been Fourcade's idea – order, actually. He wanted to know every word that was spoken between them, wanted to hear every nuance in Renard's voice. The tape would never be admissible in court, but if it gave them something to go on, it was worth the effort.

'So, you said Detective Fourcade violated the restraining order,' she began, taking out her notebook and pen.

'Well, not exactly.'

'Exactly what, then?'

'He was careful to stay back from the property line. But the fact that he came that near was upsetting to my family. We called the sheriff's office, but by the time the deputy arrived, Fourcade was gone and the man wouldn't so much as take a statement.' He dabbed at the corner of his mouth with a neatly folded handkerchief.

'If the detective didn't commit a crime, then there was no statement to take,' Annie said. 'Did Fourcade threaten you?'

'Not verbally.'

'Did he threaten you physically? Did he show a weapon?'

'No. But his presence was a perceived threat. Isn't that a part of the stalking law – perceived threats?'

The fact that he, of all people, would try to make use of the statute against stalking turned her stomach. It was all she could do to school her features into something like neutrality.

'That particular law leaves a great deal of room for interpretation,' she said. 'As you must be well aware by now, Mr Renard –'

'Marcus,' he corrected her. 'I'm aware that the authorities will bend any rule to suit them. These people have no respect for what's right. Except you, Annie. I was right about you, wasn't I? You're not like the others. You want the truth.'

'Everyone involved in the case wants the truth.'

'No. No, they don't,' he said, leaning forward. 'They had their minds made up from the first. Stokes and Fourcade came after me and no one else.'

'That's not true, Mr Renard. Other suspects were considered. You know they were. You were singled out by the process of elimination. We've been over this.'

'Yes, we have,' he said quietly, sitting back again. He studied her for a moment. His eyes were more visible today, like a pair of marbles set into dough. 'And you did state you believe in my guilt. If that's so, then why are you here, Annie? To try to trip me up? I don't think so. I don't think you'd bother, knowing nothing I say to you could be used against me. You have doubts. That's why you're here.'

'You claim you've been treated unfairly,' Annie said. 'If that's true, if the detectives have overlooked or ignored something that might exonerate you, why hasn't your own investigator – Mr Kudrow's investigator – cleared up these details for you?'

Marcus looked away. 'He's one man. My funds are limited.'

'What is it you think we should be looking at?'

'The husband, for one.'

'Mr Bichon has been thoroughly investigated.'

He changed tacks without argument. 'No real effort has been made to find the man who helped me get my car going that night.'

Annie consulted the notes she'd brought with her. 'The man whose name you didn't ask?'

'I wasn't thinking.'

'The man who was driving "some kind of dark truck"

225

with a license plate that "may have" included the letters *F* and *J*?'

'It was night. The truck was dirty. I had no reason to take note of the tags, anyway.'

'What little you gave us to go on was liberally put forth by the media, Mr Renard. No one came forward.'

'But did the sheriff's office *try* to find him? I don't think so. Fourcade never believed anything I told him. Can you imagine him wasting his time to check it out?'

'Detective Fourcade is a very thorough man,' Annie said. Fourcade also had tunnel vision when it came to Renard. He had been thorough in his efforts to prove Renard's guilt. Had he been as thorough in trying to corroborate the man's claim of innocence? 'I'll look into it, but there isn't much to go on.'

Renard let out a sigh of relief that seemed out of proportion with her offer. 'Thank you, Annie. I can't tell you how much it means to me to have you do this.'

'I told you, I don't expect anything to come of it.'

'That's not the point. Tea?' He reached for the pitcher that sat in the center of the table beside a pair of glasses and a small vase sprouting daffodils.

Annie accepted the drink, taking a moment between sips to look around the yard. Pony Bayou was a stone's throw away. Downstream it branched around a muddy island of willows and dewberry. Somewhere to the south, beyond the dense growth of woods where the spring birds were singing, was the house where Pam had died. Annie wondered if the burly fisherman sitting in his boat down by the fork realized that or if he might have come here because of it. People were strange that way.

Panic surged through her. Could the fisherman have been someone from the SO? What if Noblier had reinstated the surveillance? What if Sergeant Hooker had come to this spot on his day off in search of bass and *sac-a-lait*? If someone saw her with Renard, she was going to be way up shit creek.

'Got anything in that boathouse?' Nodding to a small, low shed of rusting corrugated metal that jutted out over the bayou, she shifted the position of her chair, turning her back more squarely to the fisherman.

'An old bass boat. My brother likes to explore the bayou. He's something of a nature buff. Aren't you, Victor?'

Victor stepped out from behind a swath of drapery inside the French door Marcus had left cracked open. There was no guilt on his face, no embarrassment at having been caught spying. He stared at Annie, turning his body sideways, as if that might somehow fool her into thinking he wasn't looking at her.

'Victor,' Marcus said, rising gingerly, 'this is Annie Broussard. Annie saved my life.'

'I wish you wouldn't keep saying that,' Annie muttered.

'Why? Because you're modest or because you wish you hadn't?'

'I was doing my job.'

Victor sidled toward the table for a better look at her. He was dressed in pants an inch too short and a plaid sport shirt buttoned to the throat. He resembled Marcus in his normal, unremarkable state: plain features, fine brown hair neatly combed. Annie had seen him around town from time to time, always in the company of either Marcus or his mother. He held himself too carefully and stood too close to people in lines, as if his sense of space and the physical world were distorted.

'It's nice to meet you, Victor.'

He squinted in suspicion. 'Good day.' He glanced at Marcus. 'Mask, no mask. Sound and sound alike. *Mimus polyglottos*. Mockingbird. No. *No*.' He shook his head. '*Dumetella carolinensis*. *Suggest* the songs of other birds.'

'What does that mean?' Annie asked.

Marcus attempted a bland smile. 'Probably that you remind him of someone. Or more precisely, that you resemble someone you aren't.'

227

Victor rocked himself a little, muttering, 'Red *and* white. Now *and* then.'

'Victor, why don't you go get your binoculars?' Marcus suggested. 'The woods are full of birds today.'

Victor cast a nervous look over his shoulder at Annie. 'Change, *interchange*, mutate. One and one. Red *and* white.'

He held himself still for a moment, as if waiting for some silent signal, then hurried back into the house.

'I expect he sees a resemblance between you and Pam,' Marcus said.

'Did he know her?'

'They met at the office once or twice. Victor periodically expresses a curiosity in my work. And of course he saw her picture in the papers after ... He reads three newspapers every day, cover to cover, every word. Impressive until you realize he'll be held in thrall by the sight of a semicolon while the bombing of the federal building in Oklahoma City meant nothing whatsoever to him.'

'It must be difficult to deal with his ... condition,' Annie said.

Marcus looked to the open door and the empty dining room beyond. 'Our cross to bear, my mother says. Of course, she takes great satisfaction from having to shoulder the load.' He turned back toward Annie with another wan smile. 'Can't pick your relatives. Do you have family here, Annie?'

'In a manner of speaking,' she said evasively. 'It's a long story.'

'Family stories always are. Look at Pam's daughter. What a family story she'll have, poor little thing. What will become of her grandfather?'

'You'd have to ask the DA,' she said, though she thought she could give an accurate guess as to what would become of Hunter Davidson: nothing much. The outcry against his arrest had been considerable. Pritchett would never risk the wrath of his constituents by pressing for a trial. A deal would likely be cut quickly and quietly – maybe already had

228

been – and Hunter Davidson would be doing community service for his attempted sin.

'He tried to kill me,' Renard said with indignation. 'The media is treating him like a celebrity.'

'Yeah. There's a lot of that going around. You're not a well-liked man, Mr Renard.'

'Marcus,' he corrected her. 'You're at least civil to me. I'd like to pretend we're friends, Annie.'

The emotion in his eyes was soft and vulnerable. Annie tried to imagine what had been in those eyes that black November night when he had plunged a knife into Pam Bichon.

'Considering what happened to your last "friend," I don't think that's a very good idea, Mr Renard.'

He turned his head as quickly as if she had slapped him, and blinked away tears, pretending to focus on the fisherman down the bayou.

'I would never have hurt Pam,' he said. 'I've told you that, Annie. That remark was deliberately hurtful to me. I expected better from you.'

He wanted her contrition. He wanted her to give him another inch of control, the way he had when he had asked to use her name. A little thing on the surface, but the psychological sleight of hand was smooth and sinister. Or she was blowing it out of proportion and giving this man more credit than he deserved.

'It's just healthy caution on my part,' she said. 'I don't know you.'

'I couldn't hurt you, Annie.' He looked at her once again with his watery hazel eyes. 'You saved my life. In certain Eastern cultures I would give you my life in return.'

'Yeah, well, this is South Lou'siana. A simple thanks is sufficient.'

'Hardly. I know you've been suffering because of what you did. I know what it is to be persecuted, Annie. We have that in common.'

'Can we move on?' Annie said. The intensity in his

expression unnerved her, as if he had already determined that their lives would now be intertwined into eternity. Was this how a fixation began? As a misunderstanding of commitment? Had it been this way between him and Pam? Between him and his now-dead girlfriend from Baton Rouge?

'No offense,' she prefaced, 'but you have to admit you have a bad track record. You wanted to be involved with Pam, and now she's dead. You were involved with Elaine Ingram back in Baton Rouge, and she's dead.'

'Elaine's death was a terrible accident.'

'But you can see how it might give pause. There's a rumor that she was going to break off your relationship.'

'That's not true,' he insisted. 'Elaine could never leave me. She loved me.'

Could never, not *would* never. The choice of words was telling. Not: Elaine would never leave him of her own accord. But: Elaine *could* never leave him if he wouldn't allow it. Marcus Renard wouldn't have been the first man to use the 'if I can't have her, no one will' rationale. It was common thinking among simple obsessionals.

Doll Renard chose that moment to come onto the terrace. She wore a dotted polyester dress twenty years out of date and an enormous kitchen apron. The ties wrapped around her twice. She was thin in the same way Richard Kudrow was thin – as if her body had burned away from within, leaving bone and tough sinew. She offered no smile of welcome. Her mouth was a thin slash in her narrow face.

Annie thought she saw Marcus wince. She rose and extended her hand.

'Annie Broussard, sheriff's office. Sorry to disturb your Sunday, Mrs Renard.'

Doll sniffed, grudgingly offering a limp hand that collapsed in Annie's like a pouch of twigs. 'Our Sunday is the least of what you people have disturbed.'

Marcus rolled his eyes. 'Mother, please. Annie isn't like the others.'

'Well, *you* wouldn't think so,' Doll muttered.

'She's going to be looking into some things that could help prove my innocence. She saved my life, for heaven's sake. Twice.'

'I was just doing my job,' Annie pointed out. 'I *am* just doing my job.'

Doll arched a penciled-on brow and clucked her tongue. 'You've managed to misread the situation yet again, Marcus.'

He looked away from his mother, his color darkening, tension crackled in the air around him. Annie watched the exchange, thinking maybe she was better off not having any blood relatives. Her memories of her mother were soft and quiet. Better memories than a bitter reality.

'Well,' Doll Renard went on, 'it's about time the sheriff's office did *something* for us. Our lawyer will be filing suit, you know, for all the pain and anguish we've been caused.'

'Mother, perhaps you could try not to alienate the one person willing to help us.'

She looked at him as if he'd called her a filthy name. 'I have every right to state my feelings. We've been treated worse than common trash through all of this, while that Bichon woman is held up like some kind of saint. And now her father – all the world's calling him a martyred hero for trying to murder you. He belongs in jail. I certainly hope the district attorney keeps him there.'

'I really should be going,' Annie said, gathering her file and notebook. 'I'll see what I can find out on that truck.'

'I'll walk you to your car.' Marcus scraped his chair back and sent his mother a venomous look.

He waited until they were along the end of the house before he spoke again.

'I wish you could have stayed longer.'

'Did you have something more to say pertinent to the case?'

'Well – ah – I don't know,' he stammered. 'I don't know what questions you might have asked.'

'The truth isn't dependent on what questions I ask,' Annie said. 'The truth is what I'm after here, Mr. Renard. I'm not out to prove your innocence, and I certainly don't want you telling people that I am. In fact, I wish you wouldn't mention me at all. I've got trouble enough as it is.'

He made a show of drawing a fingertip across his mouth. 'My lips are sealed. It'll be our secret.' He seemed to like that idea too well. 'Thank you, Annie.'

'There's no need. Really.'

He opened the door of the Jeep, and she climbed in. As she backed up to turn around, he leaned against his Volvo. The successful young architect at leisure. *He's a murderer*, she thought, *and he wants to be my friend.*

A glint of reflected sunlight caught her eye and she looked up at the second story of the Renard home, where Victor stood in one window, looking down on her with binoculars.

'Man, y'all make the Addams family look like Ozzie and Harriet,' she said under her breath.

She thought about that as she drove north and west through the flat sugarcane country. Behind the face of every killer was the accumulated by-product of his upbringing, his history, his experiences. All of those things went to shape the individual and guide him onto a path. It wasn't a stretch to add up those factors in Renard's life and get the psychopathology Fourcade had spoken about. The portrait of a serial killer.

Marcus Renard wanted to be her friend. A shiver ran down her back.

She flicked on the radio and turned it up over the static of the scanner.

'... and I just think all these crimes, these rapes and all, are a backlash against the women's lib.'

'Are you saying women essentially ask to be raped by taking nontraditional roles?'

'I'm sayin' we should know our place. That's what I'm sayin'.'

'Okay, Ruth in Youngsville. You're on KJUN, all talk all the time. In light of last night's reported rape of a Luck woman, our topic is violence against women.'

Another rape. Since the Bichon murder and the resurrected tales of the Bayou Strangler, every woman in the parish was living in a heightened state of fear. Rich hunting grounds for a certain kind of sexual predator. That was the rush for a rapist – his victim's fear. He fed on it like a narcotic.

The questions came to Annie automatically. How old was the victim? Where and how was she attacked? Did she have anything in common with Jennifer Nolan? Had the rapist followed the same MO? Were they now looking at a serial rapist? Who had caught the case? Stokes, she supposed, because of the possible tie to the Nolan rape. That was what he needed – another hot case to distract him from the Bichon homicide investigation.

The countryside began to give way to small acreages interspersed with the odd dilapidated trailer house, then the new western developments outside of town. The only L. Faulkner listed in the phone book lived on Cheval Court in the Quail Run development. Annie slowed the Jeep to a crawl, checking numbers on mailboxes.

The neighborhood was maybe four years old, but had been strategically planned to include plenty of large trees that had stood on this land for a hundred years or more, giving the area a sense of tradition. Pam Bichon had lived just a stone's throw from here on Quail Drive. Faulkner's home was a neat redbrick Caribbean colonial with ivory trim and overflowing planters on the front step.

Annie pulled in the drive and parked alongside a red Miata convertible with expired tags. She hadn't called ahead, hadn't wanted to give Lindsay Faulkner the chance to say no. The woman had put her guard up. The best plan would be to duck under it.

No one answered the doorbell. A section of the home's interior was visible through the sidelights that flanked the

233

door. The house looked open, airy, inviting. A huge fern squatted in a pot in the foyer. A cat tiptoed along the edge of the kitchen island. Beyond the island a sliding glass door offered access to a terrace.

The lingering aroma of grilled meat hooked Annie's nose before she turned the corner to the back side of the house. Whitney Houston's testimonial about all the man she'd ever need floated out the speakers of a boom box, punctuated by a woman's throaty laughter.

Lindsay Faulkner sat at a glass-topped patio table, her hair swept back in a ponytail. A striking redhead in tortoiseshell shades came out through the patio doors with a Diet Pepsi in each hand. The smile on Faulkner's face dropped as she caught sight of Annie.

'I'm sorry to interrupt, Ms Faulkner. I had a couple more questions, if you don't mind,' Annie said, trying to resist the urge to smooth the wrinkles from her blazer. Faulkner and her companion looked crisp and sporty, the kind of people who never perspired.

'I do mind, Detective. I thought I made myself clear yesterday. I'd rather not deal with you.'

'I'm sorry you feel that way, since we both want the same thing.'

'Detective?' the redhead said. She set the sodas on the table and settled herself in her chair with casual grace, a wry smile pulling at one corner of a perfectly painted mouth. 'What have you done now, Lindsay?'

'She's here about Pam,' Faulkner said, never taking her eyes off Annie. 'She's the one I was telling you about.'

'Oh.' The redhead frowned and gave Annie the once-over, a condescending glance intended to belittle.

'If I have to deal with you people at all,' Faulkner said, 'then I'd sooner deal with Detective Stokes. He's the one I've dealt with all along.'

'We're on the same side, Ms Faulkner,' Annie said, undaunted. 'I want to see Pam's murderer punished.'

'You could have let that happen the other night.'

'Within the system,' Annie specified. 'You can help make that happen.'

Faulkner looked away and sighed sharply through her slim patrician nose.

Annie helped herself to a chair, wanting to give the impression she was comfortable and in no hurry to leave. 'How well do you know Marcus Renard?'

'What kind of question is that?'

'Did you socialize?'

'Me, personally?'

'He claims you went out together a couple of times. Is that true?'

She gave a humorless laugh, obviously insulted. 'I don't believe this. Are you asking if I *dated* that sick worm?'

Annie blinked innocently and waited.

'We went out in a group from time to time – people from his office, people from mine.'

'But never one-on-one?'

Faulkner flicked a glance at the redhead. 'He's not my type. What's the point of this, Detective?'

'It's Deputy,' Annie clarified at last. 'I just want a clear picture of y'all's relationship.'

'I didn't have a "relationship" with Renard,' she said hotly. 'In his sick mind, maybe. What –'

She stopped suddenly. Annie could all but see the thought strike her – that Renard could have fixed on her as easily as on Pam. Judging by the shade of guilt that passed across her face, it wasn't the first time she had considered her good fortune at her friend's expense. She passed a hand across her forehead as if trying to wipe the thought away.

'Pam was too sweet,' she said softly. 'She didn't know how to discourage men. She never wanted to hurt anyone's feelings.'

'I'm curious about something else,' Annie said. 'Donnie was making noise about challenging Pam for custody of Josie, but I can't see that he had any grounds. Was there something? Another man, maybe?'

Faulkner looked down at her hands on the tabletop and picked at an imagined cuticle flaw. 'No.'

'She wasn't seeing anyone.'

'No.'

'Then why would Donnie think –'

'Donnie is a fool. If you haven't figured that out by now, then you must be one, too. He thought he could paint Pam as a bad mother because she sometimes worked nights and met with male clients for drinks and dinner, as if the realty was just a front for a personal dating service. The idiot. It was ridiculous. He was grasping at straws. He would have used the stalking against her if he could have.'

'Did Pam take him seriously?'

'We're talking about custody of her child. Of course she took him seriously. I don't see what this has to do with Renard.'

'He says Pam told him she didn't dare date until the divorce went through because she was afraid of what Donnie might do.'

'Yes, well, it turned out it wasn't Donnie she needed to be afraid of, was it?'

'You said she had a hard time discouraging men who were interested in her. Were there many sniffing around?'

Faulkner pressed two fingers against her right temple. 'I've been over all this with Detective Stokes. Pam had that girl-next-door quality. Men liked to flirt with her. It was reflexive. My God, even Stokes did it. It didn't mean anything.'

Annie wanted to ask if it hadn't meant anything because Pam was no longer interested in men. If Pam and Lindsay Faulkner had become partners beyond the office and Donnie found out, he certainly would have tried to use it in the divorce. That kind of discovery – the ultimate insult to masculinity – could have pushed a man on the edge *over* the edge. A motive that applied to Renard as easily as to Donnie.

She wanted to ask. Fourcade would have asked. Blunt,

straight out. *Were you and Pam lovers?* But Annie held her tongue. She couldn't afford to piss off Lindsay Faulkner any more than she already had. If Faulkner complained about her to the sheriff or to Stokes, she'd be pulling the graveyard shift in detox for the rest of her broken career.

She pushed her chair back and rose slowly, pulling a business card from the pocket of her jacket. She had scratched out the phone number for the sheriff's office and replaced it with her home phone. She slid the card across the table toward Faulkner. 'If you think of anything else that might be helpful, I'd appreciate it if you'd call me. Thank you for your time.'

She turned to the redhead. 'I'd get those tags renewed on the Miata if I were you. It's a nasty fine.'

Out in the Jeep, Annie sat for a moment, staring at the house and trying to glean something useful from the conversation. More what-ifs. More maybes. Stokes and Fourcade had been over this ground enough to wear it smooth. What did she think she was going to find?

The truth, the key, the missing piece that would tie everything together. It was here in the maze somewhere, half hidden beneath some rock they hadn't quite over-turned, lurking amid the lies and dead ends. Someone had to find it, and if she worked hard enough, looked long enough, dug a little deeper, she would be that someone.

23

The Voodoo Lounge had come into being as the indirect result of a gruesome murder, a fact that attracted the local cops in a way no other bar could. For years the place had been known as Frenchie's Landing, the hangout of farmhands and factory workers, blue-collars and rednecks. It was known for boiled crawfish, cold beer, loud Cajun music, and the occasional brawl. Still known for all of those things, the place had changed ownership in the fall of 1993, some months after the murder of Annick Delahoussaye-Gerrard at the hands of the Bayou Strangler. Worn-out with grief, Frenchie Delahoussaye and his wife had sold out to local musician and sometime bartender Leonce Comeau.

The cops had started hanging out there immediately after the murder, a show of respect and associated guilt that had quickly turned into routine. The habit lived on.

The parking lot was two-thirds full. The building stood on the bank of the bayou, raised off the ground on a sturdy set of stilts for times when the bayou rushed nearer. A new gallery was under construction around three sides of the building. Loud rocking zydeco music blasted through the walls, the volume rising as the screen door swung open and a pair of couples descended the steps, laughing.

Nick let himself in, walking past the framed photographs of celebrities and pseudocelebrities that had come here over the last four years to soak up the atmosphere. He took the place in at a glance. The house band, led by the bar's owner, belted out Zachary Richard's 'Ma Petite Fille Est Gone', Comeau contorting his face and body like a man with a neurological disorder. The dance floor was swarming with couples young and old bouncing and swinging to the infectious beat. Smoke hung in the air over the bar and tables. The smell of frying fish and gumbo was like a heavy perfume.

Stokes was in his usual spot, standing at the corner of the bar that afforded a view of the place and all the women in it. He wore a gray mechanic's shirt from a Texaco station with the name LYLE on a patch over the pocket. His porkpie hat perched on the back of his head like a mutant yarmulke. He caught sight of Nick and raised his glass.

'Hey, brothers, if it ain't our tarnished comrade!' he called, his square smile flashing bright in the center of his goatee. 'Nicky! Hey, man, you decide to go social or something?'

Nick wove his way between patrons, tolerating the slaps on the back that came from two different cops whose names he couldn't have said on pain of death. He stepped around a waitress with a tight T-shirt and inviting smile as if she were a post set into the floor.

Stokes shook his head at the wasted opportunity. He kissed the cheek of the bleached blonde on the stool next to him and gave her ass a farewell squeeze.

'Hey, sugar, how 'bout you go powder that pretty nose and let my man Nicky here take a load off. He's a legend, don'tcha know.'

The blonde slid down off the stool, letting her breasts graze Nick's arm. 'Hope you're back on the job soon, Detective.'

Stokes elbowed him as the woman walked away, her ass packed into a pair of jeans a size too small for comfort, just right for lust. 'That Valerie. Man, that girl's some piece of poontang, let me tell you. Got a pussy like a Vise-Grip. If I'm lyin', I'm dyin'. You ever done her?'

'I don't even know her,' Nick said with strained patience.

'She's Noblier's secretary, for Christ's sake. Hot for cops. Man, Nicky, sometimes I swear your hormones have gone dormant,' he declared with disgust. 'You could have your pick of the chicks in this joint, you know.'

Ignoring the vacant stool, Nick leaned against the bar,

ordered a beer, and lit a cigarette. He didn't give a shit about Stokes's assessment of his sexual appetites. He didn't believe in sex as a casual pastime. There needed to be meaning, significance, intensity. But he made no effort to explain this to Stokes.

Up on the stage, the band had announced a break, dropping the decibel level in the bar to something slightly more conducive to conversation. Danny Collett and the Louisiana Swamp Cats blared out of the juke up front. Half the dancers didn't bother to leave the floor.

'You missing the job?' Stokes asked. He'd had a few. There was a vagueness in his pale eyes, an artificial glow on his cheeks.

'Some.'

'Gus say when he's bringing you back?'

'Depends on whether or not I take the big vacation to Angola.'

Stokes shook his head. 'That bitch Broussard. There's a chick more trouble than she's worth. I been thinking on that lesbian thing with her, and I don't see it. I think she just needs her pump primed, you know what I'm saying?'

Nick looked right at him. 'Quit ragging on Broussard. She stood up and did what she had to do. That took balls.'

Stokes's eyes popped. 'What's the matter with you, man? She put your dick in the wringer –'

'*I* put my dick in the wringer. She just happened to be there at the time.'

Stokes gave a snort. 'You're singing a new tune. What's up with that?' A sly look swept across his face. He leaned closer, stroking his goatee. 'Maybe you got to looking and decided you wanna do the honors for her, huh? Give her an attitude adjustment with the old joystick? There's a challenge to rise to, if you know what I mean.'

'You know, Chaz, they say a mind is a terrible thing to waste,' Nick said. He pulled on his cigarette and exhaled twin jet streams through his nose. 'You been using yours at all lately or have you turned over all the duties to that piece of meat hanging between your legs?'

'I alternate between the two. Christ, who put the bug up your ass tonight?'

'Ah, this one's been there for a few days, *mon ami*, and I'm still not sure where it came from. Maybe you could help me with that, no?'

'Maybe. If I knew what the hell you're talking about.'

Nick leaned a little closer. 'Let's go take us a little walk in the night air, Chaz. We'll chat.'

Stokes forced an apologetic grin. 'Hey, Nicky, I got an agenda here tonight, man. I'll swing by tomorrow. We'll talk a blue streak. But tonight –'

Nick stepped in close and caught hold of his pride and joy in a crushing fist. 'Alternate, Chaz,' he ordered, his voice a low growl. 'You're getting on my nerves.'

As he let go, Stokes fell back a step, his face slack and pale with astonishment. He sucked in a gasp and shook himself like a wet cat, glancing around for witnesses. Life was moving on for everyone else in the bar. Fourcade's move had been too slick to draw notice.

'Fuckin' *A*!' he exclaimed in an outraged whisper. 'What the hell's wrong with you, man? You can't do that! You just grab my willy and give it a yank? What the fuck's wrong with you? You can't do that to a brother!'

Nick took a swig of Jax and wiped his mouth with the back of his hand. 'I just did it. Now that I got your attention, let's go get some air.'

He headed for a side door and Stokes moved with him, hesitant, wary, petulant. They stepped out onto the half-finished gallery where a sawhorse and a KEEP OUT! sign blocked the way to the bayou side of the building. Nick ignored the warning.

The gallery facing the bayou had no railing at this point in the construction. The drop was about twelve feet. Enough for the average drunk to fall and break his neck. Nick stepped to the edge of the platform and stood with his hands on his hips, thinking *calm, center*. Force was a tool of surprise in dealing with Stokes. Something to knock him off balance. A tool to be used sparingly, carefully. His goal was truth.

Still agitated, Stokes paced back and forth. 'Man, you are fuckin' crazy, grabbing my dick. What goes through that head of yours, Nick? Jesus!'

'Get over it.'

Nick lit another cigarette and stared out at the bayou. The moon shone down on half a dozen pontoon houseboats moored down the way, weekend retreats for people from town and from as far away as Lafayette. There were no lights in the windows tonight.

The music from inside the bar came through the wall in a muddled bass vibration. If he blocked it from his mind and focused, he could just hear the chorus of frog song and the slap and splash of a fish breaking the water. Lightning cracked the sky to the east – a storm sucking up along the Mississippi from the Gulf. A distant storm.

He thought of Marcotte. The distant storm.

'So why ain't you bending my ear, pard?' Stokes said, calming down. He propped a shoulder against a support post and crossed his arms over his chest. 'You're the one wanted to chat.'

'I heard there was another rape.'

'Yeah. So?'

'You catch it?'

'Yeah, I caught it. Looks like it's the same sicko did that Nolan woman the other night. Broke in about one A.M., knocked her around, tied her up, raped her, made her take a shower after. He's a smart son of a bitch, I'll give him that. We got diddly-squat to go on.'

'No semen?'

'Nope. He's taking it with him one way or another. Probably uses a condom. Maybe the lab'll find some latex residue on one of the swabs, but big fuckin' deal, you know? What'll that prove? He prefers Trojans?'

'He wear a mask?'

'Yeah. Spooked the shit out of these women, that mask did. Shades of the Bayou Strangler and all that crap.'

'And Pam Bichon.'

'And Bichon,' he conceded. 'Confuses the issue, you know what I'm saying? The mask was Renard's thing. So if Renard ain't this rapist, then is this rapist the one did Pam Bichon, folks wanna know. People are so fuckin' stupid. I mean, it's all over the news about that mask Renard left on Pam. This guy's an opportunist, that's all.'

'Who was the woman?'

'Kay Eisner. Mid-thirties, single, lives over near Devereaux, works at a catfish plant up in Henderson. What's your interest in all this?' he asked, fishing a cigarette out of the shirt pocket beneath the LYLE patch. 'I was you, Nicky, I'd be spending my free time a little better.'

'Just curious,' Nick said. He dropped his cigarette butt on the floorboards, ground it out with the toe of his boot.

Inside the bar, the band had come back onstage. Leonce Comeau wailed the intro to 'Snake Bite Love'. The drummer pounded the opening and the rest of the band jumped in at a run.

'The past overshadows the present foreshadows the future.'

Stokes blinked at him like a man nodding off in church. 'Nicky, man, I ain't drunk enough for philosophy.'

'We all got a past we drag around behind us,' Nick said. 'Sometimes it sneaks up and bites our ass.'

The shift in the tension between them was subtle, but there. A tightening of muscles. A heightened awareness. Nick watched Stokes's eyes like a poker player.

'What are you saying, Nicky?' Stokes said softly.

Nick let the silence hang, waited.

'I hear teeth snapping behind me,' he said. 'I feel that shadow on my back.' He stepped closer. 'All of a sudden a name is turning up again and again like a damn bad penny. Me, I find myself in a bad position and I keep on hearing

243

that name. And I'm thinking there's no such thing as coincidence.'

'What name?'

'Duval Marcotte.'

Stokes didn't blink.

Anticipation tightened in Nick's belly like a knot. What did he want? The flash of recognition? For Stokes to be guilty? For another cop to have betrayed him? He wanted Marcotte. After all this time, after all the work to put it behind him, he wanted Marcotte – even at the cost of another man's honor. The realization was as heavy as stone, hard and abrasive against his conscience.

'Is he in this thing, Chaz?' he asked. 'It would have been a simple errand, piece a' cake. Get me to Laveau's, fill me up with liquor and ideas, point me in the right direction, see if I go off like a cocked pistol. Easy money, and hell, he's got plenty of it.'

The expression on Stokes's face softened and he laughed to himself. He looked out toward the bayou and beyond, where the storm was an eerie glow inside black clouds.

'Man, Nicky,' he whispered, shaking his head. 'You are one crazy motherfucker. Who the hell is Duval Marcotte?'

'Truth, Chaz,' Nick said. 'Truth, or this time I walk away with your cock in my pocket.'

'Never heard of him,' Stokes murmured. 'If I'm lyin', I'm dyin'.'

Annie's eyes crossed and her head bobbed. The autopsy report blurred and came back into focus. She rubbed a hand over her face, swept the straggling tendrils of hair behind her ears, and consulted her watch. Fourcade had no clocks. Fourcade was one with time, she supposed – or he didn't believe in the concept of time, or God knew what philosophy he embraced regarding the subject. It was after midnight.

She had been sitting at the big table in his study four hours. Fourcade had not made an appearance. He had entrusted her with a key to the house and ordered her to study everything he had on the case. She asked if there would be a quiz. He wasn't amused.

Where he was was anyone's guess. Annie told herself she was grateful for his absence. And still she kind of missed his blunt interrogation, his complex insights, and odd mystic philosophies.

'My Lord, you must be getting desperate for friends, girl,' she muttered at the thought.

It was probably true. She'd been shut out at work, cut off from A.J. by necessity. People she didn't even know were insulting her on her answering machine. She was a social creature – by necessity, she sometimes thought. There was a small sense of aloneness in her that dated back to childhood, a feeling she had always feared reflected her mother's detachment, and so she sought out the company of others in an attempt to keep the aloneness from growing and swallowing her whole.

She wondered if maybe that was what had happened to Fourcade.

Needing to move, Annie forced herself up from the chair and stretched. She made a circuit of the loft, checking out the bookcases, looking out the dormer windows, wandering into the small corner Fourcade had set aside for sleeping and changing clothes. There were no personal items on the dresser, not even the cast-off miscellany from pockets. Though the temptation was certainly there, she made no move to open a drawer. She would never have invaded someone's privacy without a warrant. Besides, she knew without looking that every sock, every T-shirt, would be folded neatly and arranged in an orderly manner. The bed was made military-style, the covers tight enough to bounce quarters on.

She wondered what he looked like sleeping. Did he attack sleep with the same ferocious focus as he attacked everything else in his life? Or did unconsciousness soften the hard edges?

'Thinking of spending the night, *chère*?'

Annie spun around at the sound of his voice. Fourcade stood well inside the room, hands on his hips, one leg cocked. She hadn't heard so much as the creak of a hinge or a step on the stairs.

'Don't you know better than to sneak up on a woman when there's a rapist out running around loose?' she demanded. 'I could have shot you.'

He discounted the possibility without comment.

'I was just stretching my legs,' she said, walking away from the bed, not wanting him to imagine she had been thinking about him in it. 'Where've you been? Renard's?'

'Why would I go there?' he said, his tone flat.

'Let's put that past tense,' Annie suggested. 'Why *did* you go there? My God, what were you thinking? He could have had you thrown back in jail.'

'How's that? You weren't on duty.'

Annie shook her head. 'Don't pull that attitude with me, thinking I'll back off. You already know I'm not repentant for running you in, other than that it's made my life a living hell. You must have come here straight from his house last night and you didn't say a word to me.'

'There was nothing to say. I was out in the boat. I ended up in the neighborhood. I didn't cross the property line. I didn't touch him. I didn't threaten him. In fact, *he* approached me.'

'And you didn't think any of this would be of interest to me, *partner*?'

'The encounter was irrelevant,' he said, moving away, dismissing Annie and her argument. She wanted to kick him.

'It's relevant in that you didn't share it with me.' She pursued him to the long table where she had been studying. 'If we're partners, we're partners. There's an expectation of trust, and you've already managed to break it.'

246

He sighed heavily. 'All right. Point taken. I should have told you. Can we move on?'

It was on the tip of Annie's tongue to demand an apology, but she knew Fourcade would somehow make her feel like a fool in the end.

He had turned his attention to the papers on the table. He picked up the discarded wrapper of a Butterfinger from among the files, frowned at it, and tossed it in the trash. 'What'd you learn tonight, 'Toinette?'

'That I probably need reading glasses, but I'm too vain to go to the eye doctor,' Annie said dryly.

He looked at her sideways.

'Joke,' she stated. 'A wry remark intended to lighten the moment.'

He turned back to the statements and lab reports.

She sighed and rubbed the small of her back with both hands. 'I learned that no fewer than a dozen people swore to Donnie's level of intoxication the night of the murder – some of them friends of his, some not. Doesn't necessarily let him off the hook.

'I learned there was no semen found during the autopsy. The mutilation made it difficult to find out if she'd been raped, but then again, it just may not have been there. That makes me nervous.'

'Why is that?'

'This jerk running around out there now. I responded to the first call – Jennifer Nolan. No semen and the guy was wearing a Mardi Gras mask. Pam Bichon: no semen and a Mardi Gras mask left behind.'

'Copycat,' Fourcade said. 'The mask was common knowledge.'

'And he also knew not to come?'

'There's a certain rate of dysfunction among rapists. Maybe he couldn't come. Maybe he used a rubber. The cases are unrelated.'

'That's what I like about you, Nick,' Annie said sarcastically. 'You're so open-minded.'

247

'Don't become distracted by irrelevant external incidents.'

'Irrelevant? How is a serial rapist not relevant?'

'From what I've heard, there are more differences than similarities in the cases. One's a killer, one's a rapist. The rape victims were tied up. Pam was nailed down – thank Christ we managed to keep that out of the papers. The rape victims were attacked in their homes, Pam was not. Pam Bichon was stalked, harassed. Were the others? It's simple, sugar: Marcus Renard killed Pam Bichon, and someone else raped these women. You better make up your mind 'bout which is your focus.'

'My focus is the truth,' Annie said. 'It's not my job to draw conclusions – or yours, Detective.'

'You saw Renard today,' he said, dismissing her argument and her point once again.

Annie gritted her teeth in frustration. 'Yes. He left a message on my answering machine last night, asking for my assistance in dealing with your little chance encounter. It seems the deputy who answered the call yesterday was unsympathetic.'

'Where's the tape?'

She dug the cassette recorder out of her purse, turned the volume up, and set the machine on the table. Fourcade stared down at the plastic rectangle as if he could see Renard in it. He seemed to listen without breathing or blinking. When it was done, he nodded and turned toward her.

'Impressions?'

'He's convinced himself he's innocent.'

'Persecution complex. Nothing is his fault. Everybody's picking on him.'

'He's also convinced himself I'm his friend.'

'Good. That's what we want.'

'That's what *you* want,' she muttered behind his back. 'As a family they'd make great characters on *The Twilight Zone*.'

'He hates his mother, resents his brother. Feels shackled

248

to the both of them. This guy's head is a psychological pressure cooker full of snakes.'

She couldn't argue with Fourcade's diagnosis. It was his vehemence that bothered her.

'What he said about that truck – the guy that supposedly helped him with his car that night,' she said. 'Did you check it out?'

'Ran the partial plate through DVM. Got a list of seventy-two dark-colored trucks. None of the owners helped a stranded motorist that night.' He gave her a sharp look. 'What you think, *chère* – you think I don't do my job?'

Annie chose her words carefully. 'I think your focus was proving Renard's guilt, not verifying his alibi.'

'I do the job,' he said tightly. 'I want my arrests to stand up in court. I do the job. I did it here. I don't just *think* Renard is guilty. He *is* guilty.'

'What about New Orleans?' The words were out before she could consider the folly of pushing him. The necessity of trusting him and the reluctance to trust him were issues too important to ignore, especially after his sin of omission regarding his visit to Renard.

'What about it?'

'You thought you knew who did the Candi Parmantel murder –'

'I did.'

'The charges against Allan Zander were dismissed.'

'That doesn't make him innocent, sugar.' He strode over to a neat stack of files on a corner of the table, digging down to pull one out. 'Here,' he said, thrusting it at her. 'The DMV list. Call 'em yourself if you think I'm a liar.'

'I never said I thought you were a liar,' Annie mumbled, peeking inside the cover. 'I just need to know you didn't run through this case with blinders on, that's all.'

'Renard, he winning you over, *chère*?' he asked sardonically. 'Maybe that's what this is all about, huh? He thinks you're pretty. He thinks you're cute. He thinks you'll help him. Good. That's just what I want him to think. Just don't *you* believe it.'

She *was* pretty, Nick thought, letting that simple truth penetrate his temper. Even with her hair a mess and a cardigan two sizes too big swallowing her up. There was an earnest quality to her that the job would eventually rub off. Not naïveté, but the next thing to it: idealism. The thing that made a good cop try harder. The thing that could drive a good cop toward the line so that obsession could pull her over it.

He skimmed his fingertips down the side of her face. 'I could tell you you're pretty. That's no lie. I could tell you I need you, take you to my bed even. Would you trust me then more than you trust a killer?' he asked, leaning close.

The edge of the table bit into the backs of Annie's thighs. His legs brushed against hers. His thumb touched the corner of her mouth and everything inside her turned hot and sensitive. She tried to catch a breath, tried to make sense of her response with a mind that felt suddenly numb.

'I don't trust Renard,' she said, her voice thready.

'Nor do you trust me.' His mouth was inches from hers, his eyes burning black. He traced his thumb down her throat to the hollow at the base of it where her pulse throbbed.

'You're the one who said trust is of no use in an investigation.'

He arched a brow. 'You investigating me, *chère*?'

'No. This isn't about you.' Even as she said it, she wondered. The case was about one woman's death and one man's guilt, but it was also about so much more.

'No,' Nick said, though he wasn't certain whether he was just repeating her answer or issuing a command to himself. He took half a step back to break contact, to distance his senses from the soft, clean scent of her.

'Don't you help him, 'Toinette,' he said, brushing back a stray lock of her hair. 'Don't let him use you. Control.' He curled his hand into a fist as he pulled it from her cheek. 'Control.'

I'm not the one in danger of losing it, Annie thought, ignoring the telltale shiver that ran through her. Fourcade dug a cigarette out of a stray pack on the table and walked away, trailing smoke. The truth was, she didn't feel she'd ever had control. The case had swept her up and swept her along, taking her places she hadn't expected to go. To this man, for instance.

'I should go,' she said, talking to his back as he stood at one of the dormer windows. 'It's late.'

'I'll walk you down.' His mouth twitched as he turned around. 'Check that Jeep for snakes.'

The night was soft with humidity, cool as a root cellar and rich with the fecund scent of earth and water. In the blackness beyond the fall of Fourcade's porch light, a pair of horned owls called in eerie harmony.

'Uncle Sos used to tell all the kids the stories about the *loup-garou*,' she said, looking off into the darkness. 'How they prowled the night looking for victims to cast their spells on. Scared the pee out of us.'

'There's worse things out there than werewolves, sugar.'

'Yeah. And it's our job to catch them. Somehow that seems a more daunting prospect in the dead of night.'

'Because the darkness is their dimension,' he said. 'You and I, we're supposed to walk the edge in between and pull them from their side to the other, where everyone can see what they are.'

It sounded like a mythic task that would require Herculean strength. Maybe this was why Fourcade had shoulders like a bull – because of the strain, the weight of the world.

She climbed up into the Jeep and tossed the DMV records on the passenger's seat.

'You watch yourself, 'Toinette,' he said, closing the door. 'Don't let the *loup-garou* get you.'

24

It wasn't a fictitious creature she had to worry about, Annie thought as she drove the road that cut through the dense woods. All the trouble she was facing had to do with mortal men: Mullen, Marcus Renard, Donnie Bichon – and Fourcade.

Fourcade.

He was as enigmatic as the *loup-garou*. A mysterious past, a nature as dark and compelling as his eyes. She told herself she didn't like that he had touched her, but she had allowed it and her body had responded in a way that wasn't smart. Her life was enough of a mess at the moment without getting involved with Fourcade.

'Don't go down there, Annie,' she muttered to herself.

She tuned in to the scanner to let the chatter distract her. Nothing much going on Sunday night. What bars were open at all closed early, and the usual troublemakers refrained out of token deference to the commandments. There was no traffic. The only life she encountered was a deer darting across the road and a stray dog eating the carcass of a dead armadillo. The world seemed a deserted place, except for the lonely souls who called in to the talk radio station to speculate about the possible return of the Bayou Strangler. No one had been strangled, but people seemed confident it was just a matter of time.

Annie listened with a mix of fascination and disgust. The level of fear in the population was rising, and the level of logic was falling in direct proportion. The Bayou Strangler had come back from the dead. The Bayou Strangler had killed Pam Bichon. Conspiracy theories were plentiful. Most centered on the cops having planted evidence four years ago to pin the murders on Stephen Danjermond after he was already dead, which tied in neatly with current theories about planted evidence implicating Renard and damning Fourcade.

Annie wondered if Marcus Renard was listening. She wondered if the rapist was out there somewhere soaking up the satisfaction of his infamy, smiling to himself as he listened. Or was he out there somewhere selecting his next victim?

Spooked, she pulled the Sig from her duffel bag when she turned into the lot at the Corners. She locked the Jeep and went up to her apartment, her senses tuned to catch the slightest noise, the slightest movement. She twisted sideways as she worked the lock with one hand, and looked out over the parking lot and past it. There were no lights on at Sos and Fanchon's house. There seemed to be nothing stirring, and yet she couldn't shake the feeling of eyes on her. Nerves strung too tight, she thought as she let herself into the house.

She had left a light on in the apartment and added more to it as she made a systematic check of the rooms, gun in hand. Only after that task was finished did she put the Sig Sauer away and let go the anxiety that had gathered in tight knots in her shoulders. She pulled a bottle of Abita from the refrigerator, toed off her sneakers, and went to the answering machine.

With all the angry calls since the Fourcade incident hit the airwaves, she had considered unplugging the thing. What was the sense of offering convenience to people who wanted only to abuse her? But there was always the chance of a call on the case, or so she hoped.

The tape spilled its secrets one at a time. Two reporters wanting interviews, two verbal-abuse calls, a breather, and three hang-ups. Each call was unnerving in its own way, but only one ran a shiver down her back.

'Annie? It's Marcus.' His voice was almost intimate, as if he had called from his bed. 'I just wanted to say how pleased I was that you stopped by today. You can't know what it means to me that you're willing to help. Everyone's

253

been against me. I haven't had an ally except for my lawyer. Just to have you listen ... to know you care about the truth ... You can't know how special –'

'I don't want to know,' she said, but stopped herself from touching the reset button and pulled the cassette out instead. Fourcade would want to hear it. If things progressed with Renard, it could conceivably be deemed evidence. If he became infatuated with her ... If the attraction evolved into obsession ... Already he thought she was his friend.

'Don't you help him, 'Toinette. ... Don't let him use you.'

'And just what do you think you're doing, Fourcade?' she murmured, slipping the tape into her sweater pocket.

The faint scent of smoke clung to her sweater. She let herself out the French doors onto the balcony for a breath of cool air.

Far out in the swamp an eerie green glow wobbled in the darkness – gases that had been ignited by nature and were burning off untended. Nearer, something splashed near the shore. Probably a coon washing his midnight snack, she told herself. But the explanation had the hollow ring of wishful thinking and the sense of a larger presence touched her like eyes.

Hair rising on the back of her neck, Annie did a slow scan of the yard – what she could see of it – from Sos and Fanchon's house, along the bank and past the dock where the swamp tour pontoons were tied up, to the south side of the building, where a pair of rusty Dumpsters stood. Only the finest grains of illumination from the parking-lot security light reached back here. Nothing moved. And still the sensation of a presence closed like a hand on her throat.

Slowly, Annie backed into the apartment, then dropped to her belly on the floor and crawled back onto the balcony to peer between the balusters. She did the scan again, following the same route, slowly, her pulse thumping in her ears.

The movement came at the Dumpsters. Faint, with a

whisper of sound. The shape of a head. An arm reaching out. Black – all of it. A solid shadow. Moving toward the side of the building, toward the stairs to her apartment.

Annie scuttled backward into the apartment, pushed the doors shut, and scrambled to her bedroom, where she had left the Sig. Sitting on the floor, she checked the load in the gun as she called 911 and reported the prowler. Then she waited and listened. And waited. And waited. Five minutes ticked past.

She thought about the prowler, what his intentions might be. He could have been the rapist, but he could as easily have been a thief. A convenience store on the edge of nowhere would seem an easy target, and had been a target several times in the past. Uncle Sos had taken to keeping the cash box under his bed and a loaded shotgun in the closet – all against Annie's advice. If this was a burglar and he didn't find what he wanted in the store ... if he went to the house in search of the money ...

The potential for disaster turned Annie's stomach. She'd seen people shotgunned for fifty bucks in a liquor-store cash register. When she worked patrol in Lafayette, she'd seen a sixteen-year-old with his skull caved in because another kid wanted his starter jacket. She couldn't sit in her apartment and wait while some creep drew a bead on the only family she'd ever had.

She slipped her sneakers on and padded quietly to the bathroom and to the door behind the old claw-foot tub. The hinges groaned as she eased it open. She slipped through the door onto the seldom-used staircase that dropped steeply down into the stockroom of the store. Back pressed to the wall, gun in hand, raised and ready, she strained to listen for any sound of an intruder. Nothing. Slowly she descended one step at a time.

The light from the parking lot fell in the store's front windows like artificial moonlight. Annie moved down the short rows of goods like a prowling cat. Her hands were

255

sweating against the Sig. She quickly dried one and then the other on the leg of her jeans.

The front door seemed the least risky place to exit. A thief would try to break in through the stockroom door on the south side, out of sight from the house and from the road. And if this wasn't a thief, if he was looking to gain access to the apartment, the only way up was the stairs on the south side of the building.

Annie let herself out quickly and slipped around the corner to the north side of the building. Where the hell was the radio car? It had to have been fifteen minutes since the call. They could have sent the cavalry from New Iberia in less time.

She made her way along the building, ducking beneath the gallery as soon as she could, hoping she was putting herself between the prowler and the house. She wanted to drive him away from it, not toward it. To scare him off toward the levee road seemed safest, though that was a likely spot for him to have hidden his vehicle.

The smell of dead fish was strong as she crept down the slope, holding herself steady against the foundation of the building with one hand and stepping with caution to keep from skidding on the crushed rock and clamshell. At the corner post of the gallery a cat hunched over scavenged fish entrails, growling low in its throat.

Annie could see no movement in the direction of the house. Adjusting her grip on the gun, she took a deep breath and stuck her head out around the corner. Nothing. Another deep breath and she turned the corner, leading with the Sig. The Dumpsters sat past the south end of the gallery.

She moved quickly toward them, still close to the building. Sweat beaded on her forehead and she resisted the urge to wipe it away. She was close now, she could feel it, could feel the presence of another being. Her senses sharpened, heightened. The sound of water dripping somewhere near seemed loud in her ears. The stench of gutted

256

fish nearly made her gag. The scent seemed wrong somehow, but this wasn't the time to process that information.

She held up at the southeastern corner of the building, listening for the scrape of a foot on the ground or on the staircase to her apartment. She gathered herself to move around the corner, her mind racing ahead to visualize leading with the gun, focusing on her target, shouting out the warning to hold it. But as she drew breath to call out, a voice boomed behind her.

'Sheriff's deputy! Drop the gun!'

'I'm on the job!' Annie yelled, uncocking the Sig and tossing it to the side.

'On the ground! Now! Down on the ground!'

'I live here!' she called, dropping to her knees. 'The prowler's around the side!'

The cop didn't want to hear it. He rushed up like a charging bull and clocked her between the shoulders with his stick. 'I said, get down! Get the fuck down!'

Annie sprawled headlong on the ground, starbursts lighting up behind her eyes. The deputy yanked her left hand around behind her back and slapped on the cuff, twisted her right arm back and did the same.

'I'm Deputy Broussard! Annie Broussard.'

'Broussard? Really?' The surprise wasn't quite genuine. He rolled her onto her back and shone his flashlight in her face, blinding her. 'Well, what d'ya know? If it ain't our own little turncoat in the flesh.'

'Fuck yourself, Pitre,' Annie snapped. 'And get the cuffs off while you're at it.' She struggled to sit up. 'What the hell took you so long? I called this in twenty minutes ago.'

He shrugged, unconcerned, as he unlocked the handcuffs. 'You know how it is. We gotta prioritize calls.'

'And where did this rank? Somewhere below you paging through the latest *Penthouse*?'

'You really shouldn't insult your local patrol officer, Broussard,' he said, rising, dusting off the knees of his uniform. 'You never know when you might need him.'

'Yeah, right.'

Annie scooped up the Sig and pushed to her feet, biting back a groan.

She rolled her shoulders to try to dissipate the burning pain. 'Great job, Pitre. How many home owners do you normally assault in the course of a shift?'

'I thought you was a burglar. You didn't obey my commands to get down. You oughta know better.'

'Fine. It's my fault you whacked me. Now how about helping me look for the crook? Though I'm sure he's long gone after all your bellowing.'

Pitre ignored the gibe, sniffing the air as they walked up around the corner to the south side of the building. 'Jesus, what's that smell?' he said, shining the light ahead of them. 'You been killing hogs or something?'

Annie pulled her own flashlight from the back waistband of her jeans. *Dripping*. She could still hear dripping. It hit her as she walked beneath the staircase – a drop, and then another – falling from the stairs that led up to her apartment. She held her hand out and shone the beam of the flashlight on her palm as another drop hit, and another. Blood.

'Oh my God,' she breathed, bolting out from under the grisly shower.

'Christ Almighty,' Pitre muttered, backing up.

The crushed shell beneath the staircase was red with it, as if someone had rolled an open can of paint down the steps. And hanging down between the treads like ghoulish tinsel were animal entrails.

Annie wiped her hand on her T-shirt and moved to the end of the staircase. Shining her light up to the landing, she illuminated a trail of bloody carnage, intestines strung like a garland down the steps.

'Oh my God,' she said again.

A memory surfaced from a dark corner of her mind: Pam Bichon – stabbed and eviscerated. Then a possibility struck her like a bolt of lightning and the horror was magnified tenfold. *Sos. Fanchon.*

'Oh, God. Oh, no. No!' she screamed.

She wheeled away from Pitre and ran, feet slipping and skidding on the crushed shell, down the slope toward the dock. The beam of the flashlight waved erratically in front of her. *Sos. Fanchon. Her family.*

'Broussard!' Pitre shouted behind her.

Annie threw herself at the front door of the ranch house, pounding with the flashlight, twisting the doorknob with her bloody hand. The door swung open and she fell into Sos as a living room lamp went on.

'Oh God! Oh God!' she stammered, wrapping her arms around him in a frantic embrace. 'Oh, thank God!'

It's pig innards,' Pitre announced, poking at an intestine with his baton. 'Lotta pigs getting butchered this time of year.'

Annie was still shaking. She paced back and forth at the base of her steps, fuming. Pitre had found the five-gallon plastic bucket the stuff had come in and set it off to the side, in view by the light now coming from the front window of the store. Annie wanted to kick it. She wanted to pick it up and beat Pitre with it because he was handy and he was a jerk. He was probably in on the joke. If it was a joke.

'I wanna hear it from the lab,' she said.

'What? Why?'

'Because if a human body turns up two days from now missing its plumbing, someone's gonna want it back, Einstein.'

Pitre made a disgruntled sound. If it was evidence, he would have to deal with it, scrape it back into the bucket, and haul it away in his car.

'It's pig innards,' he insisted again.

Annie glared up into his face. 'Are you so sure because you don't wanna deal with it or because you *know*?'

'I don't know nothin',' he grumbled.

'If Mullen is behind this, you tell him I'll kick his ass all the way to Lafayette!'

'I don't know nothing about it!' Pitre griped. 'I answered your call. That's all I did!'

'Who's this Mullen, *chère*?' Sos demanded. 'Why for he'd do somethin' like dis to you?'

Annie rubbed a hand across her forehead. How could she possibly explain? Sos had never been happy with her choice of profession in the first place. He'd love to hear how deputies were trying to run her out of the department. And if it wasn't Mullen, then who?

'A bad joke, Uncle Sos.'

'A joke?' he huffed, incredulous. '*Mais non.* You didn' come laughin' to me, *chérie*. Ain' nothin' funny 'bout dis.'

'No, there isn't,' Annie agreed.

Fanchon looked up the stairs where half a dozen cats had come to feast on the entrails. 'Dat's some mess, dat's for sure.'

'Deputy Pitre and I will clean it up, Tante. It's evidence,' Annie said. 'You both go on back to bed. This is my mess. I'm sorry I woke you.'

It took another five minutes of arguing to convince them to go home and leave the mess. Annie didn't want them touched by this act any more than they had been. As they finally walked away, a residual wave of the panic she had felt for them washed through her. The world had gone mad. That she could have thought someone could have butchered Sos and Fanchon was proof of it. Deep inside, she was just as afraid as everyone else in the parish that evil had leached up from hell to contaminate their world and devour them all.

She wished for more reasons than one that she could pin this undeniably on Mullen. But the more she thought on it, the less certain she felt. Keying her out on the radio was simple, anonymous. The snake in her Jeep had been easily managed, but this ... Too much chance of being caught red-handed, literally. And the correlation to Pam Bichon was unnerving.

At Annie's insistence, Pitre hiked up onto the levee road with her and shone his light around. Animal eyes glowed red as the beam cut across woods and brush. If there had ever been a car parked along here, it was long gone now. There were no bloody footprints. Tires made no useable impression on the rock road.

It was nearly three A.M. by the time Annie trudged back up to her apartment via the in-store stairs. Her muscles ached. The pain between her shoulder blades where Pitre had struck her had a knifelike quality. At the same time, she was too wired to sleep.

She pulled another Abita from the fridge, washed down some Tylenol, and plopped down in a chair at the kitchen table, where her own notes on Pam Bichon's homicide were still spread out.

She picked up the chronology and glanced over the entries.

10/9 1:45 A.M.: Pam again reports a prowler. No suspect apprehended.

10/10: On leaving house for school bus, Josie Bichon discovers the mutilated remains of a raccoon on the front step.

Marcus Renard wanted to be her friend. He had wanted to be Pam Bichon's friend, too. Pam had rejected him. Annie had called him a killer to his face. Pam was dead. And Annie was lining herself up to take Pam's place in his life. Because she wanted to play detective, because she needed to find justice for a woman trapped in the shadowland of victims.

She had never imagined she might run the risk of ending up there herself.

25

I was thinking maybe I could go into Records and Evidence,' Annie said as she slid into the chair in front of Noblier's desk. She'd had all of three hours' sleep. She looked like hell already; lack of sleep wasn't going to alter the package noticeably.

The sheriff had apparently spent Sunday recuperating from the lousy past week. His cheeks and nose were sunburned, evidence of a day in his bass boat. He looked up at her as if she'd volunteered to clean toilets.

'Records? You *want* to go to Records?'

'No, sir. I *want* to stay on patrol. But if I can't do that, I'd like to go somewhere I haven't been. Learn something new.'

Annie struggled for visible enthusiasm. Sworn personnel were seldom wasted on jobs like records, but he was going to waste her no matter where he put her.

'I suppose you can't hardly cause any trouble there,' he muttered, petting his coffee mug.

'No, sir. I'll try not to, sir.'

He mulled it over while he took a bite out of his blueberry muffin, then nodded. 'All right, Annie, Records it is. But I've got something else I need you to do first today. Another learning experience, you might say. Go see my secretary. She'll lay it all out for you.'

McGruff the Crime Dog?'

Annie stared in horror at the costume hanging before her in the storage room: furry limbs and a trench coat. The giant dog head sat on top of the giant dog feet.

Valerie Comb smirked. 'Tony Antoine usually does it, but he called in sick.'

'Yeah, I bet he did.'

Noblier's secretary handed her a schedule. 'Two appearances this morning and two this afternoon. Deputy York will do the presentation. All you have to do is stand around.'

'Dressed up like a giant dog.'

Valerie sniffed and fussed with the chiffon scarf she had tied around her throat in a poor attempt to hide a hickey. 'You're lucky you got a job at all, you ask me.'

'I didn't.'

'You got ten minutes to get to Wee Tots,' she said, sauntering toward the door. 'Better shake a leg, Deputy. Or is that wag your tail?'

'You'd know more about that than I would,' Annie muttered under her breath as the door closed, leaving her with her new alter ego.

A learning experience.

She learned she would rather have worn the giant head out of the closet and down the halls of the station, thereby disguising herself completely and avoiding humiliation. But she also learned that she couldn't put the head on without help. It was as heavy and unwieldy as a Volkswagen bug. Her one attempt to get it on threw her off balance, and she staggered into a steel shelving unit, bounced off, and went dog headfirst into the paper recycling bin.

She learned she couldn't drive wearing giant dog feet. She learned there was no ventilation inside the suit, and the thing smelled worse than any real dog she'd ever encountered.

She learned York the Dork took his McGruff-detail duties far too seriously.

'Can you bark?' he asked as he adjusted her head. They stood in the small side parking lot at the Wee Tots Nursery School. His uniform was spotless, starched stiff. The creases in his pants looked sharp enough to slice cheese.

Annie glared out of the tiny eyeholes in McGruff's partly opened mouth. 'Can I what?' she asked, her voice muffled.

'Bark. Bark like a dog for me.'

'I'm going to pretend you didn't say that to me.'

York's little paintbrush mustache twitched with impatience. He moved around behind her and adjusted the brown tail that stuck out the back vent on the trench coat. 'This is important, Deputy Broussard. These children are depending on us. It's our job to teach them safety and to teach them that law enforcement personnel are their friends. Now say something the way McGruff might.'

'Get your hands off my tail or I'll bite you.'

'You can't say that! You'll frighten the children!'

'I was talking to you.'

'And your voice has to be much deeper, more growly. Like this.' He moved before her once again and prepared himself physically for the role, hunching his shoulders and making a face that looked like Nixon. 'Hello, boys and *girrr*ls,' he said in his best cartoon dog voice, which *sounded* like Nixon. 'I'm McG*rrr*uff the Crime Dog! Together we can all take a bite out of c*rrr*ime!'

'Yeah, you're a regular Scooby-Doo, York. You wanna wear this outfit?'

He straightened himself at the affront. 'No.'

'Then shut up and leave me alone. I'm in no mood.'

'You have an attitude problem, Deputy,' he declared, then turned on his heel and marched toward the side entrance of the school in his stick-up-the-butt gait.

Annie waddled along behind, tripped on the steps, landed on her giant dog snout. York heaved a long-suffering sigh, righted her, and guided her into the building.

A learning experience.

She learned that she had no mobility in a dog suit and no dexterity wearing paws. She learned that she was at a gross disadvantage being able to see only a small square of the world through McGruff's mouth. Toddlers existed entirely beneath that field of vision – and they knew it. They stomped on her feet and pulled her tail. One leapt from a desktop, yodeling like Tarzan and grabbed the big pink tongue lolling out of McGruff's mouth. Another sneaked in close and peed on her foot.

By the time they finished their program at Sacred Heart Elementary that afternoon, Annie felt like a pinata that had weathered the beating of one too many birthday revelers. York had stopped speaking to her altogether – but not before assuring her he would be reporting her uncooperative behavior to Sergeant Hooker and possibly even to the sheriff. According to him, she was a disgrace to crime dogs everywhere.

Annie stood on the sidewalk outside Sacred Heart with her McGruff head under her arm and watched York storm off to his cruiser. School was letting out. A herd of third graders dashed past her, barking. A bigger kid grabbed her tail and spun her around, never breaking stride on his way to the bus.

'This doesn't look good,' Josie said soberly. She stood on the steps with her arms around her backpack, her hair swept away from her face with a wide purple band.

'Hey, Jose, where y'at?' Annie said.

The girl shrugged, casting her gaze at the ground.

'You're gonna miss your bus.'

Josie shook her head. 'I'm supposed to go to the lawyer's office. Grandma and Grandpa Hunt are having a meeting. They let him out of jail yesterday, you know. We went to get him instead of going to church. I guess hardly anybody that breaks the law has to stay in jail, huh?'

'They let him out on bail?' Annie asked. Who would have thought Pritchett would move on Sunday? No one – that was the point. The offices were officially shut down, which made it a perfect day for clandestine maneuvers. The family didn't want the press making hay off them. Pritchett didn't want to upset the Davidsons any more than necessary. The Davidsons had a great many more friends among the voting constituency than Marcus Renard.

Josie shrugged again as she descended the steps and headed for the playground. 'I guess. I don't understand, but nobody wanted to talk about it. Grandpa Hunt especially. When he got home, he went fishing all alone, and when he came back he went into his study and didn't come out.'

Instead of going to the empty swing set, she sat down on a fat railroad tie that edged a patch of pansies beneath the shade of a live oak. Annie dropped the McGruff head on the asphalt and sat down beside her, rearranging her tail as best she could. On the other side of the school, the buses were roaring off.

'I know it's confusing for you, Jose. This is confusing for a lot of grown-ups, too.'

'Grandma says that detective tried to beat up the guy that killed my mom, but you stopped him.'

'He was breaking the law. Cops are supposed to enforce the law; they shouldn't ever break it. But just because I stopped Detective Fourcade doesn't mean I won't still try to get the guy that killed your mom. Do you understand?'

Josie turned sideways and reached out to touch a lavender pansy with her fingertip. A single tear slipped down her cheek and she whispered, 'No.'

She hung her head a little lower, her curtain of dark hair falling to hide her face. When she finally spoke, her voice was tiny and trembling. 'I ... I really miss my mom.'

Annie reached out with a paw and gathered Josie close to her side. 'I know you miss her, sweetheart,' she said against the top of Josie's head. 'I know exactly how much you miss her. I'm so sorry any of this had to happen to you.'

'I want her back,' Josie sobbed out against the trench coat. 'I want her to come back and I know she's never going to and I hate it!'

'I know you do, honey. Life shouldn't have to hurt so much.'

'Sister Celeste says I sh-shouldn't be mad at G-God, but I am.'

'Don't you worry about God. He's got a lot to answer for. Who else are you mad at? Are you mad at me?'

The little girl nodded.

'That's okay. But I want you to know I'm doing my best to help, Jose,' she murmured. 'I promised you I would, and I am. But you have every right to be mad at whoever you want. Who else are you mad at? Your dad?'

She nodded again.

'And your grandma?'

Another nod.

'And Grandpa Hunt?'

'N-no.'

'Who else?'

Josie went still for a moment. Annie waited, anticipation born of hard experience thickening in her chest. A desultory breeze stirred the heads of the pansies. A painted bunting flitted down from an azalea bush to pluck at a crust of bread some child had peeled from a lunch sandwich and abandoned.

'Who else, Jose?'

The answer came in a small voice brimming with pain. 'Me.'

'Oh, Josie,' Annie whispered, hugging her tight. 'What happened to your mom wasn't your fault.'

'I-I w-was g-gone to Kristen's h-house. Maybe if if I h-had been home ...'

Annie listened to the stammered confession, feeling nine years old inside, remembering the horrible burden of guilt no one had even suspected she carried. She had been with her mama always, had watched over her during the bad spells and prayed for God to make her happy. And the first time she'd gone away from home, Marie had ended her own life. The weight of that had pressed down on her until she thought it would crush her.

She remembered going down the levee road, the taste of bitter tears as she had thrown her stuffed Minnie Mouse into the water. The toy she had so cherished from her first-ever vacation trip, the trip that had marked the end of her mother's life. And she remembered Uncle Sos fishing the toy out of the reeds and sitting on the bank with her on his

267

lap, both of them crying, the soggy Minnie Mouse squished between them.

'It wasn't your fault, Josie,' she murmured at last. 'I thought that, too, when my mom died. That maybe if I had been home I could have stopped it from happening. But we can't know when bad things are coming to our lives. We can't control what other people do.

'It's not your fault your mom died, honey. That's someone else's fault, and he's going to be made to pay. I promise. All I ask is for you to believe me when I tell you I'm your friend. I'll always be your friend, Josie. I'll always try to be here for you and I'll always try my hardest for you.'

Josie looked up at her. She tried to smile. 'Then how come you're dressed up like a dog?'

Annie made a face. 'A temporary setback. It won't last. I'm told I make a crummy crime dog.'

'You were pretty bad,' Josie admitted. She wrinkled her nose in distaste. 'You smell really gross, too.'

'Hey, watch the insults,' Annie teased. 'I'll sic all my fleas on you.'

'Yuck!'

'Come on, munchkin,' she said, standing slowly. 'I'll walk you downtown. You can help me carry my head.'

Lake Pontchartrain shone metallic aqua, as flat as a coin and stretching north as far as the eye could see, bisected by the Pontchartrain Causeway toll bridge. Several boats skimmed the surface in the middle distance, their pilots playing hooky from the usual Monday rigors of work. The view from this stretch of shore was expensive. Real estate along this part of the lake was in the category of 'if you have to ask, you can't afford it.' Duval Marcotte could afford it.

His mansion was Italianate in design, looking like something that would be more at home in Tuscany than Louisiana. Soft white stucco and a red tile roof. Straight, elegant lines and tall slim windows. An eight-foot-tall wall surrounded the property, but the iron gates stood open, affording passersby a view of emerald lawn and lavish flower gardens. A black Lincoln Town Car sat in the drive near the house. A surveillance camera peered down from atop a gatepost.

Nick drove past and circled around. The service entrance stood open, as well. A florist's van sat near the kitchen entrance of the house with its doors gaping wide. Nick parked his truck outside the gate and walked to the house, grabbing an enormous arrangement of spring flowers out of the van.

The kitchen was a hive of activity. A thin woman was overseeing two aproned assistants in the making of canapés. Two more women were unloading trays of champagne glasses onto the granite top of another work island. A brawny boy of twentysomething emerged from a door with a case of champagne and carried it to a table at the direction of a small effeminate blond man in gold-rimmed glasses, who then swung toward Nick. 'Take that to the red parlor. It goes on the round mahogany table near the fireplace.'

A maid swung the kitchen door open for him.

He had been in this house twice and had memorized the layout, could see in his mind's eye every stick of antique furniture and every painting that hung on the walls. The red parlor was on the left at the front of the house, a room that looked as if it might have hosted Napoleon, the decor Second Empire, ornate and ostentatious.

Nick set the arrangement on the round mahogany table and walked quickly down the hall of the east wing, his running shoes all but silent against the polished floor. He bypassed the main staircase in favor of the stairs at the far end of the hall. Marcotte's office was on the second floor of the east wing. A man of habit, he worked from home Mondays and Fridays. Business associates Marcotte wouldn't be seen with at his offices on Poydras Street in the central business district of New Orleans came to his home on a regular basis. Nick thought of the Town Car in the drive and frowned.

He would have been better off waiting, coming in late to surprise Marcotte in his bed, but that would have given Marcotte too good an excuse to shoot him or have him shot as an intruder. He was here for business, not revenge, he reminded himself as he ducked into a bathroom and shut the door behind him.

He stared at himself in the mirror above the pedestal sink. He wore a loose-fitting black sport coat over his white T-shirt, the cut of the jacket hiding the shoulder rig and the Ruger P.94 semiautomatic. His color was high along his cheekbones. His pulse was pounding a little too hard, and anticipation coated his mouth with a taste like copper. He hadn't seen Marcotte in more than a year, hadn't planned to see him ever again. He had done his best to close the door on that chapter of his life, and now he found himself sneaking back through it.

Closing his eyes, he breathed deeply, filled his lungs, and tried to still his mind. *Calm, center, focus.* Why was he here? Nothing visible tied Marcotte to the Bichon case. He had checked out every New Orleans number on Donnie's phone records from before the murder, finding no direct link to Marcotte. A relief. He didn't want to strengthen Donnie's motive for killing Pam when he knew in his gut Renard was the murderer. If Donnie had contacted Marcotte after Pam's death, Nick had no way of knowing. There was no cause to confiscate Bichon's phone records for that period of time. And if Donnie had contacted Marcotte after the fact, that took Marcotte out of the loop for the murder.

But even after reciting that logic, the uneasiness lingered. The spectre of Marcotte loomed in the shadows at the periphery of the case. Donnie needed Pam's case closed before he could move on plans to sell the realty. If Renard were taken out, the case would likely go away. If Nick was the one to take Renard out, and if he went down for doing the deed, he would then be removed from Marcotte's new playing field.

He let the air escape slowly between his lips. *Calm, center, focus*. He couldn't let the past press into this. He had to isolate the present, deal with the moment, think forward. *Control*. He stepped back into the hall and walked down to the lacquered cypress double doors.

Marcotte's young male secretary sat at a French desk in the small outer office. 'Can I help you?'

'I'm here to see Marcotte.'

The secretary took in Nick's appearance with suspicion and disapproval. 'I'm sorry, you don't have an appointment.'

'Don't be sorry. He'll see me.'

'Mr Marcotte is a very busy man. He's in a meeting.'

Nick leaned across the desk and grabbed hold of the man's necktie just below the knot, twisting it tight around his fist. The secretary's eyes went wide and a strangled sound of surprise leaked out of him.

'You're being very rude, college boy,' Nick said softly. They were nearly nose to nose. 'Lucky for you I'm such a patient guy. Me, I believe in giving people a second chance. Now why don't I unchoke you, and you can buzz Mr Marcotte? You tell him Nick Fourcade is here on business.'

Nick let him go and the secretary fell back in his chair, sucking in air. He reached for the phone and pressed the intercom button.

'I'm sorry to interrupt you, Mr. Marcotte.' He tried to clear his throat, but the raspy edge remained in his voice. 'There's a Nick Fourcade here to see you. He was adamant that I let you know.'

No reply issued from the machine. Nick tapped his toe impatiently. A moment later the double doors to Marcotte's inner sanctum swung open and four men stepped out.

Nick assessed the company quickly, stepping toward the nearest wall. First came Vic 'The Plug' DiMonti, a mob boss of middling rank in greater New Orleans. He was built like a small cube with stubby legs and arms. In contrast, the muscle that flanked him was oversized, a matched set of steroid-pumped knee busters with crew cuts, no necks, and round Armani sunglasses.

Marcotte stayed in the open doorway as the wiseguys walked out. He looked like the most ordinary of men in dress trousers and a pin-striped shirt with the sleeves rolled up, his tie a neat blood red strip. Slim, sixty, bald on top. He was famous for his smile. His eyes were kindly. And inside his chest, his heart was a small black atrophied lump. He was lavishly benevolent, impressively humble, secretly vicious. He had bought and paid handsomely for a sterling image, and the few people in New Orleans's high circles who knew that gladly looked the other way.

'Well, if it isn't my old friend, Nick Fourcade!' he said, chuckling, jovial, flashing the kind of bonhomie reserved for old and dear acquaintances. 'This is a surprise!'

'Is it?'

'Come in, Nick,' he offered with a grand gesture. 'Evan, bring us coffee, will you?'

'I won't be staying,' Nick said as he stepped past his host into the office.

He was impressed against his will by the view of the lake through the Palladian window that centered the main wall. The room itself was no less impressive. The carpet was plush gray, a shade lighter than the walls. Objets d'art were displayed at intervals along the walls. The furnishings were museum quality.

'You've got a long drive back home,' Marcotte said, rounding his massive desk. 'I hear you've made quite a name for yourself out there in the Cajun nation.'

Nick made no comment. He positioned himself behind a Louis XIV armchair at one end of the desk, with the doors in view. He rested his hands on the back of the chair. Marcotte was the antithesis of everything he believed in: morality, justice, personal accountability. Nick had dreamed of punishing Marcotte for it, but there was no way of doing it without corrupting himself. The catch only fueled his anger.

'What brings you to my neck of the woods, Detective?' Marcotte asked. 'Aside from incredible nerve, that is.'

Elbows braced on the arms of his executive's chair, he pressed his fingertips into a pyramid and swiveled the chair slowly back and forth. 'I'd say it might be the party I'm throwing tonight, but I'm afraid your name is not on the guest list. Can't be official business: you are far out of your jurisdiction. Besides, I understand you've had a little professional setback recently.'

'What do you know about that?'

'What I read in the papers, Nick, my boy. Now what can I do for you?'

Marcotte's calm amazed him. The man had ruined him and he sat here as if there could be no hard feelings, as if it had meant nothing to him.

'Answer me a question,' he said. 'When did you first discuss the possible sale of Bayou Realty with Donnie Bichon?'

'Who is Donnie Bichon?'

'You're reading the papers, you know who he is.'

'You have some reason to believe I've spoken with him? Why would I be interested in some little backwater real estate company?'

'Oh, let me think.' Nick touched two fingers to his temple to emphasize the effort of concentration. 'Money? Making money. Hiding money. Laundering money. Take your pick. Maybe your friend Vic The Plug, he's looking for a little lightweight investment. Maybe you got some senators in your pocket, ready to bring riverboat gambling to the basin. Maybe you know something the rest of us don't.'

Marcotte's face went flat. 'You're offending me, Detective.'

'Am I? Well, hell, what else is new?'

'Nothing. You are as tedious as ever. I'm a well-respected businessman, Fourcade. My reputation is above reproach.'

'What kind of money does it take to buy a reputation like that? You pay extra depending on what crooks you wanna consort with?'

'Mr DiMonti owns a construction firm. We're developing a project together.'

'I'll bet you are. You gonna bring him and his goons out to Bayou Breaux with you?'

'You're mentally deranged, Fourcade. I have no interest in some snake-infested swamp town.'

Nick lifted a finger in warning. 'Ah. Watch what you say, Marcotte. That's *my* snake-infested swamp town – the one you drove me to. I don't wanna see your face there. I don't wanna smell the stink of your money.'

Marcotte shook his head. 'You don't learn, do you, swamp rat? I've been a perfect host to you, and you abuse me. I could have you arrested if I wanted to. How would that look in your file? Like you've lost your marbles, I'd say. Beating up suspects, driving all the way to New Orleans to harass a well-known businessman and philanthropist. You annoy me, Fourcade, like a mosquito. The last time I swatted you away. Don't pester me again.'

The door swung open, and the secretary carried in a silver tray set with a small coffee urn and bone china demitasse cups. The dark aroma of burned chicory filled the room.

'Never mind the coffee, Evan,' Marcotte said, never taking his eyes off Nick. 'Detective Fourcade has worn out his welcome.'

Nick winked at the secretary as he moved toward the door. 'You drink mine, *mon ami*. I hear it's good for a sore throat.'

He went back down the side stairs and let himself out through the solarium to avoid the crowd in the kitchen. The florist's van was gone. Vic DiMonti's thugs were not.

One stepped out from behind a potting shed to block the path to the gate. Nick pulled up ten feet from them and assessed his options. Stand his ground or run back the way he'd come, though he had the sinking feeling Meathead Number Two had already eliminated the second choice. The scuff of large feet on the brick path behind him confirmed the reality. Then DiMonti himself emerged from the potting shed with a hickory spade handle balanced in his thick paws.

'I got no quarrel with you, DiMonti,' Nick said. He kept his weight on the balls of his feet and his eyes on the thug in front of him. He could see the reflection of the twin in the man's sunglasses.

'I remember you, Fourcade,' DiMonti said. His accent was the near Brooklynese of the Irish Channel part of town, befitting a movie mobster. 'You're some kind of head case. They threw you off the force.' He barked a laugh. 'That's gotta take some doing – getting thrown off the NOPD.'

'It was nothing,' Nick said. 'Ask your friend Marcotte.'

'That's a good point you bring up, Fourcade,' DiMonti said, tapping the spade handle against his palm. 'Mr. Marcotte is a close personal friend of mine and a valued business associate. I don't want him upset. You see where I'm going with this?'

'Absolutely. So tell Tiny here to step aside and I'll be on my way.'

DiMonti shook his head sadly. 'I wish it were that simple, Nick. Can I call you Nick? You see, I think you got what they call a pattern of behavior here. You maybe need a little lesson from Bear and Brutus here to break you from that. Make you think twice before you come back here. You see what I'm saying?'

He saw Brutus behind him looming larger in Bear's sunglasses.

A spinning kick caught Brutus in the face, broke his nose and sunglasses, and sent him down on the brick path like a felled tree. Nick spun the other way, blocking a roundhouse right and popping Bear hard in the diaphragm. It was like hitting brick.

The thug caught him with a solid jab, and blood filled Nick's mouth. He brought his right foot up and hit Bear square in the knee, forcing the joint to bend in a way nature never intended. Howling, clutching at the knee, the thug doubled over, and Nick hit him with a combination that split his lip and sprayed a fountain of blood.

All he needed was Bear to go down and he could break for the gate. He didn't want to pull the Ruger. DiMonti hadn't come here to kill him and he wouldn't want the complications, but neither would he hesitate to do it. The Plug had dumped his share of bodies in the swamp. One more punch and Bear would be gone. But before Nick could draw back, DiMonti swung the spade handle like a baseball bat and caught him hard across the kidneys.

DiMonti swung again and Nick staggered forward, struggling to keep his feet under him, to keep moving. If he could run –

The thought was cut short as Brutus tackled him from behind and he went down face-first on the bricks. Then the world went black, and Nick's final thought was that it was probably just as well.

26

Annie blew out a sigh and dug through the stacks of paperwork, unearthing a packet of microcassette tapes labeled RENARD in Fourcade's bold caps. Interview tapes, no doubt made in his pocket. The official tapes would never have been allowed out of the sheriff's department, but Fourcade lived by his own set of rules – some of which she condoned, and others ...

It made her uneasy thinking about it. Where would she draw the line? And where would he? She was breaking rules by involving herself in this case, but she felt it was justified, that she owed her allegiance to a higher authority. And was that what Fourcade had been thinking when he'd confronted Renard in that parking lot? That justice was a higher power than the law?

Where the hell was he? she wondered as she dug through her purse for her tape recorder. For a man who had been suspended and warned off the case, he certainly got around.

'Maybe he's out planting evidence for you to find, Annie,' she muttered, then chided herself for it.

She didn't believe he had planted the ring just because he'd been accused of doing it before. No one had proven the allegations made during the Parmantel murder investigation. Fourcade had resigned from the NOPD before anyone got the chance. The hoopla had died down and the case had gone away.

That right there made Annie think something was hinky about the charges. The case had gone away and no civil suit had been filed. Anybody with half a beef against the cops these days filed a civil suit. Allan Zander, the man Fourcade had accused of killing the hooker, Candi Parmantel, had just faded back into anonymity.

She told herself none of that mattered as she loaded tape number one into the player. Fourcade wanted to keep his past to himself, and all she wanted was to close this homicide. The rest was just baggage.

She hit the play button and set the machine on the table.

Fourcade titled the interview with Marcus Renard. He stated the date, time, and case number; his own name, rank, and badge number. Stokes stated his name, rank, and badge number. Chairs scraped against the floor, papers were shuffled.

Fourcade: 'What'd you think of that murder, Mr Renard?'

Renard: 'It's – it's horrible. I can't believe it. Pam ... My God ...'

Stokes: 'Can't believe what? That you could butcher a woman that way? Surprised yourself, did you?'

Renard: 'What? I don't know what – You can't think *I* could do that! Pam was – I would never –'

Stokes: 'Come on, Marcus. This is your ol' buddy Chaz you're talking to. I didn't fall off the turnip truck yesterday. You and me, we been having this same conversation now for what – six, eight weeks? Only this time you did something more than just look. Am I right? You got sick of looking. You got sick of her turning you down.'

Renard: 'No. It wasn't –'

Stokes: 'Come on, Marcus, get straight with this.'

Fourcade: 'Let's give him the benefit, Chaz. You tell us, Mr Renard. Where were you last Friday night?'

Renard: 'Am I being charged with something? Should I have a lawyer present?'

Fourcade: 'Me, I dunno, Mr Renard. *Should* you have a lawyer present? We just want you to set us straight, that's all.'

Renard: 'You have nothing to tie me to this. I'm an innocent man.'

Stokes: 'You wanted her, Marcus. I been here all along, remember? I know how you followed her around, sent her little notes, little presents. I know that was you calling her up, hanging around her house. I know what you did to that woman, and you might as well confess, Marcus, 'cause you can bet your ass we're gonna prove it, Nicky and me. If I'm lyin', I'm dyin'.'

The rumble of an engine broke Annie's concentration. She clicked the cassette player off and listened for a car door slamming. When the sound didn't come, she rose from her chair, sliding the Sig out of her purse.

The small window on the end of the house afforded a view of nothing. The night was black as pitch. Fourcade's retreat was stuck in the hip pocket of civilization, readily accessible to the animals that prowled the swamp – a fair number on two legs. Poachers and thieves and worse. Society's ragged fringe.

Last night came back to her in a rush. Who would be her enemy here?

No one could have followed her without her knowing it, which eliminated anyone from the department. A random attack by the roving rapist seemed unlikely. That predator knew the lifestyles and habits of his victims. He hadn't chosen them by accident.

Something thumped hard against the floor of the gallery. Leading with the Sig, Annie let herself out onto the landing.

'Nick? That you?'

She waited, debating, knowing she had already tipped her hand. Then came a low groan, the unmistakable sound of pain.

'Fourcade?' she called, easing down the stairs. 'Don't make me shoot you. I've got a big gun, you know.'

He lay on the gallery floor, the light spilling out the window illuminating his battered face.

'Oh my Lord!' Annie stuck the gun in her waistband and dropped down beside him. 'What happened? Who did this?'

Nick cracked open an eye and looked up at her. 'Never

announce yourself until you know the situation, Broussard.'

'Man, even half dead you're bossy.'

'Help me up.'

'Help you up? I should call an ambulance! Or I suppose I could shoot you and put you out of your misery.'

He winced as he tried to push himself up onto his hands and knees. 'I'm fine.'

Annie made a rude sound. 'Oh, excuse me, I mistook you for someone who'd had the shit beat out of him.'

'*Mais* yeah,' he mumbled. 'That'd be me. It ain't the first time, sugar.'

'Why does that not surprise me?'

He straightened slowly, pain rippling through his body. 'Come on, Broussard, quit gawking and help me. If we're partners, we're partners.'

Annie moved around beside him and let him hook an arm around her shoulders. 'I don't mind saying you're more than I bargained for, Nick.'

He leaned heavily against her as she helped him into the house. They lurched past the front parlor like a pair of winos. Annie glanced at the blood that dyed the front of his T-shirt and muttered an expletive.

'Who did this?'

'Friend of a friend.'

'I think you need somebody to redefine that term for you. Where are we going?'

'Bathroom.'

She steered him down the hall and nearly fell into the tub as she lowered him to sit on the closed lid of the toilet.

'God, are you sure you're alive?' she said, squatting down in front of him.

'Looks worse than it is.'

'I suppose you're gonna tell me I should see the other guy.'

'They were ugly to start with.'

'They? Plural?'

'Nothing's broke,' Nick said, fighting off another groan as the muscles in his back seized up. 'I'll be pissing blood tomorrow, that's all.'

He leaned his forearms on his thighs and tried to concentrate on clearing away the dizziness. His head was banging like a ten-pound hammer on a cast-iron pot.

'Get me a whiskey,' he grumbled.

'Don't boss me around, Fourcade,' Annie said, digging through the small medicine cabinet. 'I have it on good authority you should never piss off your medical personnel.'

'Get me a whiskey, *please*, Nurse Ratched.'

She peered over her shoulder with a look of amazement. 'You *must* have a concussion. You just made a joke.'

'It's in the kitchen,' he ground out between his teeth, three of which felt loose. 'Third cupboard on the right.'

She went out and came back moments later with a tumbler of Jack Daniel's. She took the first shot herself.

'I want an explanation, Fourcade. And don't jerk me around. I've got a bottle of peroxide and I know how to use it.'

She set the whiskey on the sink and started to help him out of his jacket.

'I can do it,' he protested.

'Oh, God, don't be such a man. You can hardly move.'

Nick gave in and let her remove his jacket and his shoulder rig with the Ruger.

He was disgusted with himself. He should have anticipated DiMonti's attack, should have known better than to go out the same way he'd come in. He should have been fighting off the knuckle hangover with greater success. He shouldn't have needed someone to take care of him, and he couldn't allow himself to get used to it. He wasn't the kind of man who could expect that kind of comfort. His was a solitary existence by necessity. He had pared away the need for companionship to better focus on building the broken pieces of himself into something whole.

But the job was far from finished, and he was tired and battered, and Annie Broussard's touch felt too welcome.

He started to pull the bloodstained T-shirt off himself, until the pain cracked across his back again, as if DiMonti were right there with that damned spade handle.

'I thank God daily that I don't have testicles,' Annie grumbled. 'They obviously impair common sense.'

She began jerking the T-shirt up his back, but her hands stilled before she was halfway. Angry red welts lashed across the small of his back, blood pooling beneath them in bruises as dark as thunderheads.

'Jesus,' she breathed. She had to have hurt him just putting her arm around him to help him into the house, and he hadn't made a sound. Damned stubborn man, she thought. He'd probably gotten exactly what he deserved.

'It's nothing,' he snapped.

She didn't comment but moved more carefully as she peeled the T-shirt up. His skin was hot, the scent of him masculine with a feral undertone. Sweat and blood, she told herself. There was nothing sexual in it, nothing sexual in the act of undressing him.

Her knuckles grazed his collarbone. He was eye level with her breasts. The room suddenly seemed as small as a phone booth.

Fourcade leaned back as she stepped away, as if he may have felt it, too – the strange magnetic pull. He pulled the T-shirt off his arms and threw it on the tile floor. His chest was wide and hard-looking, covered with a mat of dark hair that trailed down the center of a six-pack of stomach muscles and disappeared into the waistband of his jeans.

Annie swallowed hard and moved to the sink.

'I'm waiting for that explanation,' she said. She waited another few minutes while she filled the sink with warm water and soaked a washcloth.

'I went to see Marcotte. A friend of his took exception to my visit.'

'Gosh, imagine that.' She dabbed gingerly at the blood

282

that had crusted along a cut on his cheekbone. 'I'm sure you were your usual charming self – spouting paranoid delusions, accusing him of being the devil. What were you doing there in the first place? Did you find something in Donnie's phone records?'

'No, but I don't like Marcotte's smell hanging around this. I wanted to rattle his cage.'

'And you got your bell rung, instead. Careless.'

It was. He had said so himself countless times on the endless drive home. He was rusty, and beyond that, he didn't think straight when it came to Marcotte.

'So who were these "friends"?'

'A couple of knee busters belonging to Vic DiMonti.'

'Vic DiMonti. The wiseguy Vic DiMonti?'

'C'est *vrai*. You got it in one, angel. Didn't think a fine upstanding citizen like Marcotte would know anyone like that, did you? Well, you'll never see them on the society page together, that's for damn sure.'

He took a sip of the whiskey while she rinsed the blood out of the washcloth. The liquor stung the inside of his mouth where his teeth had cut into the soft tissue. It hit his empty stomach with an acidic hiss that was followed closely by a warm, numbing glow. He took another drink.

'This should have stitches,' Annie muttered, staring at the cut that sliced his left eyebrow.

She'd thought he was insane when he'd first brought up the subject of Marcotte. She'd thought Marcotte was just part of the baggage of his past that he dragged around behind him and wouldn't let anyone see inside of. But if Marcotte was Donnie's secret buyer, and if Marcotte consorted with mob types ... maybe Fourcade wasn't so crazy after all.

'So what did Marcotte have to say?'

'Nothing. I didn't like the quality of his silence.'

'But if Donnie wasn't in contact with him before the murder, then he's not a motive. What Donnie does with his half of the company now is his own business.'

283

He took hold of her wrist and pulled her hand away from his split chin. 'The devil comes knocking at your door, 'Toinette, don'tcha turn your back on him just 'cause he's late for the first dance.'

Annie's breath caught at the leashed strength in his grip, at the dark fire in his eyes. This was what she had warned herself away – from his intensity, his obsessions.

'I'm in this to close the homicide,' she said. 'Marcotte is your demon, not mine. I don't even know what he did to win that exalted place in your heart.'

She had just finished telling herself she didn't want to know, and yet she found herself holding her breath as she waited for the explanation.

'If we're partners ...' she whispered.

The silence, the moment, took on a strange density, as clear and thick as water. The air of expectation: too heavy to breathe, charged with electricity. The weight of it was more than he wanted, the import beyond what he would have allowed himself to consider. He wondered if she felt it, if she could recognize it for what it was. Then he took a deep breath and stepped off that inner ledge.

'I went looking for justice,' he said softly. 'Marcotte bent it over my head like a tire iron. He showed me a side to the system as tangled and oily as the innards of a snake.'

'You think Marcotte killed that hooker?'

'Oh, no.' He shook his head slightly. 'Allan Zander killed Candi Parmantel. Marcotte, he made it all go away – and my career along with it.'

'Why would he do that?'

'Zander is married to a cousin of Marcotte. He's nobody, no social climber, just another jerk-off white-collar working stiff. Frustrated with his job, disappointed in his marriage, looking to take it all out on somebody. He left that girl, that fourteen-year-old runaway who was selling her body so she could eat, dead in a back-alley Dumpster like she was so much refuse. And Duval Marcotte covered it up.'

'You know this?' Annie asked carefully. 'Or you think it?'

'I know. I can't prove it. I tried, and everything I tried turned back around on me. I wasn't the one who tampered with the evidence or lost the lab work.'

'Nobody else thought it was strange – all this stuff going wrong on one case?'

'Nobody cared. What's another dead hooker besides bad press? Besides, it didn't any of it look that big. A bad test here, a piece of evidence gone there. You know what they say: New Orleans is a marvelous place for coincidence.'

'But you weren't the only detective on the case. What about your partner?'

'He had a kid with leukemia. Big-time medical bills. Who do you think he cared more about – his child or some dead prostitute? I was the only player in the game who gave a damn about that girl. I didn't want Marcotte's money, I wanted Marcotte, and most of all I wanted Zander. Marcotte snapped me like a twig, and I couldn't prove a goddamn thing. The more noise I made, the crazier I looked. The chief wanted my ass on a platter. The captain wanted me out on a psych charge. My lieutenant stuck his neck out and let me resign. I hear he's working security for some oil company in Houston now.'

Wincing, he leaned over and dug his cigarettes and lighter out of his discarded jacket. He shook one out and lit up.

'Duval Marcotte, he does something like that for a little nothing/nobody turd like Zander, what you think he'd do for someone like Vic DiMonti?'

Annie sat down on the edge of the tub and stared at her hands. Fourcade wasn't telling her he had crashed and burned in a big way. The rumors that had filtered out of New Orleans on the blue grapevine had whispered words like *crazy, paranoid, drunk, violent.* She thought of what he had said that night at Laveau's.

'You afraid of me? ... You don't listen to gossip?'

'I take it for what it's worth. Half-truths, if that.'

'And how do you decide which half is true?'

285

'Do you believe me, 'Toinette?' he asked.

For a moment the only sound was the insect buzz of the fluorescent lights that flanked the medicine chest. It had been a long time since he'd cared if anyone believed him – not facts and evidence, *him*. He had put away that need, but now he felt the strange stirrings of hope in his chest, foreign fingers touching him in a way that was intrusive and seductive, and ultimately disturbing.

'It doesn't matter,' he said, stubbing his cigarette out on the rim of the sink.

'Yes, it does,' Annie corrected him. 'Of course it does.' She raked a hand back through her hair and exhaled. 'It must have been hell. I can't – No, I *can* imagine ... a little bit. I've been learning lately about standing on the wrong side of an issue.'

'And I put you there, didn't I, *chère*?' He reached out to touch her chin. His smile was bitter and sad. 'What a helluva team we make, huh?'

She tried a smile to match his. 'Yeah. Who'd believe it?'

'No one. But it's right, you know. We want the same thing ... need the same thing ...'

His voice died to a whisper as he realized the conversation had shifted onto a new plane, that what was between them was attraction; that what he needed, what he wanted, was Annie. And she knew it. He could see it in her eyes – the surprise, apprehension, anticipation.

He slid his fingers into her hair, leaned forward, and touched his mouth to hers experimentally. A jolt went through him, a deep current that pulled at him, pulled him closer to her. He settled his mouth against hers and tasted her, whiskey warm and sweet with a kind of innocence he could barely remember. His hand cradled the back of her head and he kissed her deeply, without reserve, his tongue sliding against hers.

Annie sat frozen, paralyzed by the emotions and sensations unleashed by his kiss. Heat, fear, need, a dangerous excitement. It shocked her that she allowed him this intimacy, that she wanted it. That she wanted him. Her tongue moved against his and he groaned low in his throat.

The sense of power that rose within her, the passion that rose with it, terrified her. Fourcade was a man of dragons and deep secrets. If he wanted more than sex, he would want her soul.

She pulled away from the kiss, turned her face away, and felt his lips graze her cheek.

'I can't do this,' she whispered. 'You scare me, Nick.'

'What scares you? You think I'm crazy? You think I'm dangerous?'

'I don't know what to think.'

'Yes, you do,' he murmured. 'You're just afraid to admit it. I think, *chère*, you scare yourself.'

He touched her chin. 'Look at me. What do you see in me that scares you? You see in me what you're afraid to feel. You think if you go that deep you might drown, lose yourself ... like me.'

A fine chill threaded through her. She pushed herself past it, pushed to her feet, kicked awake what wits hadn't gone entirely numb.

'You should be in bed – and not with me,' she said, letting the plug out of the sink. Her heart was beating too fast. She couldn't quite get her breath. She fumbled with the stopper and dropped it on the floor. 'Take some aspirin. Take a cold shower. You probably shouldn't drink too much in case you've got a –'

He caught hold of her wrist as if holding her physically could stop her from prattling on. Annie looked at him with suspicion. She had let him cross a barrier, and suddenly he could touch her. If he could touch her, he could pull her toward him, literally and figuratively. She told herself she didn't want that. She couldn't handle him, didn't know if she could trust him. She'd stood on the edge of a dark parking lot and watched him beat a suspect senseless.

'I need to go,' she said. 'After last night, God knows what might be on the agenda tonight.'

'What happened last night?' he asked, coming slowly to his feet.

Annie backed into the hall, trying to pass off a casual attitude she didn't feel. She told him in the briefest detail, the way she would write a report – without emotion. Nick propped himself up in the bathroom doorway, the near-empty glass of whiskey in his hand. He seemed to concentrate on every word she said.

'What did the lab say about the entrails?'

'Nothing yet. They'll call tomorrow. Pitre insisted it was pig intestines. It probably was. It was probably Mullen and his band of merry jerks just trying to rattle me, but ...'

'But what?' Fourcade demanded. 'You got a feeling, 'Toinette, let's hear it. Speak your mind. Don't be shy.'

'Someone, presumably Renard, left a mutilated animal on Pam's doorstep back in October. Now I'm working the case and *this* happens.'

'You think it could have been Renard.'

'I don't know. Does that make sense? He didn't start harassing Pam until she'd rejected him. She rejected him, he punished her. He thinks I'm his champion. Why would he do something to jeopardize that?'

'Maybe punishment wasn't his goal with Pam,' Nick suggested. 'He was always quick enough to offer his concern after she had something bad happen.'

Annie nodded, considering. *'I know what it is to be persecuted,'* Renard had said to her just yesterday. *'We have that in common.'*

'Whoever did it – I'd like to wring their neck,' she muttered. 'It scared me. I hate being scared. It pisses me off.'

Nick almost smiled. She was working hard to be tough, to be a cop. But she'd never found herself involved in anything like this – not with the case, not with him. He'd seen the uncertainty in her eyes. He had to give her points for pushing past it.

'Call me when you get home,' he ordered. 'Partner.'

Annie looked up at his battered face and felt that strange pull toward him. It scared her. And it pissed her off. In ten days she would have to testify against him.

'I have to ...' She moved her hand in the direction of the door.

He nodded slightly. 'I know.'

As she walked out of his house, she had the distinct feeling that their parting words hadn't been about leaving at all.

All she wanted was to do the job, to find some closure for Josie, for Pam. She had never meant to fall into this ... this – God, what could she even call this thing with Fourcade? Attraction. It wasn't a relationship. She didn't want a relationship. She didn't want ... to go that deep.

Shit.

There was still a light on in the store when she pulled in at the Corners, though closing had come and gone an hour ago. Sos had probably been regaling his cronies with the tale of the past night's adventure. But if he had had company, they'd gone home. There were no other cars in the lot. Down the way, the light burned low in the Doucets' living room. Tante Fanchon would be settling in for the news, soaking her bunions in the minispa foot bath Annie had given her for Christmas two years ago.

Annie turned the Jeep off and sat looking up at the apartment, her thoughts drifting back in time to her mother. Lovely Marie, so unto herself, so complicated, so mysterious ... so deep. So deep she had drowned in herself, swamped by the intensity of her emotions.

There was nothing wrong in not wanting that. There was nothing wrong in staying safe on the ledge above that abyss.

She took a cleansing breath, feeling silly for having overreacted. She barely knew Fourcade. He'd stolen a kiss. Big deal.

She wanted him. *Big* deal.

She locked the Jeep, slung her duffel bag over her

shoulder, and started toward the building as Sos came out onto the porch.

'Hey, *chère*, what you doin', draggin' in dis hour?' he asked, grinning. 'You on a hot date or what?'

'I could ask you the same,' Annie retorted, shuffling toward the edge of the gallery. Sos had left the security lights on, something he rarely did because he had a grudge against the electric company.

'*Mais non!*' He laughed. '*T'es en erreur.* Your *tante* Fanchon, she'd take a stick after me, *chère*. You know it.'

Annie managed a smile.

'You been out with Andre?'

'No.'

'Why not? How you ever gonna marry dat boy, you never see him?'

'Uncle Sos ...' She couldn't bring herself to go into the speech, partly because of fatigue and partly because of a vague sense of guilt she had no desire to explore.

Sos stepped down off the porch, his boots scuffing on the rock. 'Hey, *'tite chatte*,' he said softly, his face creasing into lines of concern. He touched her cheek with callused fingers. 'You and Andre have another fight?'

'You've got A.J. on the brain,' Annie muttered. 'I'm just tired, that's all.'

He sniffed, indignant, and pulled her with him to the steps. 'Come on. You sit your pretty self down here with your uncle Sos and tell all about it.'

Annie sat down beside him and leaned her head against his shoulder, wishing she could just tell Uncle Sos and sort it all out, the way she had done when she was small. But life had grown so much more complicated than when she was ten and didn't have a mother to take her to the mother-daughter tea at school. Sos and Fanchon had been there for her then, always. She didn't want them touched by what was going on in her life now. She would protect them any way she could.

Sos clucked his tongue softly and hugged her against

him. 'Like pullin' hen's teeth with a pliers, gettin' a story outta you. You all the time like dat, you know, even when you was just a tiny li'l thing. You don' wanna bother no one. How many times I gotta tell you, *chérie*, dat's what family is for, huh?'

Annie closed her eyes. 'It's just the job, Uncle Sos. Things are hard for me right now.'

'Because you stop that detective from killing that man what ever'one says is guilty?'

'Yeah.'

He hummed a note. 'Well, I'd like to see him dead, too, but that don' mean you did wrong. Somebody wanna say different, they can come to me.

'Dat horse's ass Noblier, he don' deserve you for a deputy, *chère*. You can always come work for your uncle Sos, you know. I'll give you a quarter you come seine the shiners out my bait tanks.'

Annie found a chuckle for his teasing, then turned and hugged him fiercely. 'I love you.'

Sos patted her back and kissed the top of her head. '*Je t'aime, cherie*. You get some sleep tonight. Leave the rascals to me. I got fresh buckshot in the gun.'

'Oh, that's a comfort,' Annie muttered dryly.

She dragged herself up the stairs to the apartment. A small package waited for her on the landing, wrapped in paper sprigged with tiny violets and tied with a lavender bow. Automatically suspicious, she picked it up with care, listened to it, shook it a little, then carried it inside.

The light on the answering machine was blinking impatiently. She hit the message button and listened as she unwrapped the box.

'It's me,' A.J. said. 'Where you been? I thought maybe we could do that movie tonight, but … uh … I guess not, huh? Are you still pissed at me? Call me, will you?'

The confusion in his voice dragged at Annie's heart.

The machine beeped and a reporter came on asking for a

few minutes of her time. He might as well have asked her to hit herself on the head with a hammer.

'This is Lindsay Faulkner.'

Annie's hands stilled on the white gift box.

'I've been thinking about some of the questions you asked the other day. I'm sorry if I've seemed uncooperative. That wasn't my intent. This has just dragged on, and I – Please call me when you get a chance.'

Annie looked at the cat clock on the kitchen wall. 10:27. Not too late. Abandoning the package on the table, she paged through the phone book, then dialed the number. The telephone on the other end rang four times before it picked up.

'Hello, Ms Faulkner, this is –'

'This is Lindsay Faulkner. I can't take your call right now, but if you'll leave your name, number, and a brief message at the tone, I'll get back to you as soon as I can.'

Annie blew out a breath in frustration, waited for the tone, and left her name and number. The expectation that had shot upward at the sound of Lindsay Faulkner's voice dropped like a rock, and she was left with nothing but questions that couldn't be answered.

She had felt all along that the woman was holding back on her. But when she'd read over the statements from the file, they seemed very straightforward. Stokes had not included any notes regarding concerns about Faulkner's candor or anything else. He, rather than Fourcade, had dealt with her during the murder investigation because he had already established a relationship with her during the stalking investigation. Asking him for his opinion was out of the question.

Resigning herself to waiting for Lindsay's revelations, she hit the message button on the answering machine again.

The next one began to play – a snickering, sniveling stream of profanity and lewd suggestions. Annie raised her eyes heavenward and made a mental note never to appear in front of a television camera again.

She turned her attention to the box, lifting the lid carefully, braced for the possibility of unpleasant surprise. Another dead muskrat, perhaps. Another live snake. But nothing sprang out at her. No aroma of death assaulted her senses. Nestled in layers of tissue was a sheer silk scarf, ivory printed with tiny blue flowers.

Frowning, she took it out and ran it through her hands, the cool, sensuous feel of it having the opposite of its desired effect. The card read: 'Something lovely for a lovely person. With thanks and gratitude – again. Marcus.'

Among the gifts he had given Pam Bichon was a silk scarf.

It appeared he had taken the bait Annie had never intended to dangle.

She set the scarf aside and picked up the phone to call Fourcade.

27

Our topic tonight: double standards in the justice system.
You're tuned to KJUN, home of the giant jackpot giveaway.
This is your *Devil's Advocate*, Owen Onofrio. We've learned
today that Hunter Davidson of rural Partout Parish, the
father of murder victim Pamela Bichon, was released from
jail this weekend after an unprecedented private bond
hearing. Sources in the DA's office say a deal was struck late
today that will likely sentence Davidson to little more than
community service for the attempted assault of murder
suspect Marcus Renard.

'What do you think out there? Everyone with a TV saw it
on the news last week: Mr. Davidson charging down the
courthouse steps with a gun in his hand as the man accused
of killing his daughter walked away on a technicality. Curtis
from St Martinville, speak your mind.'

'Is it a double standard? I mean, they let Renard go. Why
shouldn't they let Davidson go too?'

'But the court has yet to prove Renard guilty of a crime.
Davidson committed his crime in front of a crowd of
witnesses. Doesn't Davidson's obvious intent to kill deserve
worse than a slap on the wrist and community service?
Instead, we've been touting this man as a hero and turning
him into a celebrity. He's reportedly had offers from Maury
Povich, Larry King, and Sally Jessy to appear on their
shows.'

Lindsay listened with disgust as she drove toward Bayou
Breaux. She detested Owen Onofrio. The man's sole purpose in life seemed to be irritating people to the point of
outburst. She disliked his devil's advocate game. She had no
time for people without solid convictions, and yet she
listened to the program more often than not on her drive
home from the Association of Women Realtors meetings in

Lafayette. The elevation in her blood pressure kept her from falling asleep at the wheel.

Without Pam for company, she had come to dread the monthly trip. They had always used the drive back for girl talk – True Confessions Time, Pam had called it – the kind of talks best held in the dimly lit interior of a car on a dark stretch of road. Soul-searching, souls-bared kinds of talks about life, love, motherhood, sisterhood.

She glanced at the empty passenger seat and felt a bottomless ache in her soul. She couldn't look at the night out here where houses were scarce and the only laws were nature's without thinking of Pam, alone with her killer where no one could see, no one could hear her cries for help.

Needing anger to fight off the despair, she hit the speed dial button on the car phone. As much as she hated Owen Onofrio, he had become a part of her self-therapy.

'You're on KJUN. All talk all the time.'

'This is Lindsay from Bayou Breaux.'

'Hey, Lindsay, it's Willy,' the assistant said, his voice a little too oily and intimate for her liking. 'If you don't win that jackpot soon, it won't be for lack of trying.'

'I'll donate it to Pam's daughter. Consider it payment for KJUN throwing her family into the public arena like the Christians to the lions.'

'Hey, you're on the line, aren't you?'

'Let me talk to Owen.'

'You're up next, Lindsay. That's just because I love the sound of your voice.'

Lindsay heaved a sigh into the receiver.

Onofrio's voice came on the line. 'Lindsay in Bayou Breaux, what's your opinion tonight?'

'I'd like to point out that there's a tremendous difference between a psychopath committing a brutal, sexual murder to satisfy some depraved personal appetite and a law-abiding, productive member of the human race being

295

driven by the inadequacies of our justice system to commit a desperate act.'

'So you're condoning vigilante justice?'

'Of course not. I'm simply saying the crimes involved here are not interchangeable. It would be ridiculous, to say nothing of cruel, to send Hunter Davidson to jail. He did not, in fact, kill Marcus Renard. And hasn't he suffered enough? He's already been sentenced to the memory of his daughter's hideous death.'

'A thought-provoking point. Thank you, Lindsay.'

After confirming her address for the jackpot, Lindsay hung up and changed the station. She'd had her say, made her daily defense for Pam. She wondered when it would stop – the pain, the anger, the need to fight back.

The pain wasn't as intense as it had been at first. She couldn't maintain that level of fury and keep her own sanity. So it had found a more manageable level. She wondered how long she could get by calling it healthy, wondered how long she would be able to hold on to it. Her fear was that without the pain, without the outrage, there would be only emptiness. The prospect terrified her.

Maybe she should sell the business, move to New Orleans. Start fresh. Meet new people, renew old acquaintances from college. God knew Bayou Breaux offered little in the way of culture or a glitzy social life. What kept her there besides memories and spite?

Memories and friends. A simple way of life. Social obligations that meant hands-on involvement with the community. She loved it here. And then there was Josie, her goddaughter. She couldn't leave Josie.

The dashboard clock glowed 12:24 as she neared the turnoff to her home. She shouldn't have stayed so late after the meeting. She'd been in no mood for cheery chitchat and social niceties, and yet she had lingered, putting off the long, lonely drive home. Now it was too late to call Detective Broussard back. There was no real hurry. She could do it tomorrow. What she had was nothing, really.

Just a thought, and one she didn't want to give credence to. Still, she felt guilty keeping it to herself.

She hit the garage door opener and parked the BMW beside the new bike she'd bought to force herself into a hobby. She dropped her briefcase on the dining room table and went straight to her bedroom, ignoring the blinking light on the answering machine. It was too late. She was too tired. Even the routine of washing her face and moisturizing her skin seemed too much effort, but she forced herself because, as her mother reminded her at regular intervals, she wasn't getting any younger. The strain of the past few months was showing beneath her eyes and in the lines around her mouth.

Exhausted, she climbed into bed, turned out the lights, and lay there, eyes open, a dull throb pounding in her temples. A weight hit the mattress beside her, curled into the crook behind her knees, and began purring. Taffy, the cat she had adopted from the Davidsons the year she and Pam had set up the business. The cat was asleep instantly, snoring softly.

Lindsay knew from too many nights of experience she wouldn't be so lucky. The headache wouldn't just go away, she wouldn't just go to sleep. She had tried meditation, relaxation tapes, reading a dull book. The only thing that worked was the sleeping pill her doctor had prescribed after Pam's murder. She was on her third refill, and he had made it clear there would be no more. She hated to think what she would do then.

The cat complained loudly as she threw the covers back. 'Yeah, well, be glad I never taught you how to fetch,' Lindsay mumbled.

She kept all her medications in a kitchen cupboard because she had read in *Cosmo* that the humidity in the bathroom was bad for the quality of pills and capsules. She didn't bother turning lights on as she went down the short hall to the kitchen. She had left the light in the range hood on, and it was plenty bright enough to see by. Bright enough, in fact, so that, as she turned the corner into the kitchen/dining area, she clearly saw the man coming in through the patio door.

He looked straight at her, and she saw the feathered mask. Time held fast for an instant as they recognized one another as predator and prey. Then the hold snapped, and the world was suddenly a blur of sound and motion.

Lindsay grabbed the first thing she could put her hands on and hurled it at him. He batted the pewter candlestick to the side and charged her, toppling a chair from its place at the table. She turned to run. If she could make it to the front door and onto the lawn – What? Who would look out and see her? It was after one in the morning. Her neighbors were tucked in bed, their houses were tucked back on the exclusive little properties she had sold them. If she screamed, would they even hear her?

A fleeting thought of Pam went through her mind like a lance, and she did scream for help.

He hit her from behind, knocking her to the floor. The Berber hall runner seared the skin of her knees and knuckles as she scrambled, trying to stand, trying to grab hold of something, anything to use as a weapon. Her fingers closed on the edge of the hall table that held the telephone and an array of framed family photos. Her attacker came down on her as she tried to pull herself up, and the table rocked sideways, dumping its contents with a crash.

Lindsay grabbed hold of the body of the telephone and swung back awkwardly at her assailant. He caught hold of her wrist and twisted her arm savagely. She surged up beneath him, her body bucking, legs kicking, free hand clawing at him, raking at the mask.

The word *No!* roared from her throat again and again as she fought. The sound of it wasn't even language to her own ears, but a cry of survival, of outrage.

He leaned back, dodging her hands, and grunted hard as her knee made contact with his groin. 'Fucking bitch!'

Lindsay shoved herself backward on the floor as his weight momentarily lifted. The door was only a few feet away. She twisted over onto her knees again and struggled to push to her feet. If she could get to the door –

Her arm stretched out toward the knob as something hit her as hard as a brick between the shoulder blades. She landed on her face, her chin bouncing on the hardwood. The next blow struck the back of her head with savage force. With the third she lost consciousness. Her last vague thought as she slipped toward the void was if she would see Pam on the other side.

28

The scarf wound around her wrists, the kiss of silk like cool breath against her fevered skin. It tightened and held her. It pulled her arms above her head. She was naked. Exposed, vulnerable. She couldn't escape, she couldn't fight.

Fourcade lowered his head to her breast, dragged his mouth slowly down across her belly. She groaned and twisted her body, feeling swept away on the racing tide of her pulse. She couldn't escape. It made no sense to fight.

His tongue touched her femininity, shooting heat through her veins. Then the head lifted, and Marcus Renard smiled at her.

Choking, Annie jerked awake. The sheets were tangled around her. The T-shirt she had slept in was soaked through with sweat. She knocked the alarm off the night-stand, silencing it, and sat up, fighting the urge to throw up. Dragging herself out of bed, she stumbled into the bathroom and splashed cold water in her face, trying to wash the images out of her memory – all of them.

Her workout lived up to its name. She felt every move in every muscle fiber. Live right, exercise, die anyway. She directed a few scathing thoughts at the Higher Power as she struggled for sit-up number forty. What was the point in following the rules, personally or professionally, if all that would bring her was pain and suffering? Then she thought of Fourcade, who broke the rules with impunity and would be lucky if he could crawl out of bed today. Maybe God was an equal-opportunity bully after all.

The time she'd spent tending Nick's wounds had become a surreal memory with the passing of the night. Maybe she hadn't really touched his naked chest. Maybe she hadn't let him play tonsil hockey. Maybe she hadn't dreamed about him. She tried to put it out of her head as she grabbed hold of the chin-up bar and dragged her body upward, straining every inch.

She thought instead of the story Fourcade had told her about New Orleans and Duval Marcotte. It didn't matter, she decided. Donnie Bichon had not contacted Marcotte before Pam's death, therefore Marcotte was not a motive for Donnie to have killed her. Unless *Marcotte* had contacted *him*. Unless their conversations had taken place over pay phones. Which made Donnie smarter than he let on. Who knew what his potential might be? She couldn't see him doing what had been done to Pam, but Fourcade's beating at the hands of DiMonti's men raised the unpleasant possibility of hired help.

She headed for the door, stopping as the scarf on the kitchen table caught the corner of her eye. What was she doing mapping out conspiracy scenarios when she had a suspected murderer leaving her tokens of his affection? Maybe she would have been better off with Fourcade's tunnel vision. Maybe whatever Lindsay Faulkner had to offer her would help put her on track.

She hit the trail at a slow jog. The ground fog was waist high, like something from an old horror movie. The sun was a huge fuchsia ball rising up through it in the east. Islands of trees seemed to float on it in the distance. Annie ran through it down the levee road. Fifty yards ahead a squadron of five blue herons leapt from the reeds and skimmed the top of the fog bank to a willow island, their spindly legs trailing behind them like fine streamers.

She ran two miles that seemed like ten, showered and dressed, then joined Fanchon and Sos for breakfast in the café.

'Someone left a package for me yesterday,' Annie said, stirring milk into her coffee. 'Did either of you happen to see him?'

'A secret lover?' Sos bobbed his eyebrows, mischief lighting his face. 'Dat's gotta be Andre, no? Sends you flowers, brings you presents. Dat boy's got it bad for you, *'tite chatte*. You listen to your Uncle Sos.'

Annie gave him a look. 'It wasn't A.J. I know who brought it. I was just wondering if either of you saw him.'

Sos scowled and muttered something under his breath.

Fanchon waved off the possibility. *'Mais non, chère*. We was so busy here, me, I thought I was chasin' myself. Two busloads of chil'run from Lafayette for the boat tours. Dat's like turnin' a hundred li'l raccoons loose in the store. Why for you wanna know?'

'No reason. It's not important.' Annie grabbed her coffee mug and pushed back from the table. She kissed them each on the cheek. 'I gotta go.'

'So who was he?' Sos called, his curiosity winning out over his pique.

Annie snatched a Snickers from the box as she passed down the candy aisle and waved goodbye with it. 'No one special.'

Just a likely stalker and murderer.

She didn't like the idea of Renard showing up here, trespassing on her private life, coming into contact with Sos and Fanchon. It seemed impossible Renard could have become fixated on her so quickly. She'd given him no encouragement, had in fact tried to *dis*courage him. Just as Pam had … and Pam Bichon had never saved his life.

She swung west at the edge of town, hoping to catch Lindsay Faulkner before she left for the office. Annie couldn't help but think her patience and persistence had paid off. She had appealed to Faulkner woman to woman and now she was going to get something Faulkner hadn't given the male detectives. She allowed herself a moment's smugness as she turned down Cheval Court.

Faulkner's garage door was closed. The front drapes were drawn. Annie walked up to the house and punched the doorbell as she leaned close to peer in the sidelight.

Lindsay Faulkner lay on the entry floor, her nightgown bunched up beneath her chin, her right arm reaching toward the portable handset of a phone that lay on the floor with an assortment of debris. Blood caked her golden hair at the roots. Her face was covered with it. Her ginger cat lay curled beside her, sleeping.

Swearing, Annie ran back to the Jeep and grabbed the radio mike.

'Partout Parish 911. Partout Parish 911. Requesting officers and an ambulance at 17 Cheval Court. Please hurry. And notify the detectives. This is a probable 261. Over.'

She confirmed the information as requested, giving her name and rank. Then, grabbing her gun out of her duffel in case the assailant was still on the premises, she ran back to the house to see if Lindsay Faulkner was alive.

The front door was locked, but the assailant had obligingly left the patio door standing wide open. Annie covered Lindsay's body with a blanket hastily dragged from the guest bedroom and knelt beside her, monitoring her weak pulse.

'Hang in there, Lindsay. The ambulance is on its way,' she said loudly. 'We'll have you to the hospital in no time. You've gotta hang tough. We'll need you to tell us who did this to you so we can catch the guy and make him pay. You've gotta hang on so you can help us with that.'

There was no response. Not a movement of eyelids or lips. Faulkner seemed to be clinging to the finest thread of life. The only good sign was that she had not gone into a fetal posture indicative of severe brain damage, but that didn't mean she couldn't die.

Annie stared at the face some animal had battered into unrecognizability. If this was the work of their serial rapist, why had he singled out Lindsay Faulkner? For the obvious reasons? That she was single, attractive, lived alone? She was also connected to a murder investigation. Just yesterday she'd found something relevant to say in regard to that murder. Had someone shut her up before she could tell it? The possibilities made Annie's nerves twitch.

The wail of approaching sirens penetrated the silence of

the house. The EMTs stormed the place first, followed closely by Sticks Mullen. He scowled at Annie. She scowled at him.

'What the hell are you doing here, Broussard?'

'I could ask you the same thing,' Annie said, glancing at her watch. 'You're usually stuffing your face with doughnuts about this time. Lucky me, you picked today to be diligent instead of delinquent.'

She stepped back into the living room, out of the way of the EMTs, one eye on the paramedics as they worked.

'It looks to me like the attacker cracked her head with the base unit of the phone.' She pointed to where it lay bloody on the floor among scattered broken picture frames. 'She put up a fight.'

'For all the good it did her,' Mullen muttered.

'Hey, some jerk comes after me, I go down swinging,' Annie said. 'I'll make the guy wish he'd never set eyes on me.'

'There's plenty of that going around anyway.'

'Don't start with me,' Annie snapped.

She dared him with a glare, then started for the dining area. 'He came in here through the patio door. She must have heard him, came out of her bedroom, and confronted him.'

'Should have stayed put and called 911.'

'Wouldn't have done her any good. The phone's dead. You'll find the line cut, I imagine. Just like the others.'

The EMTs hefted up their stretcher and rolled it out the front door with Lindsay Faulkner motionless beneath the blanket. As they left, Stokes walked in, a gray fedora sitting back on the crown of his head, a slip of toilet paper glued to his left cheek with a dot of blood. His light eyes were shot through with red.

'Man, I hate these early calls,' he grumbled.

'Yeah, how inconsiderate of people to be attacked during your off-hours,' Annie said. 'At least she waited until morning to be found raped, beaten, and unconscious.'

Stokes scowled at her. 'What're you doing here, Broussard? Somebody call for McGruff?'

'I found her.'

He took a moment to digest that, his gaze sharpening. 'And I say again, what are you doing here? How'd you know her? You two playing 'Bump the Doughnut' or something?'

Mullen snickered. Annie rolled her eyes.

'You know, Chaz, I hate to break it to you, but just because a woman won't have sex with you doesn't mean she's a lesbian. It just means she has standards.'

'Stop. You're spoiling my fantasies.' He nodded to Mullen. 'Go see if the phone line's cut. And see if there's any good footprints in the yard. Ground's soft. Maybe we can get a cast.'

Mullen went out the front. Stokes hiked up his baggy brown trousers and squatted down amid the junk that had toppled from the hall table.

'You gonna answer my question, Broussard?' he asked as he pulled on a pair of rubber gloves and picked up the bloody phone unit.

'She's my real estate agent,' Annie said automatically. 'I'm thinking of buying a house.'

'Is that right?' he said flatly. 'So why come all the way out here to see her when her office is – what? – all of four blocks from the department?'

'She wanted to show me something out this way.'

'This neighborhood's a little out of your price range, isn't it, Deputy?'

'A girl can dream.'

'Uh-huh. And when did y'all set this up?'

'Lindsay called me last night and left a message on my machine.' Her eyes went to Faulkner's answering machine. Her own voice would be on the tape. Thank God she'd left nothing more than her name and number.

'I tried to call her back about ten-thirty, but the machine answered. Why all the questions?' she asked, turning it

305

back around on him. 'You think I raped her and beat her head in?'

'Just doing my job, McGruff.' He narrowed his eyes as if he were visualizing Lindsay Faulkner's body on the floor. He rubbed his goatee and hummed a note. The puddle of blood that had leaked from her skull had dried dark on the honey-tone oak. Spatters and smears had soaked into the off-white Berber runner. 'He did her right here, huh?'

'Looked that way. Her nightgown was pulled up around her shoulders. There was a lot of bruising on her body.'

'So is this the work of our friendly neighborhood serial rapist?' Stokes said more to himself than to Annie. 'He did the other two in bed, tied them up.'

'It looks to me like she heard him coming,' Annie said. 'He didn't get the chance to surprise her in bed. And he didn't have to tie her up because he knocked her out with the phone.'

She squatted down beside the rug, her gaze zooming in on a patch of dark fibers embedded in the carpet runner where Faulkner's body had lain. She scratched at the spot gingerly with a fingernail and plucked at the loose end that came up, bringing it up close before her eyes.

'Looks to me like a piece of black feather,' she said, looking at Stokes as she held it out toward him. 'That answer your question for you?'

Don't you bend them papers shoving them in that way,' the records clerk snapped, his voice at a pitch that rivaled screeching chalk on a blackboard.

Annie twitched. 'Sorry, Myron.'

'That's *Mr* Myron. You on the other side of my counter, you call me Myron. You on *my* side of my counter, you call me *Mr* Myron. You are in *my* domain. You are *my* assistant.'

Myron jammed his hands at his belt and nodded sharply. A slight, prim black man, he wore a clip-on polyester tie every day and had his gray hair trimmed like a shrub every other Friday. He had worked records and evidence for

306

twenty years and saw the presence of a uniform behind his counter as a direct threat to his kingdom.

'Don't let it go to your head,' Annie muttered. To Myron she gave her earnest face and said, 'I'll do my best.'

Myron gave her the skunk eye and went back to his desk.

Annie let his presence fade from mind as she concentrated on the facts of Lindsay Faulkner's attack. She was tempted to think this attacker was a copycat of their rapist, who was a copycat of sorts of Pam Bichon's killer, someone who had taken advantage of the first two rapes to silence Faulkner for his own reasons. Perhaps it had been his intent to murder her. He may well have believed she was dead when he left her.

But if that was the case, then who was this copycat? Renard would seem to be free from suspicion. Debilitated by the pounding Fourcade had given him, he couldn't have had the strength or the mobility to attack a strong, healthy woman like Lindsay. If not Renard, then who? Donnie? It was no secret he disliked Lindsay. If she was standing in the way of a deal for the real estate company ...

Could he kill her? Make it look like rape? If it was Donnie, then did that mean he was involved in Pam's murder? If he had murdered Pam, killing Lindsay would have been easy by comparison.

The fragment of black feather was the sticking point for the copycat theory. That feather had been no plant left to implicate someone else. It appeared to be just the opposite, in fact. Something left behind by accident, hidden by his victim's unconscious body. Their boy had certainly left nothing else behind to incriminate himself.

Then again, the feather may not have come from a mask. It could have been part of a cat toy. It could have been tracked in by a visitor. They wouldn't know whether or not they had a match to the feather in the Nolan case until they heard back from the lab in New Iberia.

'Hey, Myron, what'd you do to deserve this, man?' Stokes

asked, snickering as he set the rape kit on the counter. 'Who sicced the crime dog after you?'

Annie gladly abandoned her filing and went to the counter. 'Yeah, Chaz, we all got that joke the first ten times you made it. Is this Faulkner's? It took you long enough.'

'Hey, it takes how long it takes, you know what I'm sayin'. The doctors had to get her stabilized. Don't matter nohow. We got nothing from it. There was nothing under her nails. There's not gonna be anything on the swabs, and pubic hair all looks alike to me. This joker's good.'

'He sure seems to know what we'll look for,' Annie said. 'I'll bet he's got a record. Have you checked with the state for known offenders? Run the MO past NCIC?'

Stokes switched his attitude up a notch. 'I don't need you to tell me how to run an investigation, Broussard.'

'I believe my remark was in the form of a question, Detective,' she said with stinging sweetness. 'I know how swamped you are dealing with these rapes and the Bichon homicide, and what all. I might have offered to make those calls for you.'

Myron moved his head like an outraged banty rooster. 'That ain't your job!'

Annie shrugged. 'Just trying to be helpful.'

'Just trying to stick your nose in where it don't belong,' Stokes muttered. 'I told you before, Broussard, I don't need your kind of help. You stay the hell away from my cases.'

He turned to Myron. 'I need to get this stuff logged in and back out again. I'm taking it down to New Iberia myself, *personally*, so they can rush it through the lab and tell me I ain't got squat, just like I ain't got squat on those two other rapes.'

'Who's working them besides you?' Annie asked.

He glanced at her from under the brim of his fedora. 'I don't need this shit from you. These are my cases. Quinlan's helping with the background checks on the other two women – who they worked with and like that. Is that acceptable to you, *Deputy*?'

Annie raised her hands in surrender.

'I mean, I know you don't think *I'm* acceptable,' he went on with an edge in his voice. 'But hey, who's in plain clothes here and who's going around town in a goddamn dog suit?'

Myron looked up from the paperwork to glare at her, clearly unhappy with her for bringing the stigma of the dog suit into his realm.

Coming down the hall, Mullen let out a hound-dog howl. Annie tried not to grind her teeth.

'I always said you should be wearing a flea collar, Mullen,' she said, moving down the counter away from Stokes and Myron.

'You're moving down in the world, Broussard,' he said with glee as he set a plastic pee-cup on the counter, full to the lid with some drunk's donation to forensic science. 'Take a bite outta crime lately? You can wash it down with this.'

Annie yawned as she pulled out an evidence card and began to fill it out. 'Wake me up when you have something original to say. Does this urine belong to someone, or did you bring me this to impress me with your aim?'

Thwarted again, he momentarily stuck to facts. 'Ross Leighton. Another five-martini lunch at the Wisteria Club. But you got him beat, don't you, Broussard? Nipping Wild Turkey on the way to work.'

The pen stilled on the form. Annie raised her head. 'That's a lie and you know it.'

Mullen shrugged. 'I know what I saw in that Jeep Saturday morning.'

'You know what you *put* in my Jeep Saturday morning.'

'I know the sheriff pulled you off patrol and I'm still driving,' he said smugly, flashing his ugly yellow teeth. He put his hands on the counter and leaned in, the gleam in his eye as mean as a weasel's. 'Just what kind of witness are you gonna make against Fourcade?' he whispered. 'I hear you were drinking that night too.'

Annie held back her retort. She'd had a drink before dinner at Isabeau's that night. A glass of wine with the meal. The bartender at Laveau's could testify she had been in the bar. Maybe he wouldn't remember whether he'd served her or not. Maybe someone would make it worth his while to lose his memory. She had by no means been intoxicated that night, but Fourcade's lawyer would have a field day insinuating that she may have been. What that would do for his case would be dubious; what it would do for her reputation would be obvious.

She gave a humorless half-laugh. 'I gotta say, Mullen, I wouldn't have given you credit for being that smart,' she murmured. 'I oughta shake your hand.'

As she reached out, she backhanded the specimen cup, knocked the lid askew, and sent Ross Leighton's urine spewing down the front of Mullen's pants.

Mullen jumped back like a scalded dog. 'You fuckin' bitch!'

'Oh, gee, look,' Annie said loudly, snatching the cup off the counter. 'Mullen wet his pants!'

Four people down the hall turned to stare. One of the secretaries from the business office stuck her head out the door. Mullen looked at them with horror. 'She did it!' he said.

'Well, that'd be a hell of a trick,' Annie said. 'I'd need a hose attachment. They know what they're looking at, Mullen.'

Fury contracted the muscles of his face. His thin lips tightened against his mouth, making his teeth look as big as a horse's. 'You'll pay for this, Broussard.'

'Yeah? What're you gonna do? Spill another bucket of pig guts down my steps?'

'What? I don't know what you're talking about. You done pickled your brain, Broussard.'

Hooker bulled his way through the gawkers. 'Mullen, what the fuck are you doing? You pissed yourself?'

'No!'

'Jesus Christ, clean up the mess and go change.'

'Don't forget the Depends!' someone called from down the hall.

'Broussard made the mess,' Mullen groused, bristling at the laughter. 'She ought to clean it up.'

Annie shook her head. 'That's not my job. The mess is on your side of the counter, Mr Patrol Deputy. I'm back here on my side of the counter, Myron's lowly assistant.'

The clerk looked up from his paperwork with the dignity of a king. '*Mr* Myron.'

It became quickly apparent to Annie that there were few advantages to working in records and evidence. Her one perk of the day came in the form of a fax from the regional lab in New Iberia: the preliminary results on the tests of the entrails that had been draped down her steps Sunday night. No detective had been assigned to the case, which meant the fax came into the machine in records and evidence to be passed on to the case deputy. By being right there when the message rolled out of the machine, Annie bypassed any contact with Pitre.

She held her breath as she read the report, as if the words had the power to bring back the smell. The scene flashed through her mind: the blood dripping, the gory garland of intestines, the fear for Fanchon and Sos.

Preliminary findings reported the internal organs to be from a hog. The news brought only a small measure of relief. The lab couldn't tell her where the stuff had come from. Hogs got butchered every day in South Louisiana. Butcher shops sold every part of them to people who made their own sausage. No one kept records of such things. Nor could the lab tell her who had dumped the viscera down her steps. If it hadn't been Mullen, then who? Why? Did it have anything to do with her investigation of Pam's murder?

Did Pam's murder have anything to do with Lindsay

Faulkner's attack? The questions led one into another, into another, with no end in sight.

By late afternoon Lindsay Faulkner's status was listed as critical but stable. Suffering from a skull fracture, fractures to a number of facial bones, multiple contusions, and shock, she had not regained consciousness. The doctors were arguing over whether or not she should be transferred from Our Lady of Mercy to Our Lady of Lourdes in Lafayette. Until they could decide which apparition of the Virgin would prove more miraculous, Faulkner remained in Our Lady of Mercy's ICU.

News of the attack had hit the civilian airwaves. The sheriff scheduled a press conference for five. Scuttlebutt around the department was that a task force would be set up to appease the panicking public. With few leads to go on, there would be little for them to concentrate on, but all the ground would be covered again and again until they churned it to dust. If Stokes, who would head the task force, hadn't already checked with the state for recent releases of sex offenders or with the National Crime Information Center to cross-reference MOs of known sex offenders, that would happen now. Acquaintances of the victims would all be questioned again, with the aim of finding a clue, a connection between the women who had been raped.

As Annie sat at her temporary desk in the records room, she felt a pang of envy toward the people who would be working on the task force. It was the kind of job she had set her sights on, but unless she reversed her fortunes in the department, hell would freeze over before Noblier promoted her to detective.

Closing the Bichon homicide would go a long way toward improving her status. But if anyone found out she was conducting her own investigation – and with whom she was conducting that investigation – her career would be toast.

She thought about that as Myron reluctantly left his post

for his afternoon constitutional in the men's room. What was she supposed to do if she came up with evidence? Who was she supposed to tell about Renard's apparent fixation on her? If Lindsay Faulkner had given her useful information, where would she have gone with it? Stokes didn't want her near his case, and if she gave him anything useful, he would doubtless claim the credit for himself. If she went to A.J., she would be jumping the food chain in a way that wouldn't win her points with anyone outside the DA's office. Should she go to the sheriff with any findings and risk his wrath for overstepping her boundaries? Or would Fourcade take the opportunity to put his own career back on track and leave her in the dust?

Maybe that was what that kiss had been all about. The closer he pulled her to him, the easier it would be to shove her behind him when he had what he needed.

She doodled on her notepad as her brain ran the slalom of possibilities. She had taken advantage of Myron's absence to pull some of the Bichon homicide file: Renard's initial statement, wherein he related the improbable story of his alibi, for which he had no corroborating witnesses. He had sent Fourcade on a wild-goose chase with his phantom Good Samaritan motorist, and he was trying to send her on the same pointless quest. A test of her loyalty, Annie supposed. Renard believed she was some kind of savior sent to deliver his life from the jaws of hell – or Angola penitentiary, not that there was a big difference between the two.

Mr Renard states motorist was driving a dark-colored pickup of undetermined make. Louisiana plates possibly bearing the letters FJ.

FJ. Annie traced the letters on her scratch pad over and over. Fourcade had run this piddling information through the DMV, had checked the resulting list and come up with nothing. *FJ.* She worked the *J* into a fish hook and drew a bug-eyed fish below it with the word *witness* incorporated into the scales. Renard didn't believe Fourcade had done anything with the information, and turned a blind eye to the fact that his own attorney hadn't come up with an alibi witness for him either. What did he think she would do that no one else had done for him?

She exaggerated the serifs on the F and added one at the bottom. E. *E.* She sat up a little straighter. Renard had said that it was night and the truck had been muddy.

A phone call to the DMV was simple enough. It was a morsel she could give Renard to buy another measure of his trust. She could put the request in Fourcade's name, have the list faxed directly to the machine in records, and no one would be the wiser.

She thought about the scarf lying on her table at home and the man in the shadows Sunday night, and reminded herself who she was playing games with. An accused and probable murderer. Donnie Bichon may have had motive, and the three rapes may have borne a chilling resemblance to Pam's death; the waters surrounding the case had become muddied, but Renard's fixation on Pam Bichon was a fact.

Marcus Renard had been fixated on Pam, Pam had rejected him, and Pam was dead.

She placed the call to the DMV, hanging up just seconds before Myron returned from his porcelain pilgrimage with the latest issue of *U.S. News & World Report.*

By the end of the shift Annie had half a dozen paper cuts and a headache from eyestrain. She also had two flat tires on the Jeep. The valve stems had been cut clean off. No one had seen anything. Translation: No one had seen Mullen exact his revenge. She called Meyette's Garage and was told it would be an hour before anyone could get away to help.

The afternoon was warm and muggy with the breath of a storm building out over the Gulf. Annie walked along the footpath on the bank of the bayou. The mob would be gathering for Noblier's press conference, she knew, but she wanted no part of that. She had to think the sheriff would omit her name from the story of the Faulkner attack. He wouldn't want the press taking any more interest in her than they already had. He would do what he thought was best for his department and his people, and if that meant bending or omitting the truth, then to hell with the truth.

And who am I to criticize? Annie thought as she stopped across the street from Bayou Realty. The end justified the means – as long as the end was for the good of humankind, or yourself, or someone you loved, or some higher principle.

She had expected to see a CLOSED sign in the window of the realty office, but she could see the receptionist at her desk. The woman looked up expectantly as Annie walked in and the bell jingled, announcing her.

'It's not bad news, is it?' the woman asked, her cheeks paling. 'The hospital would have called. I just spoke with – Oh, mercy.'

The last words squeezed out of her like the final breath of air leaving a balloon. She looked fiftysomething with a matron's helmet of sprayed-hard gray-blond hair. Well dressed, nails done, real gold jewelry. The placard on her desk said GRACE IRVINE.

'No,' Annie said, realizing the uniform had spooked her. 'I don't have any news. The last I heard, there hadn't been any change.'

'No,' Grace said with a measure of relief. 'No change. That was what they just told me. Oh, my.' She patted her chest. 'You frightened me.'

'I'm sorry,' Annie said as she helped herself to the chair beside the desk. 'I was surprised to see the office open.'

'Well, I didn't find out what had happened until nearly noon. Of course, I was concerned when Lindsay didn't show up at her usual time, but I assumed she had made an impromptu meeting with a client. We do that, don't we? Rationalize. Even after Pam –'

She broke off and pressed a hand to her mouth as tears washed over her eyes. 'I can't believe this is happening,' she

315

whispered. 'I tried calling her on her cellular phone. I tried the house. Finally I went out there, and there were deputies and that yellow tape across the door.'

She shook her head, at a loss for words. For an ordinary person, stumbling onto a crime scene had to be like stepping into an alternate reality.

'I kept the office open because I didn't know what else to do. I couldn't bear the thought of sitting at home, waiting, or sitting in that horrible waiting room at the hospital. The phone was ringing and ringing. There were appointments to cancel, and I had to call Lindsay's family. ... I just felt I should stay.'

'You've known Lindsay a long time?'

'I knew Pam her whole life. Her mother is my second cousin once removed on the Chandler side. I've known Lindsay since the girls were in college. Dear, both of them, absolutely dear girls. They all but took me in after my husband passed away last year. They said I needed something to do with my time besides grieve, and they were right.' She made a motion to the books spread open across her desk. 'I'm studying to get my license. I've been thinking about trying to buy Pam's share of the business from Donnie.'

She turned her face away and took a moment to compose herself, dabbing at the corners of her eyes with a linen hankie.

'I'm sorry, Deputy,' she apologized. 'I'm rambling on. What can I do for you? Are you working on the case?'

'In a manner of speaking,' Annie said. 'I'm the one who found Lindsay this morning. She had left a message on my machine last night saying that she had something to tell me in relation to Pam's case. I was wondering if she might have told you what it was.'

'Oh. Oh, no, I'm afraid not. It was hectic here yesterday. Lindsay had several appointments in the morning. Then Donnie showed up unannounced, and they had a bit of a row over the business dealings and all. They never did get along, you know. Then the new listings arrived. I had an obligation in the afternoon at my grandson's school. He's in second grade at Sacred Heart. It was law enforcement day, oddly enough. McGruff the Crime Dog came with an officer. The grandparents were invited to attend.'

'I hear that's very popular,' Annie said flatly.

'I found it rather strange, to be perfectly frank. Anyway, Lindsay and I never had a chance to talk. I know she had something on her mind, but I assumed she told the detective. You may want to ask him.'

'The –' The words caught in Annie's throat. 'Who? Which detective?'

'Detective Stokes,' Grace Irvine said. 'She saw him over the lunch hour.'

29

Mouton's was the kind of place few men entered without a gun or a knife. Squatting on stilts on the bank of Bayou Noir south of Luck, it was the hangout of poachers and thieves and others living on the ragged hem of society. People looking for trouble looked at Mouton's, where just about anything could be had for the right price and no one asked any questions.

It was the latter truth that appealed to Nick on a Tuesday afternoon. He was in no mood for the Voodoo Lounge, wanted no one patting his back or expressing their useless sympathy for his situation. He wanted whiskey, settled for a beer, and waited for Stokes to show.

He had dragged himself out of bed at noon and forced himself through the Tai Chi forms, meditating on the movement of each aching muscle, trying to force the pain out with the power of his mind. The process had been excruciating and exhausting, but his sense of being was clearer for it. His mind was sharp, his nerves coiled tight as springs, as he nursed his beer, his back to a corner.

A couple of bikers were playing pool across the room with a barfly hooker hovering around them in a short skirt and push-up bra. Nearer, a pair of swamp rats sat at a table, trading stories and drinking Jax. John Lee Hooker was moaning on the juke, black delta blues in a redneck bar. There was an illegal card game going on in the back room, and horse racing on the color television mounted over the bar. The bartender looked like Paul Prudhomme's evil twin. He watched Nick with suspicion.

Nick took a slow pull on his beer and wondered if the guy had made him for a cop or for trouble. He knew he looked like the kind of trouble no one wanted on his doorstep, his face cut and bruised, the butt of the Ruger peeking out of

318

his open jacket. He had left his mirrored sunglasses on, despite the gloom of the bar.

One of the swampers scraped his chair back and rose, scratching at the giant middle finger screened on the front of his black T-shirt. A filthy red ball cap was stuck down on his head, the brim bent into an inverted U to frame a pair of eyes too small for a bony face. Nick watched him approach, sitting forward a little on his chair, ready to move. If nothing else, the beating at the hands of DiMonti's thugs had knocked the rust off his survival instincts.

'My buddy and me, we got a bet,' the swamper said, weaving a little on his feet. 'I say you're that cop what beat the shit outta that killer, Renard.'

Nick said nothing, pulled a long drag on his cigarette, and exhaled through his nose.

'You are, ain't you? I seen you on TV. Let me shake your hand, man.' He stepped in close and popped Nick on the arm with his fist like an old buddy, as if seeing him on the news had somehow forged a bond between them. 'You're a fuckin' hero!'

'You're mistaken,' Nick said calmly.

'No way. You're him. Come on, man, shake my hand. I got ten bucks on it.' He cuffed Nick's arm again and flashed a bad set of teeth. 'I say they shoulda let you put that asshole's lights out in a permanent way. Li'l bayou justice. Save the taxpayers some money, right?'

He moved to make another friendly punch. Nick caught his fist and came up out of the chair, twisting the man's arm in a way that turned the swamper's face into the rough plank wall.

'I don't like people touching me,' he said softly, his mouth inches from his erstwhile friend's ear. 'Me, I don't believe in casual intimacy between strangers, and that's what we are – strangers. I am not your friend and I sure as hell am nobody's hero. See the mistake you've made here?'

The swamp rat tried to nod, rubbing his mashed cheek against the wall. 'Hey – hey, I'm sorry, all right? No

319

offense,' he mumbled out the side of his mouth, spittle running down his chin.

'But you see, I've already taken offense, which is why I've always found apologies to be ineffectual and the products of false logic.'

Out of the corner of his eye Nick could see the bartender watching, one hand reaching down under the bar. The screen door slammed, the sound as sharp as gunfire. The swamp rat's buddy shot up from his chair, but he made no move to come any closer.

'Now you have to ask yourself,' Nick murmured, 'do you want your friend's ten dollars only to put it toward your doctor bills, or would you rather walk away a poorer but wiser man?'

'Jesus H., Nicky.' Stokes's voice came across the room, punctuated by the sound of his footfalls on the plank floor. 'I can't leave you alone ten minutes. You keep this up, you're gonna need a license to walk around in public.'

He came up alongside Nick, shaking his head. 'What'd he do? Touch you? Did you touch him?' he asked the swamp rat. 'Man, what were you thinking? Don't cross that line. The last guy that touched him is sucking his dinner through a straw.'

He tipped his fedora back and scratched his head. 'I'm telling you, Nicky, the inherent stupidity of humankind is enough to make me give up hope on the world as a whole. You want a drink? I need a drink.'

Nick stepped back from the swamper, his temper defused and dissipating, disappointment in himself coming in on the backwash. 'Sorry I lost my cool there,' he said. The corners of his mouth twitched at the joke. 'See? It doesn't mean shit.'

Rubbing a hand against his cheek, the swamp rat stumbled back to his buddy. The pair vacated their table and moved to the far end of the bar.

'You don't play well with others, Nicky,' Stokes complained, pulling a chair out from the table and turning it backward to straddle it. 'Where'd you learn your social skills – a reformatory?'

Nick ignored him. Shaking a cigarette out of the pack, he lit it on the move, needing to pace a bit to burn off the last of the energy spike. *Control. Center. Focus.* He'd had it there for a little while, and then it slipped away like rope through a sweaty hand.

'Long as I'm asking questions, what happened to your face? You run into the business end of a jealous husband?'

'I interrupted a business meeting. Mr DiMonti took exception.'

Stokes's brows lifted. '*Vic* "The Plug" DiMonti? The wiseguy?'

'You know him?' Nick asked.

'I know *of* him. Jesus, Nicky, you're a paranoid son of a bitch. First you think I set you up. Now you think I'm on the pad with the mob. And here I am – the best friend you got in this backwater. I could get a complex.' He shook his head sadly. 'You're the one lived in New Orleans, man, not me. What's DiMonti's beef with you?'

'I went to see Duval Marcotte. Marcotte is in real estate. DiMonti owns a construction company. Donnie Bichon is all of a sudden looking to sell his half of Bayou Realty. The realty company owns a fair amount of property 'purchased' by Pam from Bichon Bayou Development to keep Donnie's ass out of bankruptcy. And now I hear Lindsay Faulkner, of Bayou Realty, was attacked last night.'

'Raped. Probably the same guy did those other two,' Stokes said, motioning to catch the bartender's attention. 'This is some hard case with his pecker in overdrive. It wasn't no mob hit, for Christ's sake. You shoulda gone into the CIA, Nicky. They would love the way your mind works.'

'I don't make it for a mob hit. Me, I just don't like coincidence, that's all. You talk to Donnie?'

He nodded, glancing at the bar again. 'Christ, you scared the bartender off. I hope you're happy,' he muttered, casting a considering glance at Nick's half-empty bottle. 'You gonna drink that? I'm dying, man.'

'What'd he have to say for himself?'

'That he wishes he'd never heard of the Partout Parish Sheriff's Office. He tells me he was at his office 'til eleven doing paperwork, stopped off at the Voodoo for a couple, then went on home alone.' He drained the beer in two long gulps. 'I told him he oughta get himself a steady girlfriend. That boy is forever without corroboration. You know what I'm saying. But then he's short on brains for a college boy. Look what he blew off so he could chase tail. Pam was a fine lady and a meal ticket to boot, and he gave her nothing but a hard time.

'Why you chewing his bone anyway?' he asked, helping himself to a cigarette from the pack on the table. 'Guy bails you outta jail, the average man would show a little gratitude. You're trying to tie him to some big boogeyman conspiracy.'

'I don't like the connections, that's all.'

'Renard did Pam. You know it and I know it, my friend.'

'The rest is an unpleasant by-product,' Nick said, finally settling into his chair. 'What else have I got to do with my time?'

'Go fishing. Get laid. Take up golf. Get laid. I'd mainly get laid if I was you. You need it, pard. Your spring's wound too damn tight, and that's a fact. That's why you're always going off on people.'

He checked his watch and sat back. The place was filling up as day edged into evening. A waitress materialized from the back room. Dyed blond curls and a tight white tank top from Hooters in Miami. He flashed her the Dudley Do-Right smile.

'A pair of Jax, darlin', and a side order of what you got.'

With a sly smirk she leaned down close and reached across in front of him for the empty, treating him with the up-close and personal view of her cleavage. He gave a tiger growl as she walked away. Across the room, the biker with

JUNIOR stitched on the breast pocket of his denim vest looked over from his pool game, scowling. Stokes kept one eye on the waitress.

'She wants me. If I'm lyin', I'm dyin'.'

'She wants a big tip.'

'You're a pessimist, Nicky. That's what happens when you look for the hidden meaning in every damn thing. You're doomed to disappointment – you know what I'm saying? Go for face value. Life's a whole hell of a lot simpler that way.'

'Like Faulkner's rape?' Nick said. 'You think it's part of the pattern because that's simpler, Chaz?'

Stokes scowled. 'I think it because it's a fact.'

'There's no change in the MO between this and the other two?'

'There's some, probably because she heard him coming. But everything else matches up. It was mean and clean, just like the others. Guy's probably got a sheet a mile long. I got a call in to the state to see what we might see.'

'Why her? Why Faulkner?'

'Why not? She's a looker, lives alone. He maybe didn't know she's a dyke.'

Nick arched a brow over the rim of his shades. 'She wouldn't sleep with you either, huh? This parish is just crawling with lesbians.'

'Hey. I call 'em like I see 'em.'

Someone had changed the channel on the television over the bar to a station out of Lafayette. The graphics said the broadcast was coming live from Bayou Breaux. Noblier's meaty face filled the screen. He stood behind a podium sprouting microphones, looking as unhappy as the proverbial cat in a room full of rocking chairs. Press conference. Every figurative rocker would be aiming for his tail.

Nick nodded toward the set. 'Why aren't you there? I hear you got the task force.'

'Hell, I *am* the task force,' Chaz muttered. 'Me and Quinlan and a few uniforms – Mullen and Compton from days, Degas and Fortier from nights. Big fuckin' deal. Quinlan tried to get the BBPD in on it – Z-Top and Riva. No way. Noblier and the chief are like dueling hard-ons on account of you. The official excuse is that the rapes have all been outside city limits. It's our turf, it's our case, it's our task force.' He shook his head and pulled on the cigarette. 'It's all for show anyway, man. We got zippo to go on. This is supposed to make the common folk feel safe.'

'So how come you're not up there reassuring all the single ladies, Hollywood?'

'Shit, I hate that media stuff,' he said. 'Bunch of hairdos asking stupid questions. I'll pass, thanks. I got a big enough headache as it is. Guess who called in on Faulkner?' he said with a pained expression. 'Broussard. Now what do you suppose she was doing there?'

Nick shrugged, the picture of disinterest. His attention had caught on the bikers. The one called Junior looked like a red-bearded upright freezer. An Aryan Brotherhood tattoo was etched into his right biceps. He stared at Stokes with reptilian eyes.

'Claims she's looking to buy a house. Yeah, right, I believe that,' Stokes sneered. 'It was just a coincidence. Like it was just a coincidence she came on you with Renard.' He shook his head as he helped himself to another smoke. 'I'm telling you, man, that chick is bad news. She's always where she hadn't oughta be. You want a conspiracy, you go see what she's up to. You know, rumor has it she's screwing the deputy DA – Doucet. There's your conspiracy.'

Junior came toward them from the pool table, intercepting the waitress and helping himself to one of the beers. Stokes swore under his breath and stood up.

'Hey, man, don't fuck with my drink.'

The biker curled his lip. 'You want a drink, go stick your head in a toilet.'

Stokes's eyes widened. 'You got a problem with me being here, Junior Dickhead? You think maybe I'm a little too brown for this bar?'

Junior took a swig of the Jax and belched. He glanced over his shoulder at his partner. 'This is the kind of trouble you get when niggers breed with white women.'

Stokes dropped a shoulder and hit him running, knocking Junior into the pool table. The biker sprawled on his back, his head banging hard on the slate. Balls bounced and scattered. The other biker stepped away, holding his cue stick like a baseball bat, as Chaz pulled his badge and shoved it in Junior's face.

'This make me any lighter, asshole?' he bellowed. 'How about this?' He pulled a Glock nine-millimeter from his belt holster and jammed the barrel into Junior's left nostril. 'You think you're the superior race, you Nazi cocksucker? What you thinkin' now?'

He slapped the biker hard on the cheek with the badge, then dropped it on the table and jammed his hand up under the man's chin. 'Don't you call me nigger! I ain't no nigger, you motherfucking cracker piece of shit! Call me a nigger and I'll blow your fuckin' head off and say you assaulted an officer!'

Junior made a strangled sound, his big face turning a shade redder than his beard.

Nick took in the wild rage in Stokes's eyes, knowing he was close to an edge, surprised by it, surprised to see it in someone else. Maybe they had something more in common than the job after all.

Nick braced his hands on the pool table, and leaned into Junior's bug-eyed field of vision. 'See what you get for being politically incorrect these days, Junior? People just don't take being abused like they used to.'

Stokes backed off and Junior rolled over, choking up phlegm on the green felt.

Stokes blew out a breath and forced a grin, twitching the tension out of his shoulders. 'Damn, Nicky, you spoiled my fun.'

Nick shook his head and started toward the door. 'And you say I'm the crazy one.'

Stokes shrugged off the responsibility. 'Hey, what can I say? He crossed my line.'

Annie sat at her kitchen table, a fork in a carton of kung pow chicken, Jann Arden singing in the background. The strange, voyeuristic lyrics of 'Living Under June' touched off thoughts of her own situation. The experiences of one person seeping into another's life, that person's life touching someone else.

Had she really believed she could become involved in this investigation and float from point to point in a bubble of invisibility? People talked to one another. The case was open and ongoing. Stokes was supposed to be working it; of course he would speak to Lindsay Faulkner. Lindsay had spoken with Annie. Why wouldn't she mention it to Stokes? She had no reason not to.

'Except that it could mean my ass,' Annie muttered.

If Stokes took this to the sheriff ... It made her stomach hurt to imagine what Noblier would have to say about it. They'd have to bury her in that damn dog suit.

But Gus had said nothing outright when he'd called her into his office about the Faulkner attack, which could only mean Stokes hadn't brought it up ... yet.

'Hooker was right,' Gus had growled, fixing her with his classic look of disgruntlement. 'It seems if there's a pile of shit around, you'll find one way or another to step in it. Just how did you come to be at Lindsay Faulkner's home, Deputy Broussard?'

She stuck with the lie she'd told Stokes, wondering too late if she'd trapped herself. There would be no paperwork at Bayou Realty to back her up. What if Stokes walked into the realty office and requested a file that didn't exist?

She would have to deal with that burning bridge when she came to it, she decided, setting her dinner aside. The question that nagged her more was this: If Stokes knew she was sniffing around his case and he didn't want her there, why hadn't he gone to the sheriff?

Maybe Faulkner *hadn't* told him about their meetings. There was no way of knowing until either Stokes made a move or Lindsay Faulkner regained consciousness.

'Why can't you just mind your own business, Annie?' she mused aloud.

Downstairs in the store, Stevie the night clerk was watching Speed again, deep in lust with Sandra Bullock. The sounds of crashes and explosions came up through the floor as if a small war were going on below. Ordinarily Annie was able to shut out the noise. Tonight she found herself wishing for the quiet of Fourcade's study, but she had no intention of seeking it out. She needed a night off, time to clear her head and take a hard look at what she'd gotten herself into. For all the good that would do her now.

Still, in spite of herself, she wondered how Fourcade was doing. She had called from a pay phone at noon and left a message on his machine about Lindsay Faulkner. He hadn't called her back. She occasionally lapsed into panicked thoughts of him lying on his floor dead from internal bleeding, but then talked herself out of them. It wasn't the first time he'd been on the receiving end of a pounding. He knew better than she did the extent of his own injuries.

He certainly hadn't kissed like a man on the brink of death.

No, he had kissed her like a blind man sensing light, like a man who needed to make a connection with another soul and wasn't quite sure how.

'Don't be stupid,' she muttered, turning her attention to the papers she had brought home with her from Nick's place the night before – the reports of the harassment Pam Bichon had endured before her murder, copies of reports from the Bayou Breaux PD on incidents that had occurred at her office.

Pam had feared for her safety and for Josie's. But her level of fear had seemed out of proportion to the officers who had taken the calls. While they had drawn no conclusions in the reports, it wasn't hard for another cop to read between the lines. They thought she was overreacting, being unreasonable, wasting their time. Why would she be afraid of Marcus Renard? He seemed so normal, so harmless. Why should she think he was the one making the breather calls? What proof did she have he was stalking the shadows of her Quail Run property? How could it possibly frighten her to receive a silk scarf from an anonymous admirer?

Gooseflesh swept down Annie's arms. She knew Renard had given Pam a number of small gifts, but the only gift ever mentioned in detail in any of the paperwork or news reports had been a necklace with a heart-shaped pendant. He tried to give it to her on her birthday, shortly before her death.

Annie pulled her binder of news clippings and paged through the pockets, hunting for the one burning in her memory. It was a piece from the Lafayette *Daily Advertiser* that had run shortly after Renard's arrest, and it spoke specifically of Pam's birthday, when she had gone into the Bowen & Briggs office with a cardboard box containing the gifts he had given her during the preceding weeks. She had reportedly hurled the box at Renard, shouting angrily for him to leave her alone, that she wanted nothing to do with him.

She had given back to him everything he had ever given her, and among those gifts was a silk scarf. Annie could find no detailed description of it. The detectives had looked for the rejected gifts during a search of Renard's home but had never found them, and didn't consider them important. How would anyone consider a lovely silk scarf proof of harassment?

Nausea swirled through Annie as an idea hit. She reached across the table for the box, lifted the scarf and ran it through her fingers, her mind racing.

'You look like her, you know,' Donnie said, his voice strangely dreamy. 'The shape of your face ... the hair ... the mouth ...'

'You fit the victim profile,' Fourcade said. '... you came into

his life, chère. Like it was meant to be. … He could fall in love with you.'

Had Pam Bichon held this very scarf in her hands, feeling the same strange sense of disquiet Annie felt right now?

The phone rang, sending her half a foot off her chair. She tossed the scarf aside and went into the living room.

The machine picked up on the fourth ring and she listened to herself advise the caller.

'If you're someone I'll actually want to talk to, leave a message after the tone. If you're a reporter, a salesman, a heavy breather, a crank, or someone with an opinion of me I don't want to hear, just don't bother. I'll only erase you.'

The warning hadn't seemed to deter anyone. The tape had been full by the time she'd gotten home. Word of her involvement in the Faulkner case had leaked out of the department like oil through a bad gasket. Three reporters had been lying in wait for her on the store gallery when she got home. But it wasn't a reporter who waited for the tone.

'Annie, this is Marcus.' His voice was tight. 'Could you please call me back? Someone took a shot at me tonight.'

Annie grabbed the receiver. 'I'm here. What happened?'

'Just what I said. Someone took a shot at me through a window.'

'Why are you calling me? Call 911.'

'We did. The deputies who came said it was a pity the guy was such a poor shot. They dug the bullet out of the wall and left. I'd like someone to look around, investigate.'

'And you'd like that someone to be me?'

'You're the only one who cares, Annie. You're the only one in that whole damn department who cares about justice being done. If it were up to the rest of them, I'd have been alligator bait weeks ago.'

He was silent for a moment. Annie waited, apprehension coiling around her stomach like a python.

'Please, Annie, say you'll come. I need you.'

Out over the Atchafalaya, thunder rumbled like distant cannon fire. He wanted her. He needed her. He was probably a killer. She had immersed herself in this case up to her chin. She took a breath and went deeper.

'I'll be right there.'

30

We were sitting here having coffee like civilized people,'
Doll Renard said, gesturing to her dining room table like a
tour guide, 'when suddenly the glass in that door shattered.
I nearly had a heart attack! We're not the kind of people
who have guns or know about guns! To think that someone
would shoot into our home! What kind of world are we
living in? To think I used to believe in the good of people!'

'Where were y'all sitting? Which chairs?'

Doll sniffed. 'The other officers didn't even bother to ask.
I was right here, in my usual place,' she said, going to the
chair at the end of the table.

'Victor was here in his usual seat.' Marcus claimed a chair
that put his brother's back to the French doors.

At the mention of his name, Victor shook his head and
slapped the palm of one hand on the table. He now sat
at the head of the table, rocking himself, muttering
incessantly. 'Not now. Not now. Very red. Enter out.
Enter out *now*!'

'He'll be ranting for days,' Doll said bitterly.

Marcus cut her a look. 'Mother, please. We're all upset.
Victor has as much reason as the rest of us. More than you –
he could have been killed.'

Doll's jaw dropped as if he'd struck her. 'I never said he
shouldn't be upset! How dare you talk to me that way in
front of a guest!'

'I'm sorry, Mother. Forgive my short temper. My manners aren't what they should be. Someone meant to kill me
earlier.'

Annie cleared her throat to draw his attention. 'Where
were you sitting?'

He glanced toward the shattered door. Dozens of insects
had flocked in through the hole and now swarmed around

331

the light fixture. Gnats dotted the ceiling like flecks of black ink. 'I was out of the room.'

'You weren't sitting here when the shot was fired?'

'No. I had left the room several moments prior.'

'Why?'

'To use the bathroom. We'd been sitting here drinking coffee.'

'Do you own a handgun or a rifle?'

'Of course not,' he said, a flush creeping up his neck.

'I wouldn't have a gun in this house,' Doll said with great affront. 'I wouldn't even let Marcus have a BB gun as a boy. They're filthy instruments of violence and nothing more. His father had guns,' she said with accusation. 'I got rid of every one of them. Temptations to violence.'

'You can't think I staged this,' Marcus said, looking hard at Annie.

'Staged it?' Doll shrilled. 'What do you mean – "staged" it?'

Annie turned her back on them and went to the wall where the slug had buried itself in the thick horsehair plaster. It looked as if the call deputies had dug the thing out with a pickax. Plaster littered the floor in crumbled chunks and fine dust. The bullet had struck a good foot above the heads of anyone seated at the table. One of the things any marksman had to consider when aiming was the drop of the bullet as it traveled away from the barrel of the gun. To hit where this shot had hit, the triggerman had to have been aiming still higher.

'Either he was a piss-poor shot or he never meant to hit anyone,' she said.

'What do you mean?' Doll asked. 'Someone *shot at us*! We were sitting right here!'

'Had you noticed anyone hanging around earlier in the day?' Annie asked. 'Today or any other day recently?'

'Fishermen go past on the bayou,' she said, fluttering one bony hand in the direction of the waterway as she clutched the bodice of her baggy housedress with the other. 'And those horrible reporters come and go, though we have nothing to say to them. They do as they will. I've never seen such an ill-mannered lot in all my life. There was a time in this country when etiquette meant something –'

Marcus squeezed his eyes shut. 'Mother, could we please stick to the subject? Annie isn't interested in a discussion of the decline of formal manners and mores.'

Doll's complexion mottled pink and white. Her face went tight, pulling skin against bone and tendon. 'Well, excuse me if my views aren't important to you, Marcus,' she said tightly. 'Pardon me if you believe *Annie* doesn't want to hear what I think.'

'This has been traumatic for all of you, I'm sure,' Annie said diplomatically.

'Don't patronize me!' Doll snapped. Her entire body was trembling with anger. 'You think we're either criminals or fools. You're no better than any of the others.'

'Mother –'

'*Red! Red! No!*' Victor shrieked, rocking so hard the chair legs came up off the floor. He slapped the tabletop over and over.

'If you believe she cares about us, Marcus, you *are* a fool.' Doll turned away from him to her other son. 'Come along, Victor. You're going to bed. No one here needs our presence.'

'*Not now! Not now! Very red!*' Victor's voice screeched upward like metal rending. He curled himself into a ball as his mother clamped a white-knuckled hand on his shoulder.

'Come along, Victor!'

Sobbing, Victor Renard unfolded his body from the chair and allowed his mother to tow him from the room.

Marcus hung his head and stared at the floor, embarrassment and anger coloring his battered face. 'Well, wasn't that lovely? Another night in the life of the happy Renard family. I'm sorry, Annie. Sometimes I think my mother

333

doesn't any more know what to do with her emotions than does Victor.'

Annie made no comment. It was more useful for her to see the Renards coming apart at the seams than to see them wrapped tightly in control. She moved toward the French doors, stepping around the broken glass. 'I'd like to look around outside.'

'Of course.'

Out on the terrace she filled her lungs with air that tasted of copper. Clouds appeared to sag to the treetops, bloated with rain that had yet to fall.

'Just to set things straight,' Marcus said, 'my mother has never believed in the good in people. She's been waiting for a lynch mob to show up on the front lawn, and never misses the opportunity to point out that it's all my fault. I'm sure she's secretly pleased by this in her own twisted way.'

'I didn't come here to discuss your mother, Mr Renard.'

'Please call me Marcus.' He turned toward her. The light that filtered out from the house softened and shadowed his bruises and stitches. With the swelling gone he was no longer grotesque, merely homely. He didn't look dangerous, he looked pathetic. 'Please, Annie. I need to at least pretend I have a friend in all this.'

'Your lawyer is your friend. I'm a cop.'

'But you're here and you don't have to be. You came for me.'

She wanted to tell him differently, had tried to set him straight, but either he didn't listen or he twisted the truth to suit himself.

It was the kind of thinking that applied to stalkers and other obsessive personalities. The unwillingness or inability to accept the truth. There was nothing overt in Renard's attitude. Nothing that could have been deemed crazy, and yet this subtle insistence to bend reality to his wishes was disturbing.

She wanted to distance herself from him. But the truth

was the closer she got to him, the more likely she was to see something the detectives had missed. He might let down his guard, make a mistake. *'He could fall in love with you ...'* and she'd be there to nail him.

'All right ... Marcus,' she said, his name sticking in her mouth like a gob of peanut butter.

He let out a breath, as if in relief, and slid his hands into his pants pockets. 'Fourcade,' he said. 'You asked if anyone had come by recently. Fourcade was here on Saturday. On the bayou.'

'Do you have any reason to believe Detective Fourcade is the one who took that shot tonight?'

He made a choking laugh, pulled a handkerchief out of his pocket, and dabbed at the corners of his mouth. 'He tried to kill me last week, why not this week?'

'He wasn't himself that night. He'd lost a tough decision in court. He'd been drinking. He –'

'You're not going to make excuses for him at the hearing next week, are you?' he asked, looking at her with shock. 'You were there. You saw what he was doing to me. You said it yourself: he was trying to kill me.'

'We're not talking about last week. We're talking about tonight. Did you see him tonight? Have you seen him since Saturday? Has he called you? Has he threatened you?'

'No.'

'And of course you didn't see the shooter because you happened to be in the bathroom at the precise moment –'

'You don't believe me,' he said flatly.

'I believe if Detective Fourcade wanted you dead, you'd be meeting your maker right now,' Annie said. 'Nick Fourcade isn't going to mistake your brother for you or put a shot in the wall a foot above your head. He'd blow your skull apart like a rotten melon, and I don't doubt but that he could do it in the dark at a hundred yards.'

'He came here in a boat Saturday. He could have been on the bayou –'

'Everybody in this parish owns a boat, and about ninety

percent of them think you should be drawn and quartered in public. Fourcade is hardly the only possibility here,' Annie argued. 'To be perfectly frank with you, Marcus, I *do* think you're a more likely candidate than Fourcade.'

He turned away from her then, staring out at the darkness. 'I didn't do this. Why would I?'

'To get attention. To get me over here. To sic the press on Fourcade.'

'You can test my hands for gunpowder residue, search the premises for the gun. I didn't do it.' He shook his head in disgust. 'That seems to be my motto these last months: I didn't do it. And while y'all are busy trying to prove me a liar, killers and would-be killers are running around loose.'

He blotted at his mouth again. Annie watched him, tried to read him, wondered how much of what he was letting her see was an act and how much of it he bought into himself.

'You know the worst part of all this?' he asked, his voice so soft Annie had to step closer to hear him. 'I never got to mourn Pam. I've not been allowed to express my grief, my outrage, my hurt, my loss. She was such a lovely person. So pretty.'

He looked down at Annie as lightning flashed and his expression was gilded in silver – a strange, glassy, dreamy look, as if he were looking at a memory that wasn't quite true.

'I miss her,' he whispered. 'I wish ...'

What? That he hadn't killed her? That she had returned his affection instead of his gifts? Annie held her breath, waiting.

'I wish you believed me,' he murmured.

'It's not my job to believe you, Marcus,' she said. 'It's my job to find the truth.'

'I want you to know the truth,' he whispered.

The intimacy in his tone unnerved her, and she stepped back from him as the wind came in a great exhalation from the heavens, rattling the trees like giant pompons.

336

'I'll keep on top of this,' she said. 'See if the deputies come up with anything. But that's all I can do. I'm in enough hot water as it is. I'd appreciate it if you didn't tell anyone I'd been here.'

He drew his thumb and forefinger across his lips. 'Our secret. That makes two.' The idea seemed to please him.

Annie frowned. 'I'm checking on that truck – your Good Samaritan the night Pam died. I'm not making promises anything will come of it, but I want you to know I'm looking.'

He tried to smile. 'I knew you would. You wouldn't want to think you saved my life for no good reason.'

'I don't want it said the investigation wasn't thorough on all counts,' she corrected. 'For the record, Detective Fourcade looked into it, he just didn't find anything. Probably because there's nothing to find.'

'You'll find the truth, Annie,' he murmured, reaching out to touch her shoulder. His hand lingered a heartbeat too long. 'I promise you will.'

Annie's skin crawled. She shrugged off his touch. 'I'm gonna go get my flashlight. I want to have a look around the yard before the rain starts.'

The yard gave up no secrets. She searched for twenty minutes. Renard watched her from the terrace for a while, then disappeared into the house, returning some time later with his own flashlight, to help her look.

Annie didn't know what she had hoped to find. A shell casing, maybe. But she found none. The shooter could have disposed of it. It may well have been in the bayou if that was where the shooter had been – if the shooter had been anyone other than Renard himself.

She mulled the possibilities over in her mind as she drove out of the Renard driveway and headed for the main road. It wouldn't hurt to know where Hunter Davidson had been at the time of the shooting, though he was an old sportsman and she couldn't imagine him missing a target.

337

Maybe he had drawn a bead on the back of Victor Renard's head, having mistaken him for Marcus, and while staring through the crosshairs of the rifle's scope had been hit with the enormity of taking a human life, then popped the shot into the wall instead.

It seemed more likely that he would have looked at Renard in his sights and pulled the trigger on a tide of emotion. Remorse, if it came at all, would come after the revenge.

Nor did it make any sense to consider Fourcade as a suspect, for the very reasons she had given Marcus. Renard himself, on the other hand, had everything to gain by staging the incident. It gave him an excuse to call her. It cast suspicion on Fourcade, could be used to draw the media. The story could have rolled on the ten o'clock news, creating a full-fledged furor by morning. That's certainly what Renard's lawyer would have wanted.

Then where were the reporters? Renard hadn't called them; he had called her.

'You're here and you don't have to be. You came for me.'

The bayou road was empty and dark, a lonely trench between the dense walls of woods that ran on either side of it. The rain had finally begun to fall, an angry spitting that would, any second, become a deluge. Annie hit the switch for the wipers and glanced in the rearview mirror as lightning flashed – illuminating the silhouette of a car behind her. Big car. Too close. No lights.

She cursed herself for not paying attention. She had no idea how long the car had been behind her or where it had pulled onto the road.

As if the driver had sensed her notice, the headlights flared on – high beams glaring into the Jeep, blinding in their sudden intensity. At the same time, the heavens opened and the rain came down in a gush. Annie clicked the wipers up to high and punched the gas. The Jeep sprinted forward with the tail car right on its bumper.

Annie nudged the gas pedal again, the speedometer

springing toward seventy. The car came with her like a dog on the heels of a rabbit. She grabbed the radio mike, then realized the cord had been severed cleanly from the base unit.

Premeditation. This was no random game. She had been chosen to play. But with whom?

There was no time to consider names. There was no time to do anything but act and react. She was outrunning her visibility, flying blind through sheets of rain. The road along here curved and bent back like a snake as it ran parallel to the bayou. Every corner tested the Jeep's traction and presented the threat of hydroplaning. Another mile and the road became a virtual land bridge between two areas of dense swamp.

The tail car swung into the left lane and roared up beside her. It was big – a Caddy, maybe – a tank of a car. Annie could sense the heft of it beside her. Too big for the curves, she thought, and hoped it would fall back. But it stayed with her, and she abandoned the distraction of hope, focusing on driving as the Jeep rocked into a turn and the wheels fought against her will.

The car had the inside of the curve and bore wide, hitting the Jeep, metal grinding on metal, trying to muscle her off the pavement. Her rear outside wheel hit the shoulder, and the Jeep jerked beneath her. Annie put her foot down and hung on, straining to hold the vehicle on course. The view through the windshield tilted, then slammed back hard onto a level plane.

'Son of a bitch!' she yelled.

She floored the accelerator as the road straightened out, and prayed there was nothing in the way. It was raining too hard for the water to run off the pavement, and plumes sprayed up from the wheels of the Jeep. The drag had to be pulling harder on the low-slung car, but it hung beside her, swerving in for another hit. Her side window shattered, chunks of it falling in on her.

Annie jerked the Jeep back into the car. The crash was

like a burst of white noise. The car held its ground, repelling the Jeep like a rubber ball. For a heartbeat she had no control as the Jeep skidded toward the shoulder and the inky blackness of the swamp beyond. The right front tire hit the shoulder and dropped. Mud spewed up across the hood, across the windshield. The wipers smeared the mess across the glass.

Annie cranked the wheel to the left and prayed at the speed of sound as the Jeep bucked along, half on the road, half off, the swamp sucking at it like a hungry monster. From the corner of her eye, she could see the car swerving toward her again, and for a split second she saw the driver – a black apparition with gleaming eyes and a mouth tearing open on a scream she couldn't hear. Then the road curved hard to the right directly in front of her and the Jeep jumped back on the pavement, bumping noses with the car, sending a shower of sparks up into the rain.

Options streaked through Annie's mind like shooting stars. She couldn't out-muscle him and she couldn't outrun him, but she had four good all-terrain tires and a machine that was nimble for its size. If she could make the levee road, she would shake him.

She hit the brakes and went into a skid, downshifting. As the car shot past her, she bent the skid into a 180-degree turn and hit the gas. In the rearview, she could see the brake lights on the car glowing like red eyes in the night. By the time he got turned around, she would be halfway to the levee – if her luck held, if the trail out to Clarence Gauthier's camp wasn't under a foot of water.

Her headlights hit the sign. Nailed to the stump of a swamp oak that had been struck by lightning twenty years ago, the sign was a jagged piece of cypress plank, hand-lettered in blaze orange: KEEP OUT – TRESPASSER WILL BE ATE.

Behind her the car was lurching around. Annie swung the Jeep onto the dirt path and hit the brakes. Ahead of her, water lay across the trail in a glossy black sheet dimpled by rain. Too late, she thought she might have been wiser to sprint the miles back to Renard's house to take refuge with one killer in order to escape another. But the car was barreling toward her now, taking advantage of her hesitation.

If she couldn't make it across to higher ground, she was his, whoever the hell he was, for whatever the hell he wanted. She'd have to go for the Sig in the duffel bag on the passenger's seat, and hold the son of a bitch off until help came along.

She gunned the engine as she let out the clutch. The Jeep hit the water, engine roaring, wheels churning. Churning and catching. Churning and sinking.

'Come on, come on, come on!' Annie chanted.

The back end of the Jeep twisted to the right as the back tire slid toward the edge of the submerged trail. The engine was screaming. Annie was screaming. In the mirror she caught a glimpse of the car pulling up on the road behind her.

Then the front tires caught hold of firmer ground, and the Jeep scrambled to safety.

'Oh, Jesus. Oh, God. Oh, shit,' Annie muttered as she sped down the twisting trail, branches slapping at the windshield.

Someone ran out of the shack where Clarence Gauthier kept his fighting dogs. Annie took a right before she got to the camp, and flinched at the sound of a shotgun going off in warning. Another half mile on the trail that was rapidly disintegrating to bog and she was finally able to climb up onto the levee road.

Clear of the woods, the rain closed around her like a liquid curtain. Only the lightning allowed her nightmare glimpses of the world beyond the beam of her headlights. Black, dead, not a living thing in sight.

She felt ill. She was shaking.

Somebody had just tried to kill her.

The Corners store was closed. The light in Sos and

Fanchon's living room glowed amber through the gloom across the parking lot. Annie pulled the Jeep in close to the staircase on the south side of the building and ran up to her landing. Her hands were trembling as she worked the lock. She struggled to mentally talk her nerves into calming down. She was a cop, after all. That someone tried to kill her probably shouldn't have bothered her so much. Maybe next time she would shrug it off entirely. Par for the course. Just another day on the job.

The hell it was.

Once inside the entry, she shed her sneakers, dropped her gear bag, and went straight to the kitchen. She pulled a chair across the floor. A dusty bottle of Jack Daniel's sat in the cupboard over the refrigerator.

She thought of Mullen as she pulled the whiskey down and set it on the counter. He would have liked this moment on videotape – evidence of her sudden alcoholism. Son of a bitch. If she found out he'd been behind the wheel of that car tonight ... what? The consequences would go far beyond having him charged with a crime.

Life should have been so much simpler, Annie thought as she unscrewed the cap from the Jack and poured a double shot. She took a long sip, grimacing as the stuff slid down.

'You gonna offer me some of that?'

Heart in her throat, Annie bolted around. The glass hit the floor and shattered.

'I locked that door when I left,' she said.

Fourcade shrugged. 'And I told you before: It's not much of a lock.'

'Where's your truck?'

'Out of sight.'

Nick grabbed a dish towel and bent down to clean up the mess. 'You're a mite on the edge tonight, 'Toinette.'

He looked up at her standing beside the jaunty gator on her refrigerator. Her face was pale as death, her eyes shining like glass beads, her hair hanging in damp strings. He could feel the tension in her like the vibrations of a tuning fork.

'I suppose I am,' she said. 'Someone just tried to kill me.'

'What?' He jerked upright and looked her over as if he expected to see blood.

'Someone tried to run me off the bayou road into the swamp. And he damn near succeeded.'

Annie looked around her kitchen, at the old cupboards and the vintage fifties table, at the canisters on the counter and the ivy plant she had started from a sprig in Serena Doucet's bridal bouquet five years ago. She looked at the cat clock, watched its eyes and tail move with the passing seconds. Everything looked somehow different, as if she hadn't seen any of it in a very long time and now found none of it quite matched the images in her memory.

The whiskey boiled in her empty stomach like acid. She could still feel its path down the back of her throat.

'Somebody tried to kill me,' she murmured again, amazed. Dizziness swept through her like a wave. With as much cool and dignity as she could muster, she looked at Nick and said, 'Excuse me. I have to go throw up now.'

31

This is not one of my finer moments.'

Annie sat on her knees in front of the toilet, propped up on one side by the old claw-foot bathtub. She felt like a withering husk, too drained for anything deeper than cursory embarrassment. 'So much for my image as a lush.'

'Did you get a look at the driver?' Fourcade asked, leaning a shoulder against the door frame.

'Just a glimpse. I think he was wearing a ski mask. It was dark. It was raining. Everything happened so fast. God,' she complained in disgust. 'I sound like every vic I've ever rolled my eyes at.'

'Tags?'

She shook her head. 'I was too busy trying to keep my ass out of the swamp.

'I don't know,' she murmured. 'I thought Renard staged the shooting just to get me over there, but maybe not. Maybe whoever took that shot hung around, watched the cops, watched me come and go.'

'Why go after you? Why not wait 'til you're gone and take another crack at Renard?'

The answer might have made her throw up again if she hadn't already emptied her system. If the assailant was after Renard, it made no sense to go after her.

'You're probably right about the shooting,' he said. 'Renard, he wanted an excuse to call you. That story he gave you is lame as a three-legged dog.'

Annie pulled herself up to sit on the edge of the tub. 'If that's true, then Cadillac Man was there for one reason – me. He had to have followed me over there.'

She looked up at Fourcade as he came into the room, half hoping he would tell her no just to ease her worry. He didn't, wouldn't, wasn't that kind of man. The facts were

344

the facts, he would see no purpose in padding the truth to soften the blows.

With a dubious look he pulled the towel away from the ceramic grasping hand that stuck out from the wall and soaked one end of it with cold tap water.

'You manage to piss people off, 'Toinette,' he said, taking a seat on the closed toilet.

'I don't mean to.'

'You have to realize that's a good thing. But you're not paying attention. You act first and think later.'

'Look who's talking.'

She pressed the cold cloth to one cheek, then the other. He looked concerned rather than contrite. She would have been better off with the latter. She was safer thinking of him as a mentor than pondering the meaning of these odd moments when he seemed to be something else.

'Me, I always think first, *chère*. My logic is occasionally flawed, that's all,' he said. 'How you doing? You okay?'

He leaned forward and pushed a strand of hair off her cheek. His knee brushed against her thigh, and in spite of everything Annie felt a subtle charge of electricity.

'Sure. I'm swell. Thanks.'

She pushed to her feet and went to the sink to brush her teeth.

'So, who wants you dead?'

'I don't know,' she mumbled through a mouthful of foam.

'Sure you do. You just haven't put the pieces together yet.'

She spat in the sink and glared at him out the corner of her eye. 'God, that's annoying.'

'Who might want you dead? Use your head.'

Annie wiped her mouth. 'You know, unlike you, I don't have a past chock-full of psychopaths and thugs.'

'Your past isn't the issue,' he said, following her to the living room. 'What about that deputy – Mullen?'

'Mullen wants me off the job. I can't believe he'd try to kill me.'

'Push any man far enough, you don't know what he might do.'

'Is that the voice of experience?' she said caustically, wanting to lash out at somebody. Maybe if she took a few swipes at him she would be able to reestablish the boundaries that had blurred last night.

She paced the length of the alligator coffee table, nervous energy rising in a new wave. 'What about you, Nick? I got you arrested. You could go down for a felony. Maybe you don't think you've got anything to lose getting rid of the only witness.'

'I don't own a Cadillac,' he said, his face stony.

'I gotta figure if you'd try to kill somebody, you probably wouldn't have any moral problem with stealing a car.'

'Stop it.'

'Why? You want me to use my head. You want me to be objective.'

'So use your head. I was here waiting for you.'

'I came up the levee. It's slower going. You could have ditched the Caddy and beat it over here in your truck.'

'You're pissing me off, Broussard.'

'Yeah? Well, I guess I do that to people. It's probably a wonder someone didn't kill me a long time ago.'

He caught hold of her arm, and Annie jerked out of his grasp, tears stinging her eyes.

'Don't touch me!' she snapped. 'I never said you could touch me! I don't know what you want from me. I don't know why you dragged me into this –'

'I didn't drag you. We're partners.'

'Oh, yeah? Well, *partner*, why don't you tell me again why you went to Renard's home Saturday? Were you scoping out a good sniper's vantage point?'

'You think I took that shot?' he said, incredulous. 'If I wanted Renard dead, sugar, he'd be in hell by now.'

'Yeah, I know. I kind of interrupted that send-off once already.'

'*C'est assez!*' he ordered, catching hold of her by both arms this time, hauling her up close.

'What're you gonna do, Nick? Beat me up?'

'What the hell's the matter with you?' he demanded. 'Why are you busting my balls here? I didn't touch Renard Saturday, I didn't take a shot at him tonight, and I sure as hell didn't try to kill you!'

He wanted to shake her, he wanted to kiss her, anger and sexual aggression bleeding together in a dangerous mix. He forced himself to stand her back from him and walk away.

'If we're partners, we're partners,' he said. 'That means trust. You have to trust me, 'Toinette. More than you trust a damn killer, for Christ's sake.'

He was amazed at the words that had come out of his mouth. He had never wanted a partner on the job, he didn't waste time trusting people. He wasn't even sure why he was angry with her. Her argument was logical. Of course she should consider him a suspect.

Annie blew out a breath. 'I don't know what to believe. I don't know who to believe. I never thought this would be so damn hard! I feel like I'm lost in a house of mirrors. I feel like I'm drowning. Someone tried to kill me! That doesn't happen to me every day. I'm sorry if I'm not reacting like an old pro.'

They stood across the length of the room from each other. Whether it was the distance or the moment, she looked small and fragile. Nick felt a strange stirring of compassion, and an unwelcome twinge of guilt. He had doubted her motives from the start, questioned the source of her interest in the Bichon case, when she was exactly what she appeared to be: a good cop who wanted to be better, who wanted to find justice for a victim. Simple and straightforward, no ulterior motives, no hidden agenda.

'It wasn't me, 'Toinette,' he murmured, closing the distance between them. 'I don't think you believe that it was. You just don't wanna think more than one person in this world might want you gone from it, *oui?* You don't wanna dig in that hole, do you, *chère?*'

'No,' she whispered as the fight drained out of her. She shut her eyes as if she could wish it all away. 'God, the things I get myself into.'

'You're in this case for good reason,' he said. 'It's your challenge, your obligation. You're in over your head, but you know how to swim – suck in a breath and start kicking.'

'Right now, I'd rather climb out of the water, thanks anyway.'

'No. Seek the truth, 'Toinette. In all things, seek the truth. In the case. In me. In yourself. You're not a child and you're nobody's pawn. You proved that when you stopped me from pounding Renard into the here-fucking-after. You're in this case because you want to be. You'll stick it out because you know you have to. Hang on. Hang tough.'

He raised a hand and touched her cheek, stroked his fingertips down her jaw. 'You're stronger than you know.'

'I'm scared, that's what I am,' she whispered. 'I hate being scared. It pisses me off.'

Annie told herself to turn away from his touch, but she couldn't make herself do it. His show of tenderness was too unexpected and too needed. He was too strong and too near.

'I'm sorry,' she murmured. 'I was scared I'd lose my job. That was bad enough. Now I have to be scared I'll lose my life.'

'And you're scared of me,' he said, his fingers curling beneath her chin.

She looked up at him, at the battered face, at the eyes bright with the intensity that burned inside him. She had told him just last night that he frightened her, but the fear wasn't of him.

'No,' she said softly. 'Not that way. I don't believe you were in that car. I don't believe you took that shot. I'm sorry. I'm sorry.'

She murmured the words again and again as the trembling came back.

His embrace seemed to swallow her up. He stroked a hand over her hair and down her back. He kissed the side of her neck, her cheek. Blindly, she turned her mouth into his, and he kissed her with the kind of heat that flared instantly out of control.

She opened her mouth beneath his and felt a wild rush as his tongue touched hers. She ached and trembled with the sensations of life, too aware she could have been dead. Heat blushed just beneath her skin and pooled thick and liquid between her legs. She could taste the need – his and her own. She could feel it, wanted to give in to it and obliterate everything else from her mind. She didn't want thought or reason or logic. She wanted Fourcade.

His hands slipped beneath her T-shirt and skimmed up her back. The shirt came off as they sank to their knees on the rug. He discarded his own between kisses. They came together, fevered skin to fevered skin, mouths and hands exploring. Annie pulled him down with her, arched into the touch of his lips on her breast, moaned at the feel of his tongue rasping against her nipple.

She allowed awareness of nothing but his touch, the strength of him, the masculine scent of his skin. She gave herself over entirely to sensation – the texture of his chest hair, the smooth hardness of his stomach muscles, the feel of his erection in her hand.

He stroked his fingers down through the dark curls between her thighs and tested her readiness. And then he was inside her, filling her, stretching her. She dug her fingertips into his back, wrapped her legs around his hips, let the passion and the urgency of the act consume her. She let her orgasm blind her with a burst of intensity borne of fear and the need to reaffirm her own existence.

She cried out at the strength of it. She held tight to Nick as her body gripped his. His arms were banded around her. His voice was low and rough in her ear, a stream of hot, erotic French. He rode her harder, faster, bringing her to climax again and finding his own end as he drove deep within her. She felt him come, felt the sudden rigidity in the muscles of his back, heard him groan through his teeth. Then stillness ... the only sound their ragged breathing. Neither of them moved.

Recriminations rose in Annie's mind like flotsam as the rush of physical sensation ebbed. Fourcade was the last man she should have allowed herself to want. Certainly one of the last she should have allowed herself to have. He was too complicated, too extreme. She had seen him commit a crime. She had questioned his motives, had questioned his sanity more than once. And yet she could find no genuine regret for crossing this particular line with him.

Maybe it was the stress of the situation. Maybe it was the inevitable eruption of the sexual tension that had pulled between them all along. Maybe she was losing her mind.

As she considered the last possibility, Nick raised his head and stared at her.

'Well, that took the edge off, *c'est vrai*,' he growled, his arms tightening around her. 'Now, let's go find a bed and get serious.'

Midnight had ticked past when Annie slipped from the bed. As she belted her old flannel robe, she studied Fourcade in the soft glow of the bedside hula-dancer lamp, surprised that he didn't open his eyes and demand an explanation for her sudden departure from between the sheets. He slept lightly, like a cat, but he didn't stir. His breathing was deep and regular. He looked too good in her bed.

'What have you gotten yourself into now, Annie?' she muttered as she padded down the hall.

She had no answers, didn't have the energy to search for them. But that didn't stop the questions from swarming in her mind. Questions about the case, about Lindsay Faulkner and Renard and whoever had been behind the wheel of that Cadillac. Questions about herself and her judgment and her capabilities.

Nick said she was stronger than she realized. He had also said she was too afraid to go deep within herself. She supposed he was right on both counts.

Flipping on the kitchen light, she walked slowly around the table, looking at everything she had laid out there. She reached for the scarf, needing to touch it, repulsed that a killer might have held it in his hands first, sickened that it might have been a gift to a woman who had died a horrible, brutal death.

'Renard, he sent you that, no?'

She jerked around at the sound of his voice. He stood in the doorway in jeans that were zipped but not buttoned, his chest and feet bare.

'I didn't mean to wake you.'

'You didn't.' He came forward, reaching for the strip of pale silk. 'He gave you this?'

'Yes.'

'Just like he did with Pam.'

'I have a creepy feeling it might be the same scarf,' Annie said. 'Do you know?'

He shook his head. 'I never saw the stuff. What he did with it after she gave it back to him is a mystery. Stokes might know if that's the one, but I doubt it. He'd have no reason to have taken note. It's not against the law to send a woman pretty things.'

'White silk,' she said. 'Like the Bayou Strangler. Do you think that's intentional?'

'If it was important to him that way, then I think he would have killed her with it.'

Shuddering a little at the thought, Annie hugged herself and wandered back into the living room. She hit the power button on her small stereo system in the bookcase, conjuring up a bluesy piano number. On the other side of the French doors the rain was still coming down. Softer, though. The bulk of the storm had moved on to Lafayette. Lightning ran across the northern sky in a neon web.

'Why did you go to Renard's Saturday, Nick?' she asked, watching his reflection in the glass. 'He could have had you arrested. Why risk that?'

'I don't know.'

'Sure you do.' She glanced at him over her shoulder, surprised as always by the brilliance of his sudden smile.

'You're learning, *'tite fille*,' he said, wagging a finger at her as he came to stand beside her.

He pulled open one of the doors and breathed deeply of the cool air.

'I went to the house where Pam died,' he said, sobering. 'And then I went to see how her killer was living.

'Outrage is a voracious beast, you know. It needs to be fueled on a regular basis or eventually it dies out. I don't want it to die out. I want to hold it in my fist like a beating heart. I want to hate him. I want him punished.'

'What if he didn't do it?'

'He did. You know he did. *I* know he did.'

'I know he's guilty of something,' Annie said. 'I know he was obsessed with her. I believe he stalked her. His thought process frightens me – the way he justifies, rationalizes, turns things around. So subtle, so smooth most people would never even notice. I believe he could have killed her. I believe he probably killed her.

'On the other hand, someone tried to kill Lindsay Faulkner the very night she called to tell me something that might be pertinent to the case. And now someone's tried to kill me, and it wasn't Renard.'

'Keep the threads separate or you end up with a knot, 'Toinette,' Nick said sharply. 'One: You got a rapist running around loose. He chose Faulkner because she fit his pattern. Two: You've got a personal enemy in Mullen. He wants to scare you, maybe hurt you a little. Say he follows you over to Renard's and this gets him crazy – you not only turned

352

on one of your own, you're consorting with the enemy. It pushed him over the line.'

'Maybe,' Annie conceded. 'Or maybe I'm making somebody nervous, poking around this case. Maybe Lindsay remembered something about Donnie and those land deals. You're the one who drew the possible connection between Donnie and Marcotte,' she reminded him. 'You're willing to look at that, but only in how it relates *after* the murder. Leave yourself open to possibilities, Detective, or you might shut the door on a killer.'

'I've considered the possibilities. I still believe Renard killed her.'

'Of course you do, because if Renard isn't the killer, then what does that make you? An avenging angel without motive is just a thug. Justice dispensed on an innocent man is injustice. If Renard isn't a criminal, then you are.'

The same line of thinking had drawn through Nick's mind as he drove back from New Orleans, aching from the beating DiMonti's goons had given him. What if the focus he had directed at Renard prevented him from seeing other possibilities? What did that make him, indeed?

'Is that what you think of me, 'Toinette? You think I'm a criminal?'

Annie sighed. 'I believe what you did to Renard was wrong. I've always wanted to believe in the rules, but I see them getting bent every day, and sometimes I think it's bad and sometimes I think it's fine – as long as I like the outcome. So what does that make me?'

'Human,' he said, staring out at the night. 'The rain's stopped.'

He went out onto the balcony. Annie followed, bare feet on the cool wet planks. To the north the sky was opaque with storm clouds. To the south, starlight studded the Gulf sky like diamonds.

'What are you gonna do about the Cadillac Man?' Nick asked. 'You didn't call it in.'

'I have a feeling I'd be wasting my time.' Annie swept

water off the railing, pushed up the sleeves of her robe, and rested her forearms on the damp wood. 'No one in the department wants to rush to my aid these days. I'm not saying they're all against me, but I'd get apathy at best. Besides, I don't have a tag number on the car. I'm not sure about the make. I can't describe the driver.

'I'll file a report in the morning and call around to the body shops myself, see if I can find a big car with half my paint job on the side. I could probably get better odds on the Saints winning the Super Bowl.'

'I'll check out Mullen's alibi,' Nick offered. 'It's time I had a little chat with him, anyhow.'

'Thanks.'

'I saw Stokes tonight. He says the Faulkner woman is stable but still unconscious.'

Annie nodded. 'She saw him over lunch yesterday. Did he say anything about that?'

'No.'

'Did he say anything about me?'

'That you're a pain in the ass. Same old, same old. Do you think she might have said something to him about you digging around?'

'I don't see why she wouldn't have. When I saw her Sunday, she told me she'd sooner deal with Stokes. She wasn't happy about me saving Renard's hide. So she sees Stokes over lunch, presumably to tell him something about Pam. Then she calls me that night: apologetic, wants to get together.'

'Why the change of heart?'

'I don't know. Maybe Stokes didn't think what she had to say was important. But if she *did* mention me, why didn't he call me on it?' she asked. 'I don't get that. This afternoon he told me to stay away from his cases, but why wouldn't he go to the sheriff? He knows I'm already in trouble. He might have a chance of getting me suspended. Why wouldn't he go for it?'

'But if he tells Noblier, that opens a can of worms for him

354

too, sugar,' Nick said. 'If it looks like he's not working the case hard enough, maybe Gus takes it away from him – especially now that Stokes has the rape task force. He doesn't want to give up the Bichon homicide any more than I did.'

'Yeah . . . I guess that makes sense.' She tried to shrug off her uneasiness. 'Maybe Lindsay didn't say anything. I guess I won't know 'til she comes around. *If* she comes around. I hope she comes around. I wish I knew what she wanted to tell me.'

The sounds of the night settled around them – wind in the trees, a splash in the water, the staccato *quock* of a black-crowned night heron out on one of the willow islands. The air was ripe with the smell of green growth and fish and mud.

Odd, Annie thought as she watched Fourcade watch the night, these brief stretches of calm quiet that sometimes lay between them, as if they were old partners, old friends. Other moments the air around them crackled with electricity, sexuality, temper, suspicion. Volatile, unstable, like the atmosphere in a newly forming world. The description fit both Fourcade and whatever was growing between them.

'This is where you grew up,' he said.

'Yeah. Once, when I was eight, I tied a rope to that corner post and tried to rappel down to the ground. I kicked in a screen down below and landed smack in the middle of a table of tourists from France.'

He chuckled. 'Destined for trouble from an early age.'

His words brought an unexpected image of her mother, coming here alone and pregnant, never revealing to anyone the father of her child. She had been trouble from conception, apparently. Every once in a while she felt a pinch of guilt for that, even though she'd had no say in the matter. The pain bloomed quick and bright, like a drop of blood from the prick of a thorn.

Nick watched as melancholy came over her like a veil and wondered at its source, wondered if that source was the reason she preferred the surface to the depths of life. He felt a sadness at the sudden absence of her usual spark. Was it that surface light in her that attracted him or the reserves of strength she had yet to tap?

'Me, I grew up out that way,' he said, pointing off to the southeast. 'The middle of nowhere was the center of my world. At least until I was twelve.'

Annie was surprised that he had offered the information. She tried to picture him as a carefree swamp kid, but couldn't.

'How did you go from there to here?' she asked.

The expression in his eyes turned remote and reflective. His voice sounded road-weary. 'The long way.'

'I actually thought you might have died last night,' she admitted belatedly.

'Disappointed?'

'No.'

'Some folks would be. Marcotte, Renard, Smith Pritchett.' He thought back to the comment Stokes had made that afternoon. 'What about Mr Doucet with the DA's office?'

'A.J.?' she said, looking puzzled. 'What's he got to do with you?'

'What's he got to do with *you*?' Nick asked. 'Rumor has it you're an item, you and Mr Deputy DA.'

'Oh, that,' Annie said, cringing inwardly. 'He'd blow a gasket if he knew you were here.'

'Because of what I did to Renard? Or because of what I did with you?'

'Both.'

'And on the second count: Does he have cause?'

'He would say yes.'

'I'm asking you,' Nick said, holding his breath as he waited for her answer.

'No,' she said softly. 'I'm not sleeping with him, if that's what you're asking.'

'That's what I'm asking, 'Toinette,' he said. 'Me, I don't like to share.'

'That's not to say I think this is such a great idea, Nick,' Annie admitted. 'I'm not saying I regret tonight. I don't. I *should*.' She sighed and tried again. 'It's just that . . . Look at the situation we're in. It's complicated enough, and – and – I don't just *do* this kind of thing, you know –'

'I know.' He stepped closer, settling his hands on her hips, wanting to touch her, to lay claim in a basic way. 'Neither do I.'

'I sure as hell shouldn't be doing it with you. I –'

He pressed a forefinger to her lips, silencing her. 'This isn't about the case. This has nothing to do with what happened with Renard. Understand?'

'But –'

'It's about attraction, need, desire. You felt it that night at Laveau's. So did I. Before any of the rest of this ever started. It's a separate issue. It has to make its own sense outside the context of the situation we're in. You can accept it or you can say no. What do you want, 'Toinette?'

Annie moved away from him. 'It must be nice to be so sure of everything,' she said. 'Who's guilty. Who's innocent. What you want. What I know. Aren't you ever confused, Nick? Aren't you ever uncertain? I am. You were right – I'm in over my head, and if one more thing weighs me down, I'll never come up for air.'

She looked for a reaction but his face was as impassive as granite.

'You want me to go?' he asked.

'I think what I want and what's best are two different things.'

'You want me to go.'

'No,' she said in exasperation. 'That's not what I *want*.'

He came toward her then, serious, purposeful, predatory. 'Then we'll deal with the rest later because I'm telling you, *chère*, I *know* what I want.'

Then he kissed her, and Annie let his certainty sweep them both away. He carried her back inside, back to bed, leaving the balcony an empty stage with an audience of one shrouded in shadows of midnight.

'*I saw her with him.*
    Touching him.
    Kissing him.
    THE WHORE.
    She has no loyalty. Just like before. It made me wish I had killed her.
    Love.
        Passion.
            Greed.
                Anger.
                    Hatred.
    Around and around the feelings spin, a red blur.
    You know, sometimes I can't tell one from the other. I have no power over them. They have all power over me. I wait for their verdict.
    Only time will tell.'

32

The black of the night sky was fading to navy in the east
when Nick let himself out of Annie's apartment. He didn't
want anyone finding him here come first light. Which was
why he had parked his truck on a secluded boat landing off
the levee road a quarter mile away. If word leaked of an
association between the defendant and the key witness in
the brutality case, there would be hell to pay for both of
them.

He didn't wake Annie. He had no desire to wrestle with
more questions. She had needed him, he had wanted her –
it was as simple and as complex as that.

He didn't want to wonder where it would go from here.
He didn't want to wonder why Antoinette, of all women,
when he had allowed himself no woman in longer than he
could remember. He had spent the last year trying to
rebuild himself. There had been nothing left to give beyond
what he gave to the job. He wouldn't have said he had
anything to give now, when he was backed into yet
another corner and in danger of losing not only his career
but his identity. And yet, he found himself drawn to this
woman. His accuser.

Antoinette, young, fresh, unspoiled. He was none of
those things. Was that it? Did he simply want to touch
something good and clean? Or was it about redemption or
salvation or coercion?

'*Aren't you ever confused, Nick? Aren't you ever uncertain?*'
'All the time, *chère*,' he whispered as he drove away.

There was only one Mullen listed in the Bayou Breaux
phone book. K. Mullen Jr lived a block north of the cane
mill in a clapboard house built in the fifties and painted
once since. Trees kept the lawn as sparse as an adolescent

360

boy's beard. The garage sat back from the house; a bass boat and a Chevy truck were parked on the cracked concrete in front of it.

Nick walked back along the side of the building, peering into windows that hadn't been cleaned in this decade. The space was crammed with junk – old tires, a motorcycle, three lawn mowers, a mud-splattered all-terrain four-wheeler. No Cadillac. At the back of the building, a pair of speckled hunting dogs had worn two crescents of yard to dirt, pacing out to the ends of their chains to crap. The dogs lay tucked into balls between their two small shelters. They didn't crack an eye at Nick.

He went to the back door of the house and let himself in with no resistance from a lock. The kitchen was a depressing little room with dirty dishes on most of the available counter space. Junk mail was stacked up on the small table beside half a loaf of Evangeline Maid white bread, an opened sack of barbeque potato chips, and three empty long-neck bottles of Miller Genuine Draft. Mullen's Sig Sauer lay in its holster on top of the latest *Field & Stream*.

Nick searched through the cupboards and refrigerator, pulling out a cheap frying pan, eggs, butter. As the skillet was heating, he cracked eggs into a bowl, sniffed the milk to check it, then added a splash along with salt and pepper, and whipped it together with a fork. The pan gave a satisfying hiss as the liquid hit the surface.

'Hold it right there!'

Nick glanced over his shoulder. Mullen stood in the doorway in uniform trousers, a shotgun pressed into the hollow of his pasty white shoulder.

'You would hold a gun on me after you've presumed me to be your good friend?' Nick said, scraping a spatula through the bubbling eggs. 'That's bad manners, Deputy.'

'Fourcade?' Mullen lowered the gun and shuffled a little farther into the room, as if he didn't trust his eyes from a distance of five feet. 'What the hell are you doing here?'

'Me, I'm making a little breakfast,' Nick said. 'Your

361

kitchen is a disgrace, Mullen. You know, the kitchen is the soul of the house. How you keep your kitchen is how you keep your life. Looking around here, I'd say you have no respect for yourself.'

Mullen made no comment. He laid the shotgun down on the table and scratched at his thin, greasy hair. 'Wha – ?'

'Got any coffee?'

'Why are you in my house? It's six o'clock in the goddamn morning!'

'Well, I figure we're such good friends, you won't mind. Isn't that right, Deputy?' Giving the eggs one last stir, he slid the pan from the burner, and turned around. 'Sorry, I don't have your first name down, but you know I didn't realize we were so close and so I forgot to ever give a shit about it.'

Mullen's expression was an ugly knot of perplexity. He looked like a man straining on the toilet. 'What are you talking about?'

'What'd you do last night' – Nick leaned over the table and scanned the mailing label on an envelope boasting YOUR NEW NRA STICKER ENCLOSED! – 'Keith?'

'Why?'

'It's called small talk. This is what buddies do, I'm told. Why you don't tell me all about what you did last night?'

'Went out to the gun club. Why?'

'Shot a few rounds, huh?' Nick said, dousing the eggs with Tabasco from the bottle sitting on the back of the stove. 'What'd you shoot? This handgun you've so carelessly left on your kitchen table?'

'Uh ...'

'How about rifles? You shoot some clay?'

'Yeah.'

'You have no clean plates,' Nick announced with disapproval, picking up the frying pan by the handle. He tasted the eggs and forked up a second mouthful. 'You hear about someone taking a shot at Renard last night?'

'Yeah.' The uncertainty was still clear in his small mean

eyes, but he had decided to pretend a bit of arrogance. They were *compadres* ... maybe. He crossed his arms over his bare chest. A smirk twisted his lips, revealing crowded bad teeth. 'Too bad he missed, huh?'

'You might assume I would think that, knowing me like you do,' Nick said. 'That wasn't you trying to help justice along there, was it, Keith?'

Mullen forced a laugh. 'Hell no.'

''Cause that's against the law, don'tcha know. Now, you might say that didn't stop me the other night. Deputy Broussard stopped me.'

Mullen made a rude sound. 'That little bitch. She oughta mind her own goddamn business.'

'I hear you're trying to help her with that, no? Giving her a hard time and whatnot.'

'She don't know nothing about loyalty, turning on one of us. Cunt's got no business being in a uniform.'

Nick flinched at the obscenity, but held himself. His smile was sharp as he allowed himself to visualize swinging the frying pan like a tennis racket, Mullen's pointy head bouncing off the door frame, blood spraying from his nose and mouth.

'So, you've taken it upon yourself to avenge this wrong she committed against me,' Nick said. 'Because we're such good pals, you and me?'

'She hadn't oughta fuck with the Brotherhood.'

Nick sent the pan sailing across the kitchen like a Frisbee. It landed in the sink with a crash of glass breaking beneath it.

'Hey!' Mullen yelled.

Nick hit him hard in the chest with the heel of his hand, knocking him backward into the cupboards, and held him there, his knuckles digging into the soft hollow just below Mullen's sternum.

'I am *not* your brother,' he growled, staring into Mullen's eyes. 'The mere suggestion of a genetic tie is an insult to my family. Nor would I count you among my friends. I don't

363

know you from something I would scrape off my shoe. And you've not impressed me here this morning, Keith, I have to say. So I think you'll understand when I tell you I take exception to you acting on my behalf.

'I fight my own battles. I take care of my own problems. I won't tolerate being used as an excuse by some redneck asshole who only wants to bully a woman. You got your own problem with Broussard – that's one thing. You drag my name into it, I'll have to hurt you. You'd be smart to just leave her alone so that I don't misinterpret. Have I made myself clear to you?'

Mullen nodded with vigor. Gasping for breath, he doubled over, rubbing his hand against his diaphragm as Nick stepped back.

'I might have guessed a man with no honor would keep his kitchen this way.' Nick shook his head as he took in the sorry state of the room one last time. 'Sad.'

Mullen looked up at him. 'Fuck you. You're just as fuckin' nuts as everyone says, Fourcade.'

Nick flashed a crocodile smile. 'Don't sell me short, Keith. I'm way crazier than people think. You'd do well to remember that.'

Annie had watched his truck go down the bayou road. A hollow feeling yawned in the middle of her. She didn't fall into bed with men she barely knew. She could count her lovers on one hand and have most of her fingers left over. Why Fourcade?

Because somewhere in the dark labyrinth that was Fourcade's personality there was a man worthy of more than what his past had dealt him. He believed in justice, a greater good, a higher power. He had destroyed his career for a fourteen-year-old dead girl no one else in the world cared about.

He had beaten a suspect bloody right before her very eyes. His hearing was little more than a week away.

'God, Broussard,' she groaned, 'the things you get into ...'

Last night might have been about wanting and needing, but the future wasn't so simple. Fourcade could pretend to separate the attraction from the rest of it, but what would happen when she got up on the witness stand at his hearing and told the court she'd seen him commit a felony? And she *would* take the stand. Whatever feelings she had for him now didn't change what had happened or what would happen. She had a duty – to burn a cop on behalf of a killer.

Rubbing her temples, Annie went back into the apartment, pulled on a pair of shorts and a T-shirt, and went through her routine with the energy of a slug. She returned home from her run to the depressing sight of her half-trashed Jeep in the lot and A.J. sitting on the gallery.

He was already dressed for the office in a smart pin-striped suit and a crisp white shirt, his burgundy tie fluttering as he leaned forward with his forearms on his thighs. His eyes were on her, a ghost of a hopeful smile curved his mouth.

At that moment he'd never been more handsome to Annie, never more dear. It broke her heart to think she was going to hurt him.

'Glad to see you in one piece,' he said, rising as she came up the steps. 'That Jeep gave me a scare. What happened?'

'Sideswiped. No big deal. Looks worse than it was,' she lied.

He shook his head. 'Lou'siana drivers. We gotta stop giving away driver's licenses with Wheaties box tops.'

Annie found a smile for him and tugged on his tie. 'What are you doing out here at this hour?'

'This is what you get for never answering your phone messages.'

'I'm sorry. I've been busy.'

'With what? From what I hear, you've got time on your hands these days.'

She made a face. 'So you heard about my change in job description?'

'Heard you got stuck with crime dog duty.' He sobered just enough to make her nervous. 'Why didn't I hear it from you?'

'I wasn't exactly proud.'

'So? Since when do you not call me to whine and complain?' he said, his confusion plain, though he tried to smile.

Annie bit her lip and looked to the left of his shoulder. She would have given anything to wriggle out of this, but she couldn't and she knew it. Better to run through the minefield now and get it over with.

'A.J., we need to talk.'

He sucked in a breath. 'Yeah, I guess we do. Let's go upstairs.'

Images of her apartment flashed through Annie's head – the kitchen table spread with files from the Bichon case, her sheets rumpled from sex with Fourcade. She felt cheap and mean, a scarlet woman, a kicker of puppies.

'No,' she said, catching his hand. 'I need to cool off. Let's go sit on a boat.'

She chose the pontoon at the far end of the dock, grabbed a towel from the storage bin, and wiped the dew from the last aqua plastic bench seat. A.J. followed reluctantly, pausing to look at the tip box Sos had mounted near the gate – a white wooden cube with a window in front and a foot-long gator head fixed over the top hole, mouth open in a money-hungry pose. The hand-lettering on the side read: TIP'S (POURBOIRE) MERCI!

'Remember the time Uncle Sos pretended this gator bit his finger off and he had all us kids screaming?'

Annie smiled. ''Cause your cousin Sonny tried to sneak a dollar out.'

'Then old Benoit, he did the trick, only he really didn't have half his fingers. Sonny about wet himself.'

He slid onto the bench a few feet from her and reached

out to touch her hand. 'We got a lotta good memories,' he said quietly. 'So why you shutting me out now, Annie? What's the deal here? You still mad at me about the Fourcade thing?'

'I'm not mad at you.'

'Then, what? We're going along fine, then all of a sudden I'm persona non grata. What –'

'What do you mean, 'going along fine'?'

'Well, you know –' A.J. struggled, clueless as to what he'd said wrong. He shrugged. 'I thought –'

'Thought what? That the last hundred times I told you we're just friends I was speaking in some kind of code?'

'Oh, come on,' he said, scowling. 'You know there's more between us –'

Annie pushed to her feet, gaping at him. 'What part of no do you not understand? You spent seven years in higher education and you can't grasp the meaning of a one-syllable word?'

'Of course I can, I just don't see that it applies to us.'

'Christ,' she muttered, shaking her head. 'You're as bad as Renard.'

'What's that supposed to mean? You're calling me a stalker?'

'I'm saying Pam Bichon told him *no* eight ways from Sunday and he just heard what he wanted to hear. How is that different from what you're doing?'

'Well, for starters, I'm not an accused murderer.'

'Don't be a smart-ass. I'm serious, A.J. I keep trying to tell you, you want something from me I can't give you! How much plainer can I make it?'

He looked away as if she'd slapped him, the muscles in his jaw flexing. 'I guess that's as plain as it gets.'

Annie sank back down on the bench. 'I don't want to hurt you, A.J.,' she said softly. 'That's the last thing I want to do. I love you –'

He barked a laugh.

'– just not in the way you need me to,' she finished.

'But see,' he said, 'we've been through this cycle before, and you come around or I come around, and then –'

Annie cut him off with a shake of her head. 'I can't do this, A.J. Not now. There's too much going on.'

'Which you won't tell me about.'

'I can't.'

'You can't tell me? Why? What's going on?'

'I can't do this,' she whispered, hating the need to keep things from him, to lie to him. Better to push him away so that he wouldn't want to know.

'I'm not the enemy, Annie!' he exploded. 'We're on the same side, for crying out loud! Why can't you tell me? *What* can't you tell me?'

She dropped her face into her hands. Allying herself with Fourcade, investigating on her own, trying to get Renard to fixate on her so she could trick him into showing the ugly truth that lay beneath his bland mask – she could no more tell A.J. any of it than she could tell Sheriff Noblier. They may all have wanted the same outcome, but they weren't all on the same side.

'Oh,' he said suddenly, as if an internal lightbulb just went on in his head, bright enough to hurt. 'Maybe you didn't mean the job. Jesus.' He huffed out a breath and looked at her sideways. 'Is there someone else? Is that where you've been lately – with some other guy?'

Annie held her breath. There was Nick, but one night did not a relationship make, and she couldn't see much hope in it lasting.

'Annie? Is that it? Is there someone else?'

'Maybe,' she hedged. 'But that's not it. That's not ... I'm so sorry,' she said, weary of the fight. 'You can't know how much I wish I felt differently, how much I wish this could be what you want it to be, A.J. But wishing can't make it so.'

'Do I know him?'

'Oh, A.J., don't go there.'

He stood with his hands on his hips, looking away from her, his pride smarting, his logical mind working to make sense of feelings that seldom bent to the will of reason. He wasn't so different from Fourcade that way – too analytical, too rational, confounded by the vagaries of human nature. Annie wanted to put her arms around him, to offer him comfort as a friend, but knew he wouldn't allow it now. The feeling of loss was a physical pain in the center of her chest.

'I know what you want,' she murmured. 'You want a wife. You want a family. I want you to have those things, A.J., and I'm not ready to be the person to give them to you. I don't know that I'll ever be.'

He rubbed a hand across his jaw, blinked hard, checked his watch. 'You know –' He stopped to clear his throat. 'I don't have time for this conversation right now. I have to be in court this morning. I'll – ah – I'll call you later.'

'A.J. –'

'Oh – ah – Pritchett wants you in his office this afternoon. Maybe I'll see you there.'

Annie watched him walk away, stuffing a five in the alligator's mouth as he passed the tip box, her heart as heavy as a stone in her chest.

An old groundskeeper was scrubbing the toes of the Virgin Mary with a toothbrush when Annie wheeled into Our Lady of Mercy. Across the street, a woman smoking a pipe was selling cut flowers out of the back of a rusty Toyota pickup. Annie parked in the visitors' lot and climbed across the passenger's seat to let herself out of the Jeep. 'The Heap' she had decided to call it, trashed as it was. The impact of one of the collisions had jammed the driver's door shut.

'Dat ol' woman, she steal dem flowers,' the grounds-keeper said, shaking the toothbrush at Annie as she passed. 'She steal 'em right out the garden at the Vet'rans Park. Me, I seen her do it. Why you don't arrest her?'

'You'll have to call the police, sir.'

His dark face squeezed tight, making his eyes pop out like Ping-Pong balls. 'You *is* the police!'

'No, sir, I'm with the sheriff's office.'

'Bah! Dogs is all dogs when you calls 'em for supper!'

'Yes, sir. Whatever that means,' Annie muttered as the doors whooshed open in front of her.

The ICU was quiet except for the sound of machines. A woman with cornrows and purple-framed glasses sat behind the desk, watching the monitors and talking on the phone. She barely glanced up as Annie passed. There was no guard at the door to Lindsay Faulkner's room. Good news, bad news, Annie thought. She didn't have to get past a uniform ... and neither did anyone else.

Faulkner lay in her bed in the ICU looking like a science experiment gone wrong. Her head and face were swathed mummy-like in bandages. Tubes fed into her and out of her. Monitors and machines of mysterious purpose blinked and cheeped, their display screens filled with glowing medical hieroglyphics. The redhead with the expired license plates rose from her chair beside the bed as Annie approached.

'How's she doing?' Annie asked.

'Better, actually,' she said in a hushed tone. 'She's out of the coma. She's been in and out of consciousness. She's said a few words.'

'Does she know who did this to her?'

'No. She doesn't remember anything about the attack. Not yet, anyway. The other detective was already here and asked.'

Two miracles in one morning: Lindsay Faulkner conscious and Chaz Stokes out of bed before eight A.M. Maybe he was making an effort after all. Maybe the spotlight of the task force would bring out some ambition in him.

'Has she had many visitors?'

'They only allow family up here,' the redhead said. 'We haven't been able to reach her parents. They're traveling in China. Until we can get them here, the hospital has agreed to make exceptions to the rule. Belle Davidson has been in, Grace from the realty, me.'

'She'll need y'all to help her through this,' Annie said. 'She's got a long road ahead of her.'

'Don't talk ... about me ... like I'm not ... here.'

At the sound of the weak voice, the redhead turned toward the bed, smiling. 'You weren't here a minute ago.'

'Ms Faulkner, it's Annie Broussard,' Annie said, leaning down. 'I came to see how you're doing.'

'You ... found me ... after ...'

'Yes, I did.'

'Thank ... you.'

'I wish I could have done more,' Annie said. 'There's a whole task force looking for the guy who did this to you.'

'You ... on it?'

'No. I've been reassigned. Detective Stokes is in charge. I hear you had lunch with him the other day. Did you have something to tell him about Pam? Was that why you called me Monday?'

The silence stretched so long Annie thought perhaps consciousness had ebbed away from her again. The sounds of the monitors filled the cubicle. Annie started to draw back from the bed.

'Donnie,' Faulkner whispered.

'What about Donnie?'

'Jealous.'

'Jealous of who?' Annie asked, bending close.

'Stupid ... It wasn't anything.'

She was slipping away. Annie touched Faulkner's arm in an attempt to maintain her connection to the waking world.

'Who was Donnie jealous of, Lindsay?'

The silence hung again, like a cold breath in the air.

'Detective Stokes.'

33

Donnie was jealous of Stokes. Annie let her brain chew on that while she sorted through the faxes in the tray, pulling the one she'd requested from the DMV – a listing of trucks with Louisiana plates containing the partial sequence *EJ*.

It wasn't difficult to envision Stokes flirting with Pam. In fact, it would have been impossible not to. That was what Stokes did: spent his every spare moment honing his seduction skills. He considered it his duty to flirt with women. And, according to what Lindsay Faulkner had said Sunday, Pam brought out those qualities in men without even trying. Men were attracted to Pam, found her charming and sweet. Chaz Stokes would never be the exception to that rule.

With the stalking an ongoing thing, he would have had ample cause to see Pam on a fairly regular basis. Had Donnie gotten the wrong idea about the two of them? And what would he have done about it if he had? Confront Stokes? Confront Pam?

If Stokes knew Donnie was jealous, then he would certainly have examined that angle when Pam was murdered. She could check the statements tonight, ask Nick about it. Renard had alleged Pam was afraid of Donnie, was afraid to see another man socially because of what Donnie might do. Donnie had threatened a custody fight, as though he had grounds for challenging Pam's rights. But it wasn't as if Pam had been seeing Stokes in a social way.

Was it?

'*Stupid*,' Lindsay Faulkner had said. '*It wasn't anything.*'

But Donnie had thought otherwise. Had he heard what he wanted to hear, interpreted the situation to suit – or to rouse – his temper? Annie had seen a hundred examples in domestic abuse cases – the imagined slights, the phantom lovers, the contrived grounds for anger. Excuses to lash out, to hurt, to belittle, to punish.

No one had ever accused Donnie of abuse, but that didn't mean his mind didn't bend the same way. Pam had bruised his ego openly, publicly, kicking him out of their house, filing for divorce, trying to separate the companies. An imagined affair with Stokes might have pushed him over the edge.

He had said something derogatory about Stokes when she'd spoken with him Saturday, hadn't he? Something about Stokes being lazy. The remark had seemed almost racist, an attitude that would have yanked Stokes's chain, and rightly so. He would have been on Donnie like a pit bull. But Marcus Renard was the suspect Stokes had in his crosshairs.

She was giving herself an unnecessary headache. Nick was probably right. If she didn't keep the individual strands separate, she would end up with a knot – around her own neck. She had Renard on the hook, just the way Fourcade had predicted. If she kept her focus, she could reel him in. She decided she would swing by the hospital again at lunch and see if Lindsay could identify the scarf Renard had sent Pam.

'There is no time for dawdling, Deputy Broussard!' Myron pronounced, marching to his post with all the starch of a palace guard. 'We have our orders for the morning. Detective Stokes needs the arrest records for every man accused of a violent sexual crime in this parish dating back ten years. I will call up the list on the computer, you will then pull the files. I will log them out, you will deliver them to the task force in the detectives' building.'

'Yes, sir, Mr Myron,' Annie said with a plastic smile, sliding the fax from the DMV under her blotter.

They worked quickly, but interruptions of usual records division business dragged the task out – calls from the courthouse, calls from insurance companies, filling out the intake form on a newly arrested burglar, checking in evidence against the same burglar, checking out evidence for the trial of a suspected drug dealer.

All of it was tedious and Annie resented it mightily. She wanted to be the one receiving the files instead of the one digging for them through decades of filed-away crap. She wanted to be on the task force instead of in the paper trenches. Even working with Stokes would have been preferable to working with Myron the Monstrous.

Lunch was ten minutes with a Snickers bar and a telephone pressed to her ear, checking the local garages for any big sedans with passenger-side damage. She found none. Her adversary either had stashed the car or had taken it out of the parish for repairs. She checked the log sheet for recently stolen vehicles and found nothing to match. Expanding the parameters of her search, she started in on the list of garages in St Martin Parish.

'Hey, Broussard,' Mullen barked, leaning over the counter. 'Knock off the hen party and do your job, why don't you.'

Annie glared at him as she thanked another mechanic for nothing and hung up the phone.

'This task force is priority one,' Mullen said, puffing his bony chest out.

'Yeah? Well, how'd you get on it? You got pictures of the sheriff naked with a goat?'

He smirked, much too pleased with himself. 'I guess on account of my work on the Nolan rape.'

'Your work,' Annie said with disdain. 'I caught that call.'

'Yeah, well, you win some, you lose some.'

'You know, Mullen,' she muttered, 'I'd tell you to eat shit and die, but by the smell of your breath I guess it's already a staple of your diet.'

She expected him to snap at the bait, but he leaned back from her instead. 'Look, can I get the rest of those files now? As for our little feud, let's just let that go. No hard feelings.'

'No hard feelings?' Annie repeated. She leaned toward

374

him, holding her voice low and taut. 'You terrorize me, threaten me, cost me a small fortune in damages, cost me my patrol. I'm standing back here playing a glorified goddamn secretary while you're making hay on a case that should have been mine, and you say *no hard feelings*?

'You son of a bitch. Hard feelings are the only kind I've got right now. You'd better believe I find so much as a paint chip connecting you to that Cadillac or whatever the hell it was you tried to kill me with last night, I'll have your badge *and* your bony ass.'

'Cadillac?' Mullen looked confused. 'I don't know what you're talking about, Broussard. I don't know nothing about no Cadillac!'

'Yeah, right.'

'I didn't do nothing to you!'

'Oh, save the act,' Annie sneered. 'Take your files and get out of here.'

She gave the folders a shove and sent them over the edge of the counter, raining arrest reports all over the floor.

'Goddammit!' Mullen yelled, drawing Hooker out of his office.

'Jesus H., Mullen!' he shouted. 'You got a nerve condition or something? You got something wrong with your motor skills?'

'No, sir,' he said tightly, glaring at Annie. 'It was an accident.'

'South Lou'siana is traditionally a place of folk justice,' Smith Pritchett preached, strolling along the credenza in his office, his hands planted at his thick waist. 'The Cajuns had their own code here before organized law enforcement and judicial agencies provided a mitigating influence. The common mind here still makes a distinction between the law and justice. I am well aware that a great many people in this parish feel that Detective Fourcade's attack on Marcus Renard was an acceptable way to cure a particular social problem. However, they would be mistaken.'

Annie watched him with barely disguised impatience. This was likely the rough draft of his opening statement for Fourcade's trial, which would be weeks or months away if he was bound over. She sat in Pritchett's visitor's chair. A.J. stood across the room, arms crossed, back against the bookcase, ignoring the empty chair four feet away from her. His expression was closed tight. He hadn't spoken a word in the ten minutes she'd been here.

'People can't be allowed to take the law into their own hands,' Pritchett continued. 'We'd end up with chaos, anarchy, law*less*ness.'

The progression and conclusion pleased him enough that he paused to jot them down on a pad on his desk.

'The system is in place to mark boundaries, to draw a firm line and hold the people to it,' he said. 'There is no room for exceptions. You believe that, Deputy Broussard, or you would never have gone into law enforcement – isn't that right?'

'Yes, sir. I believe that's been established, and I've already given my statement to –'

'Yes, you have, and I have a copy right here.' He tapped his pen against a file folder. 'But I feel it's important for us to get to know each other, Annie. May I call you Annie?'

'Look, I have a job –'

'I understand you've been having some difficulties with other members of the department,' he said with fatherly concern as he perched a hip on a corner of his desk.

Annie shot a glance at A.J. 'Nothing I can't handle –'

'Is someone trying to coerce you? Dissuade you from testifying against Detective Fourcade?'

'Not in so many wor –'

'While a certain reticence on your part would be under-standable here, Annie, I want to impress upon you the necessity and the importance of your testimony in this matter.'

'Yes, sir. I'm aware of that, sir. I –'

'Has Detective Fourcade himself approached you?'

'Detective Fourcade has made no attempt to keep me from testifying. I –'

'And Sheriff Noblier? Has he instructed you in any way?'

'I don't know what you mean,' Annie said, holding herself stiff against the urge to squirm.

'He's been less than cooperative in this matter. Which is a sad commentary on the effects of his tenure in office, I'm afraid. Gus thinks this parish is his little kingdom and he can make up the rules to suit himself, but that isn't so. The law is the law and it applies to everyone – detectives, sheriffs, deputies.'

'Yes, sir.'

He stepped around behind the desk and slid into his leather chair. Slipping on a pair of steel-rimmed reading glasses, he pulled her statement from the folder and glanced over it.

'Now, Annie, you were off duty that night, but A.J. tells me your personal vehicle is equipped with a police scanner and a radio, is that correct?'

'Yes, sir.'

'He tells me the two of you had a pleasant dinner at Isabeau's that evening.' He glanced up at her with another indulgent, fatherly smile. 'A very romantic setting. My wife's personal favorite.'

Annie said nothing. She thought she could feel A.J.'s stare burning into her. While it seemed he had told Pritchett everything else about their relationship, he hadn't told him it was over. Pritchett was trying to use it as leverage to shift her loyalties. Slimy lawyer.

'Where'd you go after dinner, Annie?'

She had managed to avoid this part of the story so far. It wasn't relevant to the incident – except that Fourcade had taken a phone call and then left the bar, which might have suggested premeditation to say nothing of collusion with someone. But no one else had been beating on Renard, and Fourcade couldn't be compelled to reveal the source or the content of the call, so what was the use of talking about it?

377

On the other hand, there were witnesses who could place her at Laveau's.

'I saw Detective Fourcade's truck across the street at Laveau's. I went to have a few words with him about what had happened at the courthouse.'

Pritchett looked at A.J., clearly unhappy at being taken by surprise.

'Why wasn't this in your statement, Deputy?'

'Because it preceded the incident and had no bearing on it.'

'What condition was Fourcade in?'

'He'd been drinking.'

'Was he aggressive, angry, antagonistic?'

'No, sir, he was ... unhappy, morose, philosophical.'

'Did he speak about Renard? Threaten him?'

'No. He talked about justice and injustice.' And shadows and ghosts.

'Did he give any indication he was going to seek Renard out?'

'No.'

Pritchett pulled his glasses off and nibbled thoughtfully on an earpiece. 'What happened next?'

'We went our separate ways. I decided to stop at the Quik Pik for a few things. The rest is in my report and in the statement I gave Chief Earl.'

'Did you at any time pick up a call on your scanner regarding a suspected prowler in the vicinity of Bowen & Briggs?'

'No, sir, but I was out of the vehicle for several minutes, and then I had the regular radio on for a while and the scanner turned down. I was off duty, it was late.'

Silence hung like dust motes in the air. Annie picked at a broken cuticle and waited. Pritchett's chair squeaked as he rose.

'Do you believe there was a call, Deputy?'

If he asked her this question in court, Fourcade's attorney would object before the whole sentence was out of his mouth. *Calls for speculation*. But they weren't in court. The only person in the room who objected was Annie.

'I didn't hear the call,' she said. 'Other people did.'

'Other people *say* they did,' he corrected her. His voice rose with every syllable. He bent over and planted his hands on the arms of Annie's chair, his face inches from hers. 'Because Gus Noblier *told them* to say that they did. Because they want to protect a man who blew a major case, then took it upon himself to execute the suspect he couldn't outsmart!

'There was no call,' he said softly, pushing himself back. He sat against the desk again, his eyes on her every second. 'Did you arrest Fourcade that night and take him into custody?'

What difference did it make when the arrest had been made? What would it change? Fourcade was up on charges. Pritchett was simply looking for ammunition to use against Noblier, and Annie wanted no part of that feud.

She called up the words the sheriff himself had put in her mouth. 'I stumbled across a situation I didn't understand. I contained it. We went to the station to sort it out.'

'Why does Richard Kudrow claim he saw an arrest report that subsequently went missing?'

'Because he's a stinking weasel lawyer and he loves nothing better than to stir the pot.' She looked Pritchett in the eye. 'Why would you believe him? He lives to tie you up in knots in the courtroom. You can bet he's loving this – you and Noblier at each other's throats with cops in the middle.'

A small measure of satisfaction warmed her as she watched her strategy work. Pritchett pressed his lips together and moved away from the desk. The last thing he would want in the world would be having Richard Kudrow play him for a fool.

'How well do you know Nick Fourcade, Annie?' he asked, the driving force gone from his voice.

379

She thought of the night spent in Nick's arms, their bodies locked together. 'Not very.'

'He doesn't deserve your loyalty. And he sure as hell doesn't deserve a badge. You're a good officer, Annie. I've seen your record. And you did a good thing that night. I'm gonna trust you to do the right thing when you get up on the witness stand next week.'

'Yes, sir,' she murmured.

He checked his Rolex and turned to A.J. 'I'm needed elsewhere. A.J., would you show Annie out?'

'Of course.'

She started to get up, intending to leave on Pritchett's heels, but the door shut too quickly after him.

'He's late for his tee time,' A.J. said, not moving from the bookcase. 'Why are you lying to us, Annie?'

She flinched as if he'd spat the words in her face. 'I'm not –'

'Don't insult me,' he snapped. 'On top of everything else, don't insult me. I know you, Annie. I know everything about you. Everything. That scares you, doesn't it? That's why you're pushing me away.'

'I don't think this is the time or place for this conversation,' she muttered.

'You don't want anyone getting that deep in your soul, do you? 'Cause what if I leave or die like your mother –'

'Stop it!' Annie ordered, furious that he would use the most painful memories of her childhood against her.

'That hurts a hell of a lot more than losing someone who isn't a part of you,' he pressed on. 'Better to keep everyone at arm's length.'

'I want more than an arm's length away from you right now, A.J.,' Annie said tightly. She felt as if he had reached out unexpectedly and sliced her with a straight razor, cutting through flesh and bone.

'Why didn't you tell me you saw Fourcade earlier that night?' he asked.

'What difference does it make?'

380

'What difference does it make? I'm supposed to be your best friend! We had a date that night. You dumped me and went to see Fourcade –'

'That was not a date,' she argued. 'We had dinner. Period. You're my friend, not my lover. I don't have to clear my every move with you!'

'You don't get it, do you?' he said, incredulous. 'This is about trust –'

'*Whose* trust?' she demanded. 'You're giving me the goddamn third degree! One minute you claim to be my best friend and the next you're wondering why I didn't give you something you can use in court. You tell me we can separate who we are from what we do, but only when it's convenient for you. I've had it, A.J. I don't need this bullshit and I sure as hell don't need you taking potshots at my psyche!'

'Annie –'

He reached for her arm as she started for the door and she jerked away from him. The secretaries in the outer office watched with owl eyes as she stormed past.

The outer hall was dark and cool. Voices floated down from the third floor. The last of the day's court skirmishes had been fought, and the last of the warriors lingered in the hall, swapping stories and making deals. Annie headed for a side exit, letting herself out into sunshine that hurt her eyes. She fumbled with her sunglasses, then nearly ran into a man standing at the edge of the sidewalk.

'Deputy Broussard. This is serendipitous, I must say.'

Annie groaned aloud. *Kudrow*. He stood leaning against a *Times-Picayune* vending machine, his trench coat belted tightly around him despite the unseasonable heat and choking humidity of the afternoon. His posture suggested pain rather than laziness. His emaciated face was the color of a mushroom and glossed with perspiration. He looked as if he might die on the spot, draped over a headline heralding the approach of Mardi Gras.

'Are you all right?' Annie asked, torn between concern for him as a human and dislike of him as a person.

Kudrow tried to smile as he straightened. 'No, my dear, I am dying, but I won't be doing it here if that's what concerns you. I'm not quite ready to go just yet. There are still injustices to be corrected. You know all about that, don't you?'

'I'm not in the mood for your word games, lawyer. If you have something to say to me, then say it. I've got better things to do.'

'Like searching for Marcus's alibi witness? Marcus has told me you've taken an interest in his plight. How fascinating. This falls outside the scope of your duties, doesn't it?'

How much damage could he do with that knowledge? Sweat pooled between her shoulder blades and trickled down the valley of her spine. 'I'm looking into a couple of things out of curiosity, that's all.'

'A thirst for the truth. Too bad no one else in your department seems to share that quality. There's no evidence anyone is so much as looking into last night's shooting incident at the Renard home.'

'Maybe there's nothing to find.'

'Two people have openly tried to do Marcus harm in a week's time. Numerous others have threatened him. The list of suspects could read like the phone book, yet to my knowledge no one has been questioned.'

'The detectives are very busy these days, Mr Kudrow.'

'They'll have another homicide on their hands if they let this go,' he warned. 'This community is wound tighter than a watch spring. I can feel the air thickening with anger, with fear, with hate. That kind of pressure can only be contained to a point, then it explodes.'

A tight, rattling cough shook him and he leaned against the vending machine again, his energy spent, his eyes growing dull; an ill spectre of doom.

Annie walked away from him knowing he was right,

feeling that same heaviness in the air, the same sense of anticipation. Even in the sunshine everything looked rimmed in black, like in a bad dream. Down the side street she could see city workers hanging pretty spring flags on the light poles, sprucing up the town for the Mardi Gras Carnival, but the sidewalks seemed strangely empty. There was no one in the park south of the law enforcement center.

Three women had been attacked in a span of a week. Cops were acting like criminals, and a suspected murderer had gone free. People were terrified.

Annie thought back to the summer the Bayou Strangler had hunted here, and remembered having the same uneasy feeling, the same irrational fear, the same sense of helplessness. But this time she was a cop, and all the other emotions were being compressed by the weight of responsibility.

Someone had to make it stop.

Myron welcomed her back to the records office with a pointed stare he directed from Annie to the clock.

'This gentleman from Allied Insurance needs a number of accident reports,' he said, nodding to a round mound of sweating flesh in rumpled seersucker on the opposite side of the counter. 'You will get him whatever he needs.'

On that order he took up his *Wall Street Journal* and marched off to the men's room.

'That's the best dang thing I've heard all day!' the insurance man chortled. He stuck out a hand that looked like a small balloon animal. 'Tom O'Connor. Easy to remember,' he said with a smarmy wink. 'Tomcat O'round the Corner. Get it?'

Annie passed on the handshake. 'I get it. What reports did you need?'

He pulled a crumpled list from his coat pocket and handed it to her. 'Hey, aren't you cute in that uniform! You look like a little lady deputy.'

'I *am* a deputy.'

His eyes popped and he let loose another volley of chuckles. 'Well, shoot me dead!'

'Don't tempt me,' Annie said. 'I'm armed and it's been a very bad day.'

She looked up to heaven as she took the list to the file cabinets. 'Purgatory is a clerical department, isn't it?'

As she sent Tom O'Connor on his way with his reports, the fax machine rang and kicked on. Annie watched the cover sheet roll out, her interest piquing at the letterhead – the regional crime lab in New Iberia. The transmission was addressed to Det. Stokes, but the fax number was for records instead of for the detectives' machine – one digit off.

She watched the sheets roll into the tray, plucking them up one at a time. Preliminary lab results on the meager physical evidence collected at Lindsay Faulkner's crime scene and from Lindsay Faulkner's person. Negative. Nothing from the rape kit – no semen, no hair, no skin from under her nails, though they knew she'd put up a fight. Blood samples from the carpet runner appeared to be hers. Same type, at least. More sophisticated tests for DNA would take weeks.

Just as Stokes had predicted, they had nothing, just as they had nothing from the Jennifer Nolan rape or the Kay Eisner rape. Lack of evidence was the one thing tying the cases together. And the black feather mask – if the fragment Annie had picked off Faulkner's rug matched the one she'd found at Nolan's trailer park. Nolan and Eisner had both seen their assailant, had both seen the mask. So far, Lindsay Faulkner remembered nothing. If that situation didn't improve, then the feather from the mask could be the only link to the other attacks.

She looked back through the transmission for mention of the feather, finding none. There should have been a note, at least.

Annie glanced at the clock. Myron would be another five minutes in men's room seclusion. The world's official timekeepers could have set their watches by Myron's bowels. She dialed the number for the lab from her desk and connected with the person she needed, rattling off the case number and what she was after.

She waited, scanning through the fax pages, frustrated by the lack of evidence. They had to be dealing with a pro, someone savvy enough and cold enough to force the women to wash away all trace evidence or, in the case of Lindsay Faulkner, to wash it away himself. He knew everything they would look for, down to pubic hairs and skin under the fingernails.

She wondered if the task force had gleaned anything from the old files, wondered if Stokes had heard back from the state pen, wondered if the NCIC or VICAP computers would come up with anything. She wished she was the person who would be finding out instead of the person waiting on sweaty insurance guys in the records department.

'Excuse me?' the woman's voice came back on the line. 'You said a black feather, didn't you?'

'Yes. There was one with the Nolan case, and what might have been a fragment of a black feather with the Faulkner case.'

'Not here, there isn't.'

'What do you mean?'

'I mean, I'm looking right at the inventories and I don't see any feathers. They were never logged in here. Sorry.'

Annie thanked the woman and hung up.

'No feathers,' she murmured as Myron marched back into the office.

'Deputy Broussard, what are you mumbling about?' he demanded.

Paying no attention to him, Annie went to the drawer at the counter and pulled the evidence card for the Faulkner case. She ran her finger down the inventory of items. The black feather-like fiber was listed fourth. The last name on the chain of custody list was Det. Chs. Stokes, who had signed out the entire list of items for the purpose of turning them over to the lab for examination.

She pulled the card for Nolan and ran her finger down the lines. The feather had been listed. The evidence had been checked out to Stokes for the purpose of turning it over to the lab. But the lab had no record of any feathers being checked in.

'What are you doing?' Myron asked, snatching the card from her fingers and squinting at it.

Annie grabbed the fax sheets from her desk and started for the door.

'Where do you think you're going?' the clerk demanded.

'To see Detective Stokes. He's got some explaining to do.'

34

The detectives had their own building across the alley from the main facility. Known affectionately as the Pizza Hut for the volume of pepperoni with extra cheese pies delivered there on a regular basis, it was a low, snot green cinderblock job that had once been office space for a road construction outfit. The sheriff's office had bought the property, converted the parking yard for the heavy equipment into an impound lot, and given the building to a detective division that had outgrown its allotted space in the aging law enforcement center.

Annie buzzed the door and was let in by the detective named Perez, his name spelled out in Magic Marker across the front of the Kevlar vest he wore over a T-shirt. His dark hair was scraped back into a short rattail. The mustache that covered his upper lip was bushy enough to hide small rodents. He gave Annie a sour once-over.

'I need to see Stokes.'

'You got a warrant?'

'Screw you, Perez.'

As she walked past him, he cupped a hand around his mouth and shouted, 'Hey, Chaz, you got the right to remain silent!'

The building was as cold as a walk-in freezer. Two window air conditioners groaned at the effort to maintain the temperature while electric fans blew the chilled air around the single front room. The room that had been given over to the rape task force was at the back. It had probably been the construction foreman's office at one time. A twelve-by-twelve cube paneled in cheap wood grain. Someone had started a soda can pyramid on the ledge of the barred window. The files Annie and Myron had gathered were strewn in haphazard piles over the long table that was the room's main piece of furniture. The hard-driving Cajun-spiced rock of Sonny Landreth's 'Shootin' for the Moon' was wailing out of a boom box on top of a corner file cabinet.

Mullen was on the phone. Stokes pranced behind the table, playing air guitar and mouthing lyrics, his crumpled porkpie hat tipped back on his head.

Annie rolled her eyes. 'Oh yeah, the women of this parish will sleep better knowing you're on the job, Stokes.'

He swung toward her. 'Broussard, you are a boil on the butt of my day. You know what I'm saying?'

'Like I care.' She held the faxes up. 'Your preliminary lab results on Faulkner. Where's the feather?'

He snatched the papers away from her and scanned them, frowning.

'Don't bother to pretend you're looking for it in there,' Annie said. 'The lab says they've never seen it or the one from the Nolan scene. I want to know why.'

Mullen still had the phone receiver pressed to his head, but his eyes were on them.

'Man, I need this like I need root canal,' Stokes muttered, turning for the back door.

Annie followed him out. The area behind the building was a wasteland of crushed shell, rock, and weeds with a view of the abandoned junkers in the impound lot.

'What'd you do with them, Chaz?' she demanded.

'I told you to keep your nose out of my cases,' he snapped, thrusting a finger at her.

'So you can feel free to fuck up with impunity?'

'Shut up!' he shouted, charging her. 'Shut the fuck up!'

Annie backpedaled into the side of the building.

'I'm just about half past sick of your shit, Broussard,' he snarled, his face inches from hers. His pale eyes were neon-bright with temper. The tendons in his neck stood out like iron rods. 'I know what I'm doing. How do you think I got this job? You think I got this job 'cause I'm browner than you? You think I skated in on my color?'

Annie glared right back at him. 'No. I think you got it because you're a man and you're full of bullshit. You talk a big game, and when somebody calls you on it, then they're suddenly a racist. I've had it up to my back teeth with that game. I don't hear Quinlan calling anybody a racist. I don't hear Ossie Compton calling anybody a racist. I don't hear anybody but you, and what you got is barely a suntan.'

She ducked under the arm he had braced against the building, and backed away from him. 'You're a jerk. You'd be a jerk if you were snow white. You'd be a jerk if you looked like Mel Gibson. End of topic. I want to know what you did with the evidence I collected. You can tell me or we can take it to the sheriff.'

Stokes paced, trying to school his temper or weigh his options or both. 'Don't you threaten me, Broussard,' he muttered. 'You're nothing but a little prick-teaser trouble-maker.'

'Gus is still in his office,' Annie bluffed. 'I could have gone straight to him, you know.'

And run the risk of not only looking like a fool but renewing every hard feeling the men held toward her. Stokes would say the same thing to Gus he'd just said to her. He'd call her a troublemaker, and there wasn't a soul in the department who wouldn't believe him on some level.

'You dumped evidence,' she prodded, not wanting to give him time to think. 'What possible excuse do you have for that?'

'I didn't dump nothing,' he growled. 'The feathers went to the state lab.'

'Where's the receipt?'

'Fuck you! I don't have to answer to you, Broussard! Who the fuck do you think you are?'

'Maybe I'm the only person paying attention,' Annie shot back. 'Why would you send everything to New Iberia except the feathers?'

'Because I know a guy in the state lab and he owes me a favor. That's why. They got some brainiac fibers expert can look at a feather and tell if it came off a duck's ass in Outer Mongolia. So I sent him the goddamn feathers *and* the mask from the Bichon homicide. For all the good that'll do us.

'Those damn masks are a dime a dozen. What are we gonna do? Track down every manufacturer in Bumfuck, Thailand, and ask them what? Go to every five-and-dime and cheap-shit souvenir shop in South Lou'siana and ask them if they sold any masks to rapists? A hundred goddamn miles of legwork that'll get us jack shit.'

'Unless the feathers match up,' Annie said. 'Then you might be able to tie the first two rapes to Faulkner, at least. Even just by a thread would be more than you've got now. Faulkner doesn't remember anything about the attack. She may never.'

She knew instantly she'd made a mistake. Stokes's posture tightened, his gaze turned cold and hard.

'How do you know that?' he asked quietly.

Oh, shit. Annie jumped in with both feet. 'I went to see her this morning.'

'Fuckin' *A*!' Stokes shouted in disbelief. Then his voice dropped to a near whisper, and yet it skated sharply across Annie's nerves. 'You just do not listen, do you, bitch?

'This is *my* case,' he said, thumping a fist to his chest. 'I *will* make it. I don't have to answer to you. I find out you called the state lab to check my story, I'll haul your ass into Noblier's office – and if you think he isn't ready to cut you loose, you better think again, Broussard. You'll be working security at a gator farm by the time I'm through with you.

'Faulkner is *my* vic, *my* witness. You stay the hell away from her. You stay the hell away from my cases,' he warned, poking her sternum with a forefinger. 'You stay the hell away from me.'

He went back into the building, the barred storm door hissing shut behind him. Mullen stared out the window at her. A moment later, a car's engine roared to life on the other side of the building and tires squealed on pavement.

She caught a glimpse of Stokes's black Camaro as it shot past toward the bayou.

What now? Annie couldn't imagine Stokes being so diligent as to send the feathers to a specialist, but if she called the state lab to check, he'd have her ass on a platter. If he had in fact taken the feathers to Shreveport, he would have kept the receipt with the case file, and the case file was in his possession. And if he hadn't sent the feathers to the state lab?

He admitted he didn't want to do the legwork, didn't want to chase down the source of the feathers. The chance of getting anything useful out of it was too big a long shot. He didn't want the feathers to match up with the mask from the Bichon homicide because that might mean someone other than Marcus Renard killed Pam Bichon. He didn't want the work. He didn't want the headache. He didn't want to be proved wrong.

A wanderer on the path of least resistance, that was Stokes. His problem had absolutely nothing to do with his color or anyone's perception of his color. It had to do with his own perception of the world and his priorities regarding it. He would rather have spent his time playing air guitar than seeing through the tedious business of tracking down a long-shot lead. He would rather have spent his time flirting with Pam Bichon than doing the grunt work that could have proved her stalking case. He hadn't perceived her to be in danger, so why follow up on anything?

Annie wondered what else he might have screwed up – on this case and on Pam's case. What might he have overlooked when Pam was being stalked? Something that could have been used against Renard when Pam filed for the restraining order? How differently might things have turned out if someone else had caught Pam's case in the beginning – Quinlan or Perez or Nick?

Now Stokes had charge of a task force that could affect the lives of any number of women. They were up against a criminal who knew the system, knew procedure, had left them virtually nothing at the scenes of three rapes. Only a pro would know what they needed –

Or a cop.

The idea swept a chill over her. Fear scratched at the back of her neck, and she turned her eyes on the Pizza Hut.

A cop would know exactly what went into building a rape case.

Stokes a rapist? It was crazy. He had more women than he could keep track of. But then, rape wasn't about sex. Plenty of rapists had wives or girlfriends. Rape was about anger and power. She thought of the way Stokes had looked as he charged her moments ago; the fury in his eyes. She thought of the way he had looked months ago when she had argued with him in the parking lot at the Voodoo Lounge, the hot blue flame of hate that had flared at her rejection of him.

But it was a long jump from anger to aggression to rape. It made more sense that Stokes was lazy than a sexual predator. It made more sense that their rapist was a career criminal than a career cop.

Still ...

Stokes had control of all the evidence in three rapes that shared traits with Pam Bichon's homicide.

Stokes had investigated Pam's stalking complaints.

Donnie Bichon had been jealous of Pam's relationship with the detective. So said Lindsay Faulkner, who had met with Stokes over lunch on Monday and had her head bashed in that same night.

Donnie had been jealous of Stokes.

'*Stupid ... It was nothing,*' Faulkner had said.

Annie wondered who might have broken that news to Stokes.

She finished her shift in clerical hell, changed clothes in her makeshift locker room, and went in search of estimates for the damage to the Heap, one eye peeled for a Cadillac with matching dents. The last of the three garages sat across the street from Po' Richard's sandwich shop.

Stomach growling, she contemplated supper. Going home this early would almost certainly mean a confrontation with Uncle Sos. She had avoided him and his questions this morning, but she wouldn't be that lucky again. He would want to know why A.J. had come and gone so quickly this morning. Going to Fourcade's place would mean what? Would they sit down and talk about what was going on between them or would they just end up in his bed, solving nothing, complicating everything?

She pulled up to the drive-through window and ordered a fried shrimp po'boy basket and a Pepsi. The kid at the window didn't recognize her. He didn't look like the type to watch the news. Shunning the picnic tables that sat out in front of the restaurant and the half-dozen people taking their suppers there, she drove down the block and parked in front of a vacant lot strewn with beer cans and broken glass. As she munched her dinner she stared out her broken window across the street to Bichon Bayou Development.

The office had been closed nearly two hours, but Donnie's Lexus sat alongside the building and a light shone in two of the windows. Why had Donnie been jealous of the time Pam spent with Stokes? Had he expected Pam to turn to him instead of to the cops during the stalking? Had that been his plan – to stalk Pam himself, frighten her anonymously, get her to turn to him, and win her back? It seemed like the kind of juvenile grand plan that would appeal to Donnie's arrested adolescent ego. And when the plan failed, he would have wanted to blame someone other than himself – Stokes, or Pam herself.

Annie picked the last shrimp from the cardboard tray and chewed it slowly, thinking of Lindsay. Faulkner disliked Donnie. *Hate* may not have been too strong a word. She may have come up with her latest revelation simply to make trouble for him. According to the receptionist at the realty, Donnie and Lindsay had argued Monday morning.

Lindsay may have thought defaming Donnie would scare off his prospective buyer for the realty. And how would Donnie have reacted to that plan?

If he was capable of terrorizing the mother of his child, if he was capable of killing her, then what would stop him from beating Lindsay Faulkner's head in with a telephone?

She let herself out of the Jeep, crossed the street, and walked through the open side gate to Bichon Bayou Development. She chose a side door, near the window with the light shining through, rang the bell twice, and waited. A moment later Donnie pulled the door open and stared at her, a vague sheen glossing his eyes.

'Well, if it isn't the chick filler in my cop sandwich,' he drawled. He had shed his tie and left his shirt open at the throat, sleeves rolled up. The scent of whiskey hung on him like a faint cologne. 'I've got Fourcade on my ass, Stokes in my face, and you ... What part of me do you want, Ms Broussard?'

'How much have you had to drink, Mr Bichon?'

'Why? Is there now some law against a man drowning his sorrows in the privacy of his own office?'

'No, sir,' Annie said. 'I'm just wondering if this conversation will be worth my while, that's all.'

He raked a hand through his brown hair, mussing it, and propped a shoulder on the door frame. The smile he flashed her seemed thin and forced. He looked tired, physically, spiritually. Sad, Annie decided, though she was careful not to let the assessment taint her feelings toward him. Donnie was the type of man a lot of women would want to mother the perpetual boy in a man's body, full of charm and mischief and confusion and potential. Had it been that boyish quality that had attracted Pam? Lindsay Faulkner had said Pam had always seen the potential in Donnie, but had never imagined he wouldn't live up to it.

'Are you always so straightforward, Detective?' he asked. 'Whatever happened to those coy games women learned while under their mothers' white-gloved tutelage?'

'It's Deputy,' Annie corrected. 'My mother died when I was nine.'

Donnie winced. 'God. I can't manage to do much of anything right these days. I'm sorry,' he said with genuine contrition. He stepped back from the door and motioned her in. 'I'm not so drunk to have lost all my manners or sense, though some would say I never had much of the latter to begin with. Come in. Have a seat. I just ordered a pizza.'

A gooseneck lamp was the only light on in his office, glowing gold on the polished oak desk and giving the place an intimate feel. A bottle of Glenlivet single malt scotch sat on the blotter beside a coffee mug that declared Donnie to be #1 DAD.

'Have you seen Josie this week?' Annie asked as she walked slowly around the office, taking in the wildlife art on the walls, the framed aerial photos of the Quail Run subdivision. A photo of Josie smiling like a pixie sat on the desk near the mug.

Donnie dropped into his chair. 'Hell, no. Every night's a school night. On the weekend Belle runs off with her. Let me tell you, the only thing worse than having an ex-wife is having an ex-mother-in-law. She lies when I call – tells me Josie's in the bathtub, she's gone to bed, she's doing homework.' He poured two fingers of scotch into the mug and drank half. 'I admit, I have dark thoughts about Belle Davidson.'

'Careful who you say that to, Mr Bichon.'

'That's right. Anything I say can and will be used against me. Well, I'm past caring at the moment. I miss my little girl.'

He sipped at the scotch, stroked his fingertips over the printing on the mug. There was an air of surprise about him, as if he had never expected to face any difficulty in his life and what he was going through now was a rude and unwelcome shock. Things had come too easily for him, Annie suspected. He was handsome. He was popular. He was an athlete. He expected love and adoration, instant forgiveness, no accountability. In many ways, he was as much a child as his daughter.

'Please have a seat so I can focus my eyes, Deputy. And please call me Donnie. I'm depressed enough without having to think attractive women feel compelled to call me "sir." ' He flashed the weary smile again.

Annie took a seat in the burgundy wing chair across the desk from him. He wanted to be friends, to pretend she was here for him instead of as a cop – the way Renard kept trying to do. But she felt less anxious about it with Donnie, which could prove to be a costly mistake, she reminded herself. He had as much reason to kill Pam as Renard. More. But he was handsome, and popular, and charming, and no one wanted to think he was guilty of anything other than cheating on his wife.

If she was going to play detective, it was her role to draw him out from behind his public facade. Get him to relax, get him to talk, see what he might reveal. She could once again play off the adversarial positions Stokes and Fourcade had taken with him. She could be his friend.

'Okay, Donnie,' she said. 'What's depressing you?'

'What isn't? I'm separated from my child. I'm being stalked by a psychopathic cop who *I* bailed out of jail. Now I've got Stokes coming in here asking me did I bash in Lindsay Faulkner's head – like I even thought anything could put a dent in it. Business is ...' He let the statement trail off on a heavy sigh. 'And Pam ...'

Tears filled his eyes and he looked away. 'This isn't what I wanted,' he whispered.

'It's not working out for the best for anyone,' Annie said. 'I saw Lindsay this morning. She's in pretty rough shape.'

'But that's got nothing to do with Pam,' he declared. 'It was that rapist.'

Annie didn't comment. In the brief silence she watched his expression of certainty slip. 'I suppose you heard about someone taking a shot at Renard last night.'

'It's the talk of the town,' Donnie said. 'I believe if he'd been killed, the Rotarians would have made the shooter grand marshal of the Mardi Gras parade. People are sick of waiting around for justice to be done.'

'Are you one of those people?'

'Hell, yes. Did I pull the trigger? Hell, no, and for once I've got half a dozen witnesses to back me up. I was here last night, working on the parade float.'

'And the crew is off tonight?'

'It's finished. I'm celebrating.' He lifted the bottle and raised his eyebrows. 'Want to help me?'

'No thanks.'

'That's the second time you've turned me down. If you're not careful, I'll get the feeling you don't like me.'

'And then what?'

He shrugged and grinned. 'I'll have to try harder. I dislike rejection.'

'What about competition? Lindsay told me you were jealous of Detective Stokes spending time with Pam.'

The grin flattened. He poured a little more scotch and took the mug with him as he unfolded his lanky body from the chair. 'The guy's a jerk, that's all. He was supposed to be investigating. All he really wanted was to get in her pants.'

'Do you think he ever succeeded?'

'Pam didn't sleep around.'

'And how would it be any of your business if she had?'

'She was still my wife,' he said, his expression tightening with suppressed anger.

'On paper.'

'It wasn't over.'

'Pam said it was.'

'She was wrong,' he insisted. 'I loved her. I screwed up. I know I screwed up, but I loved her. We would have worked things out.'

His determination amazed and unnerved Annie. 'Donnie, she had filed the papers.'

'She still had my name. She still wore my ring, for

Christ's sake.' Tears welled in his eyes again and his hand trembled a little. 'And she's out with that –'

He wasn't drunk enough to finish the sentence. He shook his head at the temptation, turned away from it.

'What do you mean – out with him?' Annie prodded. 'You mean like on dates?'

'Lunch to discuss this aspect of the case. Dinner to go over that aspect of the case. I saw the way he looked at her. I know what he wanted. He didn't give a shit about the case. He didn't do anything to stop what was happening.'

'How do you know that?'

He blinked at her. 'Because I – I *know*. I was there.'

'Where?' Annie pressed, rising and stepping toward him, her instincts at attention. 'Did you follow him around? Did you talk to the sheriff? How would you know what he did or didn't do, Donnie?'

Unless you were involved.

He didn't answer for a moment, didn't look at her. 'You ask him,' he said at last. 'You ask him what he was doing. Ask him what he wanted. I can't believe he hasn't wanted the same thing from you.' His gaze moved over her face. 'Then again, maybe he has. Maybe you go for his type. What do I know?'

'His type?'

Sipping at his scotch, he moved away.

'Did you ever confront him about his interest in Pam?' Annie asked.

'He said if I had a problem with him, I should take it to the sheriff, but that I'd look like a jackass 'cause Pam sure as hell wasn't complaining.'

'How did that make you feel toward Pam?'

He didn't answer. He picked a small framed photograph off a shelf in the bookcase and looked at it as if he hadn't seen it in a very long time. A photograph of himself with Pam and Josie at about five. His family, intact.

'She was so pretty,' he whispered.

Setting the frame aside, he turned toward Annie again.

'Like you, Detective. Pretty brown eyes.' He reached up with a hesitant hand to brush her bangs to the side. 'Pretty smile.' He touched the corner of her mouth. 'Better watch out. I'll want to marry you.'

Annie held herself still, wondering how much of this talk was Donnie and how much was the liquor. Then the doorbell buzzed, and whatever had been in Donnie's head vanished.

'Pizza man,' he announced, walking out.

She wondered just how stable he was. His logic seemed perilously close to the classic pattern of the obsessive stalker everyone had pegged Renard to be. She wondered how angry he might have been seeing Pam with Stokes. She wondered how a man who reportedly chased every skirt in town could find any moral outrage at his estranged wife having lunch with another man. Even if Stokes had had designs on Pam, Pam had not reciprocated. '*It was nothing*,' Lindsay had said; she had been reluctant even to raise the subject, it seemed so insignificant.

And yet she had raised the subject with Stokes the very day she had quarreled with Donnie ... and that same night someone had tried to silence her forever.

The pieces sifted through her mind: Donnie, desperate, losing a wife and a safety net for his business. Donnie, unable to cope with the idea of rejection. Donnie, in financial straits. Donnie, angry, driven to a dangerous limit by his problems and by the sight of his wife enjoying the company of another man – a man whose race might have added to the outrage in Donnie's mind. Pushed to that thin dark line, might he have crossed it in a moment of madness? Killed her in a fit of rage and covered the crime with atrocities no one would ever attribute to him?

The sudden ringing of the telephone broke Annie's concentration. She expected an answering machine to pick up, but none did. Who called a business line at this hour? A client? A girlfriend? A legitimate associate? A not-so-legitimate associate?

She picked up the receiver when the phone stopped ringing. Eyes on the door, she dialed star 69 and waited while the call chased itself back home.

On the fourth ring a man's voice answered. 'Marcotte.'

35

When will you paint that, Marcus? I want no reminders,'
Doll said with drama. 'My nerves are still ragged tonight.
They're worse, in fact. It's as if it's all coming back to me
because of it being evening. My evenings will never be the
same. The joy of my evenings has been robbed from me. I
will never again be able to sit at this table and enjoy a cup
of coffee after dinner. Certainly not with the wall looking
that way. When will you paint it?'

'Tomorrow, Mother.'

Marcus scraped the last of the excess wet patching
compound from the wall and into the can he had used to
mix the concoction. He was no expert at repairing walls, let
alone a bullet hole, but then no expert had been willing to
do the job. Every call had been the same: They heard his
name and hung up.

He had boarded up the broken French door himself.
When the replacement glass arrived, he would have to learn
about glazing, he supposed. Until then, the heavy drapes
would be pulled across the door. Doll had closed every
shade and drape in the house to block the view of any
potential voyeur or sniper.

'The sheriff's office should have to pay for fixing that
hole,' Doll said. 'It's their fault we have people shooting at
us. The way they've railroaded you when you're guilty of
nothing but making a fool of yourself over a woman.
They're lazy and corrupt, and we'll all end up murdered in
our beds because of them.'

'They're not all that way, Mother. Annie said she'd do her
best to check into what happened last night.'

'Annie,' she said with disapproval. 'Don't delude yourself,
Marcus. You think she's some kind of angel. She's no better
than the rest.'

Tuning out his mother's droning, Marcus knelt to clean up his work area. He imagined what it would be like to move away from here and start fresh without the burden of his family or his reputation. He envisioned a house of his own design, perhaps on the Gulf Coast of Texas or Florida. Something open and bright, with a large deck facing the water.

He thought of coming home after work to cook dinner for Annie. She wasn't the domestic sort. He would take pleasure in teaching her. They would work side by side in the kitchen, and he would show her the proper way to fillet a fish. His hand would close over hers on the knife and guide her. He could almost feel the delicate bones of her hand beneath his, the smooth handle of the knife filling her palm. It would remind them both of the night before, when he had closed her hand around the shaft of his penis. Warmth flooded his groin.

'Marcus, are you listening to me?'

Doll's shrill tone tore through the fabric of his fantasy, ruining it. He briefly imagined surging to his feet with a roar, swinging the can of plaster mix, striking his mother across the face with it, plaster and blood spraying across the wall as she crumpled to the floor. But of course he didn't do that. It was only a moment's madness, there and gone. He wiped his hands on the damp towel and folded it neatly.

'What was that, Mother?'

'Will the paint match?' she asked with exasperation. 'I have a premonition that the spot will always stand out. That the color won't match no matter what we do, and every time I look at that wall I'll be taken with the fear.'

Marcus rose with the bucket in one hand and toolbox in the other. 'I'm sure it will match – so long as we allow the plaster to cure properly before we paint it.'

Doll drummed her fingertips against her sternum, frowning sourly. 'I wish you would paint it tonight.'

'If I paint it tonight, the spot will show.' He walked away as she clucked her tongue behind him.

He wanted out of the house, needed air, needed quiet. He wanted to see Annie. He had tried to call her, to thank her again for coming to his rescue, to ask her if she had made any progress on his case, but she wasn't home, which made him wonder what she was doing. As much as he didn't want to, he couldn't help but question if she was with a man tonight.

The thought aroused his jealousy. Men would want her. He did. And she might take a lover, not fully realizing yet what could be between them. He imagined tearing her from the arms of another man, striking her, punishing her, disciplining her for betraying him, taking her sexually with force and dominance. She would realize her mistake then. She would see the truth of his feelings for her. And in seeing that truth she would recognize her own feelings.

Strange, he thought as he washed the plaster residue from his hands, after Elaine had died, he hadn't wanted anyone to take her place for a long time. He hadn't expected to think of another woman after Pam's death. He still grieved for her. He still missed her. But the sharpness of that pain had faded and was being replaced by something else – hunger, need. Pam had ultimately rejected him. She had believed the lies of her husband and Stokes, and failed to see the truth of his devotion to her. He thought less and less of Pam, more and more of Annie, his angel.

He went through his bedroom to his sanctuary and turned on the lights and radio. A Haydn string quartet played softly as he took the portrait from its special place in the small secret storage cupboard hidden behind a panel of wainscoting. The cubbyhole had been there for more than a century. No telling what the original owners of the house had protected in it. Marcus lined the shelves with keepsakes he would share with no one. Treasured mementos of past loves. Things he wanted no one in his family to taint with so much as their mere knowledge of them. He touched several pieces now.

Closing the panel, he moved to his drawing table and

arranged things to his satisfaction. The sketch was taking shape nicely. He stared at it for a long time, thinking, imagining. He concentrated first on her eyes with their slightly exotic shape. Then the slim, pert nose. Then the mouth – her incredibly sexy mouth with its full lower lip and quirking corners. He imagined touching her mouth with his, imagined her mouth moving over his naked body. He imagined her hands touching him. The arousal built until he finally went back to the secret cupboard and returned with a pair of women's black silk underpants. He opened his trousers and masturbated with the panties, his eyes on the portrait. He thought of what it would be like to be inside her, to press her body down beneath his and impale his shaft between her legs again and again and again, until she screamed with the ecstasy of it.

When it was over, he washed himself at the utility sink in the corner, rinsed out the panties, and put them away with his other treasures. He watched the clock and waited, too restless to work on the drawing. When the house was quiet and he knew his mother and Victor were likely both asleep, he let his restlessness drive him from the house into the night.

Nick paced his study as Annie recounted the events of the evening to him, culminating with Marcotte's call to Donnie. Things were starting to happen. The screws were turning.

Marcotte was in it now, and Nick couldn't help but wonder if that was his own doing. That Marcotte might never have taken an interest in Bayou Breaux if he hadn't drawn the man's attention to it didn't sit well. The possibility that Marcotte had been involved from the start pleased him even less.

The focus of the investigation was broadening rather than narrowing, suggesting he hadn't done the job right the first time around, and he didn't want to believe that. He had worked too hard to come back from the debacle of New Orleans and the Parmantel case.

'I feel like I'm balancing on the head of a pin, juggling bowling balls,' Annie muttered, starting to pace as Nick slowed, as if it were essential for one of them to keep in motion.

'If Marcotte was in contact with Donnie before Pam's murder, then that only adds to Donnie's motive,' she said. 'He was angry with Pam for leaving him. I think she was probably holding his property hostage in order to get him to drop the custody threat – which Lindsay Faulkner hinted might have been about Pam seeing male clients. I know Donnie was angry over the relationship he imagined between her and Stokes. If it was imagined.

'What do you know about that?' she asked. 'Was he talking about her around the office? Did he say anything to you?'

Nick shook his head. 'Not that I recall, but I don't listen to that crap, anyway. I don't care who's screwing who unless there's a felony involved. I sure as hell didn't listen to Stokes. He's got a new one every week, at least. I know he was friendly with her. He was quieter after her murder. He might have wanted to be the primary on the case, but he was tied up with the DA the morning you found her. I caught it instead, and Noblier left it that way, even though Stokes had worked the stalking angle. It was a matter of experience. I've worked more murders than the rest of them put together.'

'But Stokes never said anything personal about Pam, about the two of them?'

'Not in a sexual way, no. He admitted he wished he had done more for her during the harassment. He didn't take it seriously enough.'

'No kidding,' Annie said sarcastically. 'I've gone over those reports. He gave her pamphlets on domestic violence and told her to call the phone company to see if she couldn't get them to put a tap on her line. Lazy son of a bitch.'

She marched back toward him, her eyes bright with anger and adrenaline. She looked ready to wrestle tigers. Her anger pleased him.

'And what if Stokes is something worse than lazy?' Annie asked quietly, giving voice to the thought for the first time. She felt as if she had just let a poisonous snake loose in the room.

Fourcade looked at her with suspicion. 'What exactly are you saying, 'Toinette?'

'I had a little run-in with Stokes today over some of the evidence in those rapes. He claims he sent it in to the lab in Shreveport for analysis, but he threatened me not to check up on it. He says he'll go to Noblier and make a formal complaint about me digging around in his cases. But what's the big deal if I call – if the stuff is really there?'

'You think he didn't send it?' Nick said. 'Why wouldn't he?'

'This rapist knows everything we'll look for – hairs, fibers, fingerprints, body fluids. He goes so far as to make the victims clean under their fingernails after he's through with them. Who would know to be that careful? A pro ... or a cop.'

'You think Stokes is the rapist? *Mais sa c'est fou!* That's crazy!' He actually laughed. Annie didn't see the humor.

'Why is that crazy?' she demanded. 'Because he's got all the women he wants? You know as well as I do it doesn't always work that way.'

'Come on, 'Toinette. Stokes is suddenly a rapist? Overnight he's a rapist? No way.'

'You think he's not capable of violence against a woman?' Annie said. 'Good ol' Chaz. Everybody's buddy. I can tell you from experience he doesn't like the word *no*.'

The import of her words struck Nick hard, awakening feelings of jealousy and protectiveness he would have said he didn't possess. 'He laid a hand on you?'

'He never got the chance,' Annie said. 'But that doesn't mean he didn't want to or that he hasn't thought about it a hundred times since. He's got an ugly temper with a touchy trigger.'

True enough, Nick thought. He'd seen Stokes's temper in action just yesterday.

'You thought he turned on you,' Annie reminded him.

And he wasn't entirely sure it wasn't true. But Nick couldn't decide if he suspected Stokes because Stokes was deserving of it or because Nick didn't want to accept 100 percent of the culpability for beating up Renard.

'There's a big jump from selling me out to being a rapist,' he said.

'But look at the connections to Stokes in all of this,' Annie said. 'Every time I turn around, there he is. He's got control of the rape task force, has access to all the evidence. Now he's checked out the feathers from the mask in two of the rapes *and* the mask from Pam Bichon's homicide, and he doesn't want me calling the lab to check on the stuff.'

Nick lifted his hands. 'Oh, hold on, 'Toinette. You're not gonna try to tie him to Bichon.'

'Why not?' Annie said. 'Stokes investigated Pam's stalking complaints. Donnie was jealous of the time Pam spent with him – so said Lindsay Faulkner, who met Stokes over lunch on Monday and had her head bashed in that same night.'

'You're way off the beam here,' Nick said, shaking his head. 'I was there, remember. Bichon was my case. You think I wouldn't have seen that?'

'Were you looking?' Annie challenged. 'Where did Stokes steer you? To Renard.'

'Nobody steers me. I went to Renard because the logic took me there. Stokes turns up in all of this because he's a cop, for God's sake. If you follow your line of thinking, you could tie *me* to the murder, I could tie you to the rapes.'

'I'm not the one trying to hide evidence,' Annie shot back.

'You don't know that he is, either. Maybe he just wants you out of his hair.'

'And maybe I'm right and you don't wanna hear it because it would make you look like a fool.'

'I don't wanna hear it because it's a waste of time,' he said stubbornly.

'Because it's my theory and not yours,' Annie argued. 'I told you at the start of this I wouldn't be your puppet, Nick. Don't blow me off now because I'm not stuck in the same tunnel with you. I think Stokes is a legitimate suspect.'

'He's a cop.'

'So are you!' she snapped. 'It didn't stop you from breaking the law.'

Her words slapped everything to a halt. She felt a sting of guilt that aggravated her. She wasn't the one who had something to feel guilty about. And yet, she couldn't let go of the feeling that she'd hurt him. Fourcade, the granite cop, the pillar of cold logic. No one else would have thought him capable of feeling hurt.

'I'm sorry,' she murmured. 'That was bitchy.'

'No. It's true enough. *C'est vrai.*'

He went to a dormer window and stared out at nothing.

'I just think it's another possibility,' Annie said. 'It's an angle no one's considered.'

An angle he didn't want to consider, Nick admitted. For exactly the reason she had said. Bichon had been his case. If he'd worked side by side with her killer and never seen it, what kind of cop did that make him?

He ran the possibility through his mind, trying to see it as if he'd never had anything to do with the case or with Stokes.

'I don't buy it,' he said. 'Stokes has been here four or five years, suddenly he butchers a woman and becomes a serial rapist? Uh-uh. That's not the way it works.'

He turned around and walked slowly back toward Annie. 'What other evidence was there in the rapes?'

'No blood, no semen, no skin. Nothing from the rape

kits.' Then a memory surfaced. 'At the Nolan rape, I saw Stokes picking pubic hairs out of Jennifer Nolan's bathtub with a tweezers.'

'Check it out. Meanwhile, get me the case numbers on the rapes. I'll call Shreveport and tell them I'm Quinlan. See what they have to say.'

Annie nodded. 'Thanks,' she said, looking up at him. 'I'm sorry –'

'Don't be sorry, 'Toinette,' he ordered. 'It's a waste of energy. You had something on your mind, you laid it out. We'll see where it takes us, but I don't want you getting sidetracked. These rapes aren't your focus. The murder is your focus and Renard is your number one suspect. Pam Bichon herself, she told us that. You don't wanna listen to me, you listen to her.'

He was right. Pam had seen Renard for a monster and no one had listened to her. In turning away from Renard to look at other possibilities, was she also ignoring Pam's cries for help – or was she simply doing the job?

'Why couldn't I have been a cocktail waitress?' she asked on a weary sigh.

'If you weren't a cop, you wouldn't get to drive that hot car,' Nick murmured.

The humor was unexpected and welcome. Annie looked at his rugged face, the eyes that had seen too much. Logic told her to stay away from him, but the temptation to feel something other than uncertainty and apprehension was strong. He had the power to sweep it all away for a few hours, to blind her to everything but passion and raw need. A brief interlude of oblivion and obsession.

Obsession didn't seem like such a good thing to succumb to, considering where it had gotten Fourcade. But was it obsession she was afraid of or Fourcade or herself?

Annie forced herself to go to the board of crime scene photos and look at what had been left of Pam Bichon. A shudder of revulsion went through her, as sobering as a dousing of ice water.

Could Stokes have done this? With what motive? Lindsay Faulkner said he had flirted with Pam, that Donnie had been jealous. She never said that Pam had objected to Stokes's attentions. If Pam had put him off because she feared repercussions from Donnie, he had only to bide his time until the divorce went through. But Chaz Stokes was not a patient man, and not always a rational one. In a moment of blind fury could he have crossed the line?

It sounded weak to her. Maybe she wanted to look at Stokes only because he yanked her chain or because she knew he was a lazy cop.

Could Donnie have done this? In her mind's eye she could see him in the intimate light of his office, standing too close to her, that strange look of false remembrance and regret hanging crooked on his face. In a fit of anger, jealousy pushing him far beyond his limits, could he have butchered the mother of his child?

He had been drinking the night of the murder, as he had been tonight. Liquor was the key that opened the floodgates on ugly emotions. She'd seen it happen time and again. But to this level of brutality?

'You were in it from the start,' she said to Nick. 'Did you ever think Donnie could have done it?'

He joined her at the table. 'I've seen people driven to all manner of atrocities. I've seen parents kill their children, children kill their parents, husbands kill their wives, wives set their husbands on fire while they're passed out drunk. But this? I never believed he had the stomach for it. Motive, maybe, but the rest ... no, I never believed it.

'I talked to the bartender who served Donnie at the Voodoo Lounge that night.' He shook a cigarette out of the pack on the table and played with it between his fingers. 'He swore Donnie had more than his share.'

'I know. I read the statement. But it was Friday night,' Annie reminded him. 'They were busy. Can he be sure Donnie drank everything he was served? And even if he drank it, how do we know he didn't just go in the men's room and puke it all up? If he's capable of doing this to a woman, then he's clever enough to build himself an alibi.'

'There's one big stumbling block, *chère. Il a pas d'ésprit*. Donnie, he's not clever at all,' he said. 'He's a whiner not a doer, and a screwup to boot. There's no way in hell Donnie Bichon commits a crime like this and he doesn't fuck up somewhere along the way. Fingerprints, fibers, skin under her fingernails, semen, *something*. There was damn near nothing at that crime scene – on or around the body. He consented to a search of his town house – nothing. No bloody clothes, no bloody towels, no bloody footprints in the garage, no traces of blood anywhere in the house.'

'What about this possible connection to Marcotte and Marcotte's connection to DiMonti?'

'That's no mob hit,' he said. 'Mob wants somebody dead, they take 'em out in the swamp and shoot 'em. They wrap eighty pounds of chain around the body and throw it in the Atchafalaya. Bump 'em and dump 'em. No boss would have this kind of psycho on his payroll. Killer like this, he's too unpredictable, he's a risk. I've said it all along and I say it again: This was personal.'

Annie turned her back to the photos and rubbed her hands over her face. 'My brain hurts.'

'Keep your eyes on the prize, 'Toinette. Don't turn your back on Renard just because you see other possibilities. He's calling you, sending you presents – same as he did with Pam. Same as he did with that gal up in Baton Rouge. There's two dead women in his wake. You leave Donnie and Marcotte to me. Renard is your focus. You got him on the hook, *'tite fille*. Reel him in.'

And then what? she thought, but she didn't ask the question. She simply let the silence settle between them, too hot and too tired to go any further with it tonight. The loft was warm and stuffy, the unexpected heat of the day having risen up into the rafters. The ceiling fans only stirred it around.

'Had enough for one day?' Nick asked. He brought the

411

cigarette to his lips, then pulled it away and tossed it on the table beside the pack.

Annie nodded, following the move with her eyes. She wondered if he had changed his mind or if he had set it aside because he knew she didn't like it. Dangerous thinking. Foolish thinking. Fourcade did what he wanted.

'Stay the night,' he said. As if he had flipped a switch, the energy he radiated became instantly sexual. She felt it touch her, felt her own body stir in response.

'I can't,' she said softly. 'With everything that's gone on lately, Sos and Fanchon worry. I need to be home.'

'Then stay awhile,' he said, tilting her chin up. 'I want you, 'Toinette,' he murmured, lowering his head. 'I want you in my bed.'

'I wish it were that simple.'

'No, you don't. Because then it would be only sex, and you'd feel cheap and cheated and used. That's not what you want.'

'What is it, then, if it's not just sex?' Annie asked, surprised at his allusion to something more. He struck her as the kind of man who would want uncomplicated affairs, straightforward sex, no gray areas, no untidy emotions.

He stroked her cheekbone with his thumb, his expression pensive. 'It is what it is,' he whispered, touching his mouth to hers. If the answer was there, he didn't want to see it or wasn't ready to see it any more than she was ready to put a label on it.

'Stay and we can explore the possibilities,' he said against her lips.

He opened her mouth with his, touched his tongue to hers. A shiver ran through her like quicksilver.

'I want you,' he murmured, moving his hands down her back. 'You want me, yes?'

'Yes,' she admitted.

His gaze held hers. 'Don't be afraid of it, 'Toinette. Come deeper with me, *chère*.'

Deeper. Into the black water, the unknown. Sink or swim.

She thought of A.J.'s accusation that she was pushing him away because he knew her too well, and Nick's assertion that she was afraid to know herself, afraid of what might lie beneath the surface. She thought of the sense of expectation she'd been feeling for weeks, the sense that she was treading water, waiting for something.

Fourcade was reaching out to her. The unknown was whether she would buoy him or he would pull her down into his darkness so deep she would drown.

He waited. Silent. Still and as taut as a clenched fist.

'I'll stay awhile,' she said.

He swept her off her feet and carried her to the bed. They stood beside it and undressed each other, fingers hurrying, fumbling at buttons. The heat of the room pressed in on them. Skin went slick with the heat of desire. Their bodies kissed, hot and wet, flesh to flesh, man to woman. His hands explored her: the soft fullness of a breast, the pearled tip of a nipple, the moist lips of femininity. She touched everything male about him: the hard-ridged muscles of his belly, the crisp dark hair that matted his chest, the shaft of his erection, as smooth and hard as a column of marble.

They fell across the crisp sheets, a tangle of limbs, her dark hair spilling across the pillow. She arched her body into the touch of his mouth as he kissed the beads of sweat from between her breasts and followed the trail down her belly to the point of her hip, the crease of her thigh, the back of her knee. She opened herself to the touch of his hand. He took her to the brink of fulfilment and left her hanging there, aching with the need to join her body with his.

He pulled a foil packet from the drawer of the nightstand. Annie took it from his fingers. Nick sat back against the headboard and held himself still against the exquisite torture of her small hands fitting the condom over his shaft. She looked up at him, her eyes wide, her mouth swollen and cherry red from his kisses. She looked both wanton and hesitant. He had never wanted a woman more

– this woman who held sway over the fate of his career. This woman – sweet, normal Annie, who had never seen the dark side and probably never wanted to. He should have left her to her nice life, but she had wandered into his realm, and his need to touch her, to hold her to him, far outweighed his capacity for nobility.

He held his hand out to her. '*Viens ici, chérie*,' he murmured, pulling her toward him. 'Come take what you want.'

Hands at her waist, he guided her astride him. She eased herself down, taking him deep, her fingertips biting into his shoulders. They moved together. He held her tight. Their kisses tasted dark and salty-sweet.

Annie felt suspended in the rhythm of it, consumed by the intensity of it. She fell back in the support of his arms and floated while he sucked at her breast. She banded her arms around his shoulders and held tight as the urgency built.

'Open your eyes, *chère*,' he commanded. 'Open your eyes and look at me.'

Her gaze locked on his as the end came for both of them. One and then the other. Powerful. Intimate. More than sex.

In a week she would testify against him.

The thought trailed through her mind like a slug as she lay beside him. She wanted to know if his lawyer would try to cut a deal, but she didn't ask. She tried to imagine visiting him in prison. The image turned her stomach.

She supposed no jury in South Louisiana would convict him, given the false testimony any number of other officers were willing to give about the bogus 10–70 call that night, and the fact that almost everyone in Partout Parish believed Renard should have gotten worse than a beating. And so she was hoping that the justice system she had sworn to serve would corrupt itself to suit her wishes, and somehow that would be okay when Fourcade going after Renard in the first place was not.

Shades of gray, Noblier had told her. Like layers of soot and dirt. She felt it rubbing off on her.

'I have to go,' she said, a mix of reluctance and urgency struggling within her. She swung her legs over the side of the bed and sat up, reaching for her T-shirt.

Nick said nothing. He didn't expect her to stay – tonight or for the long haul. Why would she? A relationship between them would be difficult, and she had a nice tame lawyer waiting in the wings to give her a simple, normal life. Why would she not take that? He told himself it didn't matter. He was the kind of man meant to be alone. He was used to it. Solitude allowed him concentration for the job.

The job that would be taken from him forever if he was convicted of beating Marcus Renard. The hearing was a week away. The key witness stood with her back to him, scraping her dark hair into a messy ponytail. His accuser, his partner, his lover. He'd have been a hell of a lot better off hating her. But he didn't.

He climbed out of bed and picked up his jeans. 'I'll follow you home. In case Cadillac Man comes back for an encore.'

He stayed well back on the drive to the Corners. There were times when Annie thought he must have left off with the tail, and then she would catch a glimpse of his lights. He wasn't following her to prevent Cadillac Man from making another run at her, he was letting her run ahead, a rabbit to lure their predator. If her assailant took the bait, Fourcade would be there to bust the jerk.

Not exactly the way most lovers topped off a romantic interlude. But then, Fourcade was by no means typical. And they weren't exactly most lovers. Most lovers never had to face each other across a courtroom.

She turned in at the Corners and parked in front of the store. Moments later, Fourcade drove past, flashing his headlights once. He didn't stop.

She sat in the Jeep for a time, half listening to the radio –

415

an argument about whether or not women should carry handguns in these dangerous times.

'You think a rapist is just gonna stand back when y'all say, 'Oh, wait, let me get my gun out my pocketbook so I can shoot you'?' the male caller said in a high falsetto. 'Marital arts – that's what women need.'

'You mean *martial* arts?'

'That's what I said.'

Annie shook her head and pulled her keys. She climbed to the passenger seat and gathered her stuff, slinging the strap of her duffel over one shoulder and scooping the files Fourcade had sent with her into her other arm. She added the detritus of her dinner and a sandal that had worked its way out from under the seat.

Overburdened, the duffel strap slipping on her shoulder, she climbed out of the Jeep and bumped the door shut with her hip. The load in her arm shifted precariously. As she came around the back of the Jeep, the shoe slipped off the pile and took the dinner garbage with it. The duffel strap fell, the weight of the bag jerking her right arm so that the files and other junk spilled to the ground.

'Shit,' she muttered, dropping to her knees.

The sound of the rifle shot registered in her mind a split second before the bullet hit.

36

The bullet ripped through the plastic back window of the Jeep, destroyed the windshield, and shattered the front window of the store. All in less time than it took to draw a breath – not that Annie was breathing.

She dropped flat on the ground, the crushed shell biting into her bare arms as she scooted under the Jeep, dragging her duffel bag with her. She couldn't hear a damn thing for the pounding of her pulse in her ears. The heat from the Jeep pressed down on her. Hands fumbling, she dug her Sig Sauer out of the bag, twitched the safety off and waited.

She couldn't see anything but the ground. If she crawled out from under the Jeep at the front, she could make it up onto the gallery. Using the Jeep for cover, she could climb through the broken front window, get to the phone, and call 911.

A screen door slapped in the distance.

'Who's there?' Sos called, racking the shotgun. 'Me, I shoot trespassers! And survivors – I shoot them twice!'

'Uncle Sos!' Annie yelled. 'Go back inside! Call 911!'

'I'd rather unload this buckshot in some rascal's ass! Where y'at, *chère*?'

'Go back in the house! Call 911!'

'The hell I will! Your *tante*, she already called! Cops are on the way!'

And if they were lucky, Annie thought, a deputy might arrive in half an hour – unless there already was a deputy right across the road with a rifle in his hands. She thought of Mullen. She thought of Stokes. Donnie Bichon came to mind. She considered the possibility of Renard. She had accused him of shooting into his own home. Maybe this was retribution.

She adjusted her grip on the Sig and scuttled toward the

417

front end of the Jeep. The shot had to have come from the road or the woods beyond. She hadn't heard or seen a car. A shooter in the woods at night would lose himself in a hurry. It would take a dog to track him, and by the time a K-9 unit arrived, he would be long gone.

In the distance she could hear the radio car coming, siren wailing, giving all criminals in the vicinity ample warning of its imminent arrival.

Pitre was the deputy. To Sos and Fanchon, he showed a modicum of respect. To Annie he remarked that he hadn't realized there were so many poor shots in the parish. He made a laconic call back to dispatch to advise everyone of the situation, which was nothing – they had no suspect description, no vehicle description, nothing. At Annie's insistence he called for the K-9 unit and was told the officer was unavailable. A detective would be assigned the case in the morning – *if* she wanted to pursue the matter, Pitre said.

'Someone tried to kill me,' she snapped. 'Yeah, I think I don't wanna just drop that.'

Pitre shrugged, as if to say, 'suit yourself.'

The slug had passed through the front window of the store, shattered a display case of jewelry made from nutria teeth, and slammed into the old steel cash register that sat on the tour ticket counter. The cash register had sustained an impressive wound, but still worked. The slug had been mangled beyond recognition. Even if anyone ever went to the trouble of finding a suspect, they would have nothing to match for ballistics.

'Yeah, well, thanks for nothing, *again*,' Annie said, walking Pitre to his car.

He feigned innocence. 'Hey, I came with lights and siren!'

Annie scowled at him. 'Don't even get me started. Suffice it to say you're just about as big an asshole as Mullen.'

'Ooooh! You gonna go after me now?' he said. 'I heard you went after Stokes today. What is it with you, Broussard? You think the only way you'll get up the ladder is by knocking everybody else off? What ever happened to women who slept their way to the top?'

'I'd rather give bone marrow. Go piss up a rope, Pitre.' She flipped him off as he drove away.

After walking Fanchon back to the house, she used the phone in the store to call Fourcade. She chewed at a broken fingernail as she listened to the phone ring on the other end. On the sixth ring his machine picked up. He had asked her to stay the night, now the night was half gone and so was Fourcade. Where was he at one-thirty in the morning? Her mind worried at that question as she helped Sos board up the window to keep out looting raccoons.

It bothered her that she wanted Nick here for emotional reasons and not just as another cop. If she was going to get through this mess with Renard and the department and Fourcade's hearing, she had to be tougher. She needed to learn to separate the issues. She could almost hear him in her mind: *You're not dead. Suck it up and focus on your job, 'Toinette.*

And then he would put his arms around her and hold her safe against him.

As they worked on the window, she answered Sos's questions as best she could without revealing too much about the situation she had become embroiled in. But he knew she was holding things back from him, and she knew he knew.

He gave her a hard look as they walked out, his temper still up and bubbling. 'Look what you got yourself in now, *'tite fille*. Why you can't do things no way but the hard way? Why you don't just marry Andre and settle? Give your *tante* and me some grandbabies? *Mais non*, you gotta run off and do a man's job! You all the time beatin' on a hornet's nest with a stick! And now you gonna get stung. *Sa c'est de la couyonade!*'

'It'll work out, Uncle Sos,' Annie promised, feeling like a worm for lying to him. She could have been dead.

He made a strangled sound in his throat, but cupped her

face in his callused hands. 'We worry 'bout you, *chérie*, your *tante* and me. You're like our own, you know dat! Why you gotta make life so hard?'

'I don't mean to look for trouble.'

Sos heaved a sigh and patted her cheek. 'But when trouble comes lookin' for you, you ain't hard to find, *c'est vrai*.'

Annie watched him walk away. She hated that this mess had touched him and Fanchon. If her life was going to stay this complicated, maybe she would have to think about moving away from the Corners.

'If my life is going to stay this complicated, maybe I'll have to think about moving into an asylum,' she muttered as she stepped down off the gallery and turned the corner to her stairs.

A small box wrapped in flowered paper with a white bow sat on the third step from the bottom. Renard. Annie recognized the paper. It was the same as what had been wrapped around the box with the scarf in it. A too-familiar sense of unease rippled through her at the idea of him coming here as if he felt entitled to touch her private life.

She stuffed the box into her duffel bag and went up to the apartment.

The sense of violation struck her immediately. The feeling that someone had invaded her home. From her vantage point in the front entry she could see across the living room, could see that the French doors were shut, the bolt turned. The air in the apartment was stifling and stale from an unexpectedly hot day with closed windows. A faint undertone of something earthy and rotten lingered. The swamp, Annie thought. Or maybe she needed to take the garbage out. She set her duffel bag on the bench and pulled out the Sig. With the gun raised and ready, she moved into the living room and hit the message button on the answering machine. If there was someone here, and he thought she was occupied listening to the machine, he might think to take advantage and attack her from behind.

420

Images of Lindsay Faulkner flashed through her mind – lying on the floor like a broken doll; head swathed in bandages like a mummy.

The messages rolled out of the machine. A Mary Kay lady who had seen her on the news and wanted to compliment her on her complexion. A distant Doucet 'cousin' who had seen her on the news and wondered if she could help him get a job as a deputy.

She moved out of the living room and around the perimeter of the kitchen. Nothing seemed out of order. The old refrigerator hummed and groaned. The alligator on the door grinned at her. The table was clean. She had swept her notes and files together before leaving this morning and stashed them in an old steamer trunk that sat in her living room – just in case.

The answering machine continued chattering. A.J.'s psychologist sister-in-law, Serena, wanted to offer a friendly ear if Annie needed to talk. Two hang-ups.

Back in the living room, Annie made the same slow, quiet circuit, looking for anything out of place, pausing at the French doors to double-check the lock. The gator coffee table seemed to watch her as she skirted past it.

'What's the deal, Alphonse?' Annie murmured.

Silence. Then Marcus Renard's voice spoke to her.

'Annie? This is Marcus. I wish you were home. I wanted to thank you again for coming over last night.' The voice was too sincere, too familiar. 'It means so much to know you care.' More silence, and then he said, 'Goodnight, Annie. I hope you're having a pleasant evening.'

The skin crawled on the back of her neck. She crossed the room and started down the hall as the machine reported two more hang-up calls.

The bathroom was clear. Her workout room appeared undisturbed. The tension ebbed a bit. Maybe she was still just reacting to the shooting. Maybe she was just projecting her feelings of violation at Renard having left another gift

421

for her. He should never have been able to get into her home. The doors had been locked.

Then she turned the corner and opened the door to her bedroom.

The stench of decay hit her full in the face and turned her stomach inside out.

Nailed to the wall above her bed in a position of crucifixion, its legs broken and bent, hung a dead black cat. Its skull had been crushed, its entrails spilled out of the body cavity onto the pillows below. And above it one word was painted in blood – CUNT.

'People should get what they deserve, don't you think? Good or bad.

She deserves to be confronted with the consequences of her sins. She deserves to be punished. Like the others.

Betrayal is the least of her crimes.

Terror is the least of mine.'

37

He lay in wait like a panther in the night, anger and anticipation contained by forced patience. The glowing blue numbers on the VCR clicked the minutes. 1:43.1:44. The low purr of an engine approached, passed one end of the house, and slipped into the garage.

The rattle of keys. The kitchen door swung open. He waited.

Footfalls on tile. Footfalls muffled by carpet. He waited. The footsteps passed by his hiding place.

'Quite the night owl, aren't you, Tulane?'

Donnie bolted at the sound of the voice, but in a heartbeat, Fourcade materialized from the gloom of the living room and slammed him into the wall.

'You lied to me, Donnie,' he growled. 'That's not a wise thing to do.'

'I don't know what you're talking about!' Donnie blubbered, spittle collecting at the corners of his mouth. His breath reeked of scotch. The smell of sweat and fear penetrated his clothing.

Nick gave him a shake, banging his head back against the wall. 'In case you haven't noticed, Donnie, me, I'm not a patient man. And you, you're not too bright. This is bad combination, no?'

Donnie shivered. His voice took on a whine. 'What do you want from me, Fourcade?'

'Truth. You tell me you don't know Duval Marcotte. But Marcotte, he called you on the telephone tonight, didn't he?'

'I don't know him. I know *of* him,' he stressed. 'What if he called me? I can't control what other people do! Jesus, this is the perfect example – I did you a good turn and look how you treat me!'

'You don't like the way I treat you, Tulane?' Nick said, easing his weight back. 'The way you lie to me, I was tempted to beat the shit out of you a long time ago. Put in the proper perspective, my restraint has been commendable. Perspective is the key to balance in life, *c'est vrai?*'

Donnie edged away from the wall. Fourcade blocked the route to the kitchen and garage. He glanced across the living room. The furniture was an obstacle course of black shadows against a dark background; the only illumination, silver streetlight leaching in through the sheer front curtains.

Nick smiled. 'Don't you run away from me, Donnie. You'll only piss me off.'

'I've already managed to do that.'

'Yeah, but you ain't never seen me *mad, mon ami*. You don't wanna open that door, let the tiger out.'

'You know, this is it, Fourcade,' Donnie said. 'I'm calling the cops this time. You can't just break into people's homes and harass them.'

Nick leaned into the back of a tall recliner and turned the lamp beside it on low. Donnie had traded the Young Businessman look for Uptown Casual: jeans and a polo shirt with a small red crawfish embroidered on the left chest.

'Why are you wearing sunglasses?' Donnie asked. 'It's the middle of the damn night.'

Nick just smiled slowly.

'You sure you wanna do that, Donnie?' he said. 'You wanna call the SO? Because, you know, you do that, then we're all gonna have to have this conversation downtown – about how you lied to me and what all about Marcotte sniffing around the realty, wanting that land what's tied up there.

'Me,' – he shrugged – 'I'm just a friend who dropped by to chat. But you …' He shook his head sadly. 'Tulane, you just got more and more explaining to do. You see how this looks – you dealing with Marcotte? I'll tell you: It looks like you had one hell of a motive to kill your wife.'

'I never talked to Marcotte –'

'And now your wife's partner is attacked, left for dead –'

'I never laid a hand on Lindsay! I told Stokes, that son of a bitch –'

'It's just not looking good for you, Donnie.' Nick moved away from the chair, hands resting at the waist of his jeans. 'So, you gonna do something about that or what?'

'Do *what*?' Donnie said in exasperation.

'Did Marcotte contact you or the other way around?'

Donnie's Adam's apple bobbed in his throat. 'He called me.'

'When?'

'Yesterday.'

Nick silently cursed his own stupidity. 'That's the truth?' he demanded.

Donnie raised his right hand like a Boy Scout and closed his eyes, flinching. 'My hand to God.'

Nick grabbed his face with one big hand and squeezed as he backed him into another wall. 'Look at me,' he ordered. 'Look at me! You lie to God all you want, Tulane. God, He's not gonna kick your ass. You look at me and answer. Did you *ever* have contact with Duval Marcotte before Pam was killed?'

Donnie met his gaze. 'No. Never.'

And if that was the truth, then Nick had drawn Marcotte onto the scene himself. The obsession had blinded him to the possibilities. The possibility that Marcotte's interest would be piqued by Nick's ill-fated visit, and that Marcotte would be drawn to the scene like a lion to the smell of blood.

'He's the devil,' he whispered, letting Donnie go. Marcotte was the devil, and he had all but invited the devil to play in his own backyard. 'Don'tcha do business with the devil, Donnie,' he murmured. 'You'll end up in hell. One way or another.'

He dropped his gaze to the floor, reflecting on his own stupidity. There was no changing what he'd done, nothing to do but deal with it. Slowly Donnie's muddy work boots came into focus.

'Where you been tonight, Tulane?'

'Around,' Donnie said, straightening his shirt with one hand and rubbing his cheek with the other. 'I went to the cemetery for a while. I go there sometimes to talk to God, you know. And to see Pam. Then I went and checked a site.'

'In the dead of night?'

He shrugged. 'Hey, you like to go around in sunglasses. I like to get drunk and wander around half-finished construction sites. There's always the chance I'll fall in a hole and kill myself. It's kind of like Russian roulette. I don't have much of a social life since Pam was killed.'

'I suppose an unsolved murder in your past puts the ladies off.'

'Some.'

'Well ... you watch your step, *cher*,' Nick said, backing toward the kitchen. 'We don't want you to meet an untimely end – unless you deserve it.'

He was gone as quickly and quietly as he had appeared. Donnie didn't even hear the door shut. But then, that may have been due to the pounding in his head. The shakes swept over him on a wave of weakness, and he stumbled into the bathroom with a hand pressed to his burning stomach. Bruising his knees on the tile, he dropped to the floor and puked into the toilet, then started to cry.

All he wanted was a simple, cushy life. Money. Success. No worries. The adoration of his daughter. He hadn't realized how close he had come to that ideal until he'd blown it all away. Now all he had was trouble, and every time he turned around he screwed himself deeper into the hole.

Hugging the toilet, he put his head down on his arms and sobbed.

'Pam ... Pam ... I'm so sorry!'

Annie dreamed she caught a bullet in her teeth. Tied to the bullet was a string. Pulling herself hand over hand along the string, she flew through the night, through the woods, and came to a halt with a rifle barrel pressed into the center of her forehead. At the stock end of the gun stood a shimmering apparition with an elaborate feather mask covering its face. With one hand the apparition removed the mask to reveal the face of Donnie Bichon. Another hand peeled away the face of Donnie Bichon to reveal Marcus Renard. Then Renard's face was peeled away to reveal Pam Bichon's death mask – the eyes partially gone, skin discolored and decomposing, tongue swollen and purple. Nailed to her chest was the dead black cat, its intestines hanging down like a bloody necklace.

'You are me,' Pam said, and fired the rifle. *Bang! Bang! Bang!*

Annie hurled herself upright on the sofa, gasping for breath, feeling as if her heart had leapt out of her chest.

The banging came again. A fist on wood. Bleary-eyed, she grabbed for the Sig on the coffee table.

"Toinette! It's me!' Fourcade called.

He stood at the French doors, scowling in at her.

Annie went to the doors and let him in. She didn't bother to ask the obvious question. Of course Fourcade wouldn't come to the front door. Her tormentor might have been watching from the woods, returning to the scene of his crimes. She asked the second-most obvious question instead.

'Where the hell were you?'

After slamming the door shut on the atrocity in her bedroom, she had gone back to the living room and sat down, trying to think what she should do. Call the SO? Bring Pitre back here and let him soak up the gory details to spread around the department at the shift change? What good would he do? None. She had called Fourcade instead, cursing him silently as his machine picked up again.

'Taking care of some business,' he said.

428

He stared at her as she paced back and forth along the coffee table with her arms banded around her. He took in everything about her – the disheveled hair, the dirty jeans and T-shirt. Reaching out as she came toward him, he plucked the Sig from her fingers and set it aside.

'Are you all right?'

'No!' she snapped. 'Someone tried to kill me. I think we've already established that I don't take that well. Then I find out someone came into my house, wrote on my wall in blood, and nailed a dead cat above my bed. I'm not okay with that either!'

From the corner of her eye she could see Fourcade watching her. He didn't seem to know what to do except fall back on the job, the routine. She was a victim – God, but she hated that label – and he was a detective.

'Tell me what happened from the time you parked the Jeep.'

She went through the story point by point, fact by fact, the way she had been trained to testify. The process calmed her somewhat, distanced her from the violation. In her mind, she tried to separate the victim in her from the cop. For the first time she told him about the skinned muskrat that had been left in her locker room, though she didn't put the two incidents on the same plane. It was one thing to play a nasty joke at work; breaking and entering was another matter. And what had been done in her bedroom seemed more threatening, more vile, more personal. Then again, if a deputy had been behind that rifle tonight, why not this too?

Nick listened, then headed toward the bedroom. Annie followed, reluctant to face it again.

'Did you touch anything?' he asked out of habit.

'No. God, I couldn't even bring myself to go in.'

He pushed the door open and stood there with his hands on his hips, a grimace twisting his lips. *'Mon Dieu.'*

He left Annie at the door and went into the room, taking in the details with a clinical eye.

The blood had been brushed on the wall. No visible fingerprints. The word *cunt* had been chosen for what reason? As an opinion? To shock? Out of disrespect? Out of anger?

In his mind's eye he could see Keith Mullen, skinny and ugly, standing in his filthy kitchen just that morning. *'She don't know nothing about loyalty, turning on one of us. Cunt's got no business being in a uniform.'*

Was the animal symbolic? An alley cat – sexually indiscriminate. Its guts spilled down onto the bed where Annie had made love with him just the night before.

And the positioning of its body, the nails through its forepaws, the evisceration – an obvious allusion to Pam Bichon. Meant to frighten or as a warning?

He thought of how close she had come to being shot and he wanted to hit something – *someone* – hard and repeatedly.

He worked to contain the rage even as he remembered Donnie Bichon's muddy boots. He set the thought aside for the moment.

'This cat – was she yours, 'Toinette?'

'No.'

'You talked to your *tante* and uncle 'bout did they see anyone around today?'

'We had that conversation when we were talking about who might want to shoot me. They were busy today. Tourists coming in early for Mardi Gras. They had to call in extra tour guides. They didn't have time to notice anyone special.'

'How'd anyone get in here? Were your doors locked when you came up?'

'Everything was locked up tight. You might be able to pick a lock to break in, but there's no locking these doors from the outside without a key.'

'So how did this creep get in?'

'There's only one other way.' She led him into the

430

bathroom, to the door behind the old claw-foot tub. 'The stairs go down into the stockroom of the store.'

'Was it locked?'

'I don't know. I thought so. I usually keep it locked, but I went down this way Sunday night when the prowler was here. Maybe I forgot to lock it after.'

Nick stood in the tub and examined the locking mechanism in the doorknob, frowning disapproval. 'Ain't nothing but a button. Anybody could slip it with a credit card. How would anyone but family or employees know about these stairs?'

Annie shook her head. 'By luck. By chance. The rest rooms are across the hall at the bottom of the stairs. Someone going to use them might look through the stockroom and notice.'

He flicked on the light switch and descended the steep stairs, looking for any sign another person had been there – a footprint, a thread, a stray hair. There was nothing. The stockroom door stood open. Across the hall, he could see part of the door to the men's room.

'I'd say someone went out of their way to notice,' he murmured.

He went back up the steps and followed Annie to the living room. She curled herself into one corner of the sofa and rubbed her bare foot slowly back and forth under the jaw of her gator table. She looked small and forlorn.

'What d' you think, 'Toinette? You think the shooter and the cat killer are the same person?'

'I don't know,' Annie said. 'And don't try to tell me I do. Are the shooter and the cat killer one and the same? Is Renard's shooter my shooter too, or is Renard the shooter? Who hates me more: half the people I work *with* or half the people I work *for*? And what do they hate me for more: trying to solve this murder or preventing you from committing one?

'I'm so tired I can't see straight. I'm scared. I'm sick that someone would do that to that poor animal –'

Somehow, that was the last straw. Bad enough to have violence directed at her, but to have an innocent little animal, killed and mutilated for the sole purpose of frightening her was too much. She pressed her fingertips against her lips and tried to will the moment to pass. Then Fourcade was beside her and she was in his arms, her face against his chest. The tears she had fought so hard to choke back soaked into his shirt.

Nick held her close, whispering softly to her in French, brushing his lips against her forehead. For a few moments he allowed the feelings free inside him – the need to protect her, to comfort her, the blind rage against whoever had terrorized her. She had been so brave, such a fighter through all of this mess.

He pressed his cheek against the top of her head and held her tighter. It had been too long since he'd had anything of himself worth giving to another person. The idea that he wanted to was terrifying.

Annie held tight to him, knowing tenderness didn't come to him easily. This small gift from him meant more to her than she should have let it. As the tears passed, she wiped them from her cheeks with the back of her hand and studied his face as he met her stare, wondering ... and afraid to wonder.

Her gaze shifted to the gift box she had left on her coffee table. Inside the box lay a small, finely detailed antique cameo brooch. The note enclosed read: 'To my guardian angel. Love, Marcus.'

Revulsion shuddered down her back.

Fourcade picked up the box and card and studied the brooch.

'He gave Pam gifts,' he said soberly. 'And he slashed her tires and left a dead snake in her pencil drawer at work.'

'Jekyll and Hyde,' Annie murmured.

If Renard had indeed been Pam's stalker, as Pam had insisted, then he had alternated between secretly terrifying her and giving her presents; showing his concern for her,

432

claiming to be her friend. The contrast in those actions had kept the cops from taking seriously Pam's charge that Renard was the one stalking her.

Across the room the phone rang. Automatically, Annie looked at the clock. Half past three in the morning. Fourcade said nothing as she let the machine pick up.

'Annie? It's Marcus. I wish you were there. Please call me when you can. Someone just threw a rock through one of our windows. Mother is beside herself. And Victor – and I – I wish you could come over, Annie. You're the only one who cares. I need you.'

38

The flower woman was setting up at her station in the shade across the street from Our Lady, her pipe clenched between her teeth. The groundskeeper prowled the boulevard, a growling Weed Eater clutched in his hands.

'Here's the police gonna come arrest you, old witchy woman!' he screamed as Annie turned in the drive. He charged at the Jeep. 'Police girl! You gonna get her dis time or what?'

'Not me!' Annie called, driving past.

She parked the Jeep and, with the scarf and brooch in her pocketbook, headed for the building. If Pam had shown Renard's gifts to anyone, it would have been Lindsay. Annie hoped she was improved enough to tell her whether or not the things Renard had given her were the same tokens of affection being recycled to a new object of fixation.

The hospital was bustling with morning rounds for meals and medications. The strange plastic smell of antiseptics commingled with toast and oatmeal. The clang of meal trays and bedpans accented the hushed conversations and occasional moans as Annie walked down the halls.

The long, sleepless night hung heavy on her shoulders. The day stretched out in front of her like eighty miles of bad road. She would have to face an interview with the detective assigned to her shooting incident, and had already concocted a worst-case scenario in which Chaz Stokes caught the case and she would have to go to the sheriff and ask Stokes to be removed because she not only believed he was a suspect, but she also thought he could be a rapist and a murderer. She wouldn't have to worry about Stokes or anyone else killing her. She'd never make it out of Gus Noblier's office alive.

For a second or two she tried again to imagine Stokes

sneaking up to her apartment to nail a dead cat to her wall, but she couldn't see it. He might have had the temperament for it, but she couldn't believe he would take the risk. She couldn't imagine anyone in the SO would.

Who then? Who could have slipped into the store, found those stairs, made it up to her apartment and down again unnoticed?

Renard had been to the Corners to leave gifts for her twice. Fanchon hadn't noticed him either time. If he had stalked Pam, he'd done so without detection.

Annie turned the corner to the ICU, and stepped directly into the path of Stokes.

His scowl was ferocious. He descended on her like a hawk, clamping a hand on her forearm and driving her away from the traffic flow in the hall.

'What the fuck are you doing here, Broussard?'

'Who put you in charge of visitors? I came to see my real estate agent.'

'Oh, really?' he sneered. 'Is she showing you something in a nice little two-bed room on the second floor?'

'She's an acquaintance and she's in the hospital. Why shouldn't I see her?' Annie challenged.

'Because I say so!' he barked. 'Because I know you ain't nothing but trouble, Broussard. I told you to stay the hell away from my cases.' His grip tightening on her arm, he pushed her another step toward the corner. 'You think I just like to hear myself talk? You think I won't come down on you like a ton of bricks?'

'Don't threaten me, Stokes,' Annie returned as she tried to wrench her arm free. 'You're in no position to –'

Alarms sounded at the ICU desk.

'Oh, shit!' someone yelled. 'She's seizing! Call Unser!'

Two nurses dashed for a room. Lindsay Faulkner's room.

Jerking free of Stokes, Annie rushed to the room and stared in horror at the scene. Faulkner's arms and legs were flailing, jerking like a marionette on the strings of a mad puppet master. A horrible, unearthly wail tore from her,

435

accompanied by the shrieks of the monitors. Three nurses swarmed around her, trying to restrain her. One grabbed a padded tongue blade from the nurse server and worked to get it in Faulkner's mouth.

'Get an airway!'

'Got it!'

A doctor in blue scrubs burst past Annie into the room, calling, 'Diazepam: 10-milligram IV push!'

'Jesus H.,' Stokes breathed, pressing in close behind Annie. 'Jesus Fucking Christ.'

Annie glanced at him over her shoulder. His expression was likely no different from hers – shock, horror, anxious anticipation.

Another monitor began to bleat in warning and another round of expletives went up from the staff.

'She's in arrest!'

'Standard ACLS,' Unser snapped, thumping the woman on the chest. 'Phenytoin: 250 IV push. Phenobarbital: 55 IV push. I want a chem 7 and blood gases STAT! Tube and bag her!'

'She's in fine v-fib.'

'Shit!'

'Charge it up!'

One of the nurses spun around, a tube of blood in her hands. 'I'm sorry, we need you people out of here.' She herded Annie and Stokes from the door. 'Please go to the waiting area.'

Stokes's face was chalky. He rubbed his goatee. 'Jesus H.,' he said again, pulling his porkpie hat off and crumpling it with his fingers.

Annie hit him in the chest with both hands. 'What did you do to her?'

He looked as if she'd smacked him across the face with a dead carp. 'What? Nothing!'

'You come out of her room and two minutes later this happens!'

'Keep your voice down!' he ordered, reaching for her arm.

She jerked away from him. What if Stokes was the rapist? What if he was something worse?

'I went in to talk to her,' he said, as they entered the waiting area. 'She wasn't awake. Ask the nurse.'

'I will.'

'Christ, Broussard, what's the matter with you? You think I'm a killer?' he demanded, a flush creeping up his neck. 'Is that what you think? You think I'd walk into a hospital and kill a woman? You're out of your fucking mind!'

He sank down onto a chair and hung his long hands and the smashed hat between his knees.

'Maybe you oughta check yourself into this place,' he said. 'You need your damn head examined. First you go after Fourcade, now me. You're some kinda goddamn lunatic. You're like that crazy broad in *Fatal Attraction*. Obsessed – that's what you are.'

'She was better yesterday,' Annie insisted. 'I talked to her. Why would this happen?'

Stokes gave a helpless shrug. 'Do I look like George Fucking Clooney? I ain't no ER doc. It was some kind of seizure, that's all I know. Jesus, somebody bashed her head in with a telephone. What'd you expect?'

'If she dies, it's murder,' Annie declared.

Stokes pushed to his feet. 'I *told* you, Broussard –'

'It's murder,' she repeated. 'If she dies as a result of her injuries, the assault becomes a murder rap.'

'Well, yeah.' He dragged a jacket sleeve across his sweating forehead.

Annie stepped toward Faulkner's room again, trying to get a glimpse of her between the bodies of her rescue crew. The electric buzz and snap of the defibrillator was followed by another barrage of orders.

'Epinephrine and lidocaine! Dobutamine – run it wide open! Labs?'

'Not back.'

'Charging!'

'Clear!'

Buzz. Snap!

'Flat line!'

'We're losing her!'

They repeated the process so many times it seemed as if time, and hope, had become snagged in a continuous loop. Annie held herself rigid, directing her will at Lindsay Faulkner. *Live. Live. We need you.* But the loop broke. Motion in the room slowed to a stop.

'She's gone.'

'Damn.'

'Call it.'

Annie looked at the wall clock. Time of death: 7:49 A.M. Just like that, it was all over. Lindsay Faulkner was dead. A dynamic, capable, intelligent woman was gone. The suddenness of it stunned her. She had believed Faulkner would pull through, put her life back together, help solve the mysteries that had marred her life and taken her partner. But she was gone.

The staff trailed out of the room looking defeated, disgusted, blank. Annie wondered if any of them had known Lindsay Faulkner outside the walls of the hospital. She might have sold them a house or known them from the Junior League. It was a small-enough town.

The doctor came toward the waiting area, a frown digging deep into his long face. He looked fifty, his hair thick and the color of gunmetal. The name on his badge was FORBES UNSER. 'Are either of you family?'

'No,' Annie said. 'We're with the sheriff's office. I'm Deputy Broussard. I – ah – I knew her.'

'I'm sorry. She didn't make it,' he said succinctly.

'What happened? I thought she was doing better.'

'She was,' Unser said. 'The seizure was likely brought on by the trauma to her head. It led to cardiac arrest. These things happen. We did everything we could.'

Stokes stuck his hand out. 'Detective Stokes. I'm in charge of the Faulkner case.'

'Well, I hope you get the animal who attacked her,' Unser

438

said. 'I've got a wife and two teenage daughters. I barely let them out of my sight these days. Madeline wants me to keep a gun under my pillow at night.'

'We're doing everything we can,' Stokes said. 'We'll want her body transported to Lafayette for an autopsy. Standard procedure. The sheriff's office will be in touch with your morgue.'

Unser nodded, then excused himself and went back to his normal duties for the day, the death of a woman in his care just a glitch in the schedule. *These things happen.*

Annie ducked into the ladies' room as Stokes started down the hall. She washed her hands and splashed cold water on her face, trying to clear away the images of Lindsay Faulkner seizing. How could it be a coincidence that the woman had gone into arrest not ten minutes after Stokes had been in the room with her? But there would be an autopsy. Stokes knew it. He was the one who had brought it up.

Unser was just coming out of another patient's room with a chart in his hand as Annie stepped back into the hall.

'Are you all right, Deputy?' he asked. 'You look a little pale.'

'I'll be fine. It was just a shock, that's all. That didn't look like a very pleasant way to die.'

'She fought it, but it was over before we could really do anything for her.'

'Is that the way it usually happens?'

'It's always a possibility with a head trauma.'

'I guess what I'm asking is: was there anything *unusual* about her death? Any strange readings, abnormal levels of … whatever?'

Unser shook his head. 'Not that I'm aware of. The blood test never came back. You can check with the lab.' He stepped up to the counter and handed the chart to the monitor technician. 'If they haven't lost it entirely, they might be able to answer your questions.'

Annie made her way to the lab and left the number for records with a woman who seemed as if she had just dropped in and offered to mind the place while everyone else went for coffee. Did she know if the Faulkner test results were in? No. Did she know when they might be? No. Did she know the name of the President of the United States? Probably not.

'Never get sick here,' Annie muttered as she walked away.

Outside the heat was already edging toward oppressive, an unwelcome joke from Mother Nature. Summer was long enough without adding an early preview. Sweat beaded immediately between her breasts and shoulder blades. The sun burned into her scalp.

'You gonna arrest me now?'

Stokes stood beside his Camaro in the red zone, smoking a cigarette. He had shed his jacket, leaving his lime green shirt free to blind anyone looking directly at it.

'I'm sorry,' Annie said without sincerity. 'I overreacted.'

'You accused me of being a goddamn killer.' He flung the cigarette butt down on the asphalt beside a crumpled Snickers wrapper and crushed it out with the toe of his brown and white spectators. 'Personally, I take umbrage at that. You know what I'm saying?'

'I said I was sorry.'

'Yeah, well, that don't cut it by half. I've had it with you, Broussard.'

'And what are you gonna do about it?' she asked quietly. 'Shoot me?'

'I hear I'd have to get in line. I've got better things to do.'

'Like screw around with the evidence on those rape cases?'

'Don't fuck with me, Broussard. I'll have your badge. I mean it.'

He slid behind the wheel of the Camaro and started the engine with a roar. Annie stood on the sidewalk and watched him drive away. He had just lost a victim and his primary concern was getting her fired. A charming, caring individual, that Chaz.

The groundskeeper emerged from behind the statue of Mary and made a beeline for Annie with his hedge clippers. 'Police girl! Hey! I pays my taxes! I'm a vet'ran! You go, you arrest dat ol' witchy woman! Stealin' dem flowers out the Vet'rans Park!'

'I'm sorry, sir,' Annie said, her eyes on Stokes's car as it turned the corner onto Dumas. 'Has she murdered anyone?'

'What?!' he squealed. 'No, she ain't killed nobody, but –'

'Then I can't help you.'

She walked away from him toward the Jeep, her mind on Stokes, while Donnie Bichon's pearl white Lexus turned out of the parking lot behind her and drove away down the backstreet.

Donnie was shaking like a man with DTs, though it hadn't been all that long since his last drink. He'd been allowing himself a shot every hour since Fourcade had left him, in an attempt to steady his nerves. All it seemed to be doing was acting as an accelerant for the stress eating a hole in the lining of his stomach. The flecks of blood in his vomit had confirmed that suspicion.

After Fourcade's first visit, he had passed out in the bathroom and dreamed of Pam. Dark hair and shining eyes. A sunny smile. A tongue like a pit viper. Hands tipped with claws that dug into him, closed around his balls, and choked his masculinity. He loved her and he hated her. She had grown up and he never wanted to. Life had seemed best when he was twenty, when he had the world by the tail and no responsibilities. Now the world had *him* by the tail.

Then suddenly Fourcade had him by the scruff of the neck, and Donnie found himself going down face-first into a swirling pool of vomit. Startled, he tried to grab a breath half a second too late, filled his mouth, and came up choking and retching.

'Yeah, you choke on it,' Fourcade growled. He bent his body over Donnie's, all but riding him into the porcelain. 'That's what your lies taste like the second time around.'

Donnie spat into the toilet bowl. The smell of fresh urine was strong as his bladder let go. 'Jesus! God!' he gasped and spat again, trying to clear the cold chunks of vomit from his mouth.

'Where were you tonight?' Fourcade demanded.

'You're crazy!'

Nick shoved his head back in the bowl. 'Wrong answer, Tulane! Where were you tonight? Where'd you get that mud on your boots?'

'I told you!'

'Don't fuck with me, Donnie. I'm in no mood. Where were you?'

'I told you!' Donnie cried. Tears streamed down his face through the puke on his cheeks. 'I don't know what you want from me!'

'You're gonna give me the keys to your car, Tulane. And I'm gonna look through every inch of it. And if I find a rifle, I'm gonna bring it back in here, stick it up your ass, and blow your brains out. Are we clear on this?'

Donnie dug his keys out of his jeans pocket and tossed them on the floor. 'I didn't do anything!'

'You better pray to God that's the truth, Donnie,' Fourcade said as he bent to scrape up the keys. ''Cause I don't think you'd know the truth if it bit your dick off.'

Terrified and sick, disgusted with himself, Donnie forced himself to his feet and followed Fourcade out to the garage, grabbing a kitchen towel as an afterthought to wipe the mess from his face. He watched from the doorway as Fourcade popped the trunk on the Lexus and dug through the junk – a bag of golf clubs, a nail gun, a filthy Igloo cooler, gloves, crumpled receipts, a toolbox, half a dozen baseball caps with the Bichon Bayou Development logo.

'You know, you're just as rotten as everybody says, Fourcade,' he declared. 'You don't have a warrant. You got no call to treat me like this. You're not a cop; you're a goddamn jackbooted thug. I shoulda let you rot in jail.'

'You gonna wish you had, Tulane, if I find anything in this car to hook you up with taking a shot at Annie Broussard last night.'

'I don't know what you're talking about. And why should you care about Broussard?'

'I got my reasons.' He closed the trunk and moved to the passenger's side doors. 'You know, you're right for once, Donnie. I'm not a cop, I'm on suspension. That makes me a private citizen, which means I don't need a warrant to seize incriminating evidence. Ain't that a kick in the head?'

'You're trespassing,' Donnie declared as Fourcade pulled open a back door.

'Me? Trespassing in the home of my good friend who bailed me outta jail? Who would believe that?'

'Is there any law you *won't* break?'

He shut the door and strolled back toward Donnie, shining the light in Donnie's face. 'Well, I'll tell you, Tulane, me, I believe life is a journey of self-exploration, and lately I'm discovering that I have a greater concern for justice than I have for the law. Can you appreciate the difference?'

He climbed the two steps to the kitchen door and snatched hold of Donnie's shirtfront before he could backpedal. 'The law would dictate that I would have somebody else run you in tonight and interview you with regards to this shooting incident –'

'I didn't shoot anybody –'

'While justice would bypass the formalities and cut to the heart of the matter.'

'It's not for you to be judge and jury.'

'You left out executioner.' He arched a brow. 'Was that purposeful or Freudian? Not that it matters. I find it amusing that you bring the point up now, Donnie. You seemed to think it would have been just fine if I'd dispatched Renard to hell the other night. Now it's you standing on that line, and you'd just as soon I keep to the proper side of it. I'd call you a hypocrite, but I have my own problems with the black and white of it all.'

He uncurled his fist from Donnie's shirt and took half a step back. 'I'm gonna let you off with a warning, Tulane. I didn't find what I thought I might, but if I so much as hear a whisper or come across a hair that might connect you to this, I'll find you, Donnie, and I won't be in a philosophical mood.'

The crazy son of a bitch.

Donnie had gone straight back into the bathroom after Fourcade left and puked again, then sat on the edge of the tub and stared at the streaks of blood in the bowl. Scotch, nerves, and imminent financial disaster were not a good mix.

He decided what he needed was a little something of the pharmaceutical variety to settle him down so he could think his way out of this mess. Old Dr Hollier had obliged, sympathetic to the tragedy in his life. He didn't know the half of it, Donnie thought.

Lindsay Faulkner was dead and Fourcade knew about Marcotte.

With the bitch queen of Bayou Breaux gone, the way was clear to make a deal for the realty – except for one obstacle: Fourcade.

How could Fourcade have possibly known about that phone call? Paranoia had driven Donnie to an assortment of wild conclusions involving phone taps, all of which he had subsequently dismissed in a more sober moment. Fourcade knew only about a single call, last night's call, nothing else, and he was in no position to be in on any phone tap. He was suspended, awaiting trial. Assault charges. He'd nearly beaten Renard to death.

That particular reminder had Donnie reaching for the open bottle of Mylanta he'd wedged into his cup holder.

Never should have paid that bail. He had started hoping Fourcade would be bound over for trial next week, and would be thrown back in jail, but Donnie's lawyer had informed him the detective's bail would likely be continued and he would be a free man indefinitely, trial pending or no.

Pam had always told him he acted first and considered consequences too late. He wondered if she had ever realized just how right she'd been.

39

'You are late *again*.'

Myron stood at rigid attention in the middle of the room, his hands knotted together at the buckle of his skinny black belt, his expression sour with disapproval.

'I'm sorry, Myron,' Annie said, barely sparing him a glance as she entered his domain and went to the card drawer.

'*Mr* Myron,' he intoned. 'I'll have you know, I've spoken with the sheriff about your poor performance since you were assigned to me as *my* assistant. You are chronically tardy and run off at your own whim. This is a records department. Records are synonymous with stability. I cannot allow chaos in my records department.'

'I'm sorry,' she mumbled as she flicked through the evidence cards.

Myron's face pinched tight as he leaned over her shoulder. 'What are you doing, Deputy Broussard? Are you listening to me?'

Annie kept her eyes on her task. 'I'm a goof-off. You're pissed off. You want Gus to take me off this job, but I'll try to do better. Honest.'

She pulled the evidence card from the Nolan rape and ran a fingertip down the inventory. There, listed on the third line: HAIRS. The pubic hair Stokes had fished out of Jennifer Nolan's bathtub drain.

She tapped one foot impatiently. Myron moved into her field of vision again, looking a little uncertain at her lack of response to his tirade.

'What you looking at?' he asked. 'What you think you're doing?'

'My job,' she said simply, sliding the evidence card back in place.

Hairs had been logged in and checked back out to the lab. That didn't mean the hairs belonged to the rapist. Jennifer Nolan was a redhead. Her pubic hair would have stood out from any darker hair in the drain. Stokes could have picked out what he wanted and left the rest – left his own – to wash away.

Annie's stomach churned. She was on the verge of accusing a detective of being a serial rapist. If she was right, Chaz Stokes was not only a rapist but a murderer – either indirectly or directly. If she was wrong, he'd have her badge. She needed evidence, and he was in charge of every piece of it.

'Whatsa matter with you, Broussard?' Myron squawked. 'You sick or something? You been drinking?'

'Yeah, you know, I'm not feeling very well,' Annie mumbled, pushing the drawer shut. 'I might be sick. Excuse me.'

'I don't truck with drinkers,' Myron warned as she walked away. 'There ain't no place for that kind of thing in records. Alcohol is a tool of the devil.'

Annie wound her way through the halls to her locker room, went in, and sat down on her folding chair beneath the dull glow of the bare lightbulb. Someone had drilled a new hole in the wall – breast height. She would need to break out the spackling compound, but what she needed now was a few moments to untangle the threads in her mind.

'*Keep the threads separate or you end up with a knot, 'Toinette.*'

She had a knot all right, and she was trapped in the middle of it. Renard was sending her gifts. Donnie Bichon was in cahoots with Marcotte, who was in cahoots with the mob. Stokes was a bad cop at best and a killer at worst.

'You asked for it,' she muttered. 'You wanted to be a detective. You had to solve the mystery.'

One mystery at a time. Stokes seemed the most pressing

problem. If her suspicions about him were right, then other women would be in danger.

'*I'll* be in danger,' she said, a flashback of last night coming to her in jarring black and white: the ink black of the night, the pale crushed shell of the parking lot, the white papers scattering at her feet as she dropped the files. The sharp crack of the rifle, the shattering of glass.

The memory bled back into another and another. The anger in Stokes's eyes as they had argued about the missing evidence. The fury on his face that night months ago when he had fought with her in the parking lot of the Voodoo Lounge because she wasn't interested in going out with him. The aggressive way he had moved toward her, as if he meant to strike her or grab her.

He was a man capable of instant, intense rage, which he covered with loose, easy charm. He was by turns irrational and coldly logical, depending on the subject. Unpredictable. A chameleon. These were traits that had formed over the course of his life, traits he had brought with him when he had come here from Mississippi four years ago. Coincidentally, not long before the Bayou Strangler had begun his reign of terror. He may have even worked one or both of the Partout Parish murders connected to the Strangler: Annie Delahoussaye and Savannah Chandler.

That could be easily checked out, though Annie didn't see the need. Despite the gossip that had run wild since Pam's death, she didn't believe the allegations that the cops had tampered with the evidence in the Strangler case. No, that evil had been burned out of Partout Parish ... and a new one was taking root in the ashes.

What had brought Stokes here in the first place? she wondered. More important, what had he left behind? A good service record? Had his last supervisor been sad to lose him or glad to see the last of him? Had the city or county he worked in experienced a sudden drop in sex crimes after Stokes had gone? Had he left any victims in his wake?

It was rare for a man to become a sexual predator in his

thirties. That kind of behavior generally started earlier – late teens or early twenties – and continued on throughout his life. Despite the claims of various tax-sponsored programs, true sexual predators were seldom if ever rehabilitated. Their heads were wired wrong, their malevolent attitudes toward women carved forever in stone hearts.

She needed to get into Stokes's personnel file, get the name of the last force he had served on in Mississippi. Personnel files were kept in the sheriff's offices under the ever-vitriolic, blue-shadowed glare of Valerie Comb.

A fist struck the door to the locker room with the force of a hurled rock, making Annie jump.

'Broussard? You in there?'

'Who wants to know?'

'Perez.' He pulled the door open and stuck his head in. 'Shit, I figured the least I could get out of this was to see you naked.'

'Get out of what?' she said peevishly.

'The case. Your shooter. I'm your detective. Lucky fucking me. Come on. I need your statement and I ain't got all day.'

Perez was as interested in her case as he was in the politics of Uruguay. He doodled on a yellow legal pad as Annie related not only the shooting incident but her run-in with the Cadillac Man the night before, since there was the possibility the two incidents were related.

'Did you get a tag number?'

'No.'

'Did you see the driver?'

'He was wearing a ski mask.'

'Know anybody with a big car like that?'

'No.'

'Why didn't you call it in that night?'

'Would you have done anything?'

He gave her a flat look.

'I wrote it up the next day,' she said. 'Called around to

the body shops looking for the car. Nothing. Checked the log sheets for reports of a stolen Caddy, or something like a Caddy. Nothing.'

'And you didn't see the shooter last night?'

'No.'

'Didn't see his vehicle?'

'No.'

'Any ideas who it might have been?'

Annie looked at him for a long moment, knowing she couldn't name any of her prime suspects without revealing the mess she'd embroiled herself in, and certainly not without pissing Perez off by casting aspersions on two cops.

'I'm not very popular at the moment.'

'What a news flash.' He narrowed his eyes and stroked a finger across one side of his bushy mustache. 'I figured you'd point the finger at Fourcade. He's gotta hate you more than anyone else. We all know how you feel about him.'

'You don't know shit about me. It wasn't Fourcade.'

'How do you know?'

'Because Fourcade would be man enough to show his face, and if he wanted me dead, we wouldn't be having this conversation,' she said, rising from her chair. 'Are we finished, Detective? We both know this is pointless and I've got work to do.'

Perez shrugged. 'Yeah. I know where to find you ... 'til somebody wises up and boots your tight little ass outta here.'

Annie left the interview room, glad she hadn't bothered to tell him about the crucified cat. Back in records, Myron seemed in danger of spontaneous combustion.

'Look at the time!' he ranted, scurrying around the office like a windup toy gone mad. 'Look at the time! You been gone half the day!'

Annie rolled her eyes. 'Well, excuse me for being the victim of a crime. You know, Myron, you are an extremely unsympathetic individual. I practically witnessed someone dying this morning. Someone took a shot at me last night. My life is basically in the toilet here, and all you do is rag on me.'

'Sympathy? Sympathy?' He chirped the word as if it were a questionable noun from another language. 'Why should I show you sympathy? You are *my* assistant. I'm the one needs sympathy.'

'Your wife has all my sympathy,' Annie said, pulling her chair back from her desk. 'You must have about ruined all the upholstery on her furniture by now with that stick up your ass.'

Myron gave an indignant sniff. Annie ignored him. She was past currying his favor. With everything that was happening or about to happen, she figured she would be either dead or fired inside a week. Where she wouldn't be was working in this clerical hell for the rest of her life.

Two minutes later she received the summons to Noblier's office.

Valerie Comb was not at her post when Annie arrived at the sheriff's office. The room was empty, the file cabinets with the personnel records unguarded. The door to Gus's inner office was closed. Annie went to it and pressed her ear against the blond wood. No conversation sounds. No chair creaks. Nothing.

She glanced longingly at the file cabinets again. It wouldn't take more than a minute – open the S drawer, find Stokes, one glance and she'd be done. There might not be another chance.

Swallowing at the hard lump of fear wedged in her throat like a chicken bone, she crossed the room to the cabinets, reached for the handle on the S drawer.

'May I help you?'

Annie swung around at the sound of the sharp voice, hastily crossing her arms over her chest. Valerie Comb stood with one hand on the doorknob, the other holding a

451

steaming cup of coffee. Her overdone eyes were narrowed in suspicion, her mouth pressed into a thin painted line.

'I'm here to see the sheriff,' Annie said, beaming innocence.

Without comment, Valerie went to her desk, set the coffee down, and settled her fanny in her chair. Eyes on Annie, she pulled a pencil from her rat's nest of bleached hair and punched the intercom button with the eraser end of the pencil so as not to chip her slut red nails. Rumor had it she'd done half the guys in the department. She'd probably done Stokes.

'Sheriff, Deputy Broussard is here to see you.'

'Send her in!' Gus bellowed, his voice too big for the plastic box to contain.

Heart beating three steps too fast, Annie let herself into Noblier's inner sanctum. The shades were drawn. He sat back in his chair rubbing his eyes as if he might just have awakened from an afternoon nap.

'You must be out for some kind of record, Deputy,' he said, shaking his head.

'Sir?'

He waved at the chair across the desk from him. 'Sit down, Annie. Myron's been bending my ear. He says you're unreliable and you might be drinking on the job.'

'That's not true, sir.'

'That's the second time in a week I've heard your name and alcohol mentioned in the same breath.'

'I haven't been drinking, sir. I'll gladly take any test you want me to.'

'What I want is to know why two weeks ago I barely knew more than your name, now suddenly you're the burr up everybody's ass.' He leaned against his forearms on the desktop. To his right, paperwork was stacked like the Leaning Tower of Pisa. To his left lay a giant ceremonial ribbon-cutting scissors like something out of *Gulliver's Travels*.

'An unfortunate coincidence?' Annie suggested.

'Deputy, there are three things I do not believe in: UFOs, moderate Republicans, and coincidence. What the hell is going on with you? Every time I turn around you're in the middle of something you shouldn't be. You're working in records, for Christ's sake. How the hell can you get in trouble working in records?'

'Bad luck.'

'You're tripping over bodies, fighting with other deputies. Stokes was in here this morning telling me you were at the hospital when that Faulkner woman died. Why is that?'

Annie explained her absences from records as best she could, painting a picture of innocence that had been misinterpreted by Myron. She managed to depict herself as an unfortunate bystander regarding Lindsay Faulkner's attack and demise – in the wrong place at the wrong time. Noblier listened, his skepticism plain on his face.

'And this business about you getting shot at last night? What was that about?'

'I don't know, sir.'

'I sincerely doubt that,' Gus said, rising from his chair. He rubbed at a kink in his lower back as he walked away from the desk. 'Has Detective Fourcade made any effort to contact you since his release on bail?'

'Sir?'

'He's got a big ax to grind with you, Annie. As much as I respect Nick's abilities as a detective, you and I both know he's wrapped a little too tight.'

'With all due respect, sir, the harassment I've experienced since Detective Fourcade's arrest has come from other sources.'

'Yeah, you've managed to bring out the worst in a lot of people.'

Annie refrained from pointing out that blaming the victim was politically incorrect these days. The less she drew the sheriff into this mess at this time, the better. She had no proof of anything against anybody. He had already decided she was probably more trouble than she was worth.

If she started making accusations against Stokes, it might just push him beyond tolerance.

'Maybe you should take some personal time, Annie,' he suggested, coming back to the desk. He pulled a file from the top of the stack and flipped it open. 'According to your record, you carried over all your sick days from last year. You could take yourself a little vacation.'

'I'd rather not, sir,' Annie said, holding herself stiff in her chair. 'I don't think that would send a very good message. It might look to the press like you're trying to force me out because of the Fourcade thing. Punishing your only female patrol officer for stopping a bad cop from killing a suspect – that's a pretty volatile story.'

Gus's head came up and he regarded her with a piercing stare. 'Are you threatening me, Deputy Broussard?'

She did her best to look doe-eyed. 'No, sir. Never. I'm just saying how it might look to some people.'

'People after my hide,' he muttered, talking aloud to himself. He scratched at his afternoon beard stubble. 'Smith Pritchett would love that, the ungrateful swine. He'll call me corrupt, a racist, *and* a sexist. Small-minded, that's what he is. Doesn't see the big picture. All he really wants is revenge on Fourcade for screwing that search at Renard's. He wanted to prosecute the big slam-dunk, media-circus case. Mr. Big Headlines.'

He snatched a folded newspaper off his blotter and snapped a big finger against a photograph of Pritchett at the Tuesday press conference, looking stern and authoritative. The headline read: 'Task Force Named in Mardi Gras Rapist Cases.'

'Look at that,' Gus complained. 'Like it was Pritchett's task force. Like he had squat to do with trying to solve these cases. You think you know a man ...'

Annie tuned out the lament. She took the paper from the sheriff's hands as he walked away. The task force was page two news in the Wednesday *Daily Advertiser* from Lafayette.

The article gave a brief encapsulation of the news conference and details of the three attacks that had taken place in Partout Parish over the last week's time. But it was the small sidebar that drew Annie's attention. Just two paragraphs with the headline 'Task Force Leader Experienced.'

Heading the Partout Parish task force in the investigation of what has come to be called the 'Mardi Gras Rapist' cases will be Detective Charles Stokes. Stokes, 32, has been with the Partout Parish Sheriff's Office since 1993 and is described by Sheriff August F. Noblier as 'a diligent and thorough investigator'.

Prior to joining the force in Partout Parish, Stokes served with the Hattiesburg (Mississippi) Police Department, where he also worked as a detective, and was part of the team credited with solving a series of sexual assaults against female students on the campus of William Carey College.

Chaz Stokes knew all about rape cases. He'd been there before. The question was: Had he solved the William Carey College rapes cases or had he committed them?

40

The old Andrew Carnegie Library was open until nine on Thursdays. Annie hovered behind the three makeshift computer bays from about five-fifteen until the junior high geeks who used the machines to surf the Net for things they were too young to see had to go home for supper. Then she settled in at the computer farthest from prying eyes and went to work.

The computers had been a gift to the library from a well-known local author, Conroy Cooper. A new library would have been a better gift. The Carnegie had been old when Christ was in short pants. Dank and dimly lit, the place had always given Annie the creeps. The air was musty with the smell of moldering paper. Every wooden surface had either turned black with age or been worn pale from use. Even the librarian, Miss Stitch, seemed slightly mildewed.

But the computers were new and that was all that mattered. Annie was able to access the William Carey College Library, and once in that system, call up articles from the *Hattiesburg American* that related to the college rape cases in 1991 and 1992. She read them on the screen, scrutinizing for any similarities between those cases and the newly dubbed 'Mardi Gras' cases.

The victims – seven of them – had all been college students or had worked at the college. Physical characteristics of the women varied; ages hung in the late teens, early twenties. The assaults had taken place in their bedrooms late at night. Each woman lived in a ground-floor apartment. The attacks took place during warm weather, the rapist gaining entry through open windows. He used cut-off lengths of panty hose, which he brought with him, to tie his victims up. He spoke very little throughout the course of the rapes, his voice described as 'a harsh whisper'.

Though none of the women had gotten a clean look at her rapist because he had worn a ski mask, several speculated from his voice that 'he may have been black'. The rapist used a condom, which he disposed of away from the scene of the crime, and no semen or pubic hairs had been recovered for evidence. Before leaving the last of his victims, the attacker helped himself to cash and credit cards.

Evander Darnell Flood, the man arrested for the crimes, had given that victim's Visa card to his girlfriend. According to an acquaintance hauled in on unrelated drug charges, Flood had bragged to him about the rapes. While his record was not admissible in court, Evander had previously been a guest of the Mississippi correctional facility in Parchman for seven years on a rape charge. Two previous charges had been dropped due to lack of evidence.

The prosecution built a circumstantial case against Flood with evidence discovered by the Hattiesburg Police Department detectives. And, while Evander swore to the last that he was being framed, that the police had planted the evidence, the jury convicted him and the judge sent him back to Parchman for the rest of his natural life.

Annie sat back from the computer screen and rubbed her eyes. There were differences in the cases and similarities, but then the same could be said for the majority of rape cases. A certain methodology was common to the crime. The differences tended to be personal: One rapist was a talker, using foul sexual language to help get him off; the next one was silent. One might prefer to cover his victim's face to depersonalize her; another would threaten her at knifepoint to keep her eyes open so he might see her fear.

She found more similarities here than differences, but it was the circumstances surrounding Flood's arrest and conviction that made Annie uneasy. Flood swore he was innocent, like 99.9 percent of the scumbags in prison. But the case against him hadn't been that strong. The acquaintance could easily have lied as part of a deal for leniency in his own case. Witnesses who claimed to have seen a man matching Flood's description in the vicinity of several of the rapes told weak, conflicting stories. Flood claimed to have found the last victim's credit card in the hallway of his apartment building. He claimed the cops had railroaded him because he had a record and lived in the area where the crimes had taken place.

He would have been an easy target for a frame. Because of his record, the cops would have known all about Evander early on. He lived in the area, had a part-time janitorial job at the college. His live-in girlfriend worked nights, robbing him of an alibi witness.

Annie closed her eyes and saw Stokes. As a detective assigned to the cases, planting evidence would have been a simple matter for him. He had been there in Renard's home the night Fourcade had found Pam's ring. Everyone had jumped on Nick with the accusation of tampering because he had been accused before. No one had looked twice at Chaz Stokes.

She went through the steps of instructing the computer to print the articles, then turned around in her chair while the dot-matrix printer chattered away. At the far end of one row of reference books, a face stared at her, then darted back into the shadows. Victor Renard.

Annie's heart gave a jolt. The library was nearly deserted. What action there was, was on the first floor: a blue-haired ladies' reading group trying to find satanic messages in The Celestine Prophecy. The second floor, where Annie was, was quiet as a church.

Victor peeked around the end of another bookcase, saw that she was looking right at him, and darted back.

'Victor?' Annie said. Abandoning the printer to its work, she eased out of her chair and moved carefully toward the bookcases. 'Mr. Renard? You don't have to hide from me.'

She made her way slowly down one row, muscles tensing, lungs aching against the held breath. The lighting back here was poor. Gooseflesh crawled down the back of her neck.

'It's Annie Broussard, Victor. Remember me? I'm trying to help Marcus,' she said, her conscience pinching her for lying to a mentally challenged person. Would she get another day in purgatory if her ultimate goal was good? *The end justifies the means.*

She started to turn right at the end of the human sciences row and caught a glimpse of him cowering in the corner to her left.

'How are you, Victor?' she asked, trying to sound pleasant, conversational. She turned toward him slowly, not wanting to spook him.

He didn't seem comfortable with her proximity. She was no more than a yard from him. He made a small uncertain keening sound in his throat and began to rock himself from side to side.

'It's all been very hard on you, hasn't it?' Annie said, her sympathy for him genuine.

According to what little she'd read about autistics in trying to understand more about Marcus Renard's brother, routine was sacred. Yet, Victor's life had to have been an endless series of upsets since the death of Pam Bichon. The press, the cops, disgruntled citizens had all focused their scrutiny and their speculation on the Renard family. Plenty of rumors had run around town that perhaps Victor himself was dangerous. His condition baffled and frightened people. His behavior seemed odd at best, and often inappropriate.

'Mask, mask. *No* mask,' he mumbled, looking at her out the corner of his eye.

Mask. Since Pam's death the word had taken on a menacing connotation that had only been compounded by the recent rapes. Coming from someone whose behavior was so strange, someone who happened to be the brother of a murder suspect, it added to the eeriness.

459

He raised the book in his hands, a collection of Audubon's prints, to cover his face and tapped a finger against the picture on the front, a finely detailed rendering of a mockingbird. '*Mimus polyglottos. Mimus, mimic.* Mask, no mask.'

Slowly he lowered the book to peer over it at her. His eyes had a glasslike quality, hard and clear and unblinking. 'Transformation, *transmutation*, alteration. *Mask.*'

'Do you think I look like someone I'm not? Is that it? Do I remind you of Pam?' Annie asked gently. How much of what had happened could be locked inside Victor Renard's mind? What secret, what clue, might be trapped in the strange labyrinth that was his brain?

He covered his face again. 'Red *and* white. Then *and* now.'

'I don't understand, Victor.'

'I think he's confused,' Marcus said.

Annie swung toward him, startled. She hadn't heard his approach at all. They were back in the farthest, dimmest corner of the library. She had Victor on one side, Marcus on another, a wall to her back.

'That you resemble Pam, but that you aren't Pam,' Marcus finished. 'He can't decide if it's good or bad, past or present.'

Victor rocked himself and bumped the Audubon book against his forehead over and over, muttering, 'Red, red, enter out.'

'How much of his language do you understand?' Annie asked.

'Some.' He was still speaking through gritted teeth, his jaw being wired shut, but with less difficulty. The swelling was gone from his face. The bruises looked yellow and black in the poor light. 'It's a code of sorts.'

'Very red,' Victor mumbled unhappily.

'*Red* is a watchword for things that upset him,' Marcus explained. 'It's all right, Victor. Annie is a friend.'

460

'Very white, very red,' Victor said, peering over the book at Annie. 'Very white, very red.'

'White is good, red is bad. Why he's putting the two together that way is beyond me. He's been very upset since the shooting the other night.'

'I can relate to that,' Annie said, turning her attention more squarely on Marcus. 'Someone took a shot at me last night.'

'My God.' She couldn't tell if his shock was genuine or not. He took a step toward her. 'Were you hurt?'

'No. I ducked, as it happened.'

'Do you know who did it? Was it because of me?'

'I don't know.' *Was it you?* she wondered.

'It's terrible someone would want to hurt you, Annie,' Marcus said, his gaze a little too intent. He inched closer to her by just shifting his weight. 'Especially when you know it was someone wanting to punish you for doing the right thing. That's the way of the world, I'm sad to say. Evil tries to eradicate good.

'Were you alone?' His voice softened. 'You must have been frightened.'

'That would be a mild understatement,' she said, resisting the urge to step away from him. 'I suppose I should be getting used to that kind of thing. I seem to be a favorite target all of a sudden.'

'I can empathize. I know exactly what you went through, Annie,' he said. 'Having a stranger reach into your life and commit an act of violence. It's a violation. It's rape. You feel so vulnerable, so powerless. So alone. Don't you?'

A shudder vibrated just under Annie's skin. He said nothing threatening, nothing menacing. He offered her his understanding and concern … in a way that was just a little too intense. He dabbed at the corners of his mouth with his handkerchief, as if the subject matter were making him salivate. Something about the light in his eyes seemed almost excitement, a secret. No one would have understood

– except Pam Bichon. And possibly Elaine Ingram before her.

'I know what it's like,' he said. 'You know I do. You've been there for me so many times. I wish I could have been there for you. I feel so selfish now – calling you about someone throwing a rock through one of our parlor windows last night, wondering why you didn't call me back. And all the while you were in danger.'

'You called the sheriff's office, didn't you? About the rock?'

'I shouldn't have bothered,' he said bitterly. 'They're probably using the rock for a paperweight today. I'm sure they threw the note away.'

'What note?'

'The one bound to the rock with a rubber band. It said YOU DIE NEXT, KILLER.'

Victor made his strange squealing sound again and covered his face with his book.

'It was terribly upsetting,' Marcus went on. 'Someone is terrorizing my family, and the sheriff's office has done nothing. I'm being stalked just as surely as Pam was stalked by some deranged person, and the sheriff's office would be just as happy if someone killed me. You're the only one who cares, Annie.'

'Well, I'm afraid last night I was busy caring about not getting killed myself.'

'I'm so sorry. The last thing I want is to see you hurt, Annie – especially on my account.' He shifted closer, tilting his head down to an angle for sharing secrets. 'I care a great deal about you, Annie,' he murmured. 'You know that.'

'I hope you don't mean that in a personal way, Marcus,' she said, testing him. There were people just one floor down and his brother standing ten feet away, watching them over the edge of his picture book. He wouldn't risk anything here. 'I'm working on your case. That's all.'

He looked stunned for a split second, then smiled in

relief. 'I understand. Conflict of interest. Your saving my life – twice – was merely in the line of duty.'

'That's right.'

'And your looking into my alibi and coming to the house the other night, even though it wasn't officially your case – that was just because you're a good cop.'

'That's right,' Annie said, another ripple of unease ribboning through her. Once again, he was reading something into her actions that simply wasn't true. And yet, his response was nothing she could even have related to someone else as being inappropriate.

'I'm just a deputy,' she said. 'That's all I can be to you, Marcus. Do you understand what I'm telling you? You shouldn't be sending me gifts.'

'A simple show of my gratitude,' he said.

'Your taxes pay my salary. That's all the gratitude I need.'

'But you've gone above and beyond the call. You deserve more than you're getting.'

Victor whimpered and rocked himself. 'Then *and* now. Enter out. Time and time *now*, Marcus. *Very* red.'

'It's not appropriate for you to give me gifts.'

'Do you have a boyfriend?' he asked, straightening, a fine thread of irritation tightening his voice. 'Did it make him angry – me sending you things?'

'That would be none of your business,' Annie said. She hardly dared blink for fear she would miss some small nuance of expression that would give him away.

'*Very red!*' Victor keened. He sounded on the verge of tears. 'Enter out now!'

Marcus glanced at his watch and frowned. 'Ah, we'd better go. It's getting on toward eight. Victor's bedtime. Can't disrupt the schedule, can we, Victor?'

Victor clutched his book to his chest and hurried toward the door to the hall.

Marcus made a stiff little bow to Annie, trying to be dashing. 'May I walk you out, Annie? Obviously, you need to be careful.'

She refrained from pointing out that having him escort her would hardly be considered a safe thing. He was either a killer or possibly the target of a killer. 'I'm not leaving just yet. I've got some work to do.'

He let it go as they started down the aisle toward the front of the room and better light. 'Have you made any progress on finding that driver who helped me?'

'No. I've been very busy.'

'But you're trying.'

The DMV list was still under the blotter on her desk. 'I'll do what I can.'

'I know you will, Annie,' he said as they reached the vacant desk area, where Victor stood in the doorway facing the hall, rocking himself from side to side. 'I know you'll do your best for me, Annie. You're very special.'

Before Annie could protest again, he said, 'Will you be going to the street dance with anyone Friday?'

As if he meant to ask her, Annie thought, amazed. She took another step away from him. 'I'll be going in uniform if they hold it at all. I'm scheduled to work.'

Marcus sighed. 'Too bad. You've been working so hard lately.'

Because of you, Annie thought, but she wasn't going to be the one to bring on another round of cloying gratitude.

She watched the Renard brothers go, Victor hugging the wall of the stairwell, his bird book raised to hide his face. *Mask*.

He wanted to hide who he was behind another façade. His brother may well have been hiding an alter ego beneath his bland, ordinary face. Annie turned toward the printer and the stack of articles that involved Chaz Stokes, who used his badge as a mask to cover God knew what. *Mask*.

'Yeah, Victor,' she murmured, collecting her things. 'There seems to be a lot of that going around.'

'It doesn't match,' Doll harped. 'I told you it wouldn't match. I had a premonition.'

'It's wet, Mother,' Marcus said, dabbing at the paint with a sponge in hopes of better blending it in with the rest of the wall. 'Paint always appears lighter when dry than when wet.'

Doll scrutinized the dining room wall, her thin face pinched tight with concentration. She crossed her arms and declared, 'I don't believe it's the same color. What's it called? Is it called *forest*?'

'I don't know, Mother. The can has a number, not a name.'

'Well, it had ought to say *forest*. I distinctly remember choosing the color *forest*. If it doesn't say *forest*, then how can you know it's the same shade?'

'Because I *know* that it is.'

He could feel his patience fraying like an old rope, and he resented her for it. He had come home from the library with his head full of Annie, a pleasant warmth glowing just under his skin. Shutting out Victor's incessant noise, he had spent the drive home replaying the encounter in his mind, from Annie's look of surprise when she'd first turned to face him to the subtle messages in her tone of voice. She couldn't publicly accept his attentions until she had cleared him of Pam's murder. He understood. He would have to be discreet. It would be like a game between them, another secret only they shared.

'It's not *forest*,' Doll muttered, moving to examine the spot from another angle. 'It's just as I saw it in my premonition. The color won't match no matter what we do, and every time I look at that wall I'll be taken with the fear of that night. Fear and shame – that's all my life has become. I can barely bring myself to leave the house these days.'

Marcus bit back the words that sprang instantly to his tongue. She had hounded him all morning to take her into town because she needed to go to the drugstore and the supermarket. She didn't trust him to get the brands she liked and she refused to write them down because she

465

didn't necessarily go by names, but by the colors and graphics on the packages. And of course she couldn't take her own car and go herself on account of her nerves and the mysterious undiagnosed palsy that had been coming on her lately – because of him and the unwanted attention he'd drawn to the family.

'All because of your infatuation with that woman,' she said now, as if she was simply jumping back into the conversation they'd had nine hours ago. 'I don't know why you can't content yourself, Marcus.'

Content myself with what? With you? He looked at her out the corner of his eye as he climbed down from the step stool and began the process of cleaning up. He envisioned forcing her head into the paint can and drowning her in her damned *forest* paint, but of course he wouldn't do that any more than he would cram the paint-soaked sponge into her mouth and suffocate her, or stab her in the base of her throat with the screwdriver he'd used to open the can.

'Look what happened. Look what it's done to our lives.'

'What happened was not my fault, Mother,' he said, tapping the lid of the can down with a rubber mallet. If wielded with enough fury, would it do the same damage as a hammer?

'Of course it is,' Doll insisted. 'You were infatuated with that woman, and now she's dead and everyone naturally believes you did it. You should have left her alone.'

'It was a misunderstanding,' he said, gathering up his tools and the can. The spot would need a second application, but the paint couldn't be left out. Victor enjoyed the texture and viscosity of paint, and would put his hands into it and spill it out to watch it pool on the floor. 'Annie will clear it up for us. She's working on the case day and night.'

'Annie.' Doll shook her head, following him into the kitchen. 'She's no better than the rest of them, Marcus. You mark my words, she's not your friend.'

He stopped at the back door and stared at his mother,

466

defiant. 'She saved my life. She's going out of her way to help me. I believe that would define the word *friend*.'

He pushed the door open with his elbow and went out to the small, locked shed where he kept things like paint and power tools. A single bulb illuminated the rough cypress walls. He put the paint and tools away and shut the light off. If he waited long enough, he knew his mother would go to bed and he wouldn't have to speak to her again until morning. It was nearly ten o'clock. She had to be in her room for the start of the news, though he could never imagine why. The news never failed to agitate and disgust her for one reason or another. Ritual. She was as bound to it as Victor.

She couldn't understand about Annie, he told himself as he waited for the kitchen light to go out. What did his mother know of friends? She'd never had one that he'd ever been aware of. He doubted even his father had been a friend to her. She would never understand about Annie.

The lights went out in the kitchen, then the dining room. Cutting across the terrace, Marcus went to his workroom and let himself in through one of the French doors with the key he kept under a flowerpot. He went first into his bedroom for a Percodan, to calm both his pains and his nerves, then came back into his studio and gathered his things from his private cupboard.

The drug began to work quickly, relaxing him, giving him a vaguely floaty feeling, insulating him from both physical pain and emotional unpleasantness. Staring at his sketch, he drove everything from his mind except Annie.

Of course he was taken with her. She was pretty. She was intelligent. She was fair-minded. She was his angel. That was what he called her when he imagined the two of them together – Angel. It would be his secret name for her, another little something they would share only with each other. He drew a finger across his lips like closing a zipper, then smiled to himself. That had already become a pet signal between them. They had to be careful. They had to be discreet. She was risking so much by helping him.

He lifted the small keepsake from the drafting table and let it swing from his fingertips, smiling at the whimsy of it. It was a silly thing, hardly appropriate for a grown woman with a serious profession, and yet it suited her. She was still a girl in many respects – fresh, unspoiled, fun, uncertain. He recalled in perfect detail the uncertainty on her face as she turned and saw him tonight in the library. It made him want to hold her. Instead, he held the comical little plastic alligator with the sunglasses and red beret that he had taken down from the rearview mirror in Annie's Jeep.

She wouldn't mind that he had taken it, he reasoned. It was just another small secret between them. He pressed a phantom kiss to the alligator's snout and smiled. The Percodan felt like warm wine flowing through his veins. He closed his eyes for a moment and felt as if his body were going to drift up out of the chair.

He had brought out several of his treasures. Setting the alligator down on the ledge of the drawing table, he picked up the small, ornate photo frame and ran a fingertip along the filigreed edge, smiling sadly at the woman in the picture. Pam. Pam and her darling daughter. The things that might have been if Stokes and Donnie Bichon hadn't poisoned her against him ...

Regretfully, he set the photograph aside and picked up the locket. There would be a certain symbolism in passing it to Annie. A thread of continuity.

Holding the locket in one hand, he took up his pencil in the other and touched it to the paper.

'I knew it.'

Three words could not have held more accusation. Despite the melting effect of the drug, Marcus straightened his spine at the sound of the voice. His mother stood directly behind him. He hadn't heard her come in through the bedroom, he'd been so engrossed in his fantasies.

'Mother '

'I *knew* it,' Doll said again. She stared past him at the drawing on the tilt-top table. Tears rose in her eyes and she began to tremble. 'Oh, Marcus, not again.'

'You don't understand, Mother,' he said, sliding from his chair, the locket still dangling from his fist.

'I understand that you're pathetic,' she spat. 'You think that woman wants you? She wants you in jail! Do you belong there, Marcus?'

'No! Mama!'

Lunging past him, she grabbed the framed photograph from his table and held it so tightly in her hand that the metal cut into her fingers. She stared hard at the picture of Pam, her whole body trembling, then, sobbing, she threw the frame across the room.

'Why?' she cried. 'How could you do this?'

'I'm not a killer!' Marcus cried, his own tears burning his eyes. 'How can you think that, Mama?'

'Liar!' She slapped him hard on his chest with her open palm, staining his shirt with her blood. 'You're killing me now!'

Screaming, she turned and swept everything off the drawing table with a wild gesture.

'Mama, no!' Marcus cried, grabbing her arm as she reached for the portrait.

'Oh, Marcus!' Doll dragged her hand down her cheek, smearing her face with blood. 'I don't understand you.'

'No, you don't!' he shouted, pain tearing through his face as he strained against the wires in his jaw. 'I love Annie. You couldn't understand love. You don't know what love is. You know possession. You know manipulation. You don't know love. Get out. Get out of my room. I never asked you here. It's the one place I can be free of you. Get out! Get out!'

He screamed the words over and over while he staggered around the room, hitting things, smashing things blindly, knocking a dollhouse to the floor, where it splintered into kindling. Every blow he imagined landing on his mother's face, shattering the sour mask; striking her body and snapping bones.

Finally, he fell across his worktable, sobbing, pounding his fists, the fury running out of him. He lay there for a long time, his gaze blurry and unfocused, staring at nothing. After a while he realized his mother had gone. He straightened slowly and looked around the room. The destruction stunned him. His special things, his secrets, lay broken all around him. This was his sanctuary, and now it had been violated and ruined.

Without so much as righting the fallen chair, Marcus picked up his keys and walked out.

Victor sat among ruins and rocked himself, mewing. The house was dark and silent, which meant everyone else was asleep, which meant they had ceased to exist. Marcus forbade him to come into his Own Space, but Marcus was asleep and therefore his wishes were Off like television. Victor usually liked to come in here and sit among the small houses. Also, he knew where Marcus kept his Secret Things, and sometimes Victor would open the Secret Door and take them out just to touch them. It made him feel strong to know about the Secret Door and to touch the Secret Things without anyone else knowing. It gave him a feeling of red *and* white intensity, and that was very exciting.

Tonight all Victor felt was *very* red. He hadn't been able to shut down his own mind at all – not even during his regular time. The red colors swirled around and around, cutting and poking at his brain. And his Controllers – the little faces he pictured inside his mind, the arbiters of emotion and etiquette only watched, their expressions disapproving. The Controllers were always angry when he couldn't stop the red colors. Red, *red, red*. Dark *and* light. Around and around. Cutting and cutting.

He had tried to soothe himself with the Audubon book, but the birds had looked at him angrily, as if they *knew* what was in his mind. As if they had heard the voices. Emotion filled him up like water, drowning him in intensity. He felt he couldn't breathe.

He had heard the voices earlier. They had come up through the floor into his room. *Very* red. Victor didn't like voices with no faces, especially red voices. He heard them from time to time, and what they said was never white, *always* red. He'd sat on his bed, keeping his feet off the floor, because he was afraid the voices might go up his pajama legs and get into his body through his rectum.

Victor waited for the voices to go away. Then he waited some more. He counted to the Magic Number three times by sixteenths before he left his room. He had come down to Marcus's Own Space, drawn by the need to see the face, even though it upset him. Sometimes he was like that. Sometimes he couldn't stop from hitting his fist against the wall, even though he knew it hurt him.

The disorder of the room upset him. He couldn't abide broken things. It hurt him in his brain to see broken glass or splintered wood. He felt he could see every torn molecule, and feel the pain of them. And yet he stayed in the room because of the face.

He closed his eyes and saw the face, opened them and saw the face again – the same, the same, the same, but different. Mask, no mask. The feeling it gave him was *very* red. He closed his eyes again and counted by fractions to the Magic Number.

Annie. She was The Other but *not* The Other. Pam, but *not* Pam. Elaine, but *not* Elaine. Mask, no mask. It was like before, and that was *very* red.

Victor rocked himself and whimpered *inside* his being, *not* outside. The intensity was building. His senses were too acute. Every part of him was hard with tension, even his penis. He worried that panic would strike and freeze him, trapping the red intensity inside where it would go on and on, and no one would be able to make it stop.

He lifted his hands and touched his favorite mask and

rocked himself, tears running down his cheeks as he stared at his brother's pencil drawing of Annie Broussard, and the jagged, bloody tear that ran down the center of it.

41

Kim Young was a regular at the Voodoo Lounge. She worked three to eleven as an assistant manager at the Quik Pik on La Rue Dumas in Bayou Breaux and figured she deserved a beer or two after eight hours of clearing gas pumps, selling lottery tickets, and running teenagers off before they could shoplift the place into bankruptcy. Besides that, Icky Kebodeaux, the kid she supervised, was weird, smelled like a locker-room laundry basket, and had acne so bad she thought his whole face would explode one of these days and just ooze away. After eight hours of Icky's company, a beer was the least she deserved.

And so she always stopped off for a nightcap at the Lounge on her way home when Mike was out on the TriStar rig in the Gulf. They lived on the outskirts of Luck in a neat little brick house with a big yard. They had been married less than a year, and so far Kim found married life to be good news/bad news. Mike was a catch, but she was left alone for weeks at a time when he was on the rig. He was gone now and not due back for another week.

He was going to miss Carnival in Bayou Breaux, and Kim was feeling bitchy about that. At twenty-three she still liked to party, and she had decided she would damn well party without Mike if he wasn't willing to take the vacation days. He was always willing to take vacation days during hunting season, when *he* wanted to have some fun.

Screw him. She wasn't going to look good in tight jeans forever. She had already made arrangements to go to Carnival with Jeanne-Marie and Candace. Girls' night out. There were always plenty of guys to hook up with for fun at the street dance – if the town fathers allowed the street dance to go on this year.

Everyone was spooked about this rapist. One of the victims had died today. She'd heard it on the radio.

Kim would never have admitted it, but she hadn't been sleeping too well herself this last week. She had thought about moving in with her sister until Mike got home, but Becky had a month-old baby with colic and Kim wanted no part of that. Anyway, it wasn't as if she was helpless.

'What I want to know is if Baptists can't go to Disney World on account of the gays, can they go to Busch Gardens?' the caller on the radio asked. 'How do they know there ain't gays working at Busch Gardens or Six Flags? My brother-in-law's cousin works at Six Flags, and he's so light in the loafers he floats. It's all just silly, if you ask me. What kind of good Christian people go around trying to figure out if perfect strangers are AC or DC?'

'Ah, there's a can of worms. Any Baptists out there care to comment? This is KJUN, all talk all the time. Home of the giant jackpot giveaway. We'll be right back after these messages.'

Kim wouldn't have minded winning that jackpot. She and Mike had been talking about putting away money toward a new boat. God knew she called into this stupid show often enough. She had called just tonight from the Quik Pik to give her opinion on canceling the street dance. Stupid, that's what that idea was. Nobody was going to get raped at the street dance. The worst that ever happened was fistfights.

She swung her old Caprice in under the carport beside the house as Zachary Richard sang a zydeco jingle for a casino downriver.

The house was safe and sound, just the way she'd left it. A basket of laundry sat on the kitchen table, ready for folding. She scooped it up, carried it with her to the bedroom, and did the job while she watched a rerun of *Cheers* on the tiny color set she'd bought to have on her dresser.

She went to bed at about one-thirty and lay awake for a long while, straining to listen for sounds in the house. The wind had picked up outside, and she grew frustrated trying to tell the difference between the rustle of tree branches and the scrape of footsteps outside the window. By one-fifty she had drifted off, a scowl on her face, her right hand jammed under Mike's pillow.

At 2:19 she woke with a start. He was here. She could feel his presence, dark and menacing. Her pulse raced out of control. She lay perfectly still, waiting.

She had left the night-light on in the bathroom down the hall, and a faint shaft of illumination spilled out the partly opened door into the hallway.

She saw him coming. The black figure of doom. No features, no face, as silent as death.

Death.

Why me? Kim wondered as he slipped into the bedroom. *Why did he pick me? What did I do to deserve this?*

She would know later, she thought, as he came toward the bed. She would find out after she killed him.

In one smooth motion, and without hesitation, Kim Young sat up, swung the gun out from under her husband's pillow, and pulled the trigger.

42

The dream was washed in filtered shades of red. Soft red light as grainy as dust. Deep red shadows as liquid as blood. She stood in front of what she thought was a mirror, but the face staring back was not her own. Lindsay Faulkner looked through the glass at her, her expression accusatory, scornful. Annie reached out a hand to touch the mirror. The apparition came through the glass and passed over her, passed *through* her.

She twisted around and tried to run, but her body was bound in place by raw red muscle growing up from the floor and reaching out of the walls. Across the room, the apparition suddenly fell backward onto the floor, screaming. Then the floor heaved upward and became a wall, and the apparition became Pam Bichon, blood running like wine from her gaping wounds, her dark eyes burning blankly into Annie's.

With a shout, Annie clawed her way out of the dream, out of sleep. The sheet was twisted around her body like a sarong. She struggled free of it and sat up on the couch with her knees drawn up and her head in her hands. Her hair was wild and damp with sweat. Her T-shirt was soaked through. The air conditioner kicked on and blew its cold breath over her, raising gooseflesh. The disturbing quality of the dream clung to her like body odor. Shadows and blood. *Shadowland*.

'I'm doing the best I can, Pam,' she whispered. 'I'm doing the best I can.'

Too edgy to lie back down, she went into her bedroom and changed T-shirts. Fourcade had cleaned up the mess for her, but she hadn't been able to bring herself to sleep in the bed. Maybe after the images had some time to fade from her mind. Maybe after this was all over and she had a chance to put a fresh coat of paint on the wall and buy some new pillows ... Or maybe this was just one of the more obvious ways in which her life would never be the same.

She went to the kitchen for a drink, then pulled a Snickers bar from the freezer instead. Nibbling at the frozen chocolate, she wandered around her living room, using only the lights from the stereo system and the scanner to keep her from running into anything. Nick was outside somewhere. Stakeout duty. She didn't want to alarm him by turning on lights at two-thirty in the morning, even though it would have been nice to have some company. She was getting to like his company a little too much, she feared.

She sank down on the sofa and rubbed the taxidermized alligator's snout affectionately with her bare foot.

'Maybe I need to get a live pet, huh, Alphonse?' she muttered. The gator gave her his usual toothy grin.

Across the room the scanner scratched out a call.

'All units in the vicinity: We've got a possible 245 and a 261 at 759 Duff Road in Luck. Shots fired. Code 3.'

A possible assault and rape. All deputies were to come fast with lights and sirens.

'The caller says she shot him,' the dispatcher said. 'We've got an ambulance on the way.'

Luck was just down the road and across the bayou. And, if Annie's hunch was right, Chaz Stokes may just have been lying in a pool of blood at 759 Duff Road.

Two units made the scene ahead of her. The cars sat at flamboyant angles in the front yard of the little brick house, beacons rolling. One officer sat on the concrete front steps, either watching out for the ambulance or being sick. The latter, Annie guessed as she crossed the lawn.

He grabbed hold of the wrought iron railing to steady himself as he rose to his feet. The front-porch light gleamed off his red hair like the sun on a new copper penny and

Annie thanked heaven for small favors. This cop was a Doucet. Blood was thicker than the Brotherhood. Blood was thicker than anything in South Louisiana.

'Hey, Annie, that you?'

'Hey, Tee-Rouge, where y'at?'

'Tossing my cookies. What you doing here, *chère*?'

'Caught it on the scanner. I thought the victim might appreciate having another woman here,' she lied.

Tee-Rouge gave a snort and waved a hand in dismissal. 'That's some victim. Somebody oughta lift that li'l gal's nightie and see what kind of hairy balls she's hiding under there. She shot this son of a bitch point-blank in the face with a cut-down shotgun.'

'Youch. Who is he?' Annie asked, trying for casual, feeling anything but. In her mind's eye she pictured Stokes creeping toward the woman's bed, the woman raising the shotgun, Stokes's face exploding.

Tee-Rouge shrugged. '*Chère*, his mama wouldn't know him if he sat up and called her name. He's got no ID, but he was wearing the mask. There's feathers all over the damn scene. This is our scumbag of the season right here.'

'You call the detectives?'

'Yeah, but Stokes, he's who-knows-where. In bed with some chick, probably – no offense.'

Annie's heartbeat quickened. 'He's not answering his page?'

'Not so far. Quinlan's on his way, but he lives clear up in Devereaux. It'll take him some time to get down here.'

'Who's inside?' she asked, starting for the door.

'Pitre.'

Groaning to herself, Annie went on into the house as a third cruiser came screaming down the road. Every patrol in the parish was being abandoned in favor of the excitement of a hot crime scene. Everybody wanted in on wrapping the Mardi Gras case.

The living room was empty. There was no immediate sign of the victim. The bedroom looked to be a straight shot down the hall to the left. Pitre stood just inside the doorway, at the feet of the fallen assailant. Annie took a deep breath and marched down the hall.

'I'm not gonna want pizza any time soon,' Pitre muttered, then looked up at the source of the footfalls. 'Broussard, what the hell are *you* doing here? You're not on tonight. Hell, you're barely on the force at all.'

Annie ignored him, turning to look at the dead man. He wasn't her first. He wasn't even her first by shotgun. But he was the first hit at close range, and the sight was by no means pretty.

The rapist lay on the floor, arms outflung. He was dressed in black, covering every inch of his body, including his hands. He could have been black, white, Indian – there was no telling. There was virtually nothing left of his face. The flesh-and-bone mask that set one human being apart from the next had been obliterated. The raw meat, shattered bone, and exposed brain matter could have belonged to anyone. The hair was saturated with blood, its color indistinguishable. A fragment of the black feather mask was stuck to a jagged piece of cranium. The stench of violent death was thick in the air.

'Oh my Lord,' Annie breathed, her knees wilting a bit. The Snickers bar threatened a return trip, and she had to steel herself against spewing it all over the crime scene.

Scraps and chunks of the assailant's face had been sprayed up onto the ceiling and on the pale yellow wall. The sawed-off shotgun lay abandoned on the bed.

'If you can't take it, leave, Broussard. Nobody asked you here,' Pitre said, moving around the bed to check out the shotgun. 'Stokes won't be amused to see you.'

'Yeah? Well, maybe the joke's on him,' Annie muttered, trying to think ahead. Should she pull Quinlan aside when he arrived and tell him about the possibility? Or should she just step back and let the thing unravel on its own? No one would thank her for having suspected Stokes.

'Hey,' Pitre said with the delighted surprise of a child

finding the hidden prize in Cracker Jack. 'We know the guy had one blue eye.'

'How's that?'

A nasty grin lit his face as he leaned over the bed and stared at his find. ''Cause here it is. Would you look at that! That sucker musta popped clean out of his head when she shot him! It's just sitting here like a little egg!'

Stokes's turquoise blue orbs came clearly into focus in Annie's mind as she stepped around the body. But before she could get a look at Pitre's prize, a familiar voice sounded behind her.

'*Man Without a Face*. Anybody see that movie? This guy's uglier. If I'm lyin', I'm dyin'.'

Annie swung around, stunned. Stokes stood looking down at the body, chewing on a stick of boudin sausage, a Ragin' Cajuns ball cap backward on his head. He glanced over at her and made a face.

'Man, Broussard, you are like the goddamn clap – unwanted, unwelcome, and impossible to get rid of.'

'I'm sure you're the voice of experience,' Annie managed. She hadn't quite realized just how set she had been on Stokes's guilt until that moment. A mix of emotions swept over her as she watched him step around the body – disappointment, relief, guilt.

'Who asked you to the dance, anyway?' Stokes asked. 'We don't need any secretaries here, don't need any crime dogs.'

'I thought the victim might appreciate having another woman here.'

'Yeah, he probably would have if he wasn't dead.'

'I meant the woman.'

'Then go find her and get the hell outta my crime scene.' He looked right at her and said straight-faced, 'Can't have you messing up any evidence.'

As Annie went into the hall, Stokes leaned over the bed and looked at the shotgun. 'Man, that's what I call birth control. You know what I mean?'

Pitre laughed.

The victim, Kim Young, was in her neat little yellow kitchen, leaning back against the counter, trembling as if she had just walked out of a freezer. The pale blue baby-doll nightgown she wore barely cleared the tops of her thighs and was liberally flecked with blood and tissue. The mess had sprayed across her face and into her dishwater blond curls.

'I'm Deputy Broussard,' Annie said gently. 'Would you like to sit down? Are you feeling all right?'

She looked up, glassy-eyed. 'I – I shot that man.'

'Yes, you did.'

From where she stood, Annie could see the open patio door in the dining room, where the assailant had gained entry. A neat half-moon of glass had been cut out beside the handle.

'Did you get a look at him before you pulled the trigger?'

She shook her head, dislodging a bone fragment from her hair. It fell to the tile floor next to her bare foot. 'It was too dark. Something woke me up and and I was so *scared*. And then he was right there by the bed and I – I –'

Tears choked her. Her face reddened. 'What if it had been Mike? It could have been Mike! I just shot –'

Ignoring the blood and gore, Annie put an arm around Kim Young's shoulders as the realization dawned in the woman's mind – that she might have killed a loved one by mistake. Then, instead of being a hero, as she would certainly be touted when the press caught up with the story, she would have been portrayed as stupid and hysterical, a misguided vigilante forced to pay a terrible price. The difference was the outcome, not the action. Just another one of life's little object lessons.

The assailant's name was Willard Roache, known affectionately by his old pals in the penal system as 'Cock' Roache. He had a long, ugly history of sexual assault charges and two convictions. He'd done his last jolt in Angola and had been released in June 1996. His last address listed with the state correctional system was in Shreveport, where he had dumped his parole officer and his identity.

Calling himself William Dunham, he had moved to Bayou Breaux in late December and secured a job as a technician at KJUN Radio, using a fake résumé no one had bothered to check. Working the evening shift with Owen Onofrio, Roache had answered the phones and recorded the names and addresses of callers for the giant jackpot giveaway. It was from this list he had chosen his victims.

Evidence obtained at Roache's home included photocopies of the lists with his personal notes scrawled in the margin. Next to Lindsay Faulkner's name he had written the words 'Sexy bitch'. Also found in his home was a box containing half a dozen black feather Mardi Gras masks that had come from a novelties wholesaler in New Orleans.

The information came in piece by piece throughout the day, starting with the discovery of Roache's car parked a short distance from Kim Young's home. At the sheriff's instruction, Roache's corpse was fingerprinted at the scene and the prints sent through the state automated fingerprint system with a rush order – the rush being a press conference set for four o'clock in the afternoon. Noblier wanted the case tied up with a ribbon before the start of Carnival for maximum PR benefit.

Annie prowled the records office all day like a caged animal, wanting to be a part of the team of deputies and detectives going through Roache's trailer, running evidence to the regional lab in New Iberia, making calls to map out the rapist's background. Myron barely allowed her to help catalog the evidence that was brought into their own lockup for safekeeping.

The frustration was almost unbearable. She wanted to see the proof for herself, go through the process of identifying the components of Roache's guilt, so that she could exorcise the last of the theory that had taken root in her own mind: that Chaz Stokes could have committed the crimes and that those crimes might have led them back to Pam's murder.

A theory was all it had been. As Fourcade had pointed out to her, she had no evidence, nothing but hunches, conjecture, speculation. A detective's job was to find irrefutable proof, to build the case solid and airtight – which Stokes might have done with Willard Roache before he had the chance to attack Kay Eisner and Lindsay Faulkner and Kim Young, had Stokes been inclined to work a little harder after Jennifer Nolan's attack.

Instead, Stokes did the research on Roache after the fact and readily accepted congratulations on his detective work. Because everyone was so happy to have the terror of this man stalking the parish over and done with, so far people were choosing to ignore the fact that Roache had lived in the same trailer park as Jennifer Nolan and had not been interviewed the day of her rape. He hadn't been home the morning the investigation had begun. Annie had knocked on his door herself and reported to Stokes that he wasn't home. Neither Stokes nor Mullen had bothered to go back. If they had, they might have recognized him later, when the state had faxed in descriptions and mug shots of sex offenders released from the system in the past year.

With all the bad things that had happened in recent weeks, the department needed something to celebrate. The death of Willard Roache was treated as a triumph, even though neither the department nor the task force had had any hand in ending Roache's crime spree. If anything, Annie thought, they should have considered it an embarrassment. It had taken a 120-pound clerk from the Quik Pik with a sawed-off shotgun to stop the predator. They could have as easily been mourning Kim Young's own death if Roache had wrestled the gun from her. But no one else seemed to see it that way.

At the end of the day the sheriff presented the conclusion of the case to the press like an elaborately wrapped present. Only Smith Pritchett seemed less than overjoyed, and only because the thunder was all Noblier's and there was no villain left to prosecute. Still, he took the opportunity to pontificate and state that the world was a better place without Willard Roache in it. No charges would be filed against Kim Young for protecting herself in her own home.

Everybody's a winner, Annie thought, standing toward the edge of the pack watching the press conference on the break-room set. Everyone except Jennifer Nolan, and Kay Eisner, and Lindsay Faulkner, and Kim Young – who, despite saving herself from a worse fate, had blown a man's head off and would have to live with that for the rest of her life.

Annie wandered back to records feeling at loose ends. *Focus*, Fourcade would say. The rape cases were closed, but the rapes were not her focus. Pam's murder was her focus. To that end she had Marcus Renard and Donnie Bichon to hold her attention.

'You have got no respect for this office,' Myron greeted her dourly. 'There is work to be done, and you're off watching television.'

Annie rolled her eyes as she scooped the afternoon mail off the counter. 'Oh, Jesus, Myron, go have a bowel movement, why don't you? This is the records office. We're not guarding the ark of the covenant, for crying out loud.'

The clerk's eyes bugged out. His nostrils flared and his wiry frame quivered with outrage. 'That is *it*, Deputy Broussard! You are through in my office. I will *not* stand for any more.'

He stormed from the room, slamming the door behind him, and headed in the direction of Noblier's office. Annie leaned over the counter and shouted after him, 'Hey, ask for my old job back while you're at it!'

Guilt nipped her as he strode out of sight. She had always appreciated Myron for who he was – until she had to work with him. She had always had a respectful attitude toward her elders and her superiors, with few exceptions. Maybe Fourcade was a bad influence. Or maybe she just had more important things on her mind than kissing Myron's skinny ass.

She sorted through the mail, knowing Myron would go ballistic if she opened anything he deemed important. Most of it looked like insurance stuff: requests for accident reports and so on. One envelope bore the Our Lady of Mercy letterhead and was addressed to her.

Tearing the end open with her thumb, Annie extracted what looked to be a lab report. A copy of the chem 7 blood analysis on Lindsay Faulkner that Dr. Unser had requested during Faulkner's seizure. The test Annie had requested after Lindsay's death. The test the Our Lady lab had apparently lost.

She looked down the row of indecipherable symbols and corresponding numbers, none of it meaning anything to her. K+: 4.6 mEq/L. Cl-: 101 mEq/L. Na++: 139 mEq/L. BUN: 17 mg. Glucose: 120. It didn't matter much now. Willard Roache would likely be credited with both the attack and the death of Faulkner, unless the autopsy Stokes had requested turned up some anomaly.

'I have left my message with Sheriff Noblier's secretary,' Myron announced. 'I expect your position here will be terminated by the end of the day.'

Annie didn't bother to correct him, though she figured she had at least until Monday to be reassigned or suspended, depending on Gus's mood. Less than an hour shy of five o'clock on Friday, with a big win under his belt, the sheriff was doubtless off toasting himself with the town fathers.

'Then I might as well leave, hadn't I?' Annie said. 'As my last official act as your assistant, I'll take this report over to the detectives. Just to be kind to you, Myron.'

Annie walked into the Pizza Hut without bothering to ring the bell. On the phone, Perez looked up at her, dark eyes snapping impatience. She waved the report at him and gestured back to the task force war room.

The task force members had all been invited to the press conference so that Noblier could show them off and earn more praise for having the wisdom to select such a crack team. They had left their command center looking as if it had been ransacked by thieves. The radio on the file cabinet was blaring Wild Tchoupitoulas.

Moving along the table, Annie scanned file tabs until she came across the one marked FAULKNER, LINDSAY. It seemed pitifully thin for representing a woman's violent death. Not much would be added to it before the case was closed and it went into the drawers in Myron's domain. The autopsy report, Stokes's final report, that would be it.

She flipped the folder open and pulled the lab report Stokes had already collected, scanning the document to make certain it and the one she'd received were indeed the same item. K+: 4.6 mEq/L. CI-: 101 mEq/L. Na++: 139 mEq/L. BUN: 17 mg. Glucose: 120.

'What the hell is with you, Broussard?' Stokes demanded, striding into the room. 'Are you stalking me? Is that it? There's laws against that. You know what I'm saying?'

'Yeah? Well, who'd have thought you knew anything about it after the way you blew off Pam Bichon last fall?'

'I did not blow off Pam Bichon. Now why don't you tell me what you're doing in my face, then get out of it? I was having a damn fine day without you.'

'Our Lady sent over a dupe of the chem 7 blood test on Lindsay Faulkner. I thought it should be in the file, not that you care. Why bother following up when you barely did any work to begin with?'

'Fuck you, Broussard,' he said, snatching the report from her hand. 'It was just a matter of time before I woulda nailed Roache.'

'I'm sure that's a comfort to all the women he attacked after Jennifer Nolan.'

'Don't you have some paper clips to count?'

Mullen stepped into the doorway, cutting a glance from

486

Annie to Stokes. 'You coming, Chaz? They can't start the party without us.'

Stokes flashed the Dudley Do-Right. 'I'm there, man. I am *there.*'

Annie shook her head. 'A party to celebrate the fact that a civilian closed your case for you. You ought to be so proud.'

Stokes settled his porkpie hat back on his head and straightened his purple tie. 'Yeah, Broussard, I am. My only regret is that Roache didn't get to you first.'

He herded her from the room and from the building. Annie went reluctantly on toward the law enforcement center, her eyes on Stokes and Mullen as they climbed into their respective vehicles and tore out of the parking lot, blasting their horns in celebration.

A civilian had cleared their hottest case and Pam Bichon's killer was still roaming free. She couldn't see much to be happy about.

'Or maybe I'm just a sore loser,' she muttered.

43

'You're listening to KJUN. All talk all the time. Our topic: safety versus civil rights should prospective employees be subjected to fingerprinting? Carl in Iota –'

Nick switched the radio off and sat up behind the wheel of the truck as Donnie left his office and climbed into the Lexus. He looked as pale as the car. His hunch-shouldered walk had a little extra bend in it. The pressure was getting to him. He would make a move soon, maybe tonight, and Nick wanted to be there when he did. He crushed out his cigarette with the half dozen butts in the ashtray, put the truck in gear, and waited until the Lexus had turned the corner at Dumas.

Patience was the key word here. Essential in surveillance. Essential in all aspects of life. A useful tool that was difficult to master. Men like Donnie never got the hang of it. He had moved too quickly to get rid of Pam's business. Haste attracted unwanted attention. But then had that been Donnie's doing or Marcotte's? Or mine? Nick wondered, the idea burning in his gut like an ulcer. He hadn't completely mastered patience himself.

La Rue Dumas was busy, the curbs lined with cars, the sidewalk full of people. The Lexus was four cars ahead and waiting at the green light to make a left turn. Friday night always drew people into town. Nick had heard Bayou Breaux's Carnival celebration attracted folks from all over South Louisiana for the street dance and various parties and pageants that went on from tonight through Fat Tuesday. With the demise of the serial rapist, the atmosphere of revelry would be cranked up an extra notch, relief adding wild euphoria to the mix.

All day the news had been full of 'late-breaking information' on the shooting of Willard Roache, who had been subsequently unmasked, so to speak, as the Mardi Gras rapist. So much for Annie's theory on Stokes as a sexual predator, though Nick had to give her grudging admiration for going after the tough angle. She had a passion for the work she was only just beginning to tap. With the rapist out of the way, she would be better able to focus on tripping up Renard.

Renard was still his number one bet. Donnie was up to no good, but it had the smell of dirty money rather than the smell of death. It was Renard who made Nick's hackles rise. Every time he went over the case in his mind, the trail, the logic, wound back to Renard. Every time. The story was there. He just hadn't managed to find the key to open the book. Until Annie.

A mixed blessing, that, he mused. His initial intent had been to use her as bait to draw Renard out. But the better that plan worked, the less he liked it. In his mind's eye he could still see the gruesome tableau in her bedroom. He had made the same connection he knew she had, recalling the sight of Pam Bichon nailed to the floor of that house out on Pony Bayou.

The idea of Renard terrorizing Annie that way, the idea of Renard thinking about Annie that way, the idea of Renard touching Annie in any way, brought a rush of emotion Nick wasn't quite sure how to handle. He knew it wasn't wise, but it was there and he was loath to walk away from it.

She would testify against him in six days.

He turned on Fifth as the Lexus took a right to drive south along the bayou road.

The parking lot at the Voodoo Lounge was nearly full. Nick spotted the Lexus and parked the truck on the berm up on the road. Zydeco music was blowing through the walls of the joint. Colorful Chinese lanterns had been strung around the building. Costumed party-goers were dancing on the half-finished gallery. A curvy blonde in a green sequined mask opened her top and shook her naked breasts like a pair of water balloons at Nick as he mounted the steps. He walked past her without reaction.

'Man, Nicky, you got ice water in those veins of yours! If I'm lyin', I'm dyin',' Stokes announced, clapping him on the back.

Nick shot him a look, taking in the incongruity of a Zorro mask and a porkpie hat.

Stokes shrugged. 'Hey, cut me some slack, pard. It's a special occasion!'

'So I hear.'

'Drinks are on the house for cops. You picked the right night to come out of your cave, Nicky.'

They wound their way through the throng toward the bar. The energy level was high, an almost palpable electricity that magnified the scents of fried shrimp, warm bodies, and cheap cologne. Chaz bulled his way to the bar and bellowed for shots. Nick moved toward the nearest corner, his gaze scanning the room for Donnie, who had found a spot midway down the long side of the bar. He didn't look like a man who had come to party. He sipped at his whiskey as if he were using it for medicinal purposes.

Stokes held a shot glass out to Nick and raised his own. 'To the timely end of another scumbag.'

'You can concentrate on Renard, now,' Nick said, leaning close to be heard without shouting over the noise.

'I intend to. There's nothing I want more than to put an end to that situation, believe me.' He tossed back his drink, grimaced at the kick in his gut, and shook himself like a wet dog. 'You ain't exactly a party animal, man. What you doing out and about on a crazy night like this?'

'Keeping an eye on something,' Nick said vaguely. 'A developing situation. Gotta do something to occupy my time.'

Stokes snorted. 'You need a hobby, man. I suggest Valerie out there on the veranda. That girl is a regular devil's playground for idle hands. You know what I'm saying?'

'What's the matter? You bored with her?'

He flashed a smile that was a little hard around the edges. 'My attentions are needed elsewhere tonight.'

'So are mine,' Nick said, as Donnie pushed himself back from the bar and headed for the door, a solitary ambassador of gloom among the sea of smiling faces.

Nick turned his back as Bichon passed, setting his glass on the bar.

'Have another,' Stokes offered, always magnanimous with the money of others.

'One's my limit tonight. Catch you later.'

He worked his way out onto the gallery and spotted the Lexus backing carefully out of the lineup of pickups and beaters. He waited until it was headed toward the southern exit of the lot, then jogged up onto the road at the north end, and jumped in the truck.

Traffic was enough to keep Donnie distracted as they headed out of town. Still, Nick hung well back. Patience. He wanted to see how this would play out, give Donnie a little bit of rope to see if he would hang himself with it.

Twilight had surrendered to evening. Fog hung over the water. The Lexus turned east, crossed the bayou, then went south again, and passed down the main street of Luck. At the edge of town it turned in at a supper club called Landry's.

Nick cruised past the restaurant, his eye catching on the sleek silver Lincoln that sat apart from the other cars in the lot, the driver a hulking black shadow behind the wheel. He turned the corner two blocks down, doubled back, and drove in the service entrance at the back of the property.

He entered the restaurant through the kitchen door that stood open, letting the rich aromas of beefsteak and good Cajun cooking roll out into the night. The kitchen help chose to ignore him as he moved through their domain.

Landry's dining room was large and dimly lit. A free-standing fireplace with fake logs glowing orange for ambiance stood in the center. Perhaps two-thirds of the white-draped tables were taken, mostly by older middle class couples dressed up for their big night out. The low hum of conversation was constant, the chink of flatware against china like the sound of small bells ringing across the room.

Donnie and Marcotte sat in the wraparound banquette of a round corner table. To Marcotte's left, one of DiMonti's twin thugs sat hunched over a table for two, making it look like something from a child's tea set. DiMonti was nowhere in sight.

Nick adjusted the lightweight jacket he wore to show just the butt of the Ruger in its shoulder rig, slipped his sunglasses on, and moved toward the table with casual ease. Donnie spotted him when he was still ten feet away, and his color washed from ashen to chalk.

'Starting the party without me, Tulane?' Nick said, sliding onto the banquette beside him.

Donnie bolted sideways, nearly spilling his drink. 'What the hell are you doing here, Fourcade?' he demanded in a harsh whisper.

Nick raised his eyebrows above the rims of his sunglasses. 'Why, seeing for myself what a lying weasel you are, Donnie. I'd say I'm disappointed in you, but it's no less than I expected.'

He reached inside his jacket for cigarettes and Donnie's eyes widened at the sight of the Ruger.

'This is a no-smoking table,' he said stupidly.

Nick stared straight at him through the mirrored lenses of the shades and lit up.

Marcotte watched the exchange with mild amusement, relaxed, his forearms resting on the tabletop. He didn't look the least out of place in the setting. In a simple white shirt and conservative tie, he couldn't have been pegged for a business tycoon. In contrast, even the simplest bumpkin would recognize the muscle for what he was. The loan-a-thug turned in his seat for a better view, revealing a smashed nose, held to his face with adhesive tape. Brutus. Nick smiled at him and nodded.

'This is a private meeting, Nick,' Marcotte said pleasantly. He glanced at Donnie. 'Nick here has a bit of a learning disability, Donnie. He needs to be taught all his lessons twice.'

Nick blew smoke out his nostrils. 'Oh, no. Me, I learned my lesson the first time. That's why I'm here tonight as adviser to my good friend Donnie, who bailed me out of jail not long ago.'

'A poor choice,' Marcotte said.

'Well, Donnie, he's none too bright for a college boy. Are you, Tulane? I keep telling him he doesn't want the devil playing in his backyard, but I don't know if he's hearing me. He's too preoccupied by the sound of money fanning in his ear.'

'I don't feel well,' Donnie muttered, starting to rise. Sweat beaded on his pasty forehead.

Nick put a hand on his shoulder. 'Sit down, Donnie. Last time I saw you near a toilet, you had your head in it. We don't want you to drown ... just yet.'

'Adding coercion to your list of crimes now, Nick?' Marcotte said with an indulgent chuckle.

'Not at all. I'm just pointing out to my friend Donnie here the disadvantages of doing business with you. The scrutiny a deal with you would bring to bear on him and on the untimely death of his lovely wife.'

Tears welled in Donnie's eyes. 'I didn't kill Pam.'

His denial drew stares from two other tables.

Nick's gaze never wavered from Marcotte. He tapped the ash off his cigarette into Donnie's drink and took another long drag. 'You don't have to be guilty of something to have it ruin your life, Tulane. Nor do the guilty necessarily pay for their crimes. See how well I learn my lessons, Marcotte?

'It looks cold, Donnie – you trying to swing this deal,' he went on. 'Hell, that business ain't even yours to sell yet, technically speaking. This looks like something my friends in the sheriff's office would want to go over with a fine-tooth comb. They'll wanna dig through all your records and whatnot. You been wheeling and dealing for a while now. Who knows what else they might come up with?

'Folks catch wind of that kind of thing, they start thinking maybe you cheated them, and then they wanna sue. And, hey, you got all that money what Duval Marcotte paid you, so why shouldn't they try to get themselves a piece of it? Meanwhile, the Davidsons are talking to a lawyer about custody of your daughter.

'You see where this is going, Donnie?' he asked, still looking at Marcotte. 'Donnie, he doesn't always see the big picture. He fails to recognize the potential for disaster.'

'And you, Nick my boy, see that train coming and throw yourself in front of it anyway,' Marcotte said, shaking his head. 'You were born out of time, Fourcade. Chivalry went out a while back. It's called foolhardiness now.'

'Really?' The picture of disinterest, Nick crushed his smoke out and dropped the butt in Donnie's whiskey. 'I don't keep up with trends.'

'I have to go to the bathroom,' Donnie muttered, turning gray around the gills.

Nick slid out of the banquette. 'Take your time, Tulane. Do some thinking while you're in there.'

Donnie shuffled away from the table with one hand pressed to his stomach. Nick sat back down and stared at Marcotte. Marcotte sat back against the padded seat and crossed his arms. His dark eyes shone like polished stones.

'I believe you may have succeeded in ruining my chances for a deal, Nick.'

'I sincerely hope so. It's the least I can do, all things considered.'

'Yes, I suppose it is. And the least I can do is be gracious in defeat. For the moment.'

'You're giving up easily.'

Marcotte gave a shrug, pursing his lips. 'Que *sera sera*. It's been a diversion. I would never have come out here looking if it hadn't been for you rousing my interest, Nick. I'll draw

494

some satisfaction from knowing you have that to dwell on. And you know what? Coming out here has just reminded me how much I like the country. Simple life, simple pleasures. I just may come back.'

Nick said nothing. He had thought he'd cut Marcotte out of his life like a cancer. But just enough of the old obsession had remained to pull him back across that line, and now Marcotte would be drooling at the edge of his sanctuary like a wolf biding his time.

The waitress edged toward the table, looking at Nick with suspicion. 'Can I get you a drink, sir?'

'No, thank you,' he said, easing himself up. 'I won't be staying. The company here turns my stomach.'

Donnie was bent over the sink, crying and gagging when Nick entered the men's room.

'You fit to drive home, Tulane?'

'I'm ruined, you son of a bitch!' he sobbed. 'I'm fucking broke! Marcotte would have advanced me money.'

'And you'd still be ruined – for all the reasons I just told you out there. You don't listen so good, Donnie,' Nick said, washing his hands. Every encounter with Marcotte left him feeling as if he'd been handling snakes. 'There's better ways out of trouble than selling your soul.'

'You don't understand. Pam's life insurance isn't coming through. I've lost two big jobs and I've got a loan coming due. I need money.'

'Quit your whining and be a man for once,' Nick snapped. 'You don't have your wife here to bail your ass out anymore. It's time to grow up, Donnie.'

He cranked a paper towel out of the machine on the wall, dried his hands carefully. 'Listen – you don't know it, but me, I'm the best friend you've got tonight, Tulane. But I'm telling you, cher, I find out you've turned on me in this, I find out you're trying to get back in bed with Marcotte, I find out you took that shot at Broussard the other night, you're sure as hell gonna wish I'd never been born.'

Donnie leaned his head against the mirror, too weak to

stand unaided. 'I been wishing that for days now, Fourcade.'

Behind him, Nick heard the men's room door swish open. He could see the reflection of Brutus in a wedge of mirror. He shifted his weight to the balls of his feet and remained still.

'Everything all right in here, Mr. Bichon?' the thug asked.

'Hardly,' Donnie moaned.

'Everything's fine, Brutus,' Nick said. 'Mr. Bichon, he's just having some growing pains, that's all.'

'I didn't ask you, coonass.' Reaching inside his black jacket, Brutus pulled out a set of brass knuckles and slipped them over the thick fingers of his right hand. Nick watched in the mirror.

'I wouldn't go knocking family trees, King Kong,' he said. 'You're about to fall out of yours.'

He spun and kicked as Brutus stepped toward him, catching the big man on the side of the head. Brutus hit the paper towel machine face-first with a crash that reverberated off the tile walls. Blood gushed from his nose and mouth, and he dropped to the floor, out cold.

Nick shook his head as the manager rushed into the room to stare in horror, first at his broken towel dispenser, then at the mass of bleeding humanity lying on the tile.

'Floor's wet,' Nick said, moving casually for the door. 'He slipped.'

44

Big Dick Dugas and the Iota Playboys cranked up the volume on their battle-scarred guitars and launched into a fast and frantic rendition of 'C'est Chaud.' A cheer went up from the crowd and bodies began to move – young, old, drunk, sober, black, white, poor, and planter class.

There were easily a thousand people in the five-block length of La Rue France cordoned off for the annual event, all of them moving some part of their anatomy to the beat. Mouths smiling, faces shiny with the uncommon heat of the evening and the joy of liberation. The workweek was over, the five-day party was just starting, and the source of a collective fear had been obliterated from the planet.

The party atmosphere struck Annie as grotesque, a reaction she resented mightily. She had always loved the Mardi Gras festivities in Bayou Breaux. Unfettered pagan fun and frivolity before the dour days of Lent. The street dance, the food stands, the vendors selling balloons and cheap trinkets, the pageants and parade. It was a rite of spring and a thread of continuity that had run through her life from her earliest memories.

She remembered coming to the dance as a child, running around with her Doucet cousins while her mother stood off just to the side of the crowd, enjoying the music in her own quiet way, but never a part of the mass joy.

The memory brought an extra pang tonight. Annie felt she was in her own way apart from the rest of the revelers here. Not because of the uniform she was wearing, but because of the things she had experienced in the last ten days.

A burly bearded man tricked out in a pink dress and pearls, a cigar jammed into the corner of his mouth, tried to grab hold of her hand and drag her off the sidewalk into a two-step. Annie waved him off.

'I'm not that kind of girl!' she called, grinning.

'Neither am I, darlin'!' He flipped his skirt up, flashing a glimpse of baggy heart-covered boxer shorts.

The crowd around him roared and hooted. A woman dressed as a male construction worker gave a wolf whistle and tried to pinch his ass. He howled, grabbed her, and they danced off.

Annie managed a chuckle at the scene. As she started to turn away, she was detained by another costumed partyer, this one dressed in black with a white painted smiling mask, the classic theatrical portrayal of comedy. He held out a single rose to her and bowed stiffly when she accepted it.

'Thank you.' She tucked the stem of the rose through her duty belt, next to her baton as she walked away.

She loved the street dance less as a cop than as a civilian. Personnel from both the Bayou Breaux PD and the sheriff's office worked the Carnival events. A united front against hooliganism. The standing rule was to break up the fistfights, but arrest only the drunks stupid enough to swing at the cops. Anyone with a weapon went in the can for the night, and the DA's office had their pick of the litter come morning.

But even with the drunks and knife fights, the exuberant innocence of a small-town celebration usually outweighed the bad moments. Tonight it seemed that everyone was celebrating the shooting of Willard Roache more than they were celebrating Carnival. The air was crackling with the heady excitement of victorious vigilantism, and that struck Annie as a dangerous thing.

Crime in South Louisiana tended to be personal, confrontational. Folks here had their own sense of justice and an abundant supply of firearms. She thought of Marcus Renard and the incidents at his home in the past ten days. The shooting, the rock through the window. If he hadn't staged those incidents himself, if they had been the work of one of the many people who thought Fourcade should have been allowed to finish him off, then there was a real possibility that same someone might get carried away in the excitement of one criminal's demise and try for another's. And who in the SO, besides her, would even care?

God, maybe I am his guardian angel, after all.

The thought was not a comforting one, but neither could she let it go. The deeper she went into this case, the more complicated it became, the more options there seemed to be. It only became clearer to Annie that justice needed to be conducted through the proper channels, not doled out at random by the uninformed.

How popular that opinion would make her tonight, she thought, when everyone in the parish was heralding Kim Young as a heroine of the common folk.

She tried to look for a bright side to the shooting, thinking what a powder keg this street dance would have been if not for Kim Young and her trusty cut-down. The majority of revelers came to the dance in full Mardi Gras regalia: costumes, makeup, masks that ran the gamut from dead presidents to monsters to medieval fertility gods. Sequins and feather masks were in abundance. The celebration had its roots in ancient spring fertility rites and had retained a pervasive air of sexuality down through the centuries. Though it wasn't nearly so bawdy out here in the Cajun parishes as it was in the French Quarter of New Orleans, there would be plenty of flashes of bare skin before the night was through.

To think of a predator like Willard Roache running loose in this atmosphere was enough to make Annie's blood run cold. A rapist in a Mardi Gras mask amid a sea of masks ... and a heavily armed citizenry twitching at every shadow ... They could certainly have ended up with a morgue full of bullet-ridden corpses instead of one dead Roache.

Annie edged her way along between the crowd and the storefronts, keeping her eyes open for anyone taking an undue interest in merchandise in the display windows. A knot of little boys of nine or ten stampeded past, blasting squirt guns. She fended off a stream with her hand, turning away and coming face-to-face again with the white painted mask.

He stood no more than a foot from her, near enough that she started at the sight of him.

'Do I know you?' she asked.

His painted face grinned at her as he handed her the string of a heart-shaped helium balloon. He pressed his hands to his chest dramatically then held them out to her, symbolically giving her his heart.

Puzzled, Annie sized up her masked admirer – his height, his build. Realization dawned with an eerie chill.

'Marcus?'

He raised a finger to his painted mouth and backed away, melting into the crowd, anonymous. But she knew who it was. It made perfect sense. The mask offered both freedom and secrecy. He hadn't been able to walk down the street in this town for months without drawing unwanted attention. Now he moved unnoticed past people who would have spat on him or worse had they known he was behind the smiling mask.

And what would the good townsfolk of Bayou Breaux do to her if they saw her taking romantic tokens from Marcus Renard? What would her fellow cops do? She would be further ridiculed and punished. They already had that in common, she and Marcus.

Annie looked at the balloon. He had given her his heart, and she had accepted it. God only knew how significant that would be in his mind. He wanted to believe she cared for him, just as he had wanted to believe Pam had cared for him. He believed the job was what kept her from him, just as he had believed Donnie had been the barrier between himself and Pam. Juliet and Romeo.

She handed the balloon to a little girl with a *Pocahontas*

T-shirt and chocolate all over her face, and moved down the street.

A clown in a rainbow fright wig staggered toward her on the narrow band of sidewalk. The painted smile was lopsided beneath a rubber hog snout. Annie stepped right. The clown moved with her. She stepped left the same time he did. She turned to the side to motion him past. He swayed toward her instead, hitting her shoulder and spilling his beer down the front of her uniform.

'Hey, Bozo, watch it!' she snapped.

'Sorry, ociffer!' he declared, unrepentant.

From her left side a second drunk stumbled into her, this one wearing a Reagan mask with a vacuous idiot grin. Another eight ounces of beer cascaded down her back.

'Shit!' she yelped. 'Watch where you're going!'

'Sorry, ociffer!' he said with singsong insincerity. He looked at the clown and the pair of them chuckled like Beavis and Butthead.

Annie glared at the rubber face, which sat atop a pair of bony shoulders. She looked down at the skinny stick legs in tight jeans.

'Son of a bitch!' she swore, grabbing hold of him by the shirtfront. 'Mullen, is that you inside that empty head?'

The clown hollered, 'Shit!'

Reagan stumbled back from her, pulling himself free. The two plunged into the gyrating crowd, laughing.

'Dammit!' Annie said, half under her breath, plucking at her saturated shirtfront.

The beer trickled down into the waistband of her pants, front and back. It ran down inside her body armor in front and soaked through the back. Anyone getting a whiff of her was going to think the stories about her recent sad decline into alcoholism were more than just rumors.

'Sarge, it's Broussard,' she said into the two-way as she started up the street. 'I just got doused. I'm 10 – 7 at the station. Back in a few. Out.'

'Hurry the hell up.'

She made her way north along the back side of the crowd, intending to cut east at the corner of Seventh, where she had parked her cruiser on the side street.

'Annie!'

A.J.'s voice caught her ear and she pulled up. He had left three messages on her machine at home and had tried to get her at work twice since she had been shot at, and she had avoided calling him back. She didn't want to explain. She didn't want to lie. She didn't want him trying to tie a knot in the connection she had severed between them.

He came toward her from the yellow light of a vendor's stand, a red-checked cardboard basket of fried oysters cradled in one hand, a bottle of Abita in the other. He was still in his suit from the day's business, though his tie was jerked loose.

'I thought you were off the street.'

Annie shrugged. 'I go where they tell me. I'm on my way to the station now. I just got a beer bath.'

'I'll walk you to your car.'

He fell in step beside her and she glanced up at him, trying to gauge his mood. His face was drawn and a deep line dug in between his brows. The noise of the band and the crowd faded as they turned the corner and walked away from the bright yellow light of the party.

'Why'd you work late?' Annie asked. 'Friday night. Big dance and all.'

'I ah sorta lost my standing date.'

She kicked herself mentally for opening that door.

'Task force moved at the speed of light to get the background on Roache, didn't they?'

'Yeah,' she said. 'Too bad they couldn't have found that enthusiasm earlier. Maybe they could have nailed his ass after Jennifer Nolan.'

'You would have,' he said, setting his supper on the hood of her cruiser.

'I would have tried, at least. That's the thing that galls me most about Stokes – he skates over everything and still

502

comes out smelling like a rose. I wouldn't care how big a jerk he was if he did the job.'

A.J. shrugged. 'Some people do the job, some people live the job.'

'I don't live the job,' she snapped, not liking the correlation to Fourcade that A.J. couldn't possibly have known. 'But I hustle when I'm on it. That should count for something.'

'It should.'

But they both knew the thing that would count for her would be taking the witness stand on Thursday. Annie looked away and sighed.

'So, are you gonna tell me what that was all about the other night?' he asked. 'Someone taking a shot at you? My God, Annie.'

'Trying to scare me, that's all,' she said, still avoiding his gaze.

'That's *all*? You could have been killed!'

'It was a scare tactic. I'm not very popular as a witness for the prosecution.'

'You think it was Fourcade?' he demanded. 'That bastard! I'll get his bail revoked –'

'It wasn't Fourcade.'

'How do you know that?'

'It just wasn't,' she insisted. 'Leave it alone, A.J. You don't know anything about this.'

'Because you won't tell me! Christ, somebody tries to shoot you and I have to hear about it from Uncle Sos! You don't even bother to call me back when I try to check up on you –'

'Look,' she said, reining back her temper. 'Can we have this fight another time? I'm 10–7. Hooker's gonna chew me out if I don't go and get back.'

'I don't want to fight,' A.J. said wearily. He caught hold of her hand and hung on when she would have backed away. 'Just a minute, Annie. Please.'

'I'm on duty.'

503

'You're 10–7. Personal time. This is personal.'

She drew in a breath to protest and he pressed a finger against her lips. His expression was earnest in the filtered light of the streetlamp.

'I need to say this, Annie. I care about you. I don't want to see you hurt by anyone for any reason. I don't want to see you taking crazy chances. I want to take care of you. I want to protect you. I don't know who this other guy is –'

'A.J., don't –'

'And I don't know what he's got that I don't. But I love you, Annie. And I'm not gonna just walk away from this, from *us*. I love you.'

His admission stunned her silent. They hadn't been that close lately. There had been a time when she had expected him to say it, and he never had. Now he wanted her to say it and she couldn't – not with the meaning he wanted. The story of their lives. They were never quite in the same place at the same time. He wanted something from her she couldn't give, and she wanted a man she might just send on the road to prison in a week's time.

'I know you better than anyone, Annie,' he murmured. 'I won't give you up without a fight.'

He lowered his head and kissed her, slowly, sweetly, deeply. He pulled her against him, heedless of her beer-soaked shirt, and pressed her to him – breast to chest, belly to groin. Longing to regret.

'God, you think you mean it, don't you?' he whispered as he raised his head. 'That it's over.'

The hurt in his eyes brought tears to Annie's. 'I'm sorry, A.J.'

He shook his head. 'It's *not* over,' he pledged quietly. 'I won't let it be.'

Just like Donnie Bichon, Annie thought. Determined to hold on to Pam even after she'd served him with papers. Like Renard – seeing what he wanted to see, bending reality to open possibilities for the outcome he wanted. The difference was that she felt only frustration with A.J.'s bullheadedness, not fear. He hadn't crossed the line from tenacity to terror.

'Fair warning,' he said. Stepping back from her, he picked up his fried oysters and his beer. 'I'll see you around.'

Annie sat back against the car as he walked away. 'I need this like I need a hole in my head.'

She gave herself a moment to try to clear away the thought that she had somehow managed to become part of a romantic triangle, an idea that was too absurd for words. Instead, she tried to focus once again on the world around her: the noise of the band, the intermittent bang of firecrackers, the warm moist air, the silver light from the streetlamp, and the darkness beyond its reach.

The sensation of being watched crawled over her. The feeling that she suddenly wasn't alone on the deserted side street. She straightened slowly away from the car and strained to see into the shadows at the back of the paint store she had parked beside. At the mouth of the dark alley a white face seemed to float in the air.

'Marcus?' Annie said, straightening away from the cruiser, moving cautiously toward the building.

'You *kissed* him,' he said. 'That filthy lawyer. You *kissed* him!'

Anger vibrated in his voice. He took a step toward her.

'Yes, he kissed me,' Annie said. Pulse racing, she tried to settle her hands casually on her hips – the right one within reach of her baton, a can of Mace, the butt of her Sig. The tip of her middle finger pressed against the stem of the rose Renard had given her and a thorn bit deep into her skin, the pain sharp and surprising.

'Does that upset you, Marcus? That I let him kiss me?'

'He's – he's one of *them*!' he stammered, the words slurring as he forced them through his teeth. 'He's against me. Like Pritchett. Like Fourcade. How could you do this, Annie?'

'I'm one of "them" too, Marcus,' she said simply. 'I've told you that all along.'

He shook his head in denial, the grinning mask a

macabre contrast to the shock and fury vibrating from him in waves. 'No. You're trying to help me. The work you've done. The way you've come to my aid. You saved my life – twice!'

'And I keep telling you, Marcus, I'm only doing my job.'

'I'm not your job,' he said. 'You came to help me time and again when you didn't have to. You didn't want anyone to know. I thought ...'

He trailed off, unable to bring himself to say the words. Annie waited, marveling at the ease with which he had turned everything in his mind to fit his own wishes. It was crazy, and yet he sounded perfectly rational, as if any man would have made the same assumptions, as if he had every right to be angry with her for leading him on.

'You thought what?' she prodded.

'I thought you were special.'

'Like you thought Pam was special?'

'You're just like her after all,' he muttered, reaching into the deep pocket of his baggy black trousers.

Annie's hand moved to the butt of the Sig and slipped the lock strap free. A thousand people were having a party two hundred feet away, and she was standing alone with a probable murderer. The noise of the band seemed to fade to nothing.

'How do you mean?' she asked while her mind raced forward. Would he pull a knife? Would she have to take him down right here, right now? That wasn't how she thought it would go down. She didn't know what she had expected. A taped confession? The murder weapon surrendered without a fight?

'She took my friendship,' he said. 'She took my heart. And then she turned on me. And you're doing the same.'

'She was afraid of you, Marcus. That was you calling her, prowling around her house, slashing her tires – wasn't it?'

'I would never have hurt her,' he said, and Annie wondered if the answer was denial or guilt. 'She took my gifts. I thought she enjoyed my company.'

'And when she told you to get lost, you thought what – that maybe you could scare her anonymously and offer her comfort in person?'

'No. They turned her against me. She couldn't see how much I really cared. I tried to show her.'

'Who turned her against you?'

'Her sorry excuse for a husband. And Stokes. They both wanted her and they turned her against me. What's your excuse, Annie?' he asked, bitterly. 'You want that lawyer? He's using you to do his dirty work for him. Can't you see that?'

'He's got nothing to do with this, Marcus. I want to solve Pam's murder. I told you that from the first.'

'You'll be sorry,' he said quietly. 'In the end, you'll be sorry.'

He started to pull his hand from his pocket. Heart pounding, Annie pulled the Sig and pointed it at his chest.

'Slowly, Marcus,' she ordered.

Slowly he drew his hand free, balled into a fist, and held it out to the side.

'Whatever it is, drop it.'

He opened his fingers, letting fall something small that hit the sidewalk with a soft rattle. With her left hand, Annie pulled her flashlight from her belt and took a step closer, the Sig still raised. Renard moved back toward the alley.

'Stand right there.'

She swept the beam of the flashlight down on the concrete and it reflected back off a strand of gold chain, a necklace lying like a length of discarded string with a heart-shaped locket attached.

'I thought you were special,' he said again.

Annie holstered the Sig and picked the necklace up.

'Is this the necklace you tried to give Pam?'

He stared at her through the empty eyes of the smiling mask and took another step back from her. 'I don't have to answer your questions, Deputy Broussard,' he said coldly. 'And I believe I'm free to go.'

With that, he turned and went back down the alley.

'Great,' Annie said under her breath, closing her fist on the locket.

Her edge with him had been her similarity to Pam, the woman he had fallen in love with. She had gained his trust, his respect, his attraction. In a heartbeat that was gone. Now she was more like Pam, the woman he may have butchered.

The two-way crackled against her hip and she jumped half a foot. 'Broussard? Where the fuck are you? Are you back on or what?'

Annie plucked at her wet shirt and bit back a groan. 'On my way, Sarge. Out.'

Sucking on the fingertip the thorn had lacerated, she wove her way through the crowd across France to the old Canal gas station. The place had been closed since the oil bust, and the old pumps had been taken out long ago, leaving weeds to sprout where they had once stood. The BUSINESS OPPORTUNITY FOR SALE sign had been propped in the front window so long it had turned yellow. A herd of teenage boys in baggy clothes and backward baseball caps milled around on the cracked concrete, drinking Mountain Dew and smoking cigarettes. Eyeing Annie with suspicion, they scattered like a pack of scruffy young dogs as she passed through their midst.

She went to the side of the building, where a pay phone was still in service. She dialed Fourcade and flapped her wet shirtfront as the phone on the other end rang. His machine clicked on with a curt 'Leave a message'.

'It's Annie. I just had a run-in with Renard. It's a long story, but the bottom line is I might have pushed him over the edge. He said some things that make me nervous. Um – I'm stuck working the dance, then I'm going home. I'm off tomorrow. I'll see you when I see you.'

She hung up feeling vaguely sick. She may have pushed a killer over the line from love to hate. Now what?

She watched the party from the corner of the vacant

station, as removed from it as if she were standing behind a wall of glass. Inside her mind, she didn't hear the music of the band or the sounds from the crowd.

'I would never have hurt her.'

Not that he *hadn't* hurt Pam. He had made that verbal distinction before.

'She couldn't see how much I really cared. I tried to show her.'

How had he tried to show her? With his gifts or with the concern he had shown after he had scared her half to death? The same creepy, voyeuristic concern he had shown Annie when she'd told him about someone taking a shot at her.

'Were you alone? You must have been frightened … Having a stranger reach into your life and commit an act of violence – it's a violation. It's rape. You feel so vulnerable, so powerless … so alone … Don't you?'

Words of comfort that weren't comforting at all. He had made her feel vulnerable, made her feel violated, and he had done the same to Pam. She knew he had.

'I thought you were special.'

'Like you thought Pam was special?'

'You're just like her, after all … You'll be sorry … In the end, you'll be sorry.'

In the same way Pam must have been sorry? Sorry no one else could have seen the monster in him. Sorry no one had listened to her pleas for help. Sorry no one had heard her screams that night out on Pony Bayou.

Annie dug the necklace out of her pocket and held it up, watching the small gold locket sway back and forth. Renard had tried to give Pam a necklace for her birthday two weeks before she was killed.

'Officer Broussard?'

The soft voice broke Annie's concentration. She caught the locket in her fist and turned. Doll Renard stood beside her in a prison gray June Cleaver shirtwaist that had been intended for a woman with breasts and hips. In her hands she played nervously with the stem of a delicate butterfly-

509

shaped mask covered in iridescent sequins. The elegant beauty of the mask seemed at odds with the woman holding it – plain, unadorned, her mouth a bitter knot.

'Mrs. Renard. Can I help you?'

Doll glanced away, anxious. 'I don't know if you can. I swear, I don't know what I'm doing here. It's a nightmare, that's what. A terrible nightmare.'

'What is?'

Tears glazed across the woman's eyes. One hand left the stem of her mask to pat at her heart. 'I don't know. I don't know what to do. All this time I thought we'd been wronged. All this time. My boys are all I have, you know. Their father betrayed us, and now they're all I have in the world.'

Annie waited. In her previous meetings with Doll she had found the woman melodramatic and shrill, but the stress stretched taut in Doll Renard's voice now had the ring of genuineness. Her small, sharp nose was red at the tip, her eyes rimmed in crimson from crying.

'I knew motherhood would be a joy and a trial,' she said, rubbing a hankie under her nose. 'But all the joy of it has been robbed from me. And now I fear it's become a nightmare.' Tears skimmed down her thin, pale cheeks. 'I'm so afraid.'

'Afraid of what, Mrs. Renard?'

'Of Marcus,' she confessed. 'I'm afraid my son has done something terribly wrong.'

45

'Could we go somewhere and talk?' Doll asked, glancing anxiously around at the masked revelers that moved up and down the street. She raised her own mask to partially hide her face. 'Marcus is here somewhere. I don't want him to see me speaking to you. We had a terrible quarrel last night. It was horrible. I never left my bed today, I was so distraught. I don't know what to do. You've been so kind, so fair to us, I thought ...'

She paused, fighting the need to cry. Annie put a hand on her shoulder, torn between a woman's sympathy and a cop's excitement.

'I'm afraid I'm on duty –' she began.

'I wouldn't ask – I didn't want to – Oh, dear ...' Doll raised a hand to her mouth and closed her eyes for a moment, working to compose herself. 'He's my son,' she said in a tortured whisper. 'I can't bear the thought that he might have –' Breaking off again, she shook her head. 'I shouldn't have come here. I'm sorry.'

She turned to go, shoulders hunched.

'Wait,' Annie said.

If Marcus Renard's mother had something, anything, that could connect him to the murder, she couldn't put off getting it. It was clear Doll's conscience had won the internal battle to bring her to this point, and just as clear that in a heartbeat she could back away in order to save her son.

'Where are you parked?'

'Down the street. Near Po' Richard's.'

'I'll meet you down there in five minutes. How's that?'

She shook her head a little. Her whole body seemed to be trembling. 'I don't know. I think this is a mistake. I shouldn't have –'

'Mrs Renard,' Annie said, touching her arm. 'Please don't back down now. If Marcus has done something bad, he needs to be stopped. It can't go on. You can't let it.'

She held her breath as Doll closed her eyes again, looking within herself for an answer that had to be tearing her mother's heart in two.

'No,' she whispered to herself. 'It can't go on. I can't let it go on.'

'I'll meet you at your car,' Annie said. 'We can have a cup of coffee. Talk. We'll sort it all out. What kind of car do you drive?'

Doll sniffed into her handkerchief. 'It's gray,' she said, sounding resigned. 'A Cadillac.'

Annie couldn't find Hooker in the sea of people, which was just as well. She didn't want him to see her going off in the opposite direction of the station. Ducking into a door well on the side street, she called him on the two-way to tell him she'd been stricken ill.

'What the hell's wrong with you, Broussard? You been drinking?'

'No, sir. Must be that stomach flu going around.' She paused to groan for effect. 'It's awful, Sarge. Out.'

Hooker swore his usual blue streak, but let her off. Deputies vomiting in public were bad for the image of the department. 'If I hear you been drinking, I'll suspend your ass! Out.'

Banishing the threat from her mind, she went to the cruiser and dumped the radio, afraid the chatter might frighten or distract Doll. Grabbing her minicassette recorder, she shoved it in a pants pocket and hustled down the dark side street toward Po' Richard's.

Doll Renard drove a gray Cadillac. If the passenger's side was damaged, then Marcus was the one who had terrorized her on the road that night. That would confirm Annie's Jekyll and Hyde theory. The adrenaline rush of finally catching a break was incredible. She felt almost light-headed with it. Renard's own mother was going to give him up. To her. Because of the work *she* had done on the case. Losing Marcus's trust wouldn't matter.

As she hurried down the sidewalk between closed businesses and parked cars, she tensed at every shadow, bolted past the openings to alleys. Marcus was lurking somewhere, hurt and angry over what he saw as her betrayal.

God only knew what he might do if he saw her with his mother. The relationship there was too twisted to fathom. The mother relying on the support of a son whom she never ceased to criticize and belittle; the grown man staying out of obligation to a woman he resented to the marrow of his bones. The line between their love and hate had to be a hairbreadth. What would it trigger in him to know his mother was about to commit the ultimate betrayal? The rage, the pain, would be incredible.

Annie had seen what his rage had done to Pam Bichon.

The car was parked at the curb, just east of Po' Richard's. Doll Renard paced beside it, one arm banded across her waist as if her stomach hurt, the other hand rubbing her sternum. Even in the poor light that reached over from the restaurant Annie could see the scars along the side of the Cadillac.

'Did you have an accident, Mrs. Renard?'

Doll looked blank, then glanced at the car. 'Oh, that,' she said, moving again. 'Marcus must have done that. I rarely drive. It's such a *big* car. I can't imagine why he bought me such a *big* car. So conspicuous. It's vulgar, really. And difficult to park. It preys on my nerves to drive it.

'I've developed a slight palsy from my nerves, you know. You can't imagine the strain it's been. Wondering, wanting to believe ... Then last night ... I can't stand it anymore.'

'Why don't we sit down and talk about it?' Annie suggested.

'Yes. Yes,' Doll repeated almost to herself, as if to reinforce the decision she had made. 'I took the liberty of getting coffee. It's just over here on this table.'

513

The cheap picnic tables that sat out in front of the restaurant were deserted and poorly lit. A hand-lettered sign in the front window announced: CLOSED for CARNIVAL. TAKE out ORDER'S ONLY.

Doll settled on the bench, fussing with her skirt like a debutante at a cotillion. Annie took her seat, stirred her coffee, and tested it. Dark and bitter, as always; hot but drinkable. She took a long sip, wanting the caffeine to burn off the fatigue of too many late nights. She needed to be sharp now, though it wouldn't do to appear overeager. She left her notebook in her shirt pocket. Under the table, she pressed the record button on the minicassette recorder.

'I'm not proud of this,' Doll began. She rested one hand on the table, her handkerchief clutched at the ready. 'He's my son. My loyalty should be to my family.'

'Letting this go on won't be in the interest of your family, Mrs. Renard. You're doing what's best.'

'That's what I keep telling myself. I have to do what's best.' She paused to sip at her coffee and compose herself.

Annie took a drink and waited, rubbing absently at the cut on her fingertip. She sat with her back to the restaurant and a view of the surrounding area. Without turning her head, she scanned the street, the sidewalk, the vacant lot beyond Po' Richard's property, trying to make out every shadow. No sign of Marcus, but then he was very good at staying just out of reach, just out of sight. She imagined him watching them now, his anger building toward the boiling point.

'It's been very difficult for me,' Doll said, 'raising the two boys on my own. Especially with Victor's difficulties. The state tried to take him away from me once and put him in a home. I wouldn't have it. He'll be with me 'til I die. He's my child, my burden to bear. I brought him into this world the way he is. I blamed myself for his condition, even though the doctors say it's no one's fault. How can we truly know what gets passed along from one generation to the next?'

Annie made no comment, but thought fleetingly of her

514

own mother and the father she'd never known. 'What ever became of Mr Renard?'

Doll's face hardened. 'Claude betrayed us. Years ago. And now here I sit, about to betray my son.'

'You shouldn't think of it that way, Mrs. Renard. Why don't you tell me what it is you think Marcus has done wrong.'

'I don't know where to begin,' she said, looking down at her crumpled handkerchief.

'You said you had a fight with Marcus last night. What was that about?'

'You, I'm afraid.'

'Me?'

'I'm sure you realize Marcus has become quite taken with you. He does that, you see. He – he gets something in his head and there's no changing it. I can see it happening all over again with you. He's convinced there could be something ... *personal* between the two of you.'

'I've told him that's not possible.'

'It won't matter. It never has.'

'This has happened before?'

'Yes. With the Bichon woman. And before her – when we lived in Baton Rouge –'

'Elaine Ingram?'

'Yes. Love at first sight, he called it. Within a week of meeting her, he was completely preoccupied. He followed her everywhere. Called her day and night. Lavished her with gifts. It was embarrassing.'

'I thought she returned his feelings.'

'For a time, but it became too much for her. He did the same with that Bichon woman. He suddenly decided he had to have her, even though she wanted no part of him. And I can see it starting again, with you. I confronted him about it.'

'What did he say?'

'He became irate and went into his workroom. No one is supposed to disturb him there, but I followed him,' she

515

confessed. 'I never wanted to believe it was anything more than infatuation, what he felt for that woman, but I confess, I'd had a premonition. I'm very sensitive that way. I'd had these *feelings*, but I just wouldn't believe them.

'I watched Marcus from the door without him knowing. He went to a cupboard and got some things out of it, and I *knew*. I just *knew*.'

'What things?'

Doll bowed her head over the pocketbook in her lap. She reached into the bag and closed her hand around something, hesitating, withdrawing it slowly.

As she held the small picture frame out, Annie felt a strange rush shoot up her arms and into her head. She gripped one arm of the chair as the rush became a wave of dizziness. The picture frame that had gone missing from Pam Bichon's office. One of the items the detectives had searched for in order to at least tie Renard to the stalking charges. None of the items had ever been found.

Annie took it now and looked at it in the artificial light draining out the restaurant's front window. The frame was a delicate antique silver filigree, the glass inside it cracked. The photo was no more than two inches by three inches, but portrayed in that small space was a wealth of emotion – the love between a mother and child. Josie couldn't have been more than five, sitting on her mother's lap, gazing up at her with an angelic smile. Pam, her arms wrapped around her baby, smiling down at her with absolute adoration.

Marcus Renard had stolen this photograph and destroyed the relationship portrayed within it. He had taken a mother from her child. He had extinguished the spirit of a woman who had loved and had been loved by so many people.

The dizziness swooped through her again. A reaction to the photograph, Annie supposed. Or to the caffeine. She felt vaguely ill ... at the sure knowledge that the man who had become infatuated with her was in fact the man who had committed unspeakable acts against the woman in this photograph. Fourcade had been right all along: the trail, the logic, led back to Renard.

'Marcus stole that, didn't he?' Doll said.

'Yes.'

'There were other things too, but I was afraid to take them. I believe he's stolen things from me,' she admitted. 'A cameo that was in my mother's family. A locket I'd had for years – since Victor was born. God only knows what he did with them.'

God and me, Annie thought, shuddering inwardly. And Pam Bichon. And probably Elaine Ingram before her. A clammy chill ran across her skin. She worked to pull in a deep breath of the humid night air, and stared down at the photograph that blurred a little before her eyes as the dizziness tipped through her again.

'I didn't want to believe he would do it again,' Doll said. 'The preoccupation and all.'

'Do you think he killed those women, Mrs. Renard?' Annie asked, the words sticking on her tongue. She took another drink of her coffee to clear the taste of the question. How awful for a mother to think her son was a murderer.

Doll pressed her hand over her face and began to weep, her body quivering. 'He's my son! He's all I have. I don't want to lose him!'

And yet she'd brought forward the evidence.

'I'm sorry,' Annie murmured. 'But we'll have to take this to the sheriff.'

She pushed her chair back and stood, swaying unsteadily on her feet, the dizziness swarming around her head like a cloud of bees. She felt as if she might just float off the ground, and had no control over whether she would or would not. As she stepped away from the table the ground seemed to dip beneath her feet, and she staggered.

'Oh, my goodness!' Doll Renard's voice sounded far away. 'Are you all right, Deputy Broussard?'

'Uh, I'm a little dizzy,' Annie mumbled.

'Perhaps you should sit back down?'

'No, I'll be fine. Too much caffeine, that's all. We need to get to the sheriff.'

She attempted another step and went down hard on one knee. The picture frame fell from her hand.

'Oh, dear!' Doll gasped. 'Let me help you!'

'This is embarrassing,' Annie said, steadying herself against the older woman as she rose. 'I'm so sorry.'

Doll sniffed and wrinkled her nose. 'Have you been drinking, Deputy?'

'No, no, that was an assident.' Alarm jumped through her at the sound of her own voice, the words slurred and indistinct. Her body felt heavy, as if she were moving through a vat of Jell-O. 'I'm just not feeling well. We'll go to the station. I'll be fine.'

They moved slowly toward the Cadillac, Doll Renard on Annie's right, supporting her. The woman was so much stronger than she looked, Annie thought. Or maybe it was just that she suddenly had no strength at all. An electric buzzing vibrated in her arms and legs. The fingertip she had pricked on the rose stem throbbed like a beating heart.

The rose thorn. The rose Marcus had given her.

Poisoned. God, she'd never expected that. But it was certainly poetic that a token of love would become an instrument of death when the love was spurned. He would think that way, the twisted, sick son of a bitch.

'Mizzuz Renard?' she said as she collapsed into the passenger's seat of the car. 'I think maybe we shhhould go to the hossspital. I think I might be dying.'

He wanted to kill her. He wanted to put his hands around Annie Broussard's throat and watch her face as he choked her. She had played him for a fool. The last joke would be on her. The violent fantasy splashed in vivid color through Marcus's mind as he pushed his way through the crowd.

The noise of the party was a discordant cacophony in his ears. The lights and colors were too bright, too garish against the black of night and the black of his mood. Faces loomed in at him, laughing mouths and hideous masks. He stumbled into a Ronald Reagan pretender, spilling the man's beer in a geyser onto the sidewalk.

'Fucking drunk!' Reagan shouted. 'Watch where you're going!'

In retaliation, the man shoved him hard, and Marcus careened into another reveler in a Zorro mask and a porkpie hat. Stokes.

Stokes stumbled backward, feet scrambling. Marcus fell with him, fell on him amid the forest of legs. He wished he had a knife. He imagined himself stabbing Stokes as they fell, then getting up and walking away before anyone realized.

'Stupid motherfucker!' Stokes yelled, getting up.

Before Marcus could right himself, Stokes booted him in the ribs. Holding himself, Marcus struggled to his feet and kept going, half doubled over, laughter ringing behind him. He pressed on through the crowd, then turned the corner and hurried down the side street toward Bowen & Briggs.

The thick, humid air burned in his lungs. His chest felt banded with steel, the pressure crushing against his cracked ribs. Small, sharp pains burst through him with every breath. His face was on fire. He tore off the painted mask and threw it in the gutter. It was no disguise compared to the mask Annie had worn. Betrayal with the lawyer was the least of her crimes. The slut. He had overlooked and rationalized and made excuses for her, sure that she would see in the end how right it could be between them. She deserved to be punished for what she'd put him through. He punished her in his mind as the emotions tore through him. Love, rage, hate. She would be sorry. In the end, she would be sorry.

He felt as if he'd been eviscerated. Why did this have to happen to him time and again? Why couldn't the women he loved love him in return? Why did his feelings grab hold so hard and refuse to let go? Love, passion, need, need,

need. He was an otherwise normal man. He was intelligent. He had talents. He had a good job. Why did his need have to overwhelm him again and again?

As he let himself into the Volvo, tears rolled down his face, scalding with both pain and shame. His body was rigid and trembling with anger, the tension magnifying his various injuries, the physical pain further humiliating him. What kind of man was he? The kind other men kicked and scorned, the kind women sneered at, the kind women sought restraining orders against. He didn't think he could endure it any longer. The emotions were too much, too big, too painful. And in the back of his head he could hear his mother's mocking voice, telling him he was pathetic.

He *was* pathetic. That truth nearly crushed him with its weight.

He was sobbing as he passed the drive to the house where Pam had died. Her death would hang over him like a shadow for the rest of his life.

What kind of life was this to lead? A suspected murderer, a pathetic wretch living with his mother, spurned again and again by the women he loved. How many times had he wished himself away from here, envisioned a better life – with Elaine, with Pam, with Annie? But he would never go, and that better life would never happen. He would never live on the Gulf in a beach house and spend his evenings with Annie or any other woman. He would only become more pathetic, more isolated, be more loathed. What was the point?

He turned the Volvo down his driveway and gunned the engine. A sense of urgency had joined the other emotions writhing inside him like snakes. He slammed the car into park alongside the house and went inside.

Victor sat on the landing of the front stairs, wearing one of their mother's feather masks and rocking himself. He sprang to his feet and thundered down the steps, rushing to within inches of Marcus, shrieking, '*Red! Red! Red! Red!*'

'Stop it!' Marcus snapped, shoving him back. 'You'll wake Mother.'

'Not now. Enter out, Mother. Red! *Very* red!'

'What are you talking about?' Marcus demanded, cutting through the dining room. Against his will, he glanced at the wall. Of course the paint didn't match. 'It's after midnight. Mother is in bed.'

Victor shook his head vigorously. 'Then *and* now. Enter out, Mother. *Red!*'

'I don't know what you mean,' Marcus said impatiently. 'Where would she have gone? You know Mother doesn't drive at night. You're being ridiculous.'

Frustration grabbed hold of Victor as they reached the door to Marcus's rooms, and he stopped beside the wall and banged his head against it, keening in his throat.

Marcus grabbed hold of him by the shoulders. 'Victor, stop it! Go to your room and calm down. Go look at one of your books.'

'*Then* and now. Then *and* now. Then and *now!*' he chanted.

Marcus heaved a sigh, feeling a deep sadness for his brother. Poor Victor, locked inside his own mind. Then again, maybe Victor was the lucky one.

'Come along,' he said, quietly.

Taking Victor by the hand, he led him upstairs to his room, shushing him the whole way.

'*Red! Red!*' Victor harped in a whisper, like a bird with laryngitis.

'Nothing is red, Victor,' Marcus said, turning on the lamp.

Victor sat down on the edge of the bed and rocked himself from side to side. The peacock plumes that arched up from the corners of his mask bobbed like antennae. He looked absurd.

'I want you to count to five thousand by sixteenths,' Marcus said. 'And when you're done, you let me know. Can you do that?'

Victor stared past him, his eyes glassy. Chances were good that by the time he reached five thousand he would have forgotten the source of his distress.

Marcus left the room and paused, looking at the door to his mother's room farther down the hall. Of course she would be in there, the spider in her nest. She would always be there – physically, psychologically, metaphorically. There was only one escape for any of them.

Purposeful, he went down to his bedroom, locked the door behind him, and went to the drawer where he kept his Percodan. The doctor had written the prescription for seventy-five pills, probably hoping he would take them all at once. He'd taken a number of them in the days and nights since his beating, but there were plenty left. More than enough. If he could find the bottle. It was gone from the drawer.

Victor? No. If Victor had taken an overdose of Percodan, agitation would not be the result. He would be lethargic or dead – and better off, either way.

Marcus turned away from the bed and continued on into his workroom. He had cleaned up the mess his rage had created the night before. Everything was in its place once again, neat and tidy. The pencil portrait of Annie was on the drawing table. How fitting that it was torn, he thought, running his finger over the ragged edge of the paper. He imagined that the blood smeared across it was hers.

He turned to his worktable and the tools aligned with the precision of surgical instruments, contemplating the sharp razor's edge of the utility knife. Picking it up, he ran his thumb down the blade and watched his blood bloom along the cut, bright crimson. Tears came again, not at the physical pain, but at the enormous emotional burden of what he was about to do. He set the utility knife aside, disregarding it for his task. A butcher knife would serve the purpose, symbolically and literally. But first, he wanted the pills.

Going to the hidden panel in the wainscoting, he opened

the cupboard, confronting his past and his perversion. That was what other people would call his love for women who didn't want him – perversion, obsession. They didn't know what obsession was.

The small tokens he had taken from Elaine and Pam and Annie sat in clusters on a shelf. Memories of things that might have been. A wave of bittersweet nostalgia washed over him as he chose a beautiful glass paperweight that had belonged to Pam. He held it in his hands and touched it to his face. It was cool against his tears.

'Drop it, you slimy, sick bastard.' The voice was low and thick with hate. 'That belonged to my daughter.'

The paperweight rolled from Marcus's hands and fell to the floor as he looked up into the face of Hunter Davidson.

'I hope you're ready to go to hell,' the old man said, cocking the hammer on the .45 he held. 'Because I've come to send you off.'

46

He'd been right from the start. The trail, the logic, led back to Renard. And if he had maintained his focus, if he hadn't allowed his past to leach into his present, Marcotte would have remained a bad distant memory.

Nick lit a cigarette and drew hard on it, trying to burn the bitter taste of the truth from his mouth. The damage was done. He would deal with the repercussions if and when they arose. His focus now had to be on the matter at hand: Renard.

Annie had apparently yanked his chain a little too hard. She needed backup, which was what Nick now felt he should have been doing all along instead of running off half-cocked at shadows. *Focus. Control.* He had let himself become distracted when he should have stayed true to his gut. The trail, the logic, led back to Renard.

He parked on a side street and entered the Carnival crowd, eyes scanning the mob for Broussard. If she had pushed Renard over the edge, then she could be in trouble, and he had no intention of waiting until morning or even waiting until she was off duty to find out. Whatever confrontation had taken place had been while she was working. That meant Renard was here, watching her.

The crowd was rowdy and drunk, the music loud. The street was filled with costumes and color and movement. Nick looked only for the slate blue uniforms of the SO deputies. He worked systematically down one side of La Rue France and up the other, barely pausing to accept the inane well wishes of his colleagues for the upcoming hearing. He saw no sign of Annie.

She could have been at the jail, booking in some drunk. He could have missed her in the crowd, she was so little. Or she could be in trouble. In the past ten days, she'd spent more time in trouble than out of it. And tonight she'd called to tell him she might have pushed a killer too far.

He could see Hooker loitering near a vendor selling fried shrimp, the fat sergeant scowling but tapping his toe to the music. Hooker would know where Annie was, but Nick doubted Hooker would give the information to him. He'd see too much potential for disaster.

'Nicky! My brother, my man. Where y'at?'

Stokes swayed toward him, his porkpie hat tipped rakishly over one masked eye. Each arm was occupied around a woman in a cut-to-the-ass miniskirt – a bottle blonde in leather and a brunette in denim. They appeared to be holding one another upright.

'This is my man, Nick,' Stokes said to the women. 'He don't no more know what to do with a party than he'd know what to do with a two-headed goat. You want one of these fine ladies to be your spirit guide into the party world, Nicky? We can go somewhere and have us a party of our own. You know what I mean?'

Nick scowled at him. 'You seen Broussard?'

'Broussard? What the hell you want with her?'

'Have you seen her?'

'No, and thank God for it. That chick ain't nothin' but grief, man. You oughta know. She – Oooohhh!' he cooed, as the possibilities dawned in his booze bumbled mind. 'Turnabout is fair play, huh? You wanna give her a little scare or somethin'?'

'Or something.'

'That's cool. I'm cool with that. Yeah. The bitch has it coming to her.'

'So go over there and ask Hooker where she's at. Make up a good excuse.'

The Dudley Do-Right flashed bright across Stokes's face. 'Mind my lady friends, Nicky. Girls, you be nice to Nicky. He's a monk.'

The blonde looked up at Nick as Stokes walked away. 'You're not *really* a monk, are you?'

Nick slipped his shades on, shutting the bimbo out, and said nothing, watching as Stokes approached the sergeant. The two exchanged words, then Stokes bought himself an order of shrimp and came back chewing.

'You're outta luck, friend. She done packed up her tight little ass and gone home.'

'What?'

'Hooker says she called in sick a while ago. He thinks maybe she was drinking.'

'Why would he think that?'

Stokes shrugged. 'I don't know, man. These rumors get around. You know what I mean? Anyhow, she ain't here.'

The anxiety in Nick's gut wound tighter. 'What's her unit number?'

'What's the difference? She's not in it.'

'I came past the station. Her Jeep's in the lot. What the hell is her unit number?' Nick demanded.

Stokes's confusion gave way to concern. He stopped chewing and swallowed. 'What're you planning, man?'

Nick's patience snapped. He grabbed Stokes by both shoulders and shook him, sending fried shrimp scattering on the sidewalk. 'What the hell is her unit number!'

'One Able Charlie!'

He wheeled and bolted through the crowd, Stokes's voice carrying after him.

'Hey! Don't do nothin' I wouldn't do!'

Nick barreled through the partyers, bouncing people out of his way with a lowered shoulder and a stiff forearm. Masks flashed by in his peripheral vision, giving the scene a surreal quality. When he finally reached his truck, his breath was sawing hot in and out of his lungs. The muscles in his ribs and back, still sore from DiMonti's beating, grabbed at him like talons.

He pulled the radio mike free of its holder, called dispatch, and, identifying himself as Stokes, asked to be patched through to One Able Charlie. The seconds ticked past, each one seeming longer than the last.

'Detective?' the dispatcher came back. 'One Able Charlie is not responding. According to the log that unit is off duty.'

Nick hung up the mike and started the truck. If Annie was off duty and her Jeep was still in the lot at the station, then where the hell was she?

And where the hell was Renard?

Leaning her head against the side window, Annie tried to fight off a wave of nausea as Doll put the Cadillac in gear and it lurched forward. As they passed the vacant lot adjacent to Po' Richard's, Annie thought she caught a glimpse of Marcus's smiling white mask in the darkness, laughing at her.

They crossed France a block above the party. The color and lights glared in the distance, then vanished. Annie groaned a little as the car turned right, the change of direction exacerbating her dizziness. She wondered what the poison was, wondered if there was an antidote, wondered if the blundering morons in the Our Lady lab would be able to figure any of it out before she died a horrible, agonizing death.

She told herself not to panic. Marcus couldn't have foreseen the events of the evening. He wouldn't have planned for her absolute rejection of him. If he followed his own pattern, he had probably intended only to make her ill so that he could then later offer her comfort. That was his pattern.

The business district gave way to residences. Blocks of small, neat ranch-style houses, many with a homemade shrine to the Virgin Mary in the front yard. Old claw-foot bathtubs had been cut in half and planted on end in the ground to form grottos for totems of Mary. The totems were mass-produced in a town not far from Bayou Breaux, and lay stacked like cordwood in the manufacturing yard beside the railroad tracks. Having seen that took away some of the mystique, Annie thought, her brain waves fracturing.

They should be at the hospital soon. The old grounds-keeper would be scrubbing the toes of the giant Virgin Mary statue with a toothbrush.

'I appreciate this, Mizzuz Renard,' she said. 'I'll call the sheriff from the hospital. He'll come and pick yyyou up. Youuu did the right thing co-ming to mmme.'

'I know. I had to. I couldn't let it go on,' Doll said. 'I could see it happening all over again. Marcus becoming infatuated with you. You – a woman who would never have him. A woman who wants only to take my son from me and put him into prison – or worse. I can't let that happen. My boys are all I have.'

She turned and looked straight at Annie as they passed the turnoff for Our Lady of Mercy. The hate in her eyes seemed to glow red in the light of the dashboard.

'No one takes my boys away from me.'

47

'*I'm on my way to hell.*

Civilization passed behind them. The bayou country, ink black, vast and unwelcoming, stretched before them, a wilderness where violent death was the harsh reality of the day. Predator claimed prey here in an endless, bloody cycle, and no survivor mourned the demise of the less fortunate. Only the strong survived.

Annie had never felt weaker in her life. The nausea came in waves. The dizziness wouldn't abate. Her perceptions were beginning to distort. Sound seemed to come to her down a long tunnel. The world around her looked liquid and animated. Had to have been something in the coffee, she decided, something strong.

She tried to focus her eyes on the woman across the width of the big car. Doll Renard appeared elongated and so thin she could have been made of sticks. She didn't look as if she could have possessed the physical strength for violent rage. But Annie reminded herself that Doll Renard was younger than she looked, stronger than she looked. She was also a murderer. The frail, frumpy façade was as much a mask as the sequined domino that lay on the seat between them.

'Y*yyou* killed Pam? You dii*id* those things to Pam?' Annie said in disbelief, the gruesome images of the crime scene photos flashing through her mind, bright and bloody. She had dismissed the possibility of a woman perpetrator almost out of hand. Women didn't kill that way – with brutality, with cruelty, with hatred for their own gender.

'She got what she deserved, the whore,' Doll said bitterly. 'Men panting after her like dogs after a bitch in heat.'

'My God,' Annie breathed. 'But yyyou had to know Mmmarcus would be a sssuspect.'

529

'But Marcus didn't kill her,' Doll reasoned. 'He's innocent – of murder, at least. I watched him become obsessed with her,' she said with disgust. 'Just like with that Ingram woman. It didn't matter to him that she didn't want him. He gets these things in his head, and there's no getting them out. I tried. I tried to make *her* stop him, but he couldn't believe she would try to have him arrested. Her fear only seemed to draw him toward her.'

'Yyyou were the one ... behiind the stalking?'

'She would have taken him away from me – one way or the other.'

And so Doll had stabbed to death, crucified, and mutilated Pam Bichon. To end the obsession that had taken her son's attention away from her.

'I knew the police would question him, of course,' she went on. 'That was his punishment for trying to betray me. I thought it would teach him a lesson.'

Annie tried to swallow. Her reflexes had gone dull. Slowly she inched her right hand along the armrest, fingertips feeling for the butt of the Sig. The gun was gone. Doll had to have lifted it when she had been 'helping' Annie into the car, buckling her safely into the passenger's seat.

She glanced in the rearview, hoping against hope to see lights on their tail, but the night closed in behind them, and the swamp stretched out in front of them. Plenty of places to dump a body in the swamp.

The drug pulled at her, dragging her toward unconsciousness.

'Hhhow did yyou get Pam ... to the house?' she asked, forcing her brain to stay engaged. She couldn't save herself if she wasn't conscious, and no one else was going to do it for her. Shifting her weight, she brought her right arm across her stomach and groaned, surreptitiously moving her fingertips onto the release button of her seat belt.

'It was pathetically easy. I called her under a false name and asked her to show the property to me,' Doll said, smiling at her own cleverness. 'Greedy little bitch. She wanted everything – money, beauty, men. She would have taken my son away from me, and she didn't even want him.'

It had been as simple as a phone call. Pam wouldn't have thought twice about meeting an older woman to show a rural property, even at night. Her problems had all been with men – or so she had thought. So they all had thought. Fourcade had been right all along: The trail, the logic, led back to Renard. He just hadn't realized which Renard. No one had given a second thought to Marcus Renard's flighty, strident mother.

And now that woman is going to kill me. The thought swept around inside Annie's mind like a cyclone. She thought she could see the letters of the sentence floating in the air. She had to do something. Soon. Before the drug pulled her all the way under.

'You're no better,' Doll said. 'Marcus wants you. He can't see you're an enemy. His desire for you takes him away from me. I tried to make you stop him from wanting you. Just like I did with that Bichon woman.'

'Youuu were in the carrr that night. You came tooo my house,' Annie said, the puzzle pieces floating up to the surface of her brain. She envisioned them rising up through the goo, sticky and wet with blood. 'How did youuu … get in? Hooow did you know … about the ssstairs?'

A smirk tugged at Renard's thin lips. 'I knew your mother. She did some piecework for me one season, sewing on my costumes. That was before Claude betrayed me, before I had to take the boys away from here. Everyone wanted my costumes then.'

Doll Renard had known her mother. The admission brought another wave of dizziness crashing through Annie. Doll Renard had been in her home when she was a child. She tried to search through her mind for some memory of her and Marcus coming face-to-face as children. Could that have been possible? Could either of them have had any inkling that their paths would cross this way in adulthood?

That an acquaintance begun with an innocent encounter so long ago, then forgotten, would end in murder?

'She was whore, just like you,' Doll said. 'Blood will tell.'

Blood will tell. Annie saw the phrase flow from Doll's mouth in the form of a thick red snake.

She swallowed hard as the nausea came again, then pitched forward toward the dash and vomited on the floor. Doll made a sound of disgust. Annie hung there, free now of the seat belt, trying to get her breath, one hand braced against the dash. She had to do something. The drug was pulling her deeper into its embrace, the velvet blackness of unconsciousness seducing her.

Gathering what strength she could, she lunged across the width of the car, grabbing for the steering wheel. The Cadillac swerved hard to the right, tires screeching. Annie used the wheel to pull herself across the seat, one hand lying hard on the horn.

Doll screamed in outrage, slapping at Annie's face with one hand while she attempted to wrestle the wheel back to the left. The car dropped one front wheel off the shoulder of the road and bounced back, careening across the center line. The headlights shone on the glossy surface of black water.

Annie ducked her head to avoid the blows and clawed at the wheel again. She used her body to crowd Doll against the door, reaching across blindly with her left hand for the door handle. If she could get the door open, maybe she could push Doll out. She could see it happen in her mind's eye: Doll's brittle body hitting the asphalt like a crash-test dummy, bouncing, her head breaking open, her brain spilling out. She snagged the handle with the tips of two fingers.

The car went into a sudden, screeching skid as Doll jammed on the brakes. Annie flew into the dash, her head bouncing off the windshield, her shoulder slamming into the dashboard. The noise, the motion, the pain, the vertigo tumbled through her in an avalanche. She tried to push herself up from the floor as the car jolted onto the shoulder and stopped. She tried to get hold of something for support and orientation, tried to focus her eyes on something out in front of her – the barrel of a gun.

Her gun. In Doll Renard's hand. Three inches from her face.

Swinging wildly, she knocked the gun sideways, and the Sig went off with a deafening *pop!*, shattering a window somewhere in the car.

'Bitch!' Doll shrieked.

She grabbed Annie by the hair with her left hand and brought the gun down hard, slamming it against her temple and cheekbone once, twice.

Starbursts of color shot through Annie's head like a meteor shower. Surrendering for the moment, she dropped to the floor, crumpled and limp, blood trickling in thin fingers down across her cheek. She could feel consciousness sliding away. She thought she could feel the world sliding beneath her, but it was only the car. They were moving again, off the main road. She could hear the soft swish of grass brushing against the sides of the Cadillac, the popping sound of tires crunching over rock.

She lay still on the floor, energy spent, knowing she had to find more, had to scrape together another burst or die. *Weapons*. The thought was a dim light in her mind. *Doll has the Sig. Doll has the Sig. Doll has the Sig.* She knew there had to be something more, another answer, stupid simple, but she couldn't think.

So tired.

Her limbs were as heavy as the branches of a live oak. Her hands felt the size of catcher's mitts. She tried to swallow around a tongue as thick as a copperhead. Maybe the red snake she had seen come out of Doll's mouth had gone into her own to choke her. A taste as bitter as acid filled her mouth.

Acid. That would be a weapon, she thought. She imagined throwing it in Doll Renard's face, imagined the face burning down to the skull bones while the rest of her body danced a mad jig of death.

Acid.

The car rolled to a stop. Doll popped the lock on the trunk, got out of the car, and slammed the door. Annie reached slowly down her right side to her duty belt, feeling back from her empty holster to the slim nylon case just behind it. She pried up the Velcro tab and slipped the small cylinder free with clumsy fingers.

Behind her, the car door opened. Annie's head snapped back as Doll grabbed her by the hair and pulled her backward.

'Get up! Get up!'

Annie fell onto the ground, wincing as Doll kicked her in the back and cursed her. Curling into a ball, she tried to protect her head. The fingers of her right hand wrapped tightly around the cylinder in her palm.

The door of the Cadillac swung shut, just missing Annie's head, then Doll had her by the hair again, dragging her into a sitting position. Annie opened her eyes, reaching out to steady herself against the side of the car as the dizziness spun her brain around and around. The car's headlights provided the only illumination, but it was enough. Tipping and spinning in front of her vision was a house, run-down, with broken windows gaping like toothless spots in an old crone's smile.

They were on Pony Bayou. This was the house where Pam Bichon had had her life cut out of her.

I didn't kill Pam,' Marcus said softly.

Hunter Davidson's broad face twisted with disgust. 'Don't stand there and lie to me. There's no judge here but God. There's no technicalities, no loopholes for you and your damn lawyer to jump through.'

'I loved her,' Marcus whispered, tears coming again to stream down his cheeks.

'*Loved her?*' Davidson's big body quivered with rage.

Sweat ringed the underarms of his shirt. His thin hair was dark and shiny-wet. 'You don't know what love is. *I made her!* My wife bore her! She was our child! You don't know a damn thing about that kind of love. She was our baby, and you took her away from us!'

The irony, Marcus thought, was that he knew all about that kind of love. He had been caught in a sick mutation of it his whole life. Tonight he would have ended it. Now Pam's father would end it for him.

'You can't know how many times I've killed you,' Davidson said softly, moving forward. His eyes were glassy with the fever of hate. 'I dreamed of nailing you down and putting you through the hell my baby went through.'

'No,' Marcus whispered, crying harder now with fear. Spittle bubbled between his lips and dribbled down his chin. Against his will, his gaze darted to the big wooden table where his utility and X-Acto knives were laid out like surgical instruments. He shook his head. 'Please, no.'

'I wanted to hear you beg me for your life, the way Pam must have begged. Did she call for me when she was dying?' Davidson asked in a tortured voice. Tears as big as raindrops spilled down his ruddy cheeks. 'Did she call for her mama?'

'I don't know,' Marcus murmured.

'I hear her. *Every night.* I hear her calling for us, calling for me to save her, and there's not a damn thing I can do! She's gone. She's gone forever!'

He stood no more than two feet away now. The hand that held the gun was as big as a bear's paw, white-knuckled, trembling.

'You should die like that,' he whispered bitterly. 'But I didn't come here for revenge. I came for justice.'

The gun barked twice. Marcus's eyes widened in surprise as the force of the bullets knocked him backward. He felt nothing. Even as he fell into his drawing table, then to the floor, the back of his head bouncing off the hardwood, he felt nothing. His body jumped again and again as Davidson fired into him. Marcus felt as if he were watching the scene on a movie screen.

He was dying. Another irony. He would have taken his own life tonight. He would have ended his mother's quiet, twisted tyranny. He would have spared Victor a future without protection. Instead, he would die here on the floor, killed for a crime he didn't commit, a failure even in death.

They'll think Mmmmarrcus did it,' Annie said.

'No, they won't,' Doll corrected her. 'They'll know exactly who did it: you. Get up.'

Bracing herself against the Cadillac, Annie rose slowly, awkwardly.

Think. Try to think. Need a plan.

Thinking was as tiring and difficult as swimming upstream against a strong current. Thinking and walking simultaneously was nearly impossible. The ground rose and fell erratically beneath her feet. The house shimmered like a mirage in the glare of the headlights. Her breathing was becoming labored. She could feel her heartbeat slowing like the ticking of a clock winding down to a stop. It would be only a matter of time before the drugs pulled her under entirely, then Doll would stick the Sig in her mouth and pull the trigger. Suicide.

Her career had been in trouble. She'd been having difficulties with her co-workers. A number of people had reported she had recently developed a drinking problem. Would it be a stretch to believe she'd gone out to the house where she had found Pam Bichon's mutilated remains, taken a handful of downers, and blown her brains out with her service weapon?

'But hooow did I ... get here?' she asked, pausing at the foot of the porch steps.

'Shut up!' Doll snapped, jabbing her in the back with the Sig. 'Get inside.'

The vehicle was just a minor snag, Annie supposed, as she staggered up the steps onto the porch. Doll Renard was an old hand at murder. She'd gotten away with it twice already.

The door stood open, as if someone had been expecting them. Annie stepped into the entry, her footfalls echoing in the empty hall. The beam of a portable lantern cut through the gloom, lighting the way to her death. The floor was thick with dust. Cobwebs festooned the doorways. The nose of the Sig jabbed into her back. Annie moved down the hall, her left hand against the wall, feeling her way like a blind person.

'How many ... will youuu kill?' she mumbled. 'Hoow long before Marcus ... knows? He'll hate you.'

'He's my son. My sons love me. My sons need me. No one will ever take them from me.' The vehemence in Doll's tone sounded practiced, as if she'd chanted those words over and over and over for years and years and years.

'Who tried to take them?' Annie asked. Her legs felt like rubber. Her body wanted to sink to the floor and succumb.

She stepped through a doorway and found herself in the dining room. The beam of the lantern swept across the floor as Doll set it down, illuminating the hasty retreat of a long black indigo snake across the dirty old cypress planks. For an instant she saw Pam lying there, arms outstretched, her body savaged. The head lifted and the decaying face turned toward her, mouth moving.

'You are me. Help me. Help me. Help me!' The words turned to a shriek that pierced through Annie's brain from ear to ear.

Help me, she thought, knowing no one would, knowing help was too much to hope for. Time was running out.

She bent over at the waist, leaning her right shoulder against the wall, trying to marshal what strength she had left. Doll stood two feet in front of her. The doorway to the hall was immediately to the right of Doll, with the stairs to the second floor right there, leading up into darkness. She needed a plan. She needed a weapon.

Doll has the Sig. Doll has the Sig.

Her baton was gone. Her fingers tightened on the slim canister in her palm. She tried to breathe, tried to think, stared at her black cop shoes.

Stupid simple.

'Claude would have,' Doll said. 'He betrayed us. He would have taken my boys away from me. I couldn't let that happen.'

'Your ... husband?'

'He forced me to it. He betrayed us. He got what he deserved. I told him so,' she said. 'Right before I killed him.'

Doll came forward a step. 'It's time for you to lie down, Deputy.'

'Why the ... mask on Pam?' Annie asked, ignoring the dictate. 'It led strraight ... to youuu.'

'I don't know anything about that mask,' she said impatiently, gesturing with the gun for Annie to move. 'Over there, Deputy. Where that other cunt died.'

'I don't think I ... can move,' Annie said, watching Doll's feet as the sensible matron shoes came another step closer.

'I told you to move,' she said with authority. 'Move!'

Annie took the command as her signal, calling on the last of her reserves. With her left hand, she batted the Sig to one side. The gun barked, spitting a shot into the ceiling. At the same time, Annie brought up her right hand with the can of Mace and sprayed.

Doll screamed as the pepper spray caught her in the right eye. She stumbled back, clawing at her face with her free hand, swinging the gun back into position with the other. The Sig cracked off another round, the bullet hitting Annie low in the chest, knocking her into the wall. The impact of the slug against her ballistic vest knocked the breath from her lungs, but there was no time to recover. She had to move. Now.

Doubled over, she rushed for the stairs and threw herself up into the darkness as the gun fired again. Arms and legs flailing clumsily, she scrambled for the second floor, slipping, falling, hitting her knee, cracking her elbow. The drug had destroyed her sense of equilibrium. She couldn't tell up from down from flat. When she hit the landing on the second floor, she sprawled on her face. The sound of her chin hitting the wood was almost as sharp as the sound of the shot Doll fired at her from below – but not nearly as sharp as the searing pain of the bullet tearing through the back of her left thigh and exiting through the front.

Scuttling on her belly like a gator, Annie propelled herself through the nearest doorway. Coughing at the dust she'd raised, fighting the sobs of pain, she tipped herself upright with her back against the wall behind the door. She felt for the entrance and exit wounds, her hand coming away wet with blood, but there was no arterial bleeding – a small favor. It would take her longer to die. The dizziness wobbled her like a top. The blackness added to the sense of vertigo. The only light in the room came through a single window, faint and gray.

Time was running out. She tore at the cuff of her uniform trousers. Her fingers felt as huge and unwieldy as sausages. She thought she could hear Doll coming up the steps, the sound of footfalls alternating with the pounding of her pulse in her ears.

She pushed herself to her feet with her back against the wall for balance and waited. Her left leg was deadweight, unable to support her at all. The rush of adrenaline and the drag of narcotics fought a tug-of-war within her. Her chest felt as if someone had hit her with a forty-pound hammer. She wondered if the force of the first bullet had cracked a rib and knew it wouldn't matter if she were dead.

The Sig reported a fraction of a second before the shot splintered through the door, six inches in front of Annie's face. Biting back the cry of surprise, she flattened herself against the wall and held her breath. Her hands were sweating, her grip unsure. She said a quick prayer and promised to go to confession more often. The inevitable bargain with God. But if God hadn't listened to Pam

on's cries while Doll Renard had tortured and killed
then why would He listen now?

omewhere across the hall she could hear the scratching
of rats or coons or some other animal squatters. The Sig
cracked off another round in that direction, away from the
room where Annie stood. She held her position, hidden by
the partially opened door, the window across the room
giving her enough light to make out shapes, at least.

She would have one solid chance. She could hold herself
together long enough for one chance. And if she didn't
make good on it, she'd be dead.

Nick put his foot to the floor and ran the truck wide open
down the straight sections of road. Woods and swamp
flashed past in a blur. He was outrunning the reach of his
headlights but not of his imagination.

Annie wasn't in her unit. Her Jeep sat in the parking lot
behind the station. Her stuff was in her locker. She'd called
in sick, Hooker had said. What the hell did that mean? Had
Renard grabbed her and forced her to call in with a gun to
her head? Had she wanted to get free of duty to check
something out? Nick had no way of knowing. He knew
only that he had a fist of apprehension in his gut and
another one had him by the throat.

He hit the brakes and skidded past Renard's driveway,
slammed the transmission into reverse and roared backward. Without a thought to the restraining order against
him, he turned in the Renard drive and gunned it.

Lights glowed on the first floor toward the back of the
house. Only one upstairs window was lit. Renard's Volvo
sat at a cockeyed angle near the front veranda, the dome
light on. It struck Nick as odd. Renard was as anal retentive
as they came. To leave anything crooked or ajar was out of
character.

He killed the truck's lights and engine, and climbed out.
He had thought finding Renard at home would lessen his
fears for Annie. Surely Renard would never bring her here.

But the night air hung thick and heavy with tension around the old house. The quiet was the unnatural quiet of a world holding its breath.

And then came the shots.

The footsteps came nearer. Annie gulped a breath and wiped the sweat from her forehead with the back of her wrist. Dizzy. Sick. Weaker and weaker. Her vision was blurring. Time was running out.

'You'll die tonight one way or another.' Doll's voice sounded in the hall.

She was crying, cursing. The Mace had to be burning like a hot poker in her eye.

'You'll die, you'll die,' she promised over and over.

The footsteps shuffled nearer.

Annie could feel her on the other side of the door. And before her Pam suddenly appeared, her rotting corpse standing upright, glowing like a holy vision. Her mouth fell open and a single word spilled out on a tide of blood – *justice*.

Doll passed the door and turned, stepping into the vision. In that moment it seemed to Annie as if she had a spotlight turned on her. Doll's eyes bugged wide. Her mouth tore open. She raised the gun in slow motion.

And Annie pulled the trigger.

The nine-millimeter Kurz Back-Up bucked in her hands and Doll Renard's face shattered like glass. The force knocked her backward across the room. She was dead before she hit the floor.

Annie went limp against the wall, her head swimming, her vision fuzzing out. She blinked hard and watched as the apparition of Pam shot straight up through the ceiling and was gone.

Justice. She'd come into this looking for justice – for Pam, for Josie.

Let justice be done.

Too weak to return the Kurz to her ankle holster, she

stuck the gun in the waistband of her pants, then tried to find within herself the strength to keep from dying.

48

'He killed my baby girl,' Hunter Davidson mumbled. 'He killed my baby.'

He sat on his knees on the floor of Marcus Renard's studio, drenched in sweat, pale and trembling. He looked up at Nick, the pain in his eyes as wretched as anything Nick had ever seen.

'You understand, don't you?' Davidson said. 'I had to. He killed my girl.'

Nick kept his gun at his side, approaching the man cautious step by cautious step. A .45 hung limp in the big man's left hand, resting on his thigh. Marcus Renard lay on the floor, arms flung wide, his eyes half-open and sightless.

'Why you don't set that gun on the floor and slide it toward me, Mr. Davidson?' Nick said.

Hunter Davidson just sat there, his gaze on the man he had killed. Slowly, Nick bent down, took the .45 away from him, and stuck it in the back waistband of his jeans. He holstered his own weapon, then gently coaxed Davidson up from the floor and moved him away from the body.

'You have the right to remain silent, Mr. Davidson,' he began.

'I had to do it,' Davidson murmured more to himself than to Nick. 'He had to pay. We deserved justice.'

The system hadn't given it to him quickly enough. And now the justice meted out would be against him. The tragedy of Pam's death had just extended out another ring in the pond.

Nick looked from Renard's lifeless body to Pam's father and felt nothing but deep and profound sadness.

Victor held himself perfectly still outside the door to Marcus's Own Space. Marcus had given him a job to do. He tried always to please Marcus, even though Victor didn't fully understand what it meant to be pleased. *Pleased* was a white feeling – he knew that. But the sounds had driven him from his room before he could complete his counting task. The voices had come up through the floor – *very red*.

The house was quiet now, but the silence didn't give him a white feeling as it usually did. The Controllers in his head were frowning. *Red* seeped around the edges of his brain like bacteria. Then *and* now. Like before. Victor knew this feeling. He raised his hands to touch his special mask. The feel of the feathers against his fingertips was soft, *white*, like *running water*. And yet, he could feel the heavy *redness* all around. He could taste it in the air, feel it against his skin, pressing in on him, touching each individual hair on his body, reaching into his ears a sound that was not a sound. Tension. Sound *and* silence.

Mother was not asleep, as Marcus thought. Then *and* now. Like before. She was gone. Enter out. *Very* red. She was their mother, but *not* their mother sometimes. Mask, no mask. *Mask* equaled *change*, and sometimes *deception*. Victor had tried to tell, but Marcus didn't hear him. Marcus saw only one of Mother's faces, and he never heard The Voice. Sound and silence.

Victor stood just outside the door, staring in. He felt time pass, felt the earth move in minute increments beneath his feet. Marcus lay on the floor near the Secret Door. Asleep, but not asleep. Marcus had ceased to exist. His eyes were open, but he didn't see Victor. His shirt was red with blood. *Very red*.

Hesitant, Victor moved into the room, not looking at the other people. He kneeled down beside Marcus and touched the blood, though he didn't touch the holes. Holes were always bad. Bacteria and germs. Red holes were *very* bad.

'Not now, Marcus,' he said softly. 'Not now enter out.'

Marcus didn't move. Victor had tried to tell him about Mother and the Face Women – Elaine and Pam and Annie but Marcus didn't hear him. He had tried to tell him about the Waiting Man tonight, but Marcus didn't hear him. *Very, very* red.

Victor touched his brother's forehead with his bloody fingers and began to rock himself. He knew he wouldn't like for Marcus to not exist forever. He knew he didn't like the way his brother's face had changed. The Controllers frowned in his mind.

'Not now, Marcus,' he whispered. 'Not now enter out.'

Slowly he reached up and slipped the feather mask from his own face and placed it over his brother's.

Nick watched the strange, sad little ritual with a heavy heart. He wondered for the first time where Renard's mother was, why she hadn't come running at the sound of trouble. Then the roar of a big car engine cut into his thoughts, and he started for the front of the house, breaking into a run at the sound of metal hitting metal.

At the side of the house a Cadillac had broadsided Renard's Volvo. As Nick stepped out onto the veranda, the car's door opened and the driver fell out onto the lawn. Nick jumped down to the ground and jogged closer, that old hand of dread grabbing hold of him hard as he saw the uniform and the mop of dark hair.

''Toinette!' he shouted, sprinting the last few yards.

He dropped to the ground beside her, his trembling hands framing her face. He slid two fingers down the side of her throat to search for a pulse, praying, pleading.

Annie opened her eyes and looked up at him. Nick. It was nice to see him one last time, whether his image was real or not.

'Doll,' she murmured dreamily, a shudder quaking through her body. 'Doll killed Pam. And she killed me too.'

49

The edge of death was a place of darkness and light, sound and silence. She hovered there, slipping from one world into the next and back again.

The ambulance, the urgency of the EMTs, the lights, the sirens.

Utter stillness, a sense of calm and resignation.

The noise and motion of the ER.

The eerie peace of nonexistence.

Annie saw the landscape as bleak and still, a battlefield in the aftermath, bodies scattered across the ground, the sky hanging heavy and leaden, everything cast in the twilight colors of nightmares. Pam was there. And Doll Renard. And Marcus. Their souls rose from them like smoke from a dying fire and drifted just above the bloody ground. She stood on the sidelines and watched.

'It's cold here, no?' Fourcade whispered.

'Where?'

He raised his left hand, fingers spread, and reached out, not quite touching her. Slowly he passed his hand before her eyes, skimmed it around the side of her head, just brushing his fingertips against her hair.

'In Shadowland.'

He spoke as if he lived in this place. And yet, Annie felt herself being pulled away from him, deeper into the blackness.

'Don't leave me here, 'Toinette,' he murmured, his dark eyes filled with sadness. *'Me, I've been alone too long.'*

She stretched out her hand toward his, but couldn't quite reach. Then panic seized her as she felt herself being drawn backward, across the line between life and death. She didn't think she had the strength to break free. She was so

546

tired, so weak. But she didn't want to die. She wasn't ready to die.

The darkness, as thick and liquid as oil, began to suck her under. Tapping into a reserve of strength she didn't know she possessed, Annie focused on the surface and tried to kick free.

The first thing she saw when she opened her eyes was Fourcade. He sat beside the bed, staring at her as if looking away would break her tenuous tie to the living world. She was aware of monitors beside her bed and the night beyond her window.

'Hi,' she whispered.

He leaned closer, still staring. 'I thought I lost you there, *chère*,' he said softly.

'Where?'

'In Shadowland.'

His eyes never leaving hers, he raised her hand to his lips and kissed the back of it. 'You scared me, 'Toinette. Me, I don't like to be scared. It pisses me off.' The corners of his mouth turned up a fraction of an inch.

Annie smiled dreamily. 'Well, we've got that in common.'

He leaned closer and touched his lips to hers, and Annie drifted off to sleep with a sigh of deep relief. When she woke again he was gone.

You're tuned to KJUN. All talk all the time. Our top story at the top of the hour: Local planter Hunter Davidson, father of murder victim Pamela Bichon, will be arraigned this afternoon in the Partout Parish Courthouse for the murder of Bayou Breaux architect Marcus Renard.

'Davidson's new attorney, Revon Tallant, has suggested an insanity defense will be employed, and expects that an alleged confession made by Davidson early Sunday morning will be ruled inadmissible by the court.

'Davidson had recently been released from Partout Parish

Jail following a plea agreement on charges of attempted assault against Marcus Renard. District Attorney Smith Pritchett has been unavailable for comment. A formal statement is expected later this morning.'

Annie turned the radio off. During the two days she lay in the hospital bed, her senses had been bombarded with the story. On television, on the radio, in the newspapers. Accurate, inaccurate, twisted, and sensationalized – she'd heard every version of Hunter Davidson's drama and her own. She had been besieged with requests for interviews, all of which she had declined. It was over. Time for everyone to try to repair the damage that had been done and move on.

Dr Van Allen had reluctantly agreed to let her go home. The drug Doll Renard had dosed her with had been effectively counteracted. The blood she had lost had been replaced. The pain in her thigh was constant, but tolerable. The bullet had passed through and through, missing both the bone and the vital femoral artery. She would limp for a while, but all things considered, she was damn lucky.

Lucky to be alive. Whether or not she would be lucky enough to have a job to go back to remained to be seen.

Gus had come to her bedside on Sunday to personally take her statement regarding Doll Renard. He listened without comment while Annie related the events of the last ten days, his face lined with a tense emotion she was afraid to name.

She thought about it now as she sat down on the edge of the bed to rest a moment from the effort of getting dressed. What had been gained and what had been lost in all of this? A murderer had been unmasked and stopped. Annie had gained insights into her own strengths and abilities. But the losses seemed disproportionately heavy. She'd seen an ugly side to men she had to work with and rely upon. Lives had been altered, some damaged beyond repair.

She limped out of the hospital into a day that was cool and gray with the promise of rain, and eased herself awkwardly into the shotgun seat of the cruiser Noblier had sent for her. The deputy was Phil Prejean. He squirmed in the driver's seat like a five-year-old with a full bladder.

'I – ah – I'm sorry for what all that happened, Annie,' he said. 'I hope you can accept my apology.'

'Yeah, sure,' she said without conviction, and fixed her gaze out the window.

They drove out of the lot with an itchy silence thick in the air between them.

News vans from television stations all over Louisiana crowded the curbs out in front of the courthouse, even though the arraignment was still more than an hour away. The parking lot was clogged with cars. Annie wondered what those same reporters who had called Hunter Davidson a folk hero ten days ago would call him now that he'd killed an innocent man.

The story of a crime went so much deeper than what people read in the papers or saw on the nightly news. No reporter could cram into a column inch or a sixty-second sound bite how the repercussions rolled outward from a single violent epicenter to shake the lives of so many people – the victim's family and the perpetrator's, the cops and the community.

Josie Bichon had been left without a mother. Her grandfather would go to trial for murder. Belle Davidson had lost a daughter and stood to lose a husband. Victor Renard had lost the only people who could understand any part of the workings of his damaged mind. The people of Bayou Breaux had suffered irreparable damage to their sense of trust and safety.

Prejean pulled into a visitor's slot near the back entrance to the law enforcement center. Annie hoped it wasn't prophetic. Hooker scowled at her with suspicion as she limped past his desk, as if she had been revealed as an undercover spy on his shift. She received a variation on that same look from Myron as she passed the records counter.

Valerie Comb in Noblier's outer office still looked at her as if she were a bad piece of meat.

The sheriff had put on his funeral suit for the day's media attentions, a charcoal pinstripe that didn't hang quite right on his big-boned frame. He'd already jerked his tie loose at the throat. He looked older than Annie remembered him a week ago.

'How you doing, Annie? You okay for this?'

Alarm struck a low, vibrating note in her gut. 'That depends on what *this* is, sir.'

'Have a seat,' he offered, pointing to one of his visitor's chairs. 'The doctor released you?'

'Yes, sir.'

'He signed a release? You'll forgive my skepticism, but you've developed a bad habit of defying orders recently.'

'They didn't give me a copy of it,' Annie said, sucking a breath in through clenched teeth as she settled herself down on the edge of the chair. 'They gave me a bill.'

His point about her insubordination made, Noblier didn't press for the documentation. He settled into his own chair and looked at her hard for a moment. Annie returned his stare evenly.

'We executed a search warrant on the Renard home over the weekend,' he began at last, opening the pencil drawer of his desk. 'Among possessions found in Marcus Renard's workroom were items known to belong to Pam Bichon. We also found this.'

He tossed the plastic dancing alligator across the desk. Annie picked it up, feeling a vague embarrassment at the silliness of the thing with its leering grin and red beret. Then feeling a creepy sense of violation. Renard had taken this innocent trinket from her as a token. He'd fondled it, held it, and thinking of her, tainted it.

'Deputy Prejean recognized it. Thought you might want it back.'

'Thank you, sir.' She slipped it into her jacket pocket,

550

knowing she would throw it away the minute she left the room.

'Found in Doll Renard's bedroom was a nine-inch boning knife. Found it between her mattress and box spring,' he went on. 'Never found it before because the warrants never extended to Mrs. Renard's bedroom. The knife's been sent to the lab.'

'Was it clean?'

Noblier weighed his answer for a moment, then decided she'd earned it. 'No. It wasn't.'

The idea turned Annie's stomach. Doll Renard had kept a bloody knife beneath her mattress so that she could take it out and remind herself of the atrocities she had committed in the name of motherhood. But she appreciated the evidence for what it would provide. Closure – for Pam, for her family, for the cops who had worked the case. 'They'll be able to match blood and tissue.'

'I expect so.'

'Good.'

The sheriff went silent again, watching her, frowning. A bad sign, she thought.

'I been giving a lot of thought to this over the last couple of days, Annie,' he began. 'I can't condone my deputies going off on their own, investigating cases they ain't assigned to.'

'No, sir,' Annie murmured.

'You always have been one to stick your nose in where it don't belong.'

'Yes, sir.'

'Nothing but trouble. Creates dissension. Undermines command.'

Annie said nothing. She had a perverse need to relish the feel of her career slipping away.

'On the other hand, it shows initiative, guts, ambition,' he said, taking the pendulum back to the high side. 'Tell me this, Annie: Why'd you go after Fourcade that night?'

'Because it was the right thing to do.'

'And why'd you go after Renard on your own?'

It was Annie's turn to weigh her answer. She could have said she hadn't trusted Stokes to do the job, but that wasn't it, not really. Not on a gut level. Not in her soul, where it counted most.

'Because I felt I owed it to Pam. I was the first person to see what her killer had done to her. There was something very ... personal about that. I felt like I owed her. I found her body, I wanted to find her justice too.'

Gus nodded his head, pursing his lips. 'You haven't talked to the press.'

'No, sir.'

'At the press conference this afternoon I'll be telling them how you were working undercover to help crack this case. Your next paycheck will reflect your overtime.'

Annie's eyes widened at what sounded for all intents and purposes to be a bribe.

Noblier read her face like a clock and narrowed his small eyes. 'I won't have my authority undermined, Annie. My deputies work *for* me, not around me. The OT is a bonus – consider it hazard pay. Understood?'

'Yes, sir.'

'You got a hell of a lot to learn about how the world works, Broussard.' He had already begun his dismissal of her, his attention going to the notes he had scribbled for the press conference. 'Report back to me when you come in off sick leave. We'll do the paperwork on your reassignment ... Detective.'

Detective Broussard. Annie tried the sound of it in her mind as she hobbled back down the hall. It sounded good. She pulled the plastic alligator from her pocket and tossed it in the trash as she passed the sergeant's desk.

Fourcade was waiting for her outside the door. He stood leaning against the building, his ankles crossed, his hands in the pockets of his jacket, concern in his eyes.

'Noblier made me a detective,' she announced, hearing the ring of disbelief in her own voice.

'I know. I recommended you.'

'Oh.'

'It's where you belong, 'Toinette,' he said. 'You do good work. You dig hard. You believe in the job. You seek the truth, fight for justice – that's what it oughta be about.'

Annie made a little shrug and glanced away, uncomfortable with his praise. 'Yeah, well, I lose the cool uniform and the hot car.'

He didn't smile. Big surprise. He straightened away from the wall and touched her cheek with a gentle hand. 'How you doing, 'Toinette? You okay?'

The weight of it all pressed a sigh from her. 'Not exactly.'

She wanted to say she wasn't the same person she had been ten days ago, but she had the distinct feeling Nick would disagree with her. He would tell her she simply hadn't looked that deep inside before. She wondered what he saw when he looked that deeply within himself.

'Walk with me?' she said. 'Down to the bayou?'

Frowning, he looked across the parking lot to the strip of green boulevard fifty yards away. 'You sure?'

'I've been in bed for two days. I need to move. Slowly, but I need to move.'

She started without him. He fell in step beside her. Neither of them spoke as they crossed the distance. When they reached the bank, a small group of mallards started, then settled back onto the chocolate brown water, bobbing at the edge of the reeds like corks. Across the bayou, an old man was walking a dachshund.

Annie sat down gingerly on one end of a park bench, stretching her left leg carefully in front of her. Fourcade took the other end of the bench. The space between them was occupied by Marcus Renard.

'He was innocent, Nick,' she said softly.

He could have argued. Marcus Renard's obsession with Pam had acted as the catalyst for his mother's violence. But that wasn't the point here, and he knew it. He had followed the trail back to Marcus, stopped there, and meted out his own punishment.

'Would it have made a difference if he'd been guilty?'

Annie thought about it for a moment. 'It would have made it easier to rationalize, at least.'

'*C'est vrai,*' he murmured. 'True enough. But he wasn't guilty. I screwed up. I lost perspective. I lost control. Wrong is wrong, and a man is dead because of it. Because of me. I'll have to carry that the rest of my life.'

'You didn't pull the trigger.'

'But me, I loaded the gun, didn't I? Davidson believed so strongly that Marcus Renard killed his daughter in part because *I* believed so strongly that Marcus Renard killed his daughter. My focus became his focus. You should know how that works – I tried to force it on you too.'

'Only because it made sense. No one can fault your logic, Nick.'

He flashed the sudden smile, the edges of it hard with an inner bitterness. '*Mais* no. My faults lie deeper. I believe it's better to err on the side of passion rather than apathy.'

He cared too much, tried too hard. The job was his life, his mission. Everything else was secondary. Submerged in that obsession, he found it too easy to lose his perspective and his humanity. He needed an anchor, an alter ego, a voice to question his motives, a counterbalance to his single-mindedness.

He needed Annie.

'I hear Pritchett will drop the charges against you,' she said.

He leaned his forearms against his thighs and watched the dachshund man. '*Oui.* So, I not only indirectly caused Renard's death, I benefited from it.'

'So did I. I'm off the hook for testifying. That's no small relief,' she said, willing him to meet her eyes. He turned his head and looked at her. 'I didn't want to, Nick, but I would have.'

'I know. You're a woman of convictions, 'Toinette,' he said, offering her a smile that was softer, fond, almost sad. 'So where does that leave me?'

'I don't know.'

'Sure you do.'

Annie didn't bother to argue. He was right. He was a complex and difficult man. He would push her. He would test her. It would have been so much easier for her to turn to A.J., take what he wanted to give her, live a simple life. A nice simple life, just short of fulfilment. Maybe in time the restlessness would fade into contentment. Or maybe it was better to err on the side of passion.

'You're not an easy man, Nick.'

'No, I'm not,' he admitted, never taking his eyes off hers. 'So, you gonna help me with that, *chère*, or what? You gonna take a chance? Be bold?'

He held his breath and waited, stared at her and willed her to take the challenge.

'I don't know what I have in me to offer you, 'Toinette,' he confessed softly. 'But I'd like the chance to find out.'

Annie looked past his determination to his need. She looked at the hard face, the dark eyes burning on hers. He was too intense, too driven, too alone. But she had the distinct feeling he was what she had been waiting for. Her strongest instinct was to reach out to him.

'Me too,' she murmured, reaching across the space between them to lay her hand on his. 'If we're partners ...'

He turned his hand over and twined his fingers with hers, the contact warm and right. '... we're partners.'

Epilogue

Victor sat at the small table in his room, cutting paper with a blunt-nosed scissors. The house was not his family house. Riverview was a group home for autistic adults. It was a strange place full of people he did not know. Some were kind to him. Some were not.

There was a large lawn with a tall brick wall around it and many trees around the perimeter, and a very nice garden. A good place for watching birds, though not nearly as many species as there had been at Victor's own house. And here he couldn't take a boat out on the bayou to search for more. Nor was he allowed to go outside in the night to listen for the night birds or observe the other creatures that preferred darkness to light. There were many that did. Some were predators. Some were not.

For the most part, Victor's life in this new place was quiet and calm. Somewhere between *red and white. Gray*, he had decided. Most days he felt very gray. Like sleeping, but awake. He often thought of Marcus and wished that he had not ceased to exist. He often thought of Mother.

Setting the scissors aside, he took up the small bottle of glue and set about putting the finishing touches on his creation. Mother had ceased to exist, Richard Kudrow had told him, though Victor had not seen her and did not know for a fact that this was true. Sometimes he dreamed that she came to him in the night, as she often had, and sat beside him on his bed and stroked his hair while she talked in the Night Voice.

A low hum of tension vibrated through him as he remembered the Night Voice. The Night Voice spoke of red things. The Night Voice spoke of *feelings*. Better not to have them.

Love.

    Passion.

        Greed.

            Anger.

                Hatred.

Their power was very red. The people they touched ceased to exist. Like Father. Like Mother. Like Marcus. Like Pam.

Sometimes Victor dreamed of the Dark Night and the things he had seen. *Very red.* Mother, but *not* Mother, doing things the Night Voice talked about. Even just remembering brought on a red intensity that paralyzed him, as it had that night. He had stood frozen outside the house for hours afterward, hidden in the darkness, unable to move or speak. Finally he had gone inside to see.

Pam, but *not* Pam. She had ceased to exist. Her cries remained locked inside Victor's mind, echoing and echoing. He didn't like the way her face had changed. Slowly, he took off his mask and laid it across her eyes.

Love.

    Passion.

        Greed.

            Anger.

                Hatred.

Emotions. Better not to have them. Better to wear a mask, he thought as he put his new one on and went to his small window to stare out at a world cast in the intense colors and soft shadows of twilight.

Hatred.

    Anger.

        Greed.

            Passion.

                Love.

The line between them is thin and dark.

Glossary of Cajun French

allons	let's go
arrète	stop
c'est assez	that's enough
c'est chaud	that's hot
c'est ein affaire à pus finir	it's a thing that has no end
c'est vrai	that's true
chère 'tite bête	poor little dear
chérie, chère, cher	cherished, beloved
coonass	a sometimes derogatory slang term for Cajun
éspèsces de tête dure	you hard-headed thing
fils de putain	son of a bitch
foute ton quant dici	get away
grenier	attic, loft
ici on parle français	French spoken here
Il a pas d'ésprit	he doesn't have any sense
je t'aime	I love you
jeune fille	young girl
le grand derangement	when the Cajuns were exiled from Canada
loup-garou	Cajun myth: werewolf
ma 'tite fille	my little girl
mais	but: often used for emphasis with yes or no
mais non	but no
mais sa c'est fou	but that's crazy
merde	shit
mon ami	my friend
mon Dieu	my God
pou	louse
pur Cajun	pure Cajun
que sera sera	what will be will be

sa c'est de la couyonade	that's foolishness
si vous plâit	please
t'es trop grand pour tes cullotes	you're too big for your britches
t'es en érreur	you're mistaken
tcheue poule	chicken ass
'tite chatte	little cat
'tite belle	little sweetheart
T- or Tee	preceding a name is short for *petite* or *'tite*, and denotes a nickname
viens ici	come here

All Orion/Phoenix titles are available at your local bookshop or from the following address:

Mail Order Department
Littlehampton Book Services
FREEPOST BR535
Worthing, West Sussex, BN13 3BR
telephone 01903 828503, *facsimile* 01903 828802
e-mail MailOrders@lbsltd.co.uk
(Please ensure that you include full postal address details)

Payment can be made either by credit/debit card (Visa, Mastercard, Access and Switch accepted) or by sending a £ Sterling cheque or postal order made payable to *Littlehampton Book Services*.
DO NOT SEND CASH OR CURRENCY

Please add the following to cover postage and packing

UK and BFPO:
£1.50 for the first book, and 50p for each additional book to a maximum of £3.50

Overseas and Eire:
£2.50 for the first book plus £1.00 for the second book and 50p for each additional book ordered

---

BLOCK CAPITALS PLEASE

name of cardholder ....

address of cardholder ....

delivery address
(*if different from cardholder*)

....

....

....

postcode ....

postcode ....

☐ I enclose my remittance for £ ....

☐ please debit my Mastercard/Visa/Access/Switch (delete as appropriate)

card number ☐☐☐☐☐☐☐☐☐☐☐☐☐☐☐☐

expiry date ☐☐☐☐   Switch issue no. ☐☐

signature ....

prices and availability are subject to change without notice